Charles Warren Stoddard, John Talbot Smith, Maurice Francis Egan, Anna Hanson Dorsey, Christian Reid, William A. McDermott, Ella Loraine Dorsey, Mary Ann Madden Sadlier

A Round Table of the Representative American Catholic Novelists

At which is served a feast of excellent stories

Charles Warren Stoddard, John Talbot Smith, Maurice Francis Egan, Anna Hanson Dorsey, Christian Reid, William A. McDermott, Ella Loraine Dorsey, Mary Ann Madden Sadlier

A Round Table of the Representative American Catholic Novelists
At which is served a feast of excellent stories

ISBN/EAN: 9783337393878

Printed in Europe, USA, Canada, Australia, Japan

Cover: Foto ©Andreas Hilbeck / pixelio.de

More available books at **www.hansebooks.com**

A ROUND TABLE

OF THE

REPRESENTATIVE

AMERICAN CATHOLIC NOVELISTS,

At which is Served a Feast of Excellent Stories

BY

ELEANOR C. DONNELLY,	WALTER LECKY,
ANNA HANSON DORSEY,	CHRISTIAN REID,
ELLA LORAINE DORSEY,	ANNA T. SADLIER,
MAURICE FRANCIS EGAN,	MARY A. SADLIER,
FRANCIS J. FINN, S.J.,	JOHN TALBOT SMITH,

CHARLES WARREN STODDARD.

With Portraits, Biographical Sketches, and Bibliography.

SECOND EDITION.

New York, Cincinnati, Chicago:

BENZIGER BROTHERS,

Printers to the Holy Apostolic See.

1897

Contents.

ELEANOR C. DONNELLY.

Eleanor Cecilia Donnelly is a native of Philadelphia, where her father, Dr. Philip Carroll Donnelly, died when she was a mere infant. Dr. Donnelly was of Irish birth, but his wife, Catharine Gavin Donnelly, was born in Philadelphia, and when her husband early fell a martyr to his profession, upon her devolved the exclusive rearing and training of her seven fatherless children. Her natural abilities peculiarly fitted her for this labor of love ; and she lived to reap the harvest of her toils in the varied and carefully cul-tivated talents of her offspring. Her daughter Eleanor began to write and publish poetry before she was out of her pinafores; and her life has been devoted to the elevation and extension of the cause of Catholic literature.

Besides being a constant contributor to current literature, Miss Donnelly has published some dozen volumes of poems. Her " Life of Father Barbelin, S.J.," won from the press most flattering comment; and she has excelled in religious compilations, such as "Liguori Leaflets," "Pearls from the Casket of the Sacred Heart," " Our Birthday Bouquet," and " Little Compliments of the Season." Her latest works have been: "Poems," "Petronilla and other Stories," "A Tuscan Magdalen and other Legends and Poems," "Amy's Music Box," and "The Lost Christmas Tree." It is claimed that one of Eleanor Donnelly's poems, "The Vision of the Monk Gabriel," furnished Mr. Longfellow with the theme of his " Legend Beautiful," written eight years later.

Miss Donnelly has represented Catholic literature on all occasions of national interest wherein women have figured during the past ten years. She was selected to compose the " Odes" for the Golden Jubilee of both the Priesthood and Episcopacy of His Holiness Pope Leo XIII., receiving in return the Papal benediction. It was her pen that was selected by the American Catholic Historical Society, of which she is a valued member, to prepare an " Ode " for the Philadelphia commemoration of the adoption of our National Constitution, as also the Columbian " Ode " for her native city's celebration of the quadri-centennial of the discovery of America.

A Lost Prima Donna.

BY ELEANOR C. DONNELLY.

I.

" ONCE again," said the Italian *maestro;* and the clear, flexible young voice ran up one of Rossini's most difficult cadenzas (around which clustered curious combinations of notes, like bunches of roses around a healthy stalk), trilled, like a lark, upon high *Do*, and came down the scale with a clean and elegant finish refreshing to hear.

" Good!" said the sententious master; " that will do for to-day."

His English was excellent, but he might have said " for this evening," for the twilight had fallen an hour before, and the lights were burning red against the windows that shut out the dark night. Quite a cheery contrast to the outside gloom was that warm, bright spot, small as it was, and up three pair of stairs.   The open fire was reflected in the polished floor, as in a mirror; there were pretty rosewood desks scattered around, filled with valuable music; and a vase of heliotrope on the grand

Erard; while the high ceiling and the dark panel-
ings of the walls gave an air of foreign elegance to
all.

The young singer sighed as she closed her
solfeggi, gathered up the rest of her music in
silence, and began to draw on her gloves. She was
a girl of twenty or so, in an Astrachan cap and
rather an old-fashioned dress; her well-worn pelisse
being by far too scanty to protect her against the
inclemency of a raw November night. But her
form was slight and lissome; and a glance at her
face made one forget the details of her toilet. It
was such an odd face, more remarkable for its force
of character than for any actual beauty of feature
or complexion. The latter was neither fair nor
delicate; and her hair, which she wore very simply,
was of a neutral brown. But the piercing gray eyes
were softened by the longest and silkiest of lashes,
and when a word or a smile broke up the almost
severe repose of her face, the expression was singularly sweet, and the firm chin revealed a girlish
dimple.

The master had subsided into playing minor
chords with his velvety touch, and seemed to have
forgotten her presence altogether. She glanced
furtively at him through her long lashes. He was
in the prime of life, and strikingly handsome; a
tall, willowy presence in a faultless costume, perfectly composed and graceful in every movement.
His skin was a dark olive, lighted up by a pair of
wonderful eyes that glowed at times, like burning

coals, under his finely-arched brows; but his habitual expression was an arbitrary one. Albeit he wore his black, curling hair parted in the middle, in true artist mode, no thought of weakness or womanliness could attach itself to the manly face it framed.

The last of her glove buttons disposed of, the young lady picked up her leather *rouleau.* On it was printed in tiny letters, " *Marguerite Don Ivan.*" She balanced it in her hands and walked to the door, then hesitated, turned back, and spoke with a certain nervous timidity:

" You have not told me the hour of the train, Mr. Cellini ?"

No answer. The minor chords had melted by degrees into the intricacies of a classical sonata; and the master's impressive profile showed *en silhouette* against a dark panel beyond. She tried it again, a little louder, and with more formality:

" May I ask, Mr. Cellini, the hour of the train to-morrow ?"

" What train ?" questioned the gentleman absently.

The young girl bit her lip in discomfiture: " The train that is to take us to Washington to-morrow, sir. Have you forgotten the concert ?"

" True! " said Mr. Cellini, still playing ; and there was a silence of full five minutes more, which brought him to the end of the *adagio.* Then, without even a glance over his shoulder : " We leave the Baltimore depot in the morning at eight," he said briefly, and went on with his *allegro.*

"*Maestro !*" said the young singer, coming a step nearer, with her heart in her eyes ; " please, let me sing the *Bolero* at the concert, instead of that poor little ballad."

The master dropped his long, slender hands upon his knees, and wheeled round upon his stool; her heart beat faster and her color deepened at the expression of his face.

" The *Bolero!* " he said slowly, and then he laughed a short, mellow laugh. " The *Bolero* from the ' *Sicilian Vespers' ?* " and he laughed again, eyes and teeth lighting up his dark face as with a flash of sunshine. " Miss Don Ivan, you are jesting."

" I am in sober earnest;" and her face glowed. " I know I could do it justice. I have practised it day and night for a week, and Miss Lightwood says I do it like a bird."

" Miss Lightwood is a—goose," said the master, " and that also is a bird."

He was standing now, with folded arms, looking at her across the music desk, the amused smile still upon his face.

" But you will admit that she is a musician, that she travelled in Europe, and heard the best *prima donni* in the world ? Oh, Mr. Cellini! " cried the girl excitedly, clasping her hands and with a red flame burning in her cheeks, " say I may do the *Bolero* instead of that paltry *Robin Adair*, and I shall be forever grateful. If you will but trust me, you will yet have reason to be proud of your pupil.

I feel within me the power to be a great singer. I have that within which—which——"

"' Passeth show!'" added he; and the amused smile became a sarcastic one.

To his surprise she burst into tears. He looked annoyed and bored, shrugged his shoulders, and cast away the matter with a swift motion of his graceful hands.

" Miss Marguerite, you have vanquished with a woman's best weapon. It is the first time I have ever yielded to a pupil. You shall sing the *Bolero* instead of the ballad."

He lifted up a curtain behind the piano, and, dropping it, withdrew into an alcove, where a cup of hot coffee was always awaiting him at the end of the day's lessons.

Marguerite, through her tears, looked absently at the wall, and saw a picture there for the first time —a lovely little cabinet picture of the Sacred Heart of Jesus. It was in oil, and exquisite in design and coloring; a gift to Cellini from a good Italian priest who sought his countryman's conversion. The sweet Saviour pointed to the glowing Heart upon His breast, as if inviting her to enter therein, while pitying eyes and tender lips seemed about to speak the legend inscribed upon the margin: " *Learn of Me, for I am meek and humble of heart.*"

Words and picture, both together, brought back to Marguerite the memory of a girl in an Astrachan cap and a well-worn pelisse, kneeling in the dim confessional of the Sacred Heart chapel on just such a night as that, and hearing, between the bitter sobs, the whispered admonition: " My child, you will never be truly happy until you are truly humble."

How long ago was that ? Months, and months, and months—more than she (who had once been so faithful, who had tried so hard to please God) could reckon on all the fingers of her shapely hands. She set her lips in a hard line; her eyes took a stony look as she crushed down the pleading remorse of an awakened conscience. People in positions like hers could not be saints. The paths of pride and ambition were full of thorns, but she had elected to walk in them; and in spite of bleeding feet and aching heart it was too late now to turn back. She dried her eyes and ran quickly down the staircase. At its foot a dressy woman, some ten years her senior, was keeping guard. Her face was as innocent of expression as a waxen doll's, and her flaxen frizzes and pink-and-white complexion increased her resemblance to that pleasant toy. She caught Miss Don Ivan in her arms with emphasis: " My sweet Marguerite!" And she kissed her on both cheeks. " My precious Lightwood!" And the embrace and salute were returned with ardor. Arm in arm, the two ladies stepped into the dark street.

" Some good fairy must have sent you to me," said the young singer, squeezing her friend's hand. " I wanted so badly to see you, and you may guess about what."

" The Washington concert ?" hazarded the friend.

"Precisely; and you know you promised to chaperon me. We start to-morrow morning in the early train. And oh! my dear Lightwood, rejoice with me—Mr. Cellini says I may sing the *Bolero!*"

"You do not surprise me," said her listener. "It is just as it should be—right, and proper, and reasonable. To come before a Washington audience (the *élite*, the very *crême de la crême* of the country) with such sentimental twaddle as *Robin Adair*— you, with your magnificent voice and your faultless execution,—why, my love, I knew in my heart that Cellini never would permit you to perpetrate such an insane act. Said I to your aunt when you sang the *Bolero* yesterday: 'Such sweetness, such expression, such facile finish! I am free to say, it carries me back to the day when I was in Paris at the house of Mme. Cinti Damareau, and heard there the inimitable Piccaninni, the pupil of the divine Rossini, who——' "

"Yes, yes, dear Lightwood," interrupted Marguerite, too urgent to feast quietly even upon this delicious ambrosia, "you are the truest friend in the world, and I thank you heartily for your fond appreciation; but time presses, and what about my dress? You know I must be provided with a concert dress."

"A very grave and important matter, but rather late in the day for its consideration."

"Granted," laughed the young girl, "but, you see, Cellini has so many whims, I was not sure until this evening that the concert might not be postponed a month from date. Lily thinks I might wear my black silk, with flowers in my hair, and new gloves."

" Lily is a little foo-foo," said Miss Lightwood. " Black silk for a *débutante* at a *soirée?* Who ever heard of such madness ? My love, you would look like your grandmother."

"·But what can I do ?" queried Marguerite. " Every cent I can spare goes to pay Mr. Cellini for my lessons, and times are so hard I cannot afford a new dress until next year. Indeed, to be plain with you, I don't see very clearly how I can pay for one even then."

Lightwood's flaxen curls trembled with importance.

" And who wants you to pay for a new dress out of hand ? My child, there is such a thing as management. There is such a thing as elegant economy. And, thank fortune! there are such things in the world as *modistes* who have the Christian charity to wait for their money, or take it in monthly instalments. I think I may say with certainty that I saw your new concert dress this afternoon."

" Where ?" cried the *débutante* in amazement.

" At Mme. Fitzeasy's (a misfit of Miss Clara Cadwallader's, who, by the by, is just your height and make), the sweetest love of a white gros-grain that ever you laid an eye on. Fitzeasy said I might have it for a trifle over seventy dollars, and I'm free to say I never saw a greater bargain."

" Oh, Lightwood, let me think!" cried Miss Don Ivan, pressing her hands to her head, the color coming and going in her cheeks.

" What is there to think about ? The dress is indispensable, ready-made, of exquisite material, and will fit you like a glove."

" Oh! it is not that," half sobbed Marguerite. " Heaven knows I want a new dress bad enough, and this white gros-grain would be the very thing for the concert. (My black silk was one of aunty's made over, you know, and ten years old, if it is a day.) But the simple truth is, I cannot afford it. My music, choir and all, does not half pay me. Aunty works so hard; poor Lily, crippled as she is, is killing herself with copying; and as for Maurice——"

" Hang Maurice!" cried the homicidal Lightwood; " a plague take Maurice! Maurice, indeed, —always Maurice! Much the foreman in a foundry knows about proprieties. The man has not a soul above iron. He is not worthy of you, the dolt. He does not appreciate your genius, your glorious voice, your sublime ambition. Now, if it were Cellini——"

" Hush!" under her breath, and the girl laid a strong hand upon her friend's arm, silencing her.

" Well, as I was saying," pursued the volatile lady, " there is the white gros-grain at Fitzeasy's at your own terms, and here I go, up-town, to see about your gloves and slippers. Bless your precious heart! mightn't I just as well kill two birds with one stone, and order home the dress on my way?"

"Wait!" groaned Marguerite, but so feebly, so irresolutely, that Miss Lightwood either heard not or pretended not to hear; and away she went with an airy "*Au revoir,*" and a kiss blown backward from her gloved finger tips.

"Oh! you cruel, selfish girl!" murmured Miss Don Ivan, apostrophizing herself remorsefully: "Oh! you mean and poor-spirited coward!" And looking up in distress of mind at the starless sky, she felt some drops of water upon her forehead, and realized for the first time that it was raining.

A gentleman passing with an umbrella, and looking keenly at every chance pedestrian (as if in search of some one), saw her face in the light of a street lamp, and turned back to walk beside her.

The light of the same street lamp showed him to be a tall, broad-shouldered young man, with a frank, honest face, and earnest brown eyes.

His chestnut hair was clipped close to his well-shaped head; but his dress, while exquisitely neat, was nothing finer than a substantial business suit.

"Good-evening, Maggie," and he offered her his arm.

"Good-evening, Maurice," but she would not take it.

"Your aunt and Lily were worried at your staying so late," said his strong, even voice, "so I came in search of you."

" There was no cause for anxiety," she replied
coolly. " Mr. Cellini gave me a longer lesson than
usual this evening, in rehearsal for the concert; and
Miss Lightwood only left me a moment ago."

He started slightly.

" Maggie, you are not going to sing at that concert, after all ? "

She evidently resented the reproach in his voice,
but she controlled herself to ask:

" And why not ? "

" I have already told you my objections to the
matter," said the young man gravely; " reasonable
objections, which your aunt and sister share. But
it seems your best friends have lost, of late, the
power to advise or persuade you."

" One would think I was a child or a fool who
could not be trusted," returned his companion
bitterly (and she kept her face persistently turned
away from him). " My ' best friends,' as you call
them, have rather a curious way of consulting my
best interests."

" And what are your best interests ? Tell me
candidly, Maggie, what good is the thing going to
do you ? What do you expect to gain by singing
at this concert ? "

" I expect to gain celebrity. I expect to make
a name for myself, to establish my reputation as an
artist, to win golden opinions from all sorts of men."

" And Cellini, of course, will pay you well for
your services ? "

How heartily she longed to cast back a triumphant assent to this humiliating query! But she dared not tell an open lie. Her head drooped a little, and her voice was lower:

" To be permitted to sing at all at Mr. Cellini's *soirées* I regard as a singular privilege. To be the pupil of such a master imparts a prestige which is beyond and above a mere question of money. And furthermore, it is clear that I might go on singing in that stupid choir" (pointing to the church they were passing) " till my voice was broken and my hair turned gray, and I would never gain the *éclat* that one night's success before a Washington audience would give me!"

Her gray eyes flashed like steel, but were dimmed the next moment with tears, as she saw how reverently her companion lifted his hat in worship of the unseen Presence whose poor little temple they were passing by.

" And for this empty bubble of fame," he said after a long pause, " you will sacrifice not only your peace of heart but that of your home? You will turn your back on the friend you have known and (it is to be hoped) loved from childhood, and go over the world with this man, Cellini, who——"

" Maurice Keating!" she broke out, her voice sharp with pain, " you shall *not* insult me! If I go to Washington to-morrow, I go under the protection of Miss Lightwood, a highly respectable lady, whose reputation is beyond the shadow of reproach, and one who has been, in her day, the chaperon of some of the finest singers of Europe!"

A dark flush rose to the young man's cheek:

"You are well aware, Margaret, that I detest that woman. She is worldly and frivolous to the last degree. Weak as she is, and you, a girl of such marked character, her influence over you is simply a species of fascination for which I cannot account. (Nay, hear me out, since you goad me beyond control.) She has bewitched you; she has enslaved you; she has alienated you from your home and friends. Her folly and flattery have transformed the once noble, sensible, and unselfish Margaret Donivan into the unreal and restlessly-ambitious *Marguerite Don Ivan.* Her work was complete when she made you a pupil of that Italian adventurer, Cellini!"

Marguerite's face grew stormy.

"He is *not* an adventurer, Mr. Keating," she panted; "he is a finished artist, and a thorough gentleman, which is more than can be said of some of the friends whom I have known and (it is to be hoped) loved from my childhood! My good Lightwood was right when she declared that you had not a soul above iron."

"You have said enough, Margaret," said the young man in a low, intense voice. "God forgive you for your scorn of a true heart! A foreman in an iron-foundry should not, indeed, sit in judgment on his betters. May your good Lightwood and your gentlemanly Cellini amply compensate you, in the future, for that which I foolishly hoped might have been the glory and the crown of your life!"

They had reached the door of Miss Don Ivan's home. He quitted her abruptly, and strode down the street into the foggy darkness; and she entered the house without a word or a backward glance.

II.

Her aunt was setting the table for tea; a slender woman in shabby mourning, whose care-worn face was a faded counterpart of Marguerite's. The blast of damp air which that young lady brought in with her set the lamp to flaring on an old-fashioned writing desk in the corner, and fluttered the papers over which a girl was bending.

She was like a spirit, more than flesh and blood, that young copyist, so ethereal in form, so transparent in skin, that it did not need a glance at the crooked spine to tell that she was an invalid. Her pale face was full of purity and sweetness; her dress so simple, both in material and make, that Maurice Keating always said the wearer brought to his mind those old, old words: " Whose adorning let it not be the outward plaiting of the hair, or the wearing of gold, or the putting on of apparel; but the hidden man of the heart, the incorruptibility of a quiet and meek spirit, which is rich in the sight of God."

No such holy or soothing words came to Marguerite, however, as she threw aside her things, and sat herself down on a low stool by the fire. She was deaf to Lily's gentle, " What kept you so late, darling ?" and the older woman's, "Isn't your dress damp, my dear ? And hadn't you better change your shoes ?" She could only look from her aunt's threadbare merino to her sister's thin hand, in which the pen was trembling at its work, and think with horror of the white gros-grain at Mme. Fitzeasy's, and the gloves, and the flowers, and the slippers, and all the rest of the folly.

A few months back this had been the sunniest and sweetest hour of the Donivan day. Maurice Keating, glad to escape from the barren resources of a suburban boarding-house into a loved and most congenial atmosphere, generally came to supper every evening; and bringing Margaret safely home from the last tedious music lesson, brought with him at the same time a fund of genial talk and cheerful laughter that seemed to fill the poor little box of a house with warmth and beauty. There was always some delicacy then for slender Lily, a bird or a jelly, a bottle of wine or a few hot-house flowers; and after supper, when the poor tired girl lay resting upon the old lounge before the fire, aunty and Margaret sewed or knitted, while Maurice read aloud from some charming book. It would have been hard to find a happier or a worthier quartette. Marguerite thought of it all now till her heart swelled within her, and her eyes were wet with unshed tears. To quarrel with Maurice and wound his noble nature was bad enough; but to go in debt in such a mean, selfish, underhand way, without the faintest hope of getting out of it, was assuredly the bitterest drop in her bitter cup of retrospection. When her aunt called her to supper she could not even make a show of eating. A sob kept rising in her throat as she sipped her tea in miserable silence, and a voice that welled from a certain bleeding Heart kept sounding ever in her ears: " Learn of Me, for I am meek and humble of heart, and you shall find rest for your soul."

Rest—rest—the rest that remaineth for the people of God, the very thing for which her soul was hungering and thirsting.

Rest—rest—sweeter than the balmy slumber of the tired child, safe in its mother's arms and pillowed close to its mother's heart; purer and deeper than the twilight repose of the weary traveller after his long day's journey, stretched on a downy bed, the hush of contentment on the cozy room, and soft hands bathing his dusty, toil-worn feet.

Rest *for the soul* (was Marguerite's thought), delicious, refreshing rest. But the words must be taken with their context, and the plaintive music of the promise, like phantom bells in the desert, seemed to mock her as she shrank from the hard conditions it imposed.

Her sympathetic companions, reading her pale, stern face (without apparently looking at it), suspected a lovers' quarrel. Leaving her to herself, they kept up a kindly dialogue all the while on homely topics. They knew her too well to harass her with questions. And after the tea things were removed, Marguerite went to the old upright piano in the corner and practised the *Bolero* for hours.

It was only at bedtime, when she took up her candle to go to her room, that she nerved herself to make mention of to-morrow's journey:

"You must call me betimes in the morning, aunty, for I am going to Washington on the early train, and I have arranged to stop for Miss Lightwood on my way to the depot."

She did not look at them as she spoke, and it was never clear to her afterward how she evaded Lily's inquiries about her dress, or her aunt's mild protest against travelling to the Capital (as she meant to do) in her best black silk. The half-smothered sigh that accompanied the words was not lost upon the *débutante*, for that sigh meant unpaid rent, and a grocer's bill, and a half-empty coal bin; but she said nothing about the expensive parcel awaiting her at Miss Lightwood's. What she did say was:

"I am too tired and hoarse to help you with the Rosary to-night, Lily," and so went upstairs, leaving her sister and aunt to tell their beads alone before the little crucifix in Lily's room. Long after the lights were put out, and silence had settled on the house, she stole, in her night-dress and with noiseless feet, into that darkened room, and, kneeling by the bedside, pressed her lips gently to the pale face on the pillow. Lily was asleep; but the cheek that Marguerite kissed was wet with tears, and the regular breathing of the slumberer was broken at intervals by one of those long, shuddering sobs such as children give when, worn out with weeping, they lose all (save the vague memory of their griefs) in innocent repose.

To sleep after that was to dream of being dead and laid out in a gros-grain silk which was all wet and blistered with Maurice Keating's tears, while her aunt and Lily shook over her what seemed at first to be showers of scarlet roses, but which changed as they fell into earthworms and creeping leeches, defiling the whole of her curious shroud. So loathsome to her, in fine, were the waking thoughts of her new and costly dress, that she could not bring herself to look at it until the next evening. Miss Lightwood was with her then, and they stood together before a mirror in one of the rooms of a Washington hotel, making ready for the concert. That highly respectable lady, who had been in her day the chaperon of some of the finest singers of the Old World, had taken her *protégée* (of the New) thoroughly in hand. She had powdered the young girl's skin and rouged her cheeks; she had penciled the naturally fine brows, touched the eyelashes with some sort of an Eastern cosmetic, and built her hair into such a tower of braids and puffs and frizzles and flowers, that Marguerite's *coiffure* was something rare and mysterious to behold.

But, unfortunately, there was a drawback. The resources of the most adroit and practised of dressing-maids are but finite. Fashionable science can adorn, but not create, a subject; and when Light-wood had looped the last spray of flowers and secured the last hairpin, dissatisfaction took posses-sion of her soul. Marguerite's head was *not* a success. Human skill could do no more; it was impossible to dispute *that* fact; but it was equally impossible to dispute another and much more stub-born fact (which almost deserves, from its astound-ing character, to be put into italics). Marguerite looked better, handsomer—yea, even more distin-guished—in her own natural complexion, and her own simple everyday *coiffure*, than she did in all this artificial bravery.

" If I took it, every hair, to pieces again, I don't think I could improve on it," said Lightwood, her head on one side, like a parrot, viewing the dis-appointing effect. " Marguerite, I have never remarked it before, and I am very sorry to have to remark it now, but I am free to say you lack *style*. When your combing-sacque goes off, however, and your new dress goes on, perhaps matters will mend."

And so Marguerite's snowy horror came to light at last, was lifted out of its case, and shaken into a shining mass on Lightwood's arm. How it seemed to fill the room with its gorgeousness! The white slippers waiting their turn on the footstool, the white gloves on the bed, and the spangled fan and trinkets on the table, all sank into obscurity and annihilation before this piece of trailing elegance. Blistering tears, and earthworms and leeches, what

had they to do with such a fresh and lovely thing ?
And yet the *débutante* shuddered as it was whisked
dexterously over her head, and the dressing-maid
pro tem. (coming to the surface of her deep dejec-
tion) began to draw the silken laces. Then the
loathing took a new form:

"Oh, Lightwood! this is detestable!"

"What, my love ?" and the waxen doll looked
up, very red in the face from her unusual exertions.

Miss Don Ivan was still redder, a good, honest,
substantial blush that swallowed up the rouge and
did violence to the powder.

"Look at this corsage; it is cut low, and shame-
fully low at that!"

"My precious child, who ever saw a genuine concert dress with a high corsage ? The thing is pre-
posterous! Why, there was the inimitable Piccaninni, pupil of the divine Rossini, as pure and
modest a flower as ever bloomed on a stage, said to
be a convent graduate, wore her shoulders so
bare (exquisite shoulders she had, I am free to say)
that——"

"I don't care if a hundred Piccaninnis indorsed
it," cried Marguerite hotly. "It isn't decent,
Lightwood, and you know it as well as I do. I
would sooner give up the concert altogether than
go out on a public stage with my neck as bare as
this."

Lightwood stood with clasped hands and shoulders elevated, a picture of aggravating resignation:

" Well then, my dear, I am afraid the audience must forego that delicious *Bolero*. A thousand pities it is, when the dress is so expensive a one, and you have come so far to wear it, and may never in your lifetime have a like chance to display your superb voice to appreciative people. But that is not the worst of it."

" For mercy's sake, don't torture me!" cried Miss Don Ivan crossly. " What more are you keeping back ?"

" Nothing," sighed the exasperating Lightwood, " only Cellini will be as mad as a hornet if you leave him in the lurch for a bit of prudery: and it will be *such* a triumph to that odious Maurice Keating. You will never hear the end of his ' I told you so's,' and the rest of his humdrum platitudes."

Marguerite bit her lips till they pained her, and tapped the floor with the point of her slipper.

" Listen, Lightwood," she said after a pause, " can you not manage a *fichu* of some kind ?"

" Haven't a single thing in the valise that would answer. A common article won't do; it must be real lace, something rich and rare to correspond with the dress. And to go to buy it here in a strange city, and the clock on the minute of seven—don't talk about it! "—and the cunning chaperon elevated her hands and eyes, implying that a *fichu* at such an hour, and under such peculiar circumstances, would command a more than fabulous price.

When Wolsey said to Cromwell:

> "I charge thee, fling away ambition:
>   By that sin fell the angels ; how can man, then,
>   The image of his Maker, hope to win by't?"

he gave utterance to a sublime truth, old as the
eternal hills, which bitter personal experience has
made patent to all the sons and daughters of men
seeking preferment, since the days when Adam
and Eve ate of the primeval apple, that they might
be as gods;—has made patent to none more signally
than to those who, not being to the manor born
(and forgetful that he who exalteth himself shall be
humbled), aspire to sit in the high places of the
earth.

And so, in her little measure and degree, was
Miss Don Ivan to gain the saving knowledge which
a bitter personal experience (the agent of a divine
will and the instrument of a divine grace) alone
could bring her in her day and generation.

She made no further remonstrance. She sub-
mitted in silence to be laced into the ill-fitting
corsage by her adroit companion. She allowed
herself to be turned about like a lay figure in a
modiste's window. Gold buttons were screwed into
her ears; the satin slippers pinched her feet; a
necklace of pearls was fastened about her throat,
and bracelets and rings were adjusted; and, at last,
(the elaborate toilet complete) she saw her full-
length reflection in the swinging mirror.

Her nearest and dearest relation would not have
known her!

The face was not her own, painted and powdered

into a semblance of a wax dummy's in a barber's show-case; the form was not her own, with its naked shoulders and arms, borrowed laces and jewels; and the dress was certainly not her own, for she had not paid for it, and alas! poor victim, she did not know (under heaven) when she ever *would* be able to pay for it.

She felt herself to be what she looked, false, false, false; from head to foot, utterly and supremely false. And she despised herself.

In the small dressing-room behind the stage, she was met by Mr. Cellini. His first puzzled glance told her that he did not recognize her. The chrysalis had become such a very remarkable butterfly that the gentleman was not to be blamed for his error. He recovered himself quickly, however, and approaching Marguerite, presented her with a programme. Then he kept near her, plying her with compliments and *bonbons*, and even going so far as to detach some flowers from his buttonhole and lay them in her hand. But there was an odor of wine with it all, which the tuberoses and heliotrope could not cover.

Marguerite's face burned with embarrassment. She felt humiliated, ill at ease; and, although her admiration of her master bordered on worship, she could not disguise from herself the fact that his manner of addressing her was a trifle more familiar than it ever had been before. Instead of pleasing her vanity, this, strange to say, inspired her with a certain fear, and she thought of her aunt, and of old-fashioned Maurice Keating, with a yearning for their protecting presence that was positive pain. The brilliant eyes bending over her led her to droop her own upon the programme she held, and she began to go carefully over its contents. Then, indeed, the iron entered her soul. Her master had said little to her on the subject, but from his significant silence she had inferred flattering things, and fallen into a fatal delusion. " The Washington *soirée* " (she had said to Miss Lightwood) " is to have but *one prima donna*, and the name of that enviable being is Marguerite Don Ivan." Now, to her amazement, she read in the most desirable place on the programme " MME. ETHEL COURTNEY VIVIANI, LATE OF THE ROYAL OPERA AT VIENNA!" The paper shook in her hands. But for the *rouge*, she would have been as colorless as her dress; and in the faintness which came over her (the result of excitement, thwarted ambition, and, it must be confessed, tight lacing) she could scarcely see the obscure number which marked her own modest name on the bill. She nerved herself to look around the room. Besides Lightwood and Cellini, there were present some half-dozen men and women, all musical, all more or less engrossed with boxes of pastilles, their voices, and their gloves. But none of those unassuming ladies could be mistaken for a moment for " Mme. Ethel Courtney Viviani, late of the Royal Opera," etc. The " star of the goodly companie " had evidently not yet arisen. *The prima donna* of the night had not yet condescended to appear.

Marguerite became aware that Lightwood was winking and nodding at her in a most extraordinary and mysterious way, and immediately put her hand to her head, under the impression that some of the finery had got out of kelter.

" It is not that," whispered her friend, drawing nearer, and talking behind her fan; " you look very nice and presentable (although I might as well have let your eyebrows alone, and now that the powder has blown off, I see you are too sallow to wear white); but I heard her in Vienna, and, I am free to say, she is perfectly exquisite and sings like an angel."

" Who?" questioned Marguerite, knowing all the while what the reply would be.

" Mme. Viviani, the celebrated singer. Those people have been telling me all about her, and I *do* think it was mean of Cellini to show you such a slight."

" I don't see how Mme. Viviani can damage *me*," said the young girl proudly. " A cultivated audience will understand at once. *She* is an opera singer, and this is my first concert."

" Oh, yes! but the critics are perfectly merciless, and they always favor those who have been abroad. You might sing like a seraph to-night, but you and your clothes are not imported, and Mme. Viviani and hers are, and, I am free to say, those newspaper

men will pick you to pieces.   I don't want to dis-
courage you, my love," concluded the voluble lady,
" but do you know you are a little, just a little—
hoarse ?"

" It is this abominable dress," retorted poor Marguerite.   " I am fairly shivering with cold, and I
left my shawl in the carriage because it was too old
and shabby to be brought to the light."

" That is a thousand pities," said the chaperon.
" I would insist on your putting on this opera cloak
of mine, but I mean to slip into the hall with one
of the gentlemen whenever your solo is in order;
and it is really a very distinguished audience.   I
peeped through the curtain just now, and I assure
you they are all in evening dress."

" Miss Marguerite," interposed Cellini, bending
over her again with that familiar smile she detested,
" if you will give me this moment that little hand
of yours, we shall go out now for our *duo*."

Like one in a dream (more like one in a nightmare), she faced that sea of eyes.   All she saw was
eyes—eyes—eyes, and a mass of silks, jewels, and
waving fans.   Her long skirt tripped her twice
before she reached the piano, and the awkwardness
of her *début* threw a chill on the critical house.   No
one (who has not tried it) knows how very hard it
is to walk gracefully down a stage for the first time,
and face, simply and naturally, the fire of a battery
of eyes.   There is a difficulty (under such circumstances) with one's elbows and hands which borders
on the insurmountable; and the victim (to borrow

the words of a well-known humorist) seems, in his embarrassed imagination, to have as many feet as a centipede.

Marguerite, in her turn, felt as if all ease and comfort had forever fled.

With her first note came the consciousness that she *was* hoarse; and she grew blind with terror.

The duo was the familiar " *La ci darem* " from " Don Giovanni," of which luckily she knew her part by rote; and the powerful magnetism of Cellini bore her along with an abandon and vim that redeemed her from destruction.

But the Italian's blood was up. The fame of the *maestro* was staked upon the success of his pupil; and the latter almost shrieked aloud from the grip upon her hand.

It was hard enough for her to see that olive face bowing low to the audience at the final cadence, wreathed with smiles and melting with affected suavity; but it was simply terrible to watch it darken upon her the moment his back was turned to the people, and behold it secretly convulsed with arbitrary anger.

" I thought we were going to have a *fiasco*," he hissed between his clenched teeth (as the ghost of an applause followed them off the stage): " Miss Marguerite, you had better look sharp to your *Bolero!* "

As well might he have told a blind woman to look sharp on the brink of a precipice; or a sleep-walker to take care on the dizzy apex of a dangerous roof. For, blinded and stunned, the poor young creature sat herself down in the little dressing-room to which he led her, and heard, more than saw, him tear the music of the unfortunate duet to ribbons, and cast it from him. But, before she could say to him what was trembling on her lips, an excitement arose around the staircase leading to the street. The door was thrown open, and a French maid in a peculiar costume preceded into the apartment a lady on whom all eyes were riveted at once.

III.

She was surpassingly beautiful, and dressed with a magnificence that was simply royal. Her skin was colorless as the petals of a Calla lily, but the red of her delicate mouth, the golden brown of her large eyes, and the shining elegance of her blond hair, made ample amends for her lack of bloom. She was not tall, but moulded most symmetrically. Her jewels were diamonds of the purest water; and the clinging crape of her embroidered dress, and the simple coil of her fair hair, gave such a classical charm to her form and face that poor Miss Don Ivan felt beside her as a barnyard fowl might be supposed to feel beside a bird of paradise.

Cellini and the other gentlemen immediately surrounded her; but she ignored them all, and dropping a white velvet coat from her still whiter shoulders, she seated herself deliberately in a chair near Marguerite, and put out her foot to her maid. The Frenchwoman, on her knees, proceeded to remove the beauty's shoe, and incase the pretty member in a satin slipper which literally blazed with diamonds. And then the other foot was put forth, and the same performance gone through with equal results. Being daintily shod to her satisfaction, and her blond hair relieved of a gossamer scarf, the elegant creature condescended for the first time to look at Cellini through her glass, and to extend to him the tips of her gloved fingers.

The Italian figuratively laid himself down at her feet, and suffered her to walk over him. He devoured her with his wonderful eyes. He hung upon her charming lips. He showed himself so completely oblivious of everything and everybody, save her own sweet self, that Marguerite looked with profound amazement on his transfigured face. The pillar of ice was turned to a pillar of fire.

" My dear," whispered Lightwood in her ear, " he is evidently dead in love with her; and they say she is as rich as a queen. She was hand-in-glove with all the crowned heads of Europe, and the reigning favorite with the late Empress of France. But is it not time for her to sing her solo ? "

" It is full ten minutes since the last piece: and she is next on the programme," answered Marguerite drearily.

" Bless my heart! and how perfectly composed she is! Look at her, walking up and down with

Cellini, and fanning herself—and the audience waiting! That necklace is what I call Oriental; I'm
free to say I never saw a purer set of brilliants.
Some Caliph or Khedive, or some other old Begum
of that sort, threw it to her in a bouquet when she
was brought before the curtain ten times in the
Egyptian opera. What is she going to sing this
evening, anyway, Marguerite?''

"It is marked simply *Ballad,*" said poor Miss
Don Ivan, who was shivering visibly.

"Now, who'd have believed it? One would
think her selection might be an aria, or a cavatina,
or a——''

"*Bolero,*'' suggested Marguerite grimly.

"To be sure'' (not noticing the sarcasm);
"something operatic or classical, or even elabor-
ately ecclesiastical, you know. *Only* a ballad?
And dear me, hear how she talks French one
minute, and Italian the next, as if she had been
born in France, and raised in Italy. There! she
is going on the stage at last! My precious child,
did you ever hear such an uproar in your life?''

It was indeed a perfect tempest of applause that
greeted the appearance of the beautiful *cantatrice.*

Miss Lightwood dragged Marguerite to the stage
door, and (unseen themselves) they could see Cellini
lead the famous Mme. Ethel Courtney Viviani
down to the footlights, which seemed to blaze up
and burn brighter in honor of her approach.

The applause subsided for a second, only to break
out with redoubled vehemence as the lovely creature

stood alone in the centre of the stage and surveyed the crowded house.

Such exquisite coolness and *aplomb!* She might have been facing such throngs every night for a thousand years, for all the emotion the stirring scene seemed to awake in her. Was there no heart to beat, that the color of her creamy cheek never took the faintest blush, nor the golden-brown eyes the smallest dilation? She adjusted the diamond bracelets on her arms, calmly folded her graceful hands, and stood unmoved as a statue. When the house was so still that every man could hear his neighbor breathing, she slightly, very slightly, bent her perfect head, and sang—*Robin Adair.*

Miss Lightwood pinched Marguerite's arm till it was purple; but the girl was too absorbed to feel it. The draught from the open windows (raw, searching November wind) beat upon her uncovered neck and shoulders; and Cellini rudely jostled her in the doorway, as he applauded noiselessly with his gloved palms, and purred to himself in Italian. But Marguerite was lost to every personal discomfort. She was spell-bound, mesmerized, chained hand and foot, by the silver links of the blond one's siren voice. Never had she heard anything like it before. Never had she seen anything like this marvellous repose, this perfect control of every nerve which made " the fair with the golden hair " so graceful a contrast to her frightened and awkward predecessor. But this was not all—ah, no! just Heaven! this was not all. Out on that brilliant stage, in the presence of that elegant and æsthetic audience, the favorite of the crowned heads was singing the very song she (Margaret) had despised and rejected—the simple old *Robin Adair*, without a trill or a cadenza or a foreign flourish or any sort to mar its beauty. The voice that sang it was so superlatively lovely, so easy in its extraordinary cultivation, so full of the rich aroma its owner had brought across the seas from the land whose every breeze is musical with song—that the homely old ballad took a new and most pathetic meaning.

The audience was visibly moved. Silly, overdressed misses forgot to flirt, and found a legitimate use for their airy handkerchiefs. Tears sparkled on the cheeks of worldly-faced women, and were suffered, unchecked, to water the dry dust of treacherous cosmetics; and even the keen eyes of practical merchants, and the dull orbs of plethoric bankers and congressmen, revealed a suspicious moisture. Alas! for the listener who shivered unnoticed in the stage-door! The bitterness of a never-to-be-realized ambition dropped that hour, like burning gall, into Margaret Donivan's sore heart. " Vanity of vanities, and all is vanity, save to love God and serve but Him alone!" She saw Mme. Viviani retreating from the stage, laden with floral treasures, bouquets, baskets, crowns. The public enthusiasm had run mad and found a vent in flowers. She heard the call for madame's footman, which was answered by a colored man in livery, who came to aid in clearing the boards of their fragrant burden; while Cellini led off the triumphant *Diva* literally through a path strewn with roses. And then arose a rapturous *encore*.

"I'm free to say," whispered Lightwood, her flaxen frizzes (very moist and limp with perspiration) hanging over her brows, and her general appearance that of a much-abused doll; "I'm free to say, my love, in all my travels, I never beheld a grander ovation. I can't take my eyes off her."

Neither could Marguerite. And what she saw suggested a sick sultana lying back on her divan with a jewelled *vinaigrette* at her nostrils, and her maid fanning her with a sandal-wood fan. Nor were the slaves wanting to complete the scene. Cellini and a number of distinguished-looking men (who had come in from the audience) surrounded the languid beauty, plying her with compliments in foreign tongues, and paying her homage as to a sovereign queen.

Finally, after a delay sufficient to set the audience into a frenzy (the applause thundering all the while outside), the ex-*prima-donna* of the Royal Opera at Vienna yielded reluctantly to the *encore*, and once more condescended to show her lovely face to her admirers.

Poor Miss Don Ivan sat like a carven image in the corner. Forgotten by her companions, deserted even by the inconstant Lightwood (who had gone over with the rest to the enemy), the poor young singer was only conscious of feeling very cool in her uncomfortable dress, only conscious of a desperate longing to rush out of it all, and get home as quickly as she could to Lily and her aunt. But that awful *Bolero* was yet to come. Cellini had never looked at her nor spoken to her since Mme. Viviani's entrance; and she began to take heart of grace that he, too, had forgotten her. Now, however, he stood before her with a mask of reserve on his face, and the long slender fingers twitching viciously at his mustache. The regal blonde put up her gold-mounted glasses, and superciliously studied the situation. His manner was freezing:

"Are you aware, Miss Don Ivan, that your solo is in order, and that the audience is waiting?"

The poor girl's misery found a voice at last, but it was a very hoarse one.

"Oh, Mr. Cellini! please excuse me this evening. I am ill—I am nervous—I cannot, indeed, I cannot sing that *Bolero.*"

A wicked light came into the *maestro's* stern eyes:

"I shall *not* excuse you," he said between his teeth; "the choice of the *Bolero, signorina,* was your own. In spite of my better judgment, you insisted on selecting it, and now, *pazzerella,* you shall stick to your selection. Come!" And with his hand of iron stripped entirely of its velvet glove, the master led forth his pale and trembling pupil.

Once more the vision of eyes—eyes—eyes—staring at her out of an ambush of silks, and jewels, and waving fans. The very sweetness of the perfumed air helped to turn her sick. Losing Cellini's support (for the *maestro* had retreated again to the stage-door), Marguerite grasped at the piano, and steadied herself—literally, to face the music. The hands beside her struck the keys—a florid prelude —then an awful pause. She was mute.

A hum of surprise began to pervade the house; *lorgnettes* were levelled at the stage, and the sublime indifference of the audience was broken here and there. The critics were growing restless in their toleration of this unknown singer, who lacked both style and prestige.

"Mme. Viviani has killed her!" sighed Lightwood to a ready-made acquaintance, a youth of tender years in a dress suit and lavender gloves, on whom she was wasting her platitudes and her pastilles.

"Pwe-cithe-ly," lisped the gentle dandy.

"Oh! faithful friend, how true you are to your trust!" said a stern, even voice in her ear that made her shiver. But she failed to discover the speaker. The Nemesis was lost in the dense throng around the entrance door.

"Courage!" whispered the accommodating pianist to Marguerite; and he improvised a few more brilliant bars. Then there came another pause more awful than the first, during which audible murmurs of "What does it all mean?" "I do wish she would hurry and get through!" "Aren't you dying to hear that sweet Viviani sing again?" penetrated even to the footlights.

" Go on! " hissed Cellini in the background; and in sheer desperation from Marguerite's dry lips burst a hoarse, discordant strain.   Such a mockery of music!   There was neither time nor tune to the song; and just below her, in the orchestra chairs, a group of fashionable, but ill-bred, young ladies were shaking under her very eyes in spasms of suppressed laughter.

Could it be that all the wholesome air in the house was suddenly exhausted, and Marguerite was smothering in the dreadful vacuum ?   Could it be that the lustrous globes of the chandelier above the stage had broken loose in a crazy transport and were rushing wildly down upon her head ?

She crumpled her music in her gloved hand—took a step backward (unconscious tragedy!) in a blind, dizzy way—and fell flat at the pianist's feet in a dead faint.

Then was seen the spectacle of a tall, broad-shouldered young man with a frank, honest face and a pair of earnest brown eyes making his way from the entrance door, like a strong swimmer, through waves of excited people.

The genteel voice of Lightwood was heard to cry " Murder! " as the vigorous arm of the newcomer dealt destruction to the waxen doll and her amiable dandy; and, leaving them *hors de combat*, Maurice Keating cleared the footlights at a bound, and sprang upon the stage.

> " O sweet pale Margaret!
> O rare pale Margaret!"

She lay there like a marble statue of despair fallen from its pedestal; the broken and bruised flowers that were strewn all about her (*débris* of Mme. Viviani's triumph) mute and fitting emblems of the crushed and broken victim of a blighted ambition. It wrung his very heart to look at her, so ghastly and corpse-like in all that glittering and detestable finery; but the hero of our story did not waste his time in useless sentimentalities or adjurations *à la Romeo.* He was eminently a man of action as well as one of unpretending delicacy, and he loyally resented his maiden Margaret, his pearl, his precious one, being exposed in her hour of helpless humiliation to the profane gaze of those cold-blooded aristocrats. With the grace and agility of a young Lochinvar, he caught up the lifeless form of his poor wilful darling; and with that waxen face upon his shoulder, and the shining length of her snowy dress trailing over his arm, Maurice Keating bore away his prize. The dressing-room door stood open; Cellini and his satellites, the French maid and the colored footman (to say nothing of Lightwood, *désolée,* and supported by her amorous stripling), all pressed around him; but he scattered them, right and left. To snatch from the elegant Viviani the glass of champagne she was about to pour into her own stately throat, and to force it between the white lips of Margaret; to wrap his warm plaid about the reviving girl, and to shut the carriage-door forcibly in the face of the astounded Lightwood, were works which few save

Maurice Keating could have done as rapidly or as well.

But that wretched ride by rail that followed, the stout-hearted young foreman never forgot. The girl was burning with fever, and her strong lover was taxed to the utmost to keep her safely in the car; to soothe her out of singing snatches of that vile *Bolero* in her husky wreck of a voice; and to hide his manly emotion when she pleaded with him in moving terms to send Maurice Keating to her, that she might ask his forgiveness then and there for all her obstinacy and pride.

Before noon the next day Margaret lay in her own little white bed in her own little room, with her aunt and Lily watching anxiously by her side. It was an aggravated case of pneumonia. Disappointment, mental worriment, and the unusual exposure of her neck and chest had done the mischief; and life and death had a tough struggle of it before her naturally good constitution, with the blessing of Heaven, got the mastery. But her singing voice was gone forever.

" My pride is justly punished, dear Maurice," she whispered with a faint smile (when that gentleman at his one hundred and tenth call was admitted for the first time to a peep at the pale and interesting invalid). " The stage has lost a *prima donna*."

" But *we* have gained our Margaret, God bless her!" was the hearty response; and the speaker thought he had never seen his affianced look sweeter or lovelier than she did at that moment, with the penitent light in her eyes and the peaceful smile playing about her lips.

It was her first venture at sitting up, and they had ensconced her in the big easy-chair in aunty's room; and Lily had made her quite gay with a scarlet woollen wrapper and a breast-knot of Maurice's flowers.

She touched them with her thin hand, and the gray eyes were turned brightly on the young man:

" Your ' roses blossom the whole year round,' " she said to him, with a glance at the Christmas frost on the window pane.

" Heaven grant that they may, and that the longest-lived of all my flowers may be my sweet Queen Margaret! They have not told you my secret, dear, but God has been very good to us. The iron men have taken me into the firm this week; and I have the prettiest little nest in the world making ready for my sick bird. As soon as you are strong enough to go to church, Daisy, we will get married like old-fashioned folks, and settle down to housekeeping."

" I am not worthy of you," she said very humbly, and with moist eyes.

" Say rather I am not worthy of *you*," returned he, much moved and shading his face with his hand; and there is no telling to what lengths these mutual self-depreciations might have gone, if Lily had not burst into the room at this juncture in a state of such excitement as to startle even aunty, who, worn out with nursing, was dozing over the fire. Her usually pensive face was radiant with smiles, and she made a show of hiding something in the folds of her apron.

" Miss Lightwood has just been here with a message," she cried merrily.

Maurice's pleasant face was clouded, and the blood rose brightly in Margaret's transparent cheek.

" You need not look so cross, young gentleman," said Lily, not at all abashed at her reception. " It is all so funny, and so nice, and so romantic, that I know you will laugh instead of frowning when you hear the whole of it. *Voilà tout !* Mr. Cellini is to be married at the Cathedral, to-morrow morning, to some Mme. Vivi—Vivi—(bless me! what *was* the name anyway?) ah, yes! Viviani, Mme. Viviani; and Miss Lightwood goes to Europe with them, right after the ceremony, as companion to the bride."

" I am free to say, *Deo gratias !* " murmured Maurice under his breath.

" You would have pitied the poor old soul if you had seen her," pursued Lily, trying to straighten her smiling face into a sympathetic expression; " she was all tears and remorse over Maggie's narrow escape, and she really showed a depth of feeling for which we did not give her credit. She is desperately afraid of shipwreck on the high seas, and she left all sorts of loving adieux for the entire family, not even forgetting her ancient enemy, Mr. Maurice Keating," and Lily courtesied in his direction.

"May every blessing go with her," said that gentleman, with a very serene and sunshiny face; "and may she enjoy the delights of the Old World so thoroughly and so supremely that she may never be tempted to return to the annoyances of the New! But what are you hiding in your apron, Pussy?"

"Ah! that is the best of it," and Lily crossed the room and knelt by her sister, looking up into her pale face with eyes brimful of tenderest affection. "Maggie dear, Mr. Cellini is also very, very sorry for his share in your sufferings, and he has sent Lightwood expressly to say so, and to present you in his name with this little token of his lasting regret."

She threw aside her apron as she spoke and held up before them all the lovely little picture of the Sacred Heart of Jesus which Margaret had seen in the *maestro's* room the night before the fatal concert. Once more she beheld the sweet Saviour pointing to the glowing Heart upon His breast as if inviting her to enter into that sanctuary of love and peace; once more the pitying eyes and tender lips seemed about to speak the words inscribed upon the margin: "Learn of Me, for I am meek and humble of heart"; and *this* time (thanks to His patient and persistent mercy!) she did not reject His inspiration, she was not deaf to His pleading whispers. The happy tears were shining in her eyes as she laid the gift in her lover's hands.

"'Meek and humble of heart,'" she said softly,

looking up into his face, " and only God and my
confessor know how full *my* heart has been of anger,
and pride, and obstinate ambition.   Oh, Maurice!
how much I have to learn before I shall find rest to
my soul."

. " We will study the lesson together, dear love,"
was his grave and gentle answer; " we will go like
little ignorant children, day after day, to learn in
that sacred school; and surely at last when we ask
the Master and His holy Mother to bless our humble wedding feast, He will not refuse to change the
water into wine, but will draw us closer and closer
to Himself, and make us henceforth the faithful
servants of His meek and lowly Heart."

ANNA HANSON DORSEY.

Mrs. Anna Hanson Dorsey was born in Georgetown, D. C., December 17th, 1815, and descends from a number of the most brilliant and patriotic Colonial and Revolutionary families of Maryland. She is a convert to the Catholic faith, having been received into the Church by the Rev. Louis Regis Deluol several years after her marriage with Lorenzo Dorsey, Esq.

Mrs. Dorsey is the pioneer of Catholic light literature in the United States, and her works, from her first story, "The Student of Blenheim Forest," to her last book, "Palms," have enjoyed a never-diminishing popularity.

The list is a long one, including: ''The Oriental Pearl,'' ''May Brooke,'' ''The Young Countess,'' ''Tears on the Diadem,'' ''Woodreve Manor,'' ''The Sister of Charity,'' ''Mona the Vestal,'' ''Nora Brady's Vow,'' ''Dummy,'' ''Fair Play is a Jewel,'' ''The Flemmings,'' ''Coaina,'' ''The Old Gray Rosary,'' ''Tangled Paths,'' ''Guy the Leper,'' ''The Heiress of Carrigmona,'' ''Adrift,'' ''Zoe's Daughter,'' ''Beth's Promise,'' ''Ada's Trust,'' ''Warp and Woof,'' ''The Old House at Glenaran,'' ''The Fate of the Dane,'' ''The Mad Penitent of Todi,'' ''The Story of Manuel;'' three admirable juveniles, ''Tom Boy,'' ''Two Ways,'' ''The Snow Angel;'' and finally her crowning achievement, ''Palms,'' pronounced by all the critics to be the equal of ''Ben-Hur,'' and by some its superior.

During the late Civil War Mrs. Dorsey was an earnest lover and ardent advocate of the Union cause, and her burning patriotism found vent in two ringing lyrics: ''They're Comin,' Grandad, A Tale of East Tennessee,'' and ''Men of the Land.'' And her ''Mother and Son'' was said to be the best piece of literature evoked by the Custer Massacre.

She has been the recipient of the highest honors that the Church in America can confer, being a Lætare Medallist. Her work has been twice especially blessed from Rome, and the tribute recently paid her by the Bishops is one of the most highly-prized happenings of her life.

She has been a widow for many years and lives at her home on Washington Heights, Washington, D. C., crowned with years and honors, and surrounded by her children, her grandchildren, and her great-grandchildren.

The Mad Penitent of Todi.

BY ANNA HANSON DORSEY.

I.

IT is near sunset as two men stand talking on one
of the lower terraces of the public garden of an old
Umbrian town, which, perched on the mountain
side, looks down, with its time-worn walls and tur-
rets, like a grim warden over the beautiful valley
below, where the Tiber and the Naga unite their
waters and flow peacefully through fertile meadows
and shadowy solitudes, lending brightness to the
scene and musical echoes to the air; where, in more
shallow places, the stream, made impetuous by
obstructions, dashes in wild eddies and wreaths of
foam over the grotesque rocks which by some freak
of nature pave its bed.   The glow of sunset is over
all: a tint of rose-color here, flashes of gold there;
and farther away, on the sides of the rugged mountains, soft purple shadows creep slowly up, to throw
a twilight mantle over the shining mists that like
bridal veils crown their summits.   The perfume of
roses and jessamine makes the air drowsy with fra-

grance, and the first trills of the nightingale are heard in snatches from the leafy coverts.

Suddenly the silvery chime of a convent bell, higher up the mountain than the old city, floats out on the hushed air, repeating to heaven and earth the oft-told story of the Incarnation and the glory of Mary; then the deep-throated bell of the Cathedral, and that of St. Francis Assisi strike in, the air trembling and pulsing with their notes as the *Angelus* sweeps heavenward, while a solemn stillness falls upon the city, upon the gay pleasure-seekers in the gardens, upon the groups chattering and laughing around the fountains; upon little children, and proud cavaliers, noble dames, peasants, and the toil-worn sons of labor; and all, with one accord, saint and sinner alike, kneel in honor of that supreme moment which announced to the world a Saviour.

The two men rise from the reverently whispered prayer, and turn to ascend the broad marble steps leading to the gardens. They are near the top; but, reluctant to leave a view so beautiful, pause, and turn again towards the valley. One of them is past middle age, a man of grave, abstracted, but gentle countenance; the other, in the first glow of early manhood, with dark, soul-lit eyes, finely chiselled aquiline features, and a dreamy expression which harmonizes well with the clear pallor of his complexion. The elder man had spent his life in endeavoring to master the science of the stars. His companion, a Florentine, was already pluming his poet-wings for sublime flights which would one day fill the world with his fame. Both stand silent, the astrologer thinking of the hour which will triumphantly verify his calculations, the poet steeping his soul in the glowing loveliness outspread before him, when suddenly wild shrieks fill the air, people rush hither and thither, as if seeking safety; some, in their blind haste get too near the edge of the terrace, lose their footing and roll, spinning over and over, to the bottom; but there is no one to laugh at them—the panic is too universal.

The two friends hasten forward, and have scarcely reached the last step when two spirited Andalusian horses, harnessed to a light magnificent chariot of a new fashion, dash towards them; their driver, a handsome young man in richly embroidered garments of garnet velvet, with heavy chains of gold about his neck, his long dark hair flying backwards on the wind, trying in vain to curb them. His companion—a female—whose jewels and superb attire glitter and flash in the last level rays of the sun, with white agonized face clings shrieking to his arm, impeding his efforts to rein in the frightened animals, whose course leads direct towards a narrow belt of olives and ilex which grow on the very borders of a precipice overlooking the valley a hundred feet below.

With one impulse the friends spring forward, and at the risk of their lives seize the horses' heads, and the Florentine with a quick motion throws his cloak over their wild, fiery eyes: the sudden movement,

the sudden darkness, check their mad flight, and
they fall back upon their haunches, their silken coats
covered with foam, their limbs trembling and convulsed; then he passes his long soft hand gently
over their faces, speaking caressingly to the frightened creatures, smooths and pats them on shoulder
and flank, until at last they stand quiet. Many
persons—the danger past—now press around with
zealous offers of assistance; and the gentleman,
having descended from the chariot and led his companion to a grassy bank, directs some workmen,
who stand by, to lead the horses to his stables,
throwing them several broad gold pieces to ensure
the safe conduct of his equipage. Having seen that
his horses step off quietly, he turns—not to the
frightened woman, trembling and sobbing hysteri-
cally where he left her, and from whom other
women stand aloof—but to find his preservers, who
are just turning into a shaded alley which leads by
a short cut to the street. Walking swiftly forward,
he overtakes them, and, saluting them courteously, .
holds out his hand, and thanks them in earnest language for saving his companion and himself from a
certain and terrible death. But the outstretched
hand is unnoticed, and the older of the two men
replies in coldly courteous words that " they deserve no thanks for obeying a humane impulse."

Chagrined at the repulse, the young cavalier,
with the blood rising hotly to his face, hands them
his card, saying: " If I can ever requite the service
done me to-day, present or send this to my

address "; then, turning on his heel with haughty mien, he walks away.

" I see by the flush upon thy cheek, Alighieri, that thou art shocked by my rudeness."

" I must confess to the fact, Maestro; for that is as handsome and fair-spoken a cavalier as I ever saw."

" Yes, he's handsome, and he's fair-spoken, more's the pity; and he's not only of gentle birth, but the only son of the richest man in Umbria,— more's the pity again."

" Why, may I ask ? "

" Because his position and gold give him great power to do evil, for which he has a large capacity, and he loses no opportunity to follow the impulse."

" Dear Maestro, art thou not severe on the follies of youth? "

" Towards the *follies* of youth I am lenient, but I must judge a man by his virtues or vices. Listen, Alighieri: that man whose life we have just saved is Jacques dei Benedetti, the greatest profligate of the age; he is breaking his old father's heart by his wasteful profusion and his shameless pleasures—"

" And the lady——"

" Faugh! do not name her. She is lost to virtue, to shame, and to all womanliness, and yet he dares to flaunt her in jewels and rich raiment, which are the price of sin, before the eyes of the fair matrons and virgins of Todi. It had been better, perhaps, had we let them be dashed to pieces."

" If God, the All-seeing, were not over all!" said Alighieri, making the sign of the cross. " The future is a sealed book to us."

" Well! if Jacques dei Benedetti is preserved this day for any good end, it will be a miracle," said the elder man, laughing. " Don't understand, because I am incredulous, that I am not willing it should be so; for the Church hath saints whose beginning was not a whit better than his; but such things are hard to realize."

" The man hath touched me strangely, and I will offer a decade of *Ave Marias* daily for him," said Alighieri.

" Our blessed Lady loves to win such triumphs; may thy *Aves* be blessed!" said the Maestro, lifting his velvet cap, and glancing upward for an instant; but in that one glance he saw, pillowed on a fold of purple cloud, the evening star just risen from behind the mountain. " I would have thee come with me to my eyrie, Alighieri, but the stars are beginning to come out, and I must be vigilant lest I lose the first appearance of the new planet."

" Thou hast yet faith ? "

" Yes, unless the heavens fall," said the astrologer, fixing a look of rapt belief on the blue depths above.

This man, Bartolomeo Tasti, had spent the best years of his life in studying the movements of the heavenly bodies, and it was said that he was master of the more occult science of astrology. It is certain that many of his predictions had been verified, and the common mind regarded him with awe, as one whose knowledge of hidden things was indisputable; but he, pursuing the even tenor of his way, waited only for the appearance of the new planet, to crown his labors with triumph.

" I would fain go with thee to thy quiet eyrie, Maestro, if only to read the poetry of the heavens, but I have an engagement at the house of one of thy citizens, to whom I brought letters."

" Keep watch and ward over thy heart, Alighieri; for there's a beautiful maiden in the house of Gondolfo the banker."

" So I have heard. But how didst thou divine my destination so truly ? "

" No divination in the matter. I met Gondolfo to-day and he told me that he had invited thee this evening; but I had forgotten it until thou didst speak of thy engagement."

With a warm grasp of the hand the friends separated. The young Florentine had heard much of the beautiful Julia from Father Giovanni, a monk of St. Francis Assisi, whose monastery crowned one of the hills back of the town. " She will devote herself to Heaven," the good monk said, folding his hands with a smile of complacency; " such a soul is indeed a true daughter of our blessed St. Francis."

And Alighieri thought, as he saw her an hour afterwards moving among her guests with winning smiles and graceful mien, clothed in the rich attire befitting her station, and decorated with the old jewels of her house, that she far surpassed the ideal he had formed of her, and could but sigh that so radiant a creature should seclude herself in a convent; such perfection, his poetic mind imagined, would win more souls to Heaven in the world than she could hope to do by austerities and prayers in the cloister, the Italians even then having a saying that " a beautiful woman is the thought of God."

So, as on one set apart for Heaven, he gazed, until her fair image was imprinted on his imagination so vividly, that in later years, under the form of Beatrice, the world saw her in the " Divine Comedy."

He lingered some days longer in Todi, studying the marvellous paintings and sculptures of Guido of Sienna, of Cimabue and Giotto, and seeking in the monastery and convent chapels scenes in the life of the beloved patron Francis. And here, wandering through the delicious scenery, he pored over St. Bonaventure's " Legend of St. Francis," and felt his heart moved by the account of the saint's last hours, " when the swallows, those little birds that love the light and hate darkness, though the night was falling when he breathed his last, came in a great multitude, filling the windows and roof."

Likewise did St. Francis find immortal honor in the " Divine Comedy," which seems part of the glory with which he is crowned in heaven.

Several times after the evening spent at her house, Alighieri saw the beautiful maiden at the early Masses, sometimes coming from Holy Communion, her eyes downcast, her bared,* perfect hands folded, her countenance clothed in such peace as the world cannot give — unseeing, and unthinking of all except the heavenly Guest who abode in her heart.

And occasionally he met, either driving or on the promenade, the handsome cavalier Benedetti, always conspicuous for his perfect physique, the bold beauty of his face, his rich attire, and the good-nature which threw bows and smiles to his friends or a handful of silver to the beggars. The poet's heart was strangely drawn towards him, why he did not seek to analyze, knowing how impossible a friendship would be between them; but he never failed to whisper the *Ave Marias* he had vowed for his conversion.

II.

It is early summer, and in the three years that have glided by the world appears to have moved on without change in the old city perched on the mountain side. The games are over; it is very quiet; every one is complaining of the dulness, and weary to death for a sensation.

But it is always a deathlike stillness which precedes the earthquake, and one day a rumor suddenly shook the old city that made men turn pale and hold their breath; it was that, at last, Jacques dei

---

* In Catholic countries it is a custom for ladies to unglove during Mass.

Benedetti had ruined his father, and there was nothing left except the house that sheltered them, and that only because it had been inalienably settled upon him and his descendants by his grandfather !

One morning, shortly after this, the elder Benedetti was found seated at his desk, his account-books open before him, with pen in hand—dead. His son was instantly summoned. He had avoided his father's presence ever since the crash—the silent anguish of the old man hurting him more than the most violent reproaches would have done. He hastily entered the library, not knowing what to expect—for the servant who called him was incoherent from terror—and stood arrested by the shock, as if turned to stone. His eyes, starting from his head, gazed upon the staring eyes of the dead; his face grew white and drawn, while the veins in his temples and neck stood out like whipcords. No tear relieved the remorse that stung him, no passionate outcry relieved his grief, no whispered prayer escaped his lips, as he stood there motionless before the cold, silent figure upon whose wide-open eyes the expiring lamplight flickered, imparting to them a life-like expression of wrath and reproach. Suddenly the flame shot up and expired, and the stricken man beheld only the sad, pathetic expression left upon the dead face by the last throb of a broken heart.

With a cry of anguish Jacques threw himself upon his knees, and, lifting the cold, stiff hand, pressed it to his burning forehead, and registered a vow—a vow which he fulfilled to the letter. Then he stooped and kissed the dead man's feet; he dared not desecrate that poor, sorrowful face by a caress—he who had brought such bitterness, even death itself, to him who had never reproached or pained him by a harsh word.

He secluded himself in his own apartment, leaving to the good monks of St. Francis, to whom his father had been a generous benefactor, and a few of the most trusted servants of the house, all the necessary arrangements for the last rites. Masses were daily offered for the repose of the departed soul, and all that the faithful could do, all that the Church could do, through the communion of saints, was done to win for it a place of "refreshment, light, and peace." The funeral, as was customary in Italy, took place by torchlight. One figure wrapped in a black cloak, walked by the bier, and while the priests and monks chanted the solemn services of the dead, no tear, no sign of emotion was visible in his white, rigid face. People touched each other to notice him, and wondered at his heartlessness; "he is either turned to stone," they said, "or he is dead to all natural feeling." Ah, they did not know.

But there was one present, closely veiled, who watched him with the deepest pity, from whose eyes tears flowed, and from whose heart pure prayers ascended for his conversion and consolation. This was Julia Gondolfo, who attended the funeral with her father—between whom and the deceased a life-long friendship had existed. She beheld under the still calm of those features a stern, remorseful grief, too deep for expression, and she would fain have whispered words of sympathy; but that being impossible, she could only pray, and oh! how earnestly, for she knew he had sinned deeply, and her heart was filled with a great compassion for him, lest without consolation or divine help he might despair and end his own life. Every one was against him; all blamed him; but he had been her playmate once, and she remembered the gentle traits of his character, especially his kindness to the poor, and his merry companionship.

The gentle maiden need have had no dread on one point. Jacques had no thought of self-destruction; on the contrary, he meant to live and repair the fortune he had wasted, and the honor of his house; this was what he had vowed, and this was to be henceforth the *motif* of his existence. He would live only for this, and accomplish it, or die in the attempt.

He disappeared from men's eyes; the gay resorts of pleasure saw him no longer; his splendid horses, equipages, and jewels were sold; those who had ministered to his sinful pleasures were peremptorily, and without appeal, dismissed, and of the small remnant of a fortune inherited from his grandfather, and the result of his sales, he formed the nucleus of a new business. None so attentive to his affairs, none so exact as he, and none so frugal! To Venice, to Florence, to Marseilles and other marts he journeyed, and one or two fortunate speculations brought him immense gains. Grave and quiet in his demeanor, he was never seen in public except at Mass, or sometimes in the evening wandering alone in the more retired parts of the public gardens, his avoidance of all sympathy and companionship keeping away his former friends.

Prosperity crowned his energetic efforts, and in two or three years he had nearly retrieved his losses and the honor of his old house, which still carried on its business in his father's name. He began now to relax somewhat the severity of his self-imposed isolation from society, and one day he accepted Count Gondolfo's invitation to dine with his daughter and himself—with Julia, who yet told her beads and offered her Communions for him. Living so long apart from all social intercourse, it is not strange that he should have been at once attracted, fascinated by the exquisite loveliness and gentle grace of his young hostess; he felt as if under the influence of a mysterious spell, not only while in her presence, but afterwards; thoughts and feelings heretofore strangers took possession of his mind, and again seeking her, drawn by an irresistible impulse, he found himself even more bewildered and fascinated than at first; he could not define his sensations, nor recognize the fact that it was the dawning of the first virtuous love he had ever known.

But how one so fair and saintly in her life could ever consent to become the bride of the man whose record was stained with sins and vices which had broken his father's heart, became the topic of the day in Todi; for Jacques, determined to woo and win her, had made known his sentiments to her father, to whom he furnished proofs that he had more than retrieved his fortunes, and had put aside forever the vices of his earlier life, which, he declared, were more the result of an undisciplined youth than of a malicious preference for sin; and now he wanted a wife like Julia, who, like an angel by his side, would lead him to a better and higher life.

Count Gondolfo probed deeply the past history of his daughter's suitor, and, with stern insistence to know clearly much that had been only half revealed by rumors and gossip, questioned him without mercy. But he was equal to the ordeal; he frankly acknowledged his guilty peccadilloes, but defied the strictest investigation of his life since he had turned his back on the follies and sins of the past. The old Count, at length satisfied of his sincerity, felt that he might trust his daughter's happiness to his keeping, and consented to her receiving his addresses, saying: " Thy cause must stand upon thy own merits, Benedetti. I shall not interfere either for or against. My daughter is old enough to judge for herself, and is too precious for me to want to be separated from her; therefore do not count in the least upon me."

" Never fear, Count Gondolfo," said the other, proudly; " I must have a willing bride or none.

Julia is my first love; if she in turn loves me, I shall be the happiest man living. Good night.''

Julia did not reject her lover's suit, neither did she accept him; she only asked in shy, broken words for time to consider his proposal. The delay would have chafed his proud spirit beyond endurance, had not the soft blushes that mantled her cheeks, and the quickened throbbings of her heart, which stirred the rich lace upon her bodice, assured him; and he yielded with tender deference to her request, hopeful and confident as to what the final answer would be. Meantime the gentle maiden did not propose to settle this momentous question by her own unaided judgment. She had Masses offered, commenced a novena to St. Francis, and asked the prayers of the saintly religious of Santa Agnese and of the Franciscan monks, and of many faithful souls among her poor, for her intention.

The rumor that she was betrothed to Jacques dei Benedetti penetrated convent and cloister, and, although none questioned her, they understood what her '' intention ''was,—and, truth to say, the holy souls were opposed to it, for had they not always believed her a virgin too fair and pure for any earthly love, and that she was surely destined to become the bride of Heaven ? The Virgin without stain, the sweet Mother of Jesus, was besieged by the devotion of all who best loved Julia, and feared that she was rushing to the destruction of her earthly happiness; and on the day the novena ended, never except on a saint's *festa* had so many thronged to receive and offer Holy Communion that all danger and evil be averted from her whom many of them looked upon as a victim to the wicked designs of an unprincipled man,—notwithstanding which they prayed ardently for his conversion, for (as they said) if any one ever needed such prayers and the saving grace of God, it was Jacques dei Benedetti.

But there was no miraculous interposition—no sign vouchsafed to show either the approval or the displeasure of Heaven, and the betrothal was duly announced, and celebrated with great splendor by a superb entertainment. The nuptials followed shortly after, and never had so lovely and magnificently dressed a bride been seen in Todi; never a bridegroom so noble in appearance, so perfect in manly beauty. But as the grand nuptial Mass went on, every one felt a sensation of thankfulness, and drew a long breath of relief when they saw the Sacred Host laid upon the bridegroom's tongue; and the remark of an old woman at the church door, afterwards, represents the sentiment which had generally prevailed at the moment.

"Thanks to our blessed Lady, he's not given over body and soul to Satan, or he'd have dropped dead when he received," said she to a friend.

"They don't always," mumbled the other old crone. "Let them wait as cares to, to see the end of it. God has His ways and we have ours, and they are as far apart as the East and the West!"

That was a grand truth: '' God's ways are not as our ways.''

And of all the gossip and talk that day, there was nothing came so near the truth as the saying of that toothless old woman.

III.

The marriage was a happy one. Jacques idolized his wife, and revered in her the Christian virtues which made her life more beautiful than that of other women. He accompanied her to High Mass on Sundays and the great *festas;* because he desired to make her happy, and he loved to watch her in her rich attire, more beautiful than any pictured saint upon the walls. It was not long, however, before she discovered that although his life was morally changed he never approached the Sacraments, and whenever he alluded to religion, it was in light, careless terms, which pained and saddened her.

Benedetti was now jurisconsult of Umbria, a dignity conferred upon him by the reigning prince in reward for some successful achievement in finance which had greatly benefited the royal treasury, and he felt it to be due his position to take the lead universally conceded to him. With all his pride, he was never haughty or arrogant; the same good-nature and generosity characterized him now as in the past, and he dealt even justice in all cases over which he had jurisdiction. Upon his wife he lavished the most profuse and magnificent gifts: the richest stuffs from Genoa, from Persia, and Lyons; the most cunning embroideries from India, the most rare and costly laces from Venice and Flanders; opals, pearls, and diamonds set in rare devices in gold, he offered as love-gifts to her; the most costly equipages and the finest of Arabian horses were imported for her use, and it was his pleasure and will that she should appear in magnificent attire at the entertainments, the games, and the public gardens, where her peerless beauty made her the cynosure of every eye.

Not only was he generous in this prodigal fashion to her, but he won the hearts of the good religious on every side by his *largesse* to their charities and his alms to the poor. If a new altar was to be erected, or new mosaics were needed, another wing to be added to the monastery of St. Francis, or an orphanage established, or stained glass from Venice for an abbot's memorial, his was the hand that responded, partly because he knew it would please his wife, but more because he was by nature lavish and fond of giving; and he was blessed and prayed for as no other sinner in Todi had ever been before.

And these prayers! Do we not read in St. John's vision of golden vials in which were the prayers of the saints? Why then should one ever faint with despondency, even after years of unanswered prayers?

Within a year of her marriage, Julia's father died, leaving his daughter a large fortune; he blessed his children, for he loved Benedetti as his own son, and besought him to watch over and guard his daughter's happiness; then, fortified and consoled by the rites of the Church, he passed away in hope.

In Julia's heart, consolation mingled with grief; it was her sweet privilege, she knew, to help him by her prayers and more solemn devotions; that, although separated for a season, her intercourse with him would remain unbroken. But Benedetti, gazing sadly upon the white, drawn features of the old patrician, as the flicker of the blessed tapers trembled over their motionless calm, thought: "And is this the end ? Death, the grave, and forgetfulness! Rather let us enjoy life while it lasts; let us eat, drink, and be merry! Faugh! the thought of becoming a carcass sickens me"; and he left the death-chamber to go out into the sunshine and scented air of his garden, his only grief being the tears which he knew must flow from the eyes of his wife, and the shadow that death would throw across his home. He hated gloom; he breathed freely only when in an atmosphere of gay, stirring life, and surrounded by everything that could charm the senses or delight the taste. But the period of mourning was inevitable; it was one of the penalties of his rank and station, and he determined to go through it with the best grace he might.

One year of intolerable weariness to Benedetti passed by; several times he determined to leave home for a month or two, but he could not bear to absent himself from his gentle wife, more beautiful in her sadness than even in the sunshine of happiness, and her efforts to be cheerful for his sake were so full of pathos that he would rather have seen her weep.

A few friends were admitted during these days of mourning; and her drives usually terminated at the convent of Santa Agnese or the monastery of St. Francis, where, in sweet converse with the saintly men and women who had devoted themselves by heroic vows, body and soul, to Heaven, the hours passed swiftly and happily by. Every morning found her humbly kneeling before the altar of St. Stephen the Martyr, offering her Communion and devotions for her father and her husband. Nor were her poor forgotten: in seeking to alleviate their sufferings, and in other works of mercy, her time was well and profitably occupied.

But as the days passed on, Benedetti, who had nothing to console him beyond the perishable things of earth, grew restive. The silence and gloom of his house became more and more intolerable to him; his patience had been rare, but it was now nearly worn out, and he began to absent himself from home, frequently not returning until far into the night, and sometimes not until daydawn.

Julia observed these signs with sad surprise; he was not less kind or affectionate in his manner towards her, but—he was seeking pleasures outside his own home. Soon she noticed that under some slight pretext or other, often without any, he would hurry from her presence, leaving her lonely, and saddened by vague apprehensions. One evening he came in with reddened face, his speech thick, and his gait unsteady, doing his best in a fond, maudlin way, to conceal his real condition. She was very gentle towards him, nay, tender in her great pity; and when, under pretext of not feeling well, he retired, she was thankful.

She spent the hours of that sorrowful night in questioning her own heart severely, and praying earnestly for guidance. "I have been selfish!" was the result of her self-examination; "I have expected too much of my husband, who finds his greatest happiness in the pleasures of the world, and flies from solitude and devotion as something fit only for priests and nuns. This is no way to win an influence over him which will lead him to better and higher things. I will henceforth forget myself, and bury my griefs for his sake; and oh! Blessed Lady of Sorrows, help me by thy intercession; pray for my husband, that the fruit of thy Son's Passion and thine own unspeakable sorrows may not be lost on him."

Two or three days after this, when Benedetti had quite recovered from the fumes of the strong foreign wines he had drank that night, and to the use of which he was unaccustomed,—for with all his faults, he was temperate in the use of liquors,—he drove out, and after his return appeared on the promenade of the gardens in his usual way, elegantly attired, dignified, as became a jurisconsult, and affable to all. When he returned home, towards his dinner hour, with a sort of chill at the thought of what would meet him there, what was his surprise to find his house brilliantly lighted, and to hear the sound of music stealing through the half-closed *jalousies !* He hastily entered: the fragrance of flowers welcomed him; the sight of their glowing hues, grouped with dark greens, decorating the vases and garlanded about the pillars, filled his sensuous nature with a thrill of ecstasy. He saw no one, and ran up to his wife's dressing-room, where he found her in rich attire, decked with his favorite gems, and looking more beautiful than ever, as she came forward with smiles to greet him. He was overjoyed; never had she looked so lovely, so regal; never had such brightness and fragrance pervaded his home.

"I am thankful that at last thy penance is ended," he said, embracing her. "How beautiful thou art, *bella sposa !* and what an enchanting surprise thou hast prepared for me! Ah," he said, gazing fondly upon her, "how much more suitable to thy years, than so much praying, and fasting, and penance!"

"Penance, dear Jacques! Dost thou ever think of penance?" she asked, with a smile, smoothing the hand which still clasped hers.

"Think! Of course I think of it! How can I help it with such a devout little wife! And my father's death gave me penance enough for a life-time," he said, with a sad inflection in his voice.

"True, that was a great sorrow," she said,

raising his hand and leaning her fair cheek upon it.

" It was, and will be to my dying day, a bitter remorse. What more penance wouldst thou have the heart to ask for me, *bella sposa*, than this ? "

" Dear Jacques, my husband, let me do penance for thee. I will gladly, and mayhap our dear Lord will accept it."

" What a little enthusiast! " he said, laughing, and kissing her hand as he folded her to his breast. " How glad I am that thou didst not live in the days of Santa Agnese! Thou wouldst surely have won the palm of martyrdom. Do penance for me, *cara mia*, if it will make thee happier; only don't flog thy fair flesh, or torture it with sackcloth. I would rather not have such vicarious penance, my nightingale."

She smiled, and said sweetly, as she left the dressing-room :

" It is time for thee, dear one, to change thy dress; a party of friends are to join us at dinner, and even now I must hasten down to receive them."

" Company to dinner! " he exclaimed; " how delicious! " and she could but smile at his almost boyish delight.

A year passed by after this, and the jurisconsult led a life which completely filled out his ideal of happiness. The most beautiful woman in Italy— had not the artists and poets so crowned her ?—was his wife; they loved each other devotedly; there seemed to be nothing to cloud his felicity, and

he had retrieved himself in the opinion of his fel-
low-citizens, who, smiling, said to each other:
" Aha! our jurisconsult has sowed all his wild oats!
See what a good and beautiful wife can do for a
man!"

As we said before, he was devoted to art, and
was ever ready to assist young and struggling
artists; and he had the honor of entertaining
Alighieri. From him he heard ill news of the
astrologer Tasti. The old star-gazer had gone
blind, and his heart was broken; his star had not
yet appeared, and now he could never behold it;
he was living in actual want, without a friend to see
to his needs.

" My God!" exclaimed Benedetti, " to think I
am rolling in wealth and luxury, while the man who
saved my life is without bread! Alighieri, pledge
thyself to do me a favor."

" If I may, most gladly," answered the poet,
gravely.

" Thou mayest if thou wilt; I ask nothing that
could hurt the most sensitive scruples of a saint,"
said Benedetti, flushing.

" What wouldst thou have, friend ? " said the
sweet-voiced Florentine.

" I would have thee be my almoner; not really
to give alms, but to repay a debt I owe to Tasti by
all the laws of honor and gratitude."

" Ah, I see!" said Alighieri, a divine smile
brightening his countenance.

" I would settle an annuity upon him for life.

Let him think it is a long-delayed debt due his family—make up any harmless romance thou mayest about it. *I* must not appear; for he'd throw the money into the fire, and me after it, if he could lay hands upon me. Say, wilt thou manage this?"

"I must think it over, and see how best it can be done."

"How best? It does not require a moment's thought. So many thousand ducats are placed in thy hands by me, which thou wilt deposit in thy own name to the credit of Giovanni Tasti. What can be more plain?"

"I will, and with a thankful heart that our blessed Lady has inspired thee to so help the friendless and destitute," said the Florentine, grasping his hand.

"It is a debt, and my religion is to pay my debts," replied Benedetti, dryly. "When will thy cursed pride let me pay that which I owe thyself?"

"Should need overtake me, friend, I will not fail to call upon thee," answered Alighieri.

"I trust to thy word; and now to business, for I will not sleep until it is all settled."

And so it was done, and a divine rest filled Alighieri's compassionate heart, which had been torn and grieved beyond measure by the condition in which he had found his old friend, whose needs he had no power to relieve, his own means being barely sufficient to procure him the necessaries of life. Now he could leave him in comfort, with an attendant to care for him, and enough to provide clothing and any little luxury he might crave; and all owing to the noble generosity of a man he had once despised, and refused to know,

IV.

One bright day, at an hour when he was rarely there, Benedetti came home in a gay mood, and went with quick steps towards an apartment which opened on the garden, where his wife usually spent her mornings.   The light air he was humming died upon his lips as, looking around, he saw no signs of her except her empty chair, and a coarse woollen garment, that her fair hands had been fashioning for one of her poor, lying upon it.

" Where is your lady ? " he asked her favorite maid, who was seated in a window, busied over a piece of embroidery.

" My lady has gone to the Cathedral, signor, to offer prayers," she answered.

" The fiend fly off with so much praying! " he exclaimed, hotly. "Are you sure it is to the Cathedral she is gone? "

" Yes, signor, because she took flowers to lay on the old Count's tomb."

" How long has she been away ? "

" About a half hour, signor."

" There is some chance then of my finding her there ? "

" I think so, signor."

Chafing with impatience, Benedetti rushed off to the Cathedral, where, just as he was crossing the marble pavement of the wide portico, he heard the voice that always fell upon his ear like a strain of music say: " Here! Shall we turn back ? " And she was beside him, wondering with deep emotion if he had come thither for some pious purpose.

" Aha, runaway! is it thou ? Turn back ? Not for the world. I only came to bring thee away, for I have great news for thee, *bella sposa*."

" Good, I trust ? "

" Joyous! But I will hold thee in suspense until we get home," he answered, gayly.

The distance was short between the Cathedral and their house; and after Julia had thrown aside her veil and mantle, and seated herself, she said:

" Now I am ready for the great news."

" Great news indeed! " he exclaimed, throwing himself upon the pillow of an ivory couch that stood near her; " something that I have worn myself out to obtain. Thou knowest, *bella sposa*, that we have not had the games at Todi for five years, and the theatre is overgrown with moss and weeds, the arena a haunt for swine; but next month they are to be celebrated, by the royal order, which I obtained, in honor of the birth of a son to the king. He is so devout and keeps so many monks around him, that I had great difficulty in obtaining his consent, for he thinks such amusements are bad for the morals of the people, a belief which his spiritual advisers are at great pains to confirm; but I prevailed this time, and I am determined the games of 1268 shall be celebrated with a splendor and magnificence never seen before. What sayest thou?"

"They will make our old town very gay," she answered, with a sinking heart.

"Gay! It will be like paradise! I have ordered a new gallery to be built for a chosen company, among whom the wife of the jurisconsult will shine the fairest of them all. The Prince and Princess Doria of Rome, the great Minister, Count Taverno, and one or two other distinguished persons of the Court, I have invited to occupy the gallery with thee. It will be a splendid affair, hung with cloth-of-gold, and canopied and cushioned with Lyons silk of rose-color and blue, spangled with gold. Aha! how proud I shall be to have the world see and acknowledge thy beauty!"

"O Jacques, why so vain of me? It pains me."

"Pains thee! How can I help being proud of thee, sweet love? The very thought of possessing such a treasure—a treasure such as no monarch, if he searched the world, could hope to find—makes me supremely happy!" he replied, folding her hand to his heart.

"Such love is very sweet, but it is too much for the creature; we must remember that our God is a jealous God, and will have none preferred before Him."

He dropped her hand, and turned from her with

a cloud upon his brow, and did not speak immediately; when he did, it was not unkindly:

"We hear those sayings in the Cathedral. Leave them to the monks, and don't throw cold water, albeit it be holy water, into my face when my heart runs over with love for thee. I will be good one of these days, *bella sposa:* in fact I am not so bad a Christian as some others. Look at old Sacchi, for instance, who has prayed his knee-pans off, and often goes to Communion! Does he ever give a scudi to the poor ? Did he not turn his own son into the street, to want and beggary, because he could not pay a debt that he owed him ?"

"No, thank our dear Lord, thou art not like that!" she said, laying her long fair hand upon his head. "But we must not judge."

"What! Not when a fig tree is barren ? Why, my gardener, an ignorant peasant, would root it up and burn it with the weeds."

"Our dear Lord is patient—oh, how patient! He alone, who beholds the secrets of hearts, can judge with righteousness," she said, sweetly.

"If the devil don't get old Sacchi, what is the use of being pious ? Here am I always giving to the poor and to the Church. I love to give. I am never happier than when I am giving. Have I not just sent a piece of Venetian lace to the Cathedral for the *baldachino* of Our Lady; and did I not only yesterday send a beautiful picture, *Santa Agnese before the Proconsul*, to the convent, for their new altar ?"

" Our dear Lord will requite all that is done for
the love of Him," she said, smoothing back the hair
from his forehead, and smiling brightly. " Yes,
thou art good, my love, according to thy mind; by
and by Our Lord will show thee His way."

" Wilt thou go to the games ?" he said, abruptly,
almost as if he feared she would refuse.

" Yes, as thou dost wish it so much. What is
to be done ?"

" I can scarcely tell thee in order yet. There
will be comedies, wrestling, dancing, music, races,
mock fights between the athletes, and what more
I cannot tell; but thou wilt enjoy it all, my Julia;
I know thou wilt."

She said no more, and Benedetti, wooed by the
breeze that stole through the jessamine, fell
asleep.

" Enjoy it," he said. Alas! her splendors, and
all that her husband imagined ought to make her
the happiest woman on earth, were simply weary-
ing, irksome trials; she had but one wish upon
earth, and that was for his conversion; for that she
endured all things; for that she did penance; for
that she daily offered her very life to Almighty
God.

It must not be supposed that conversations like
the one just related were of frequent occurrence: it
was only when his mood presented the opportunity, and then only so long as he appeared willing
to listen; the moment a shadow darkened his face,
or a sneer escaped his lips, she would change the

subject for something more congenial to his gay temperament.

Keen in his perceptions, the proud, pleasure-loving man was not slow to notice this exercise of charity; he made no remarks, but it softened his heart yet more tenderly towards her, and made more holy and beautiful in his eyes the example of her virtues.

Days and weeks passed by. Todi was full of strangers,—the princely, the noble, and wealthy citizens from other parts; poets, philosophers, comedians, dancers, and wrestlers thronged thither, some to witness, others to take part in the games. Nothing else was thought of, nothing else was talked of. There were those who criticised, and others who praised the arrangements; many made themselves happy by betting on this, that, or the other, while there were not a few who predicted failure—on points which ran counter to their advice. There were whispers, too, about certain repairs at the amphitheatre having been too hastily made for safety; among them the jurisconsult's gallery, which was built upon the old beams of the original one, that had been blackening there in the sun and rains of a century; but it had been examined by competent persons, and pronounced safe; and it was being painted and gilded by artists from Rome.

*　　*　　*　　*　　*

There is a soft luminous radiance behind the mountains, about whose shadowy sides the blue mists still linger; jets of glittering light shoot up towards the violet-tinted and rose-colored clouds as if from a sea of gold; the nightingales sing sweet fitful songs in their bosky coverts; the river sweeps through the valley like a whispered prayer; the dew spangles leaf and flower. Oh, how brightly dawns this day upon the old Umbrian city—the opening day of the games!

From the side door of a lofty and elegant dwelling, a lady, closely wrapped in mantle and veil, came out. With swift, light steps, she approached the Cathedral just as one of the Fathers of St. Francis ascended the altar to begin the celebration of the Holy Sacrifice. It was Julia dei Benedetti, and those who saw her that morning when she received the Sacred Host never forgot the radiant expression of her face, a radiance so solemn and angelic that had it been the Viaticum they might have been pardoned for believing that light from the half-opened portals of heaven was shining upon her.

The jurisconsult wished his beautiful wife to appear on this the opening day of the games in her most magnificent apparel, in her rarest jewels; in obedience to his request, so emphatically made that it savored of command, she arrayed herself in robes fashioned of rare and costly silk of pale delicate color; films of Venice lace shaded her bosom and arms, and fell draped about her in misty folds; pearls and fire-opals from India gleamed in her hair, around her throat and arms, and in her ears. Never had she looked so lovely, and when

Benedetti ran up to her dressing-room to speak to her, she happened to be standing where a ray of sunshine slanted over her. He paused an instant in mute admiration and astonishment: even he had never imagined she could look like this. She held out her hand with a smile of welcome, he clasped it a moment, then, bending his knee, kissed it, saying:

" Nay! hast thou just stepped out of paradise ? I can scarcely dare more than offer homage to an angel."

" O Jacques! why so foolish? Wouldst thou turn my head with thy flatteries?" she answered, with a little laugh, making him rise. " I am only I; all these beautiful things in which I am arrayed are thy gifts and worn for love of thee. Ah! why should I be vain ?"

" If thou wert clad in sackcloth, would it change thy beauty, thy grace, thy perfect form, *bella sposa ?* No! I will then be proud and vain of thee—enough for thee and for myself."

" How soon are we to go ? " she asked.

" I just ran up, *bella sposa*, to say that it is utterly impossible for me to accompany thee to the amphitheatre. I have been appointed to receive the members of the royal family that are here; but thy cousin, the Count Pelchioni, and his wife, are coming to go with thee."

" Ah! I am sorry to lose thy attendance. But the Prince and Princess Doria—who will receive them ?"

"I forgot to mention yesterday that they have been recalled to Rome by the illness of their only son."

"Ah, how unfortunate! Our blessed Lady grant they may find him out of danger. But thou wilt join us after thy official duties are over?" she said.

"Yes, yes. The Count knows our gallery, and I have stationed a guard there to prevent those who have no right from crowding upon our party. Farewell, sweet one, until we meet again."

He kissed her almost reverently, and after one fond lingering look hurried away.

It was a glorious day, clear and balmy; the awning which formed the temporary roof of the amphitheatre tempered the glare of the sun to a pleasant light, and surely there was never assembled a gayer or more light-hearted crowd than that which filled the circular tiers of seats, from the arena to the roof. It was one shimmering, beautiful mass of color, the richly-decorated gallery of the jurisconsult being the centre of attraction when his beautiful wife entered. The comedy was a great success; the plaudits of the people and strains of music thundered together, and only subsided when a troupe of Egyptian dancing-girls floated out to perform a measure to the sound of weird, wild harmonies. Benedetti had not yet appeared; he was evidently detained by something imperative, for the royal seats were all filled; and it was not until a chariot-race began that Julia, who had been restlessly watching for him, caught a glimpse of him forcing his way towards her through the surging crowd. There was a proud smile upon his lips as he saw how conspicuously her beauty shone in that great assemblage, and how well the splendor of her surroundings became her. But just as he lifted his jewelled cap to her, there came a sudden, crackling sound, shrieks filled the air, and that richly-decorated structure, that gallery, with its freight of life and beauty, fell, a wild, heaped-up ruin, into the arena. With a piercing cry, he sprang to the rescue of his wife over the heads and shoulders of the crowd; and no man stayed his mad progress, for all knew him, and understood the awful blow which had fallen upon him.

At length he reached the spot, and on the edge of the mutilated, shrieking heap, crushed and benumbed, he found her who was all the world to him, and, lifting her tenderly, he conveyed her to a place of safety, the crowd making way and giving what assistance they could. She still breathed, and, unclosing her eyes, fixed a tender gaze upon his agonized face. He laid her down, her head still reposing upon his breast, and began to cut open her bodice, but with a blush that crimsoned even her neck, she whispered, " Not here! not here! " and indicated by a gesture that he should take her farther away from the crowd. Again raising her in his arms, and forbidding any to follow, he bore her to a green, shaded spot, cut open the pearl-embroidered tissues of her festive robe, and tore away

the fine silk and linen of her under garments, that
her heart might have no pressure upon it, that the
air of heaven could blow freely upon her; but what
did he see ?   Not the fair ivory skin that covered
the faultless symmetry of her form, but a rough
hair-shirt under which the tender flesh showed many
a stripe and scar.   A cry escaped his lips of such
bitter anguish that it recalled her from the bright
mysteries which were already dawning upon her;
there was a tremulous movement of her white, dying
lips, and, bending down his ear, he heard her whisper: "It was for thee! O Christ, make him Thine
own!"

That was all.   Her pure soul passed with the
prayer.   Then he knew how she had done penance
for him, knew that for his sins and follies this rough
garment was worn, and that by the suffering of her
tender flesh she had hoped to win mercy for him.
Many drew near and offered assistance, but he
motioned them away, and, gathering the dead form
to his bosom, he bore her back to their desolated
home, where, with speechless agony and a dumb
wonder, he watched, shedding no tear, uttering no
moan, until those who were to perform the last sad
offices for the dead came to lead him away.   Then
he touched the hair-shirt with his finger, "Leave
that as it is," he said.

V.

What was left for Jacques dei Benedetti, now ?
Sympathy, condolence, and religious help were

offered, but he would none of it. The dreadful blow had wounded the natural man unto death; it was as a sword that had " divided the bones and the marrow "; and there echoed through heart and brain one only word: Penance! Penance! Penance!

It was not as yet the solemn whisper of a new life, but the memory that stood out above all else —the penance and prayers *she* had offered for his guilty soul. Nature was, however, slowly giving place to a new-born supernatural principle, as in solitude, almost in darkness, the days went on. He refused admittance to all, except when obliged to answer questions about the funeral arrangements; and when a friend would have led him to look his last on the saintly beauty of his dead, he uttered a stern " No!" and, closing his door, flung himself prostrate while his soul leaped up in a strong cry to God. It was his first prayer, and a strange peace fell upon him, with a sentiment of humility so profound as to overwhelm him like a torrent.

Then came the magnificent funeral, and again he walked a pale, tearless mourner; but his hair had grown white, and his stately form so bowed that people questioned whether it could really be the proud, handsome jurisconsult. And when the world, weary of a week's mourning and seclusion, and even the priests—worn out with their long vigils, fasting, and the ceremonies which had occupied them so many days—hastened from the Cathedral, Jacques dei Benedetti remained in the crypt with the dead; and with his head bowed upon the coffin-lid of her whom he had so loved, he made another and holier vow than the one of years before. After this, no more grieving: here they would separate until the judgment-day; she was Heaven's own; and he then made a renunciation of tender, fruitless memories; of his sorrow, which he offered with the sufferings of the Crucified; of all the beautiful idyls of the past; of every earthly hope and desire; and thus stripped of self, he offered himself humbly to Almighty God, to be moulded and fashioned as He willed.

His next step was to resign his civic dignities, and to the almost dumb amazement of the community, he sold his goods and distributed his possessions to the poor; and then, dressed in rags, like one distraught, he haunted the churches, absorbed in devotion, looking neither to the right nor left, his head bowed upon his breast, and floods of tears streaming from his eyes. He walked the streets bareheaded, his garments old and coarse and ragged, and his bare feet often bleeding from the sharp uneven stones.

At first people were awed, and wondered at such abnegation. Some thought he would get over it and come out in renewed splendor. But when they found he did not mend his ways they nicknamed him "Jacopone"—mad Jacques. The boys shouted after him in the streets, pelted him with stones, and the people saluted him with derisive shouts; but he went his way in silence, unheeding their insults. One day, like the prophet Jeremias, who appeared in the public places of Jerusalem with a yoke about his neck, a symbol of her approaching captivity, the poor penitent showed himself on the public promenade half naked, with a saddle and bridle on his back, walking on his hands and knees like a beast of burden. Some wept; there were a few who shouted in derision; and many were touched and saddened as they beheld the miserable state to which his envied destiny had fallen. "He is mad!" they said. "He is *not* mad," observed a holy man who knew; "he is doing penance."

But people could not discern the supernatural under such a guise; they only stared and laughed at the strange spectacle, and said: "Poor Jacopone! His vagaries are harmless; but Todi misses him sorely; the place has grown as dull as a graveyard."

His palace he could not alienate; but he granted the free use of it to a branch of the Order of Mercy, founded by a saintly knight of Languedoc, Peter Nolasco; and this was considered by many as fresh evidence of his insanity. "When he recovers, there will not be a shelter for his head."

But none knew of Jacopone's hidden life,—how he went in secret to the sick and destitute poor in the hovels about the town, ministering to their necessities and performing the meanest offices for them, until some even believed that the dear Lord had sent St. Francis to their aid; none knew of his vigils in the churches, where, hidden behind a pillar or tomb, his forehead pressed against the stone floor, he meditated on the Passion of Jesus and the Dolors of Mary until the marble flags were wet with his tears.

News of his madness finally spread abroad, and strangers, many of whom had witnessed his former splendor, came to look upon him and wonder. His case was reported to and discussed at Rome, but when those were sent having authority—three men of holy lives—to note his eccentricities and question him, his answers, briefly and humbly made, convinced them that he was moved to perform his heroic acts of penance by a purely supernatural motive.

A period of ten years passed by, and one morning the porter of the Franciscan Monastery told the prior that Jacopone was at the gate and asked to be admitted to the abbot's presence. The prior frowned. He was a man of holy, ascetic life, but looked upon all novelties as a delusion and a snare of the devil.

" Didst thou tell him, brother, that the abbot is rarely interrupted at this hour ? "

" I did, Reverend Father; but he said he would wait, and went and sat upon the roadside with the beggars."

" Very well. I will let him know the abbot's pleasure."

" Our abbot does strange things, sometimes," the prior thought: " he may choose to see this mad beggar, for whom we pray as one of our benefactors. May our blessed Lady deliver us from evil. The enemy of souls *has* been known to counterfeit a penitent; didn't he so appear once to Fra Juan Garin, at Montserrat, and come near dragging his soul to hell!"

By this time he had reached the abbot's door, where he rapped, and was bid to enter.

"A mad beggar is at the gate, Reverend Father, craving admission to thy presence; I will dismiss him if thou sayest so."

"Name him," said the abbot briefly.

"Jacopone."

"Jacopone! Bring him hither, my good prior. Jacopone must never be kept waiting; it were a shame for us, whose house and church he so beautified in time past; and let me tell thee what I fear: when Christ comes some of us will be cast out of the Kingdom, while the ' mad penitent ' will be received and crowned among the saints."

The prior bowed; there was a spot of color on his pale cheeks, but he made no reply, and withdrew to do the bidding of his superior.

The abbot arose from his chair, and stood waiting, while strange emotions agitated his heart. He had known Jacopone in the days of his pride and prosperity; and he had met him saddled on the public promenade, followed by the hooting crowd; but never since his penitential days had he come to the monastery. What could be his object ?

The door opened, and Jacopone—his broad forehead pale, his temples and cheeks sunken, his beard almost white—entered and knelt while the abbot blessed and welcomed him in a voice that trembled with emotion.

" Rise, my son, and be seated," he said.

" If thou wilt, I will remain so; it is more fitting, as I have come to beg a great boon at thy hands, Lord Abbot."

" Do as it best pleases thee, my son; but what wouldst thou of me, in God's holy name ?"

" Having fulfilled a vow, I now wish to enter the Order of St. Francis," he said humbly, never raising his eyes.

" My son, dost thou understand that all who enter here have to learn the holy science of obedience?" His voice was steady now, and almost stern.

" That I know right well, Lord Abbot; it is a science I most desire to be taught."

" And dost thou know that our rule permits no singularities in devotion—no novelties in dress or manner ?"

" Aye, that also I know. I seek to enter the Order of the blessed St. Francis as a servant,— that I may work out my salvation. Pity me, my Lord Abbot, for my unworthiness is even greater than thou canst conceive; but by the grace of our dear Lord, whose mercy is infinite, I hope to be moulded like wax by the blessed rule of St. Francis, until—until—at last—I may be found worthy of reconciliation with Him." He faltered, while great tears rolled over his wan cheeks, and glistened like jewels on his gray, tangled beard. The good abbot's impulse was to kneel beside the poor suppliant, fold his arms about him and welcome him with a thousand welcomes to the Order. But he only said:

"Be comforted, my son; for, whether in the Order of St. Francis or out of it, such penitence as thine will in the end win heaven for thee. I will lay thy application before the brethren. Come hither next Monday and I will make known the decision to thee. Now, go in peace, pray for me, and may the Most Adorable Trinity bless and strengthen thee."

*   *   *   *   *

The answer was a favorable one, and thus "the old athlete of penance," as he is called, entered the great Order, and his after-life became a strange chapter in its history.

He lived long years, abating nothing of his austerities, rather adding to them; and shortly before his death, from his prison at Collazone, he gave to the world his matchless hymn the "*Stabat Mater*," which will keep alive the memory of his burning love and his mighty repentance until the sublime chants of the Church Militant blend forever with those of the Church Triumphant.

ELLA LORAINE DORSEY.

ELLA LORAINE DORSEY is the youngest child of Mrs. Anna Hanson Dorsey and her husband, the late Lorenzo Dorsey, Esq. She began her literary career when she was about 16, as special correspondent on the *Chronicle* and *Critic*, two Washington papers. Later she wrote specials—regularly for the *Chicago Tribune*, and now and then for the *Boston Journal, Cincinnati Commercial Gazette*, etc.

In April, 1886, *Harper's Magazine* published " Back from the Frozen Pole," and the *Catholic World* published " The Czar's Horses," which last was attributed to Archibald Forbes, and went around the English colonies as far as New Zealand. The same year Father Hudson published " Midshipman Bob," which was so kindly received that it was reprinted and had a large sale in England and Ireland, and was translated into Italian. From that time she devoted herself to our Catholic boys through the *Ave Maria,* trying to do for them what her mother does so nobly for the grown-ups ; and between '86 and '90 Father Hudson published: "Jet, the War Mule," "The Two Tramps," "Coppinger's Inheritance" "The Josè Maria," "Saxty's Angel," "Speculum Justitiae," "The Wharf Rat's Christmas," "The Brahmin's Christmas," "The Salem Witch," and "Tiny Tim." Before that, however, several of her sketches had been published: "The Solitary Soul," "The Son of the Widow of Naim," "The Fool of the Wood," "Bodger," "Ole Miss," etc.

In 1890 a violent and prolonged attack of grippe put a stop to her work, and since that time she has written scarcely anything, except two poems in the *Cosmopolitan,* a story in *Outing,* "Ivan of the Mask," some "specials" in the *Washington Post* and *Ave Maria,* and "Smallwood's Immortals," a historical sketch of the young paladins of the Maryland Line, who died at Long Island in 1776, that the army—the defeated, panic-stricken, routed, almost destroyed army—might live.

Her mother's prolonged illness two years ago further checked Miss Dorsey's work, and a new book on which she is now engaged will mark the recommencement of her regular work.

Miss Dorsey is a Daughter of the American Revolution, a Colonial Dame, a member of the Literary Society of Washington, the Geographical Society, and the Georgetown Convent Alumnæ Association.

Speculum Justitiæ.

BY ELLA LORAINE DORSEY.

I.

IT was a bitter night in winter. The streets had been deserted at an early hour, and the wind that raged up from the sea tore at the shutters and banged at the doors, shrieking, whistling, and roaring, till the townsfolk turned in their beds and muttered: '' God save the sailor lads this night!'' But some of the nervous old women covered their ears and said: '' The good-for-nothing vagabonds!'' For they thought the banging and shouting came from some ship's crew just landed, and hurrying to spend their money and vitality larking.

Suddenly the wind veered to the northwest, and whirling down out of the low black clouds came one soft white flake, then another, and another, until the air was as white as the surf bursting and flying out on the harbor bar.

And all the time, in a side street of this water-end of the city, a man lay face down, a knife in his back, and death on his lips and in his heart. And the snow gathered and covered the red stain that crept like a scarlet snake from the small wound, and wrapt him in a winding-sheet whiter than any flax ever spun.

And a ship drove safely into the harbor out of the storm, let go her anchor with a rattle and clank of chains, and a hearty "Yo-heave-oh!" that rang merrily through the night; and one of the sailors—refusing with a laugh to wait for daybreak—sprang into the dingy, pulled ashore through the angry water, and struck out briskly for home. Such a little box of a home, but neat as a new pin, and an old mother in it dearer than all the world to the sturdy fellow tramping through the snow.

"I told her I'd be there, and of course I will; for this here wind a-blowin', and the delay from the backin' and fillin' we had to do outside there, so 's to git a good headway on th' old gal [the ship], ull have her that uneasy I know she won't sleep a wink this blessed—hullo! what's here? Git along, old chap. 'Taint safe for a feller to be takin' naps in this here temperatoor. Whew! if there's one thing I hate it's a feller a-makin' a beast of himself a-drinkin'. Mebbe, though, I'd been there myself if it hadn't been for Father Tom; so here goes to help ' the man and brother.' My Lord A'mighty, what's this here? It's a knife, and the man's dead as a nail! Mur——"

But an iron arm had him round the neck, and an iron hand was clapped over his mouth, and he was dragged furiously here and there, while a stentorian voice rang out, "Murder! murder! murder!"

In the mad struggle that followed, David Jameson's clothing was torn from his back, and his face bruised; though he defended himself so manfully that his assailant was put to it for breath wherewith to keep up his shout of " Murder."

The harbor-watch ran panting to the scene, and before Jameson—bewildered by the sudden attack, and exhausted by the violent tussle—could speak, the man who grappled him poured out a voluble story. He had been coming along the street after spending the evening at Moreno's wine-shop, and had seen the two men struggling; this one had plunged a knife into the back of the other; he had fallen and died without a groan. Then this man stooped to—he supposed—rifle the dead man's pockets, and he had seized him.

" You lie!" shouted Davie. " The man must have been dead an hour when I saw him. He was covered with snow——"

" Shut up!" said the harbor-watch.

And Davie's captor, with an expressive shrug and a flinging out of his hands, said: " Behold the knife, signor."

The knife was a black clasp-knife, such as any sailor of any nation might carry; but the officers smiled contemptuously when Jameson declared it was not his, and told them his sheath was empty only because he had lost his knife that very night coming into port—that it had been knocked out of his hand while he was cutting away some raffle tangled up by the gale. And they carried him off with every indignity to the station-house, treating

with marked consideration the foreigner—an Italian
—who had captured the desperate murderer at such
risk and after such a fight, and thanking him with
some effusion for his offer to be at their service day
or night so long as he stayed in port, noting down
the place of anchorage of his vessel; for of course
he was the only witness for the prosecution.

Poor David!   One hour before a free, light-
hearted lad, springing home to his mother, his soul
innocent of guile, and his heart at peace with the
world.   Now disgraced, ironed at ankles and wrists,
his heart a pit of rage, and every muscle aching to
get at the man who had lied away his honesty, his
integrity, his liberty, and—it might easily come to
that—his life.

The jailer was a kind-hearted man, so when he
came into the cell in the early morning he asked
David if he had any friends he wished to see; and
he, poor lad, with a ray of hope striking across his
passion of rage and despair, cried: " Let me see
Father Fahey."

" Father Tom, is it? " asked the jailer.

" That's the one," said David, eagerly.

" Oh, I know *him!* " said the man, with a broad
smile; " and it's himself always has his joke and
his good word for everybody. I tell him, sometimes, he's sent for so constant he'd better just live
here.   Him and me'd make a good pair, and trot
well in double harness—me a-catchin' the *corpus
delictisses* " (he had his little vanities of fine language, this jailer), " and him a-nabbin' the bad

consciences. ' Gillett,' says he to me no later than last Tuesday, when I'd said as much to him,— ' Gillett, we've got responsibilities both of us, and above all we've got to keep everything clean-washed and accounted for.' ' Yes,' I cuts in, ' me to the Guv'nor and you to the Lord.' That's just what I said—' me to the Guv'nor and you to the Lord,' —and it was a pretty neat answer.''

And he rubbed his chin softly, and repeated his own words several times with intense enjoyment of their neatness.

'' When can I see him ?'' begged David.

'' To-morrow, maybe.''

'' To-morrow!'' and his face fell back to its lines of misery. '' Good Lord, man, my old mother'll hear it before that, and it'll kill her if it's broke too sudden to her! Father Tom's the only man that can do it.''

'' Well, well,'' said the jailer, '' I'll telephone round for you; but ''—with a sudden sense of responsibility—'' that was a shabby trick to play a messmate.''

'' I didn't,'' said David, simply, and he raised his honest eyes to the jailer's face. ''I never saw him till—— ''

'' There, there!'' said the jailer, soothingly; '' don't talk till your lawyer gits here.'' And off he went down the corridor, thinking as he did so: '' He looks honest, but, great Scott! you never can tell. They'll look like cheraphs and serabims '' (his biblical knowledge was slight and very mixed), "and all the time they'll be up to any dodge on the p'lice docket. This feller's cut diff'rent from the heft of my birds, though."

An hour later Father Tom stood in the cell, and he took David in his arms, and welcomed him as if he had come home laden with honors instead of crushed under the charge of crime. Then he said, gently: " Now, Davie, tell me all about it."

And David told the whole story, beginning with the start from the ship, and going circumstantially through the after-events, from the brief but terrific struggle over the dead man's body to the prison. Father Tom listened intently, and David, as he warmed up to his story, concluded with " I am as innocent of that man's blood as you are, Father Tom; but if I had that Italian here I'd strangle him."

Father Tom's only answer was to pull out the crucifix from his girdle, hold it up, and point to the agonized figure on it.

David hung his head, and with the cry, " But think of mother!" the tears burst from his dry and burning eyes.

Presently Father Tom said: " Now, Davie, let us kneel down and say a *Memorare* and the *Veni Sancte Spiritus*, and then we'll see what's to be done first."

But poor David's cry, as soon as the Amen was said, was again: " O Father Tom! my poor old mother!"

" Now look here, boy," said the priest, with some severity, " do you suppose such a good

Catholic and such a devoted servant of Our Lady as your mother is, is going to waste time mourning and weeping ? If you had been guilty, *then* she might have broken her heart; but she'll have so many prayers to say for you, and so many things to do for you—and she can come every day to see you, too,—that the time will go by almost before you know it. I'll go to her now and tell her about it. And would you like me to send your skipper or any of your shipmates to see you ?"

" Not yet," said Davie; " tell 'em, though. And, Father, tell 'em, too, I didn't do it."

" Ay, ay, lad, you may depend on that. Now, is there anything you want? Have you got tobacco, and warm flannels, and some money ? Have you got your—oh, yes, there are your beads! "

" Yes, sir," said David, " I've got them safe; but it's a wonder I didn't lose 'em in that scrimmage last night. I s'pose I would a' done it ef I hadn't strung 'em round my neck before I went aloft out yonder. The wind 'certainly was tremmenjis off the Point, and when we was piped up to cut loose a broken yard and snug down, I didn't count much on seeing home-lights again. So 's I run along the deck and began scramblin' up the shrouds, I slipped 'em over my head. I heerd a Breton sailor say once that the Blessed Lady 'd lift us safe and sound out of even a ragin' sea into heaven by 'em. Of course I knew he didn't mean the real body of us, nor the real string of beads, nor the real seas; but it seemed to me the idee was about so—that she'd lift the souls of us out of the pit o' death and tow us into port by that there hawser of prayers we'd been a-makin' and a-makin' ever sence we could toddle.''

'' And it *is* so,'' said Father Tom, heartily, laying his hand on David's shoulder; while the latter knelt as he used to do when a little lad in Father Tom's catechism class, and received his blessing.

'' Keep up your heart, keep down your temper, and trust in God,'' were the priest's parting words. '' I'll send you some papers, and I'll come back to-morrow.''

Then he went and had a little talk with the jailer, and asked such privileges as could be allowed the prisoner; and left the jail with a heavy heart, to break the news to David's mother, to get good counsel for him, to see the judge of the criminal court, whom he had so often to interview on behalf of prisoners, and to see the captain of the ship to which the young sailor belonged. And the farther he went, the more depressed he got—the hour, the circumstances, the straight story told by the Italian, all tended to push David nearer and nearer the gallows.

There was a certain sort of good luck, though; for the court was in session, and a sudden lapse in the testimony in a long-drawn bank robbery case left a free day, which the counsel seized upon, asking the judge, in view of the peculiar circumstances, to call the trial; for the only actual witness, one Manuel Ignatius Pizarro, would have to sail with his brig—the *Maria di Napoli*—on the following Wednesday for Marseilles.

There was some demur about precedent and so on, but the point was carried, and the 20th of December saw the court-room filled to hear the trial of David Jameson, seaman, for the murder of an unknown man on the night of the 13th day of that same month, in the year of Our Lord 188–. The court was opened with the usual formalities, and the case presented by the counsel for the Government. Then, after a brief citation of the facts —" the terrible facts," they were called, — the Italian, " whose tongue alone could tell the truth," was put upon the stand.

He was a tall, well-formed man, but there was a furtive trick about his eyes; and the eyes themselves, though large and brilliant, were so near together that they seemed to cross at times; the eyebrows were heavy and met at the root of the nose, which gave a sinister look to his face; and his nostrils were thin as paper, and vibrated with every breath. For the rest, he was handsome enough; and his picturesque though very theatrical costume was becoming, from the scarlet Phrygian cap, and the wide gold rings in his ears, to the curiously embroidered top-boots, and the long Spanish cloak in which he draped himself (as he entered and departed) in folds that would have done credit to an ancient Roman.

He told his story dramatically and with abundant gesture, and wound up by saying, " Doubtless, excellency, it was some secret foe; for he stabbed him with such force, such savagery; and a blow in the back—O treachery! O cruelty——''

'' Stick to facts, sir,'' said the judge, impassively.

The Italian shrugged his shoulders and bowed, but his eyes seemed to leap toward each other, and their flash belied the wide smile that displayed his teeth, white and strong as a shark's.

Then the cross-examination began.

'' At what time did you go to Moreno's ?''

'' At twenty-two hours (10 o'clock p.m.).''

'' Where were you before that ? ''

'' Aboard the *Maria di Napoli.*''

'' At what hour did you leave the ship? ''

'' At twenty-one hours and a half (9.30 p.m.).''

'' Were you alone ? ''

'' When ? ''

'' When you left the ship.''

'' No.   My mate was with me.''

'' What is his name ? ''

'' Pedro Maria Allegrini.''

'' Was he with you in the wine-shop ? ''

'' All the time.''

'' Did you leave together ? ''

'' No.''

'' Why ? ''

'' Pedro's head was heavier than his legs.''

'' Where is Pedro Allegrini ? ''

'' Here,'' and he waved his arm toward a heavy, stolid man among the audience.

His name was noted.

"When you saw the two men—the prisoner and the deceased,—what were they doing?"

"Struggling: this one actively, the other like a man heavy with wine."

And so on, and so on, with a circumstantiality of detail and a distinctness of outline that were appalling to Father Tom and David's other friends.

And when Moreno and Allegrini were called they confirmed all that Pizarro had said up to the hour of his leaving the house, at two o'clock.

The witnesses for the defence could do only negative service by testifying to David's previous good character, and this they did heartily; but the jury, after a half-hour's deliberation, returned a verdict of murder, commending the prisoner, however, to the mercy of the court.

When the foreman had spoken, a shrill, heart-broken cry rang through the room: "My son! my son! Spare him, your honor! spare him! He's as innocent as a baby!"

It was the old mother, who tore at her gray hair and beat her breast, while the slow tears of old age rolled down her cheeks.

"Poor soul!" said the judge, kindly; "I can only let the law take its course."

Then she raised her tottering frame, and, with hands and arms uplifted, she cried: "Mirror of Justice, defend us!"

It was a touching little scene, and many people in the court-room wiped their eyes; and the prisoner's drooping head, clenched fists, and laboring breath, bore witness to the anguish he endured.

Father Tom came to him, and spoke a few cheering words, then took the mother from the court-room; and the captain and some of David's ship-mates followed him to the jail to see him; but, finding they could not enter, stood about and talked in low voices of him as one already dead. During the week they came back one by one, the captain to shake hands and wish him kindly but vaguely '' well out of it ''; the sailor-men to shuffle their feet, shift their quids, and sit about awkwardly and silently, the very force of their sympathy making them as undemonstrative as wooden figure-heads.

Then they sailed away, and the *Maria di Napoli* spread her canvas wings for the Mediterranean; and the world forgot David—all except Father Tom, and his mother, and his lawyer; the latter of whom had become so deeply interested in his fate that, by incredible work and judicious appeal and present-ment of the case in the right quarters (to say nothing of catching at every technical straw that could aid him), he secured a final sentence of '' imprison-ment for life at hard labor.''

But this all took months, and it was not until the jail had blanched his face, and the confinement almost burst his heart, that David was taken to the penitentiary, and there, among forgers, murderers, and criminals of all degrees and grades, put to work out a life of misery.

II.

Again it was a night in winter, and again the wind blew and the snow flew—stinging like a swarm of white bees,—just as it had blown and flown that other night three years ago, when, in that Northern seaport town, a man had been stabbed in the street, and a young sailor was sent to the penitentiary for it;—sent to the penitentiary for life on circumstantial evidence and the testimony of—of the man who is now, on this bitter winter evening, creeping along against the houses of that same town, glancing first over one shoulder, then over the other, with terror in his eyes, and a shivering and racking of his body that made progress slow. Once or twice he stopped, panting for breath; but started up and hurried on again, looking back fearfully as if pursued.

Up the street a great block of carriages stopped the way. It was before the house of an old German merchant, who, forty years before, built his house in the then most fashionable quarter of the city; but business marched up and on, pushing the gay world farther and farther northward and westward, until now it was the only dwelling in the square. But the old merchant lived there contentedly, and on this night his youngest daughter, his golden-haired Elsa, came of age, and the birthday was celebrated by a great fancy ball.

This the Italian, of course, could not know; for

he was a stranger, and was, moreover, half crazed with drink; but what he did know was that at that point there were people, there was *life*, there was the sound of human voices, and above all there was light, beautiful light,—light that kept at bay the terrors that rent his soul when night and sleep fell on the world.

How he hated the dark! It swarmed with such ugly things; and a face—an awful face, with staring eyes and rigid lips—would start into such ghastly distinctness as soon as the sun was down. And it followed him like a shadow, hounding him from place to place, filling him with an unnatural vigor, and an activity that tired out the stoutest of his boon companions; and when they slept, exhausted, it still drove him on, tortured, agonized, panic-stricken, till the day broke, and the sight of the crowds helped him to sleep and reason.

As he reached the awning, and pressed close to the steps, a carriage dashed up to the curb; the door of the house was flung open for some parting guests, and for a few minutes a dazzling vision was revealed — fairies, shepherdesses, arquebusiers, pages, halberdiers, kings, court ladies, and queens, in gorgeous colors and flashing jewels. But the Italian saw none of these; his staring eyes fastened on a stately figure that seemed to float down toward him between the rows of orange and palm trees that lined the staircase. On it came, tall, in flowing raiment, a cloud of golden hair rippling over its shoulders from under a crown of light; in one raised hand a pair of scales, in the other a gleaming sword, whose point seemed to mark him from the throng.

" *Speculum Justitiæ!* " he shrieked; " yes, I did it—I did it! I murdered him! Take me——"

And he fell grovelling at the feet of the police-men, who had forgotten their official stolidity to stare, open-mouthed, at the lovely Angela von Henkeldyne, who in her costume of " Justice " had wrought such innocent vengeance.

On principle they seized the Italian for a rowdy; but his repeated cry, " I did it—I murdered him! " soon attracted their attention, and as he struggled in a fit, they called up the patrol wagon, and took him to headquarters. There the police surgeon took him in hand, until finally, at daybreak, he recovered consciousness. On being told that he could not live through the next night, he asked for a priest, and who but Father Tom was brought to shrive the poor wretch, and listen to the story he had to tell!

He had played, he said, in the wine-shop *that* night until midnight with a stranger, who lost heavily to him, and drank deeply as he played. But his losses did not seem to depress him, and the wines did not confuse him, and Manuel said:

" You are a gallant man, signor. You lose with grace and courage."

And he had answered, with a laugh: " I can afford to. I have fifty thousand dollars here." And he touched his breast.

Manuel raised his eyebrows.

"Don't you believe me?" asked his companion, with some heat.

Manuel bowed derisively.

"Hang it!" said the man; "I'm telling you the simple truth. Look here." And he drew out and opened a small doeskin bag slung around his neck, showing a diamond, the like of which Manuel had never beheld.

"It sent a madness to my head, Father, and I felt I must have it, if I had to wade to my eyes in blood to get it. But he tucked it away again, and rose. 'I must go,' he said; 'I have already stayed too long.' I pressed him to wait, but he got restless, and looked at me suspiciously. I asked where we might meet the next day, and drink our glass and play our little game of *mora*. But he answered he didn't know—he was here to-day, and there to-morrow, and far away the day after. I laid my hand on his arm. 'Come, crack another bottle,' I urged. But he shook me off roughly, and pushed out of the wine-shop, saying, 'Enough's as good as a feast.'

"I knew the house. There was a cellar that gave on the street he must pass. I said: 'I must have a bottle of *lachryma*, the vintage of '73.' I went below—the landlord knows me,—and I opened the cellar door, and stole after him. In the dark I tracked him, and struck as I sprang on him. I wrenched the bag from his neck, and nearly shrieked as something soft and cold, like a dead finger, touched my cheek. It was a snow-flake, and

I ran in hot haste back to the shop, so no tracks could be left. I had struck well—the blood had not spattered, there was no struggle. It was the stroke of the Vendetta. The whole affair did not take twenty minutes, and I came back into the room, and drank and played. But the diamond in my breast burned like a coal, and I thought its rays of splendid fire must be seen; and in at the windows the dead man's face seemed to look—but that was only the snow flying past; and I felt drawn back to the spot, as if he had his hand at the sleeve of my jacket. But this I fought against, until suddenly I remembered with terror I had left my knife sticking in the wound, and I knew I must have it at any risk. As I crept along I saw a sailor coming up the street. He stopped; he touched the body. Here was my chance. I sprang on him, dragging him here and there—and he fought well, that boy—like a wild-cat; and I shouted, ' Murder! murder! '

" It all turned out as I hoped. The watch— poor fools!—never thought to see whether the man was stiff; and when the coroner arrived, he was too stiff for question. Then came the trial, and there the first stone struck me."

His face was distorted with emotion.

" That boy I pitied—yes! But it was he or I, and *I* preferred to go free. The lies I swore to did not trouble me at all, for lies and I were bosom-friends; but when that old woman raised her hands and cried out, ' Mirror of Justice, defend us! ' I felt a fear; for my medal hung at my neck, and the

only prayer I had said for years was, sometimes, an
' *Ave.*'   Habit, I suppose, but it was so—I said it.
And like the thunder on the mountain came the
meaning of that prayer—*Speculum Justitiæ.*   And
from that day I was a haunted man.   Waking, that
face followed me—the face I had struck into stone
by a knife blow; and if I slept I saw always the
same thing—myself trembling before a great balance, and a sword hanging over my head; but two
hands—a Woman's hands—held down the scale-
pan, and held back the sword; and through a mist
a face sweet and sorrowful looked down at me, like
the *Dolorosa* in the home chapel where I made my
First Communion.   And my terror lest the hands
should slip or move would wake me with a start,
and there would be the dead man and—and *my
memory* waiting for me."

His voice sank to a whisper, and his .eyes stared
gloomily into space.

" What a life it has been ! " he went on, wearily.
" I dreaded to be robbed, and yet I dared not sell
for fear of detection; I could not drink for fear I
might betray myself, and for months the diamond
hung like lead on my breast.   Then I went to
South America, and from there to Paris, where I
sold it well, with a good story of how I found it at
the mines, and smuggled it away.

" But bad luck followed me.   The money went
at play—I lost, lost, lost, at everything; *rouge-et-
noir*, *vingt-et-un*, *roulette*, *mora*—all were alike
against me.   Everything I touched failed,   My

crew got the fever. My *Maria* was lost off the
Bahamas. My savings went in a bank failure.
And forever and forever Our Lady appeared when
I slept, and the dead man when I waked.

" Then I began to drink hard, and I kept jolly
fellows about me—loud fellows, boisterous fellows,
—and I would hear no word of prayer or hereafter;
for the devil ruled my soul, and I knew I was out-
cast from heaven. But—will you believe it ?—I
still wore my medal, and might have tried to say
an ' *Ave*,' but I woke too often shrieking, ' *Speculum Justitiæ!* ' and out of my own mouth I was
condemned; for what would justice mean for me ?

" To-night the end has come; for I saw with
these " (he touched his eyes), " not sleeping, not
dreaming—awake—the Mirror of Justice. But She
no longer stayed the sword, She no longer touched
the scales. She held both in Her own hands——"

He stopped, shuddering violently.

" My son," said Father Tom, " what you saw
to-night was not Our Lady, although she might well
have come from heaven to cry justice on your two-
fold crime." He told him what had really taken
place, closing with, " Now be a man and a true son
of the Church. Come back to the manhood and
the faith you have betrayed. That you repent
truly of these sins I firmly believe, but prove it by
confessing before the proper officers of the law; set
free the innocent man who drags out his days under
an unjust sentence in the penitentiary; and rest
assured when you are weighed in the great scales of

eternal justice, Our Lord's cross will outweigh your sins, and Our Lady's prayers will stay the sword.''

Manuel nodded his head, and with a great effort raised his eyes to Father Tom's. They were still far too near together for honest dealing as the spirit understands it, but there was a new light in them.

'' Father, I will, but—but—what will they think up aloft there, the good *Jesu* and *Sanctissima ?* I fear I could not do this if I did not know I was going to die. I would not have the courage. I, who call myself a gallant man—I am a coward!'' And two tears rolled down his cheeks.

Father Tom felt a knot in his own throat at this confession, courageous in its weakness, pathetic in its falterings; and, although the words of St. Augustine * seemed to stand out before him in letters of fire, he thought of that hill on which once hung three crosses, and he heard a thief cry, '' Lord, be merciful to me a sinner!'' and the Voice that answered through the gathering darkness across the shuddering earth, '' This day shalt thou be with Me in paradise.'' And while he sent for the nearest magistrate, he said such words of hope as the Church alone can breathe to the penitent, teaching as he did it the meaning of true repentance, and filling the sinner's heart with humble hope.

After all was over, Manuel begged to see David.

* Beware of delayed repentance. A sick-bed repentance is too often a sickly repentance; and a death-bed repentance, alas! is in danger of being a dead repentance.

"I dread it, but I cannot go until he forgives me," he said.

And somehow, in spite of technicalities, Father Tom managed it so the two men met on the third day; for Manuel spoke the truth when he said he could not go without forgiveness, and he lived on until then, to the amazement of the prison physician.

At first David refused outright to see him, for his heart was bitter with the load of anguish borne through those three frightful years. But Father Tom "talked to him," and his mother gave the final stroke that determined him.

"Ye *must* go, Davie," she said, as she hung on his neck. "Ye must go, boy; for the Mirror of Justice is the Mother of Mercy too."

And, oh! the thoughts of the two men as they faced each other!

*   *   *   *   *

Where is Davie now? Well, his story got about, and there was quite a *furore* of sympathy. Some good soul started a purse, and big hearts and good incomes ran the money up to enough to buy him a half share in a schooner, of which he ultimately became owner and captain. His old skipper wanted him back, but he did not need to be any man's man now, except his own—and Our Lady's.

The old mother lived to dandle his children on her knee, and to take them on sunny Sundays, sometimes to Father Tom's, and sometimes to a quiet graveyard by the shore of the bay, where they would kneel by a small slab of gray granite, and pray for him who slept below. And then, as they rested before starting home, small hands pulled the weeds from the grave, and picked the lichens from the letters of the inscription, sometimes spelling them out as they did so. And the spelling read: " Pray for the soul of Manuel Ignatius Pizarro. Mirror of Justice, defend him!"

MAURICE FRANCIS EGAN.

Maurice Francis Egan was born at Philadelphia, May 24th, 1852. He was sent to one of the first parochial schools established in his native city, but his education was chiefly conducted by his mother, a woman of excellent literary taste. He attended La Salle College for a time, but being obliged to leave on account of his health, he continued his studies at home, and was enabled to receive his degree of Master without the customary attendance. He finally took a course in philosophy at Georgetown College.

For a while he studied law, but eventually drifted into journalism, and was successively editor of *McGee's Weekly,* assistant editor of *The Catholic Review,* and associate editor of the *New York Freeman's Journal.* In 1888 he was appointed professor of English Literature at Notre Dame University, which chair he resigned seven years later to occupy a similar position in the Catholic University of America.

Mr. Egan is a member of the Authors' Club, the New York Shakespere Society, and half-a-dozen philological societies in this country, England, and Germany. He has travelled extensively and written many books, some of which, including his most successful anonymous novels, he prefers to forget. His sonnets in the *Century* have been widely copied, and have elicited praise from Longfellow, Cardinal Newman, Stedman, and Gilder. His poetry and prose differ greatly;—and this, according to Mr. Edmund Clarence Stedman, is a great advantage. '' His verse is that of a poet ; his prose direct, simple, true." And, as in the example we quote : '' How Perseus became a Star,'' he is sometimes almost painfully realistic. We give the list of his works taken from the book of the Authors' Club (1896) : '' That Girl of Mine,'' ''Preludes '' (Poems for the benefit of Notre Dame University), ''A Garden of Roses.'' '' Stories of Duty,'' '' Songs and Sonnets '' (1885 and 1894), '' The Life Around Us,'' '' The Theatre and Christian Parents,'' '' Modern Novelists,'' '' Lectures on English Literature,'' ''The Disappearance of John Long-worthy,'' ''A Primer of English Literature,'' ''A Gentleman'' (essays for boys), '' A Marriage of Reason,'' '' The Success of Patrick Desmond,'' '' The Flower of the Flock and the Badgers of Belmont,'' ''Jack Chumleigh,'' ''The Vocation of Edward Conway,'' '' Influences in Literature.''

Ibow Perseus Became a Star.

A SKETCH FROM LIFE.

BY MAURICE FRANCIS EGAN.

I.

CONE CITY is well known now because the Hon.
Perseus G. Mahaffy was born there. The noise he
made in the House of Representatives when it was
found that Golung Creek, on which Cone City has
the happiness to be placed, had been left out of the
first River and Harbor Bill is historical; for, reduced to printed symbols, it is in the *Congressional
Globe.* He was known for the last ten years of his
life as the Fixed Star of Golung Creek, and he was
supposed to equal in learning the Sage of Hastings
and in eloquence the Tall Sycamore of the Wabash.

The Cone City *Eagle* had sung his praises many
times, but when he died it exhausted itself in a
burst of adulation and appeared with a black border.
The opposition paper, the *Herald of Liberty*,
dropped its series of letters under the heading
" Why did He Change His Name ? " and a respect-
ful tear; although it said editorially that death
condones even the weakness which impels a man to
change his name from Patrick to Perseus. Both

papers had long accounts of the services which were conducted in the First Baptist Church; the lists of the floral tributes occupied a column, and among them was a star of lilies-of-the-valley from Col. Will Brodbeck, who assisted at the service, without, as he distinctly asserted, taking any part in a mummery which the world had outgrown. Still, Col. Will Brodbeck's presence at the church was looked on as a compliment to religion and as showing a very liberal spirit. The Rev. Mr. Schuyler changed his text from a passage in Isaias to one in Robert Elsmere when he saw that the Colonel was a pall-bearer; and the congregation, consisting of the best people in Cone City, divided its attention between the widow's appearance and the Colonel's face, which wore a highly decorous and non-committal expression. When the preacher alluded to the Hon. Perseus G. Mahaffy as one who had cast off the bonds of early superstition, who had seen the light lit by Luther and the Fathers of the Reformation, who had died firm in the Protestant belief, the Colonel looked scornful; and when the Colonel looked scornful, he was not pretty.

He was six feet high, and of that pale, waxy complexion which gamblers, in works of fiction, are said to possess, with keen black eyes, a mass of grayish hair, and a broad chest. He took off his white gloves supplied by the undertaker, and, of course, too large even for him, and while Mr. Schuyler made his peroration, toyed with a large diamond on the little finger of his left hand. The mocking look in his eyes became more evident as the diamond flashed with his nervous movements, for he knew why and how the Hon. Perseus G. Mahaffy had died.

The widow of the subject of Mr. Schuyler's eulogies, a handsome woman with a haughty manner and eyes like Col. Brodbeck's—she was his sister— sat with her three children near the coffin. She did not appear to be interested in the minister's discourse, and as it was known that she had had violent differences of opinion with the deceased, and that he had left a large life insurance, many of the assembly felt that she should have shown more signs of grief. Clara, her eldest daughter, a girl of sixteen, bent over the pew in front of her, a shapeless mass of black; the two boys seemed sad and bewildered rather than grief-stricken.

When the long prayer was over and the choir, assisted by the Masonic Temple Quartette, had sung "Almost Persuaded," which was hastily chosen with reference to the supposed effect of the sermon on Col. Brodbeck, the funeral procession moved slowly from the church. Nothing unusual happened until Mrs. Mahaffy reached the door.

An old woman in a bonnet and gown of rusty black bombazine rushed forward from a corner of the vestibule and caught Mrs. Mahaffy's hand. "Can you tell me—will you tell me, in the presence of the dead, how *he* died ?" she said in a hasty and trembling voice.

The widow snatched away her hand and passed

on. Clara Mahaffy unconsciously raised her head at the words, and the old woman caught sight of the gentle face, so like that of her father in his best moods.

" Oh, dear! oh, acushla! " the old woman said with a pathetic ring in her words, " maybe you can tell me—maybe *you* were told——"

But she was thrust aside by the undertaker, and the mourners passed into the street. The longing, despairing eyes of the old woman, so wretched in appearance, so wretched in heart, never left the girl's mind until the answer to that strange question was found.

II.

The opposition paper of Cone City made a mistake when it asserted that Perseus Mahaffy had dropped the name of Patrick. He often remarked that he would not have been fool enough to do that. If he had been named Patrick, it would have been money in his pocket, for the vote which is supposed to be attracted by that venerable name was strong in Cone City, and sometimes held the balance of power, but he had changed his name. His mother came from a part of Tipperary where Boethius is a cherished patronymic, and he had been called by that name. He had dropped it for Perseus Gifford, because Perseus Gifford took an interest in the clever young Irish lad, and helped him to study law, and because Perseus was an honored name in Cone City; it gave an air of "Americanism" to his surname, which, until the Irish vote became a factor in politics, he cursed with all his might. His father had died when he was eleven years of age. His mother, a rosy-cheeked, wrinkled old woman, who adored her son, had passed away about a year before Mr. Schuyler had delivered his funeral oration. He had got "beyond her," as she said towards the last, when he and his wife and her grandchildren passed the end of her little garden every evening without coming in. She shed many bitter tears over this, but she never blamed him; in her heart she laid the guilt of this desertion on his wife.

Ah! what an angel of light he would have been had it not been for this wife! she exclaimed to herself often in the twilight when she sat alone. These idle hours in the dusk were the hardest for her to bear. She could see the lights in her son's house from where she sat. There were sounds of music and of children singing—his children, her grandchildren, yet so far from her. She could never bear the music of those childish voices. She always shut the windows when they began and tried to say her beads. He was a good son still; did he not send her every week from the bank enough money —more than enough—to keep her in comfort? But oh! if she could only go back again to the old days when he was a little boy, and such an affectionate little fellow! How he used to cry when she sang an old song to him in the gloaming, after she

had done her day's work and they were waiting for
the father.   It was all about a little girl that lived
in a red house by the sea, without sister or brother
or father or mother.   She often tried to recall it:

> " I sit alone in the twilight,
>   While the wind comes sighing to me,
> And I see that dear little orphan
>   In the little red house by the sea."

Surely the loving little boy, whose eyes filled
with tears every time she sang those simple words,
could not have changed entirely.   *She* had made
his heart cold, the mother said of his wife; she had
made him forget church and priest, and even his
mother.

It must be admitted that the old woman would
not restrain herself when, soon after his marriage,
her son had often come to see her.   She had never
spared his wife, and from this fact had sprung the
coldness which prevented him from going to see
her.   It was none the less hard for the warm-
hearted old woman.   She took no pleasure in her
son's political successes; her only consolation,
besides her religious duties, was in the company of
one more unhappy, if possible, than herself.   This
was an old Irishwoman, Mrs. Carney, who lived in
an unpainted and bare-looking frame house at the
back of her garden.

Frank Carney had been in the district school with
Perseus—Mrs. Mahaffy never called him by that
name, but always " the Boy "—and he had entered

the same Lodge as that enterprising politician when the time came to cast off allegiance to the faith. Frank, a blue-eyed, light-haired, good-natured young man, was not quite so clever as Perseus, and not quite so unscrupulous. He had more conscience; but he had no firmness of will in face of a laugh. Moreover, he was fond of society; and, according to the constitution of Cone City, Catholics were not socially eligible. He was gay, cheerful, with a fatal facility for making himself agreeable. He was handsome; he could dance well, and he soon acquired those graces which Cone City had lately grasped with the " swallow tail " and other metropolitan novelties. Perseus took him into his law office, and from that time Mrs. Carney's life became bitter. Her only son dropped his habit of going to Mass with her; he seldom came home; he promised when he did come that " he'd make his soul by and by "—and this with a laugh. But when she heard that he had been promoted—Cone City looked on this as a promotion —to the friendship of Col. Brodbeck, the notorious infidel, her heart sank; she refused to be comforted.

Mrs. Mahaffy knew that her son had drawn Frank Carney from the way of peace. She never admitted it, nor did Mrs. Carney speak of it. But any one who knew the two old women could not help seeing that on one side was a desire to make amends, and on the other a determination to accept kindness simply because it relieved the one who conferred it. Each of these two old friends—they were born on the banks of the Suir, had crossed on the same ship, and had lost their husbands at the same time—bore her burden better because each thought the other's was the heavier. At last old Mrs. Mahaffy died, blessing her son. He, being absent at a political convention, was not present to receive that blessing. And so great was this admirable man's horror of superstition, and so strong his desire not to give bad example to his fellow-townsmen, that he telegraphed to his mother's pastor to bury her at once with solemn services. He did this because he wanted to be sure of his nomination and because he did not care to be seen entering the Catholic church. Old Mrs. Carney, who had never said a word against Perseus, burst out at the funeral of her friend. " If I had such a son," she cried, " I'd curse him!"

III.

Perseus had begun to be a star when he married the late Judge Brodbeck's daughter. Judge Brodbeck came of an old English family, but this would have mattered very little in the town of Cone City had not the judge made a great deal of money in railroad speculations. People said the railroads had influenced his decisions on the bench; but as he was rich there was a certain respect for him mixed with this censure. The judge had been the strictest of strict Calvinists; his two children, the colonel and Clara, hated Presbyterianism.

Clara meeting Perseus by chance at one of the dancing assemblies, found him to be a pleasant contrast to the business-sodden men around her. And the colonel, her brother, who saw that Perseus was vain as well as clever, did not object to the intimacy. When the marriage was announced Cone City was amazed. The ceremony was performed in the First Baptist Church, simply because Clara held that a religious ceremony was socially respectable.

But on that day the mother of the bridegroom knelt before the crucifix in her little room. Her son had become an apostate to gain prosperity—he, the descendant of martyrs! After this Perseus had fewer scruples; the die was cast; his mother's entreaties fell on callous ears.

Colonel Brodbeck determined to take advantage of Perseus' vanity, as well as of his cleverness. It was Perseus' misfortune that his horizon was bounded by Cone City. No parvenu who had suddenly married a princess could have been more elated than was Perseus by his marriage.

" You have given up your God, your soul," his mother had said to him, " for nothing."

" I have never seen God or my soul, mother," he had answered. " See here, mother, I want a big house, I want to be rich, I want to be one of the best people of this town, and you can't be that if you're poor; for all these reasons I've married Clara Brodbeck. I'll get the best out of life I can, and take my chances."

" And you'll turn your back on the Church and the priest for this! Sure, you've already joined a secret society."

" Everybody knows that. As soon as I learned to read I learned that I must get on or live down here in this shanty, despised—nobody. I was born of the poor; everybody looked down on the ' Irish boy '—I'm no more Irish than they are English or German or anything else—and the Irish boy had patches on his clothes, and he went to the church to which only the hewers of wood and the drawers of water went."

" And his mother was only a poor Irishwoman!" said Mrs. Mahaffy, with a flash of sarcasm.

" She couldn't help that——"

" But her son would have helped being her son, if he could."

Perseus reddened. He admitted the truth of this in his heart.

" You ought to be proud of me, mother. I've leaped over the bounds that kept me out of everything worth having. I have an assured position in the town, and my children will have all the advantages which I lacked. My wife is the most cultured woman——"

" God help us!" interjected the mother, " you'd think he was talking of Dublin after having married a great lord's daughter! You're too ignorant to know the miserable price for which you've sold your soul. Your grandmother starved in the famine rather than change her religion, or seem to change it even for a moment. Why was your father poor ? Why were we exiles ? For one reason only: we kept the faith.''

'' I've heard all this before, mother,'' he said, '' and there's no money in it.''

'' And you're leading young Frank Carney away, too,'' the old woman had said, exhausted and despondent.

Perseus only shrugged his shoulders. He was satisfied that he had done the best he could for himself. The duty of making money was the first recognized in Cone City. '' Put money in thy purse,'' the spirit of the town whispered through every medium. The churches were valued according to their financial status. The Presbyterians were in the ascendant in money matters; therefore their '' socials '' and meetings were best attended. The Catholic priest was respected because he paid his bills promptly and would not permit himself to be cheated. The Protestant-Episcopalians were poor, their minister was a Canadian of high-church proclivities, and though some '' nice people '' sat under him—people who wore diamonds and seal-skin—yet they were, as a rule, '' looked down on.''

Perseus must have been stronger than he was to have escaped the fever of money-making. He saw that in a Protestant and highly total abstaining town, Colonel Brodbeck's infidelity and moderate fondness for whiskey were condoned because of his wealth. Money could do anything, he concluded; it might even open the way socially to a Catholic, provided he were not *too* Irish. He had a somewhat better education than the other boys; for Father Deschamps taught the little school—he was too poor to pay a teacher. When Perseus had left it and gone to the district school, the kind priest, discerning the boy's talent, had made him read Cicero and Virgil. Father Deschamps was replaced by another pastor, and Perseus was left to the deadening influence around him. Having planned his career, he was somewhat relieved to have Father Deschamps go. And yet he never felt that he was ungrateful; he became so entirely absorbed in his desire to be rich that it seemed only right that all the world should aid. He became his own Buddha; he was rapidly losing himself in self.

Colonel Brodbeck admired Perseus' capabilities. "If the fellow," he said to himself, "only knew his ability, and if his confounded snobbishness did not prevent him seeing how superior he is to these Cone City chumps, he'd get away from here as soon as possible. But he looks on the Cone City settler as one of a superior race."

The colonel grinned sardonically, and opened a letter about the selling of the Cone City water-front to the new railroad company, whose stock was mostly owned in Chicago.

"Ah!" he said, "we shall find some work here for Perseus."

Perseus was sent to Congress. And just before the day of election the rival candidate brought out

the old story about his having changed his name.
Both of the Cone City papers had his mother "interviewed." According to the friendly journalist,
she was a "handsome old lady, living in opulence
provided by an adoring son." The other journal
said she was a "decent old woman, bowed down
by her son's neglect, and living in comparative
squalor." All the old woman could be induced to
say was that she "would not have cared how often
'the Boy' changed his name, if he had only stuck
to his religion."

This brought a card from Perseus. He protested
that religion had no place in politics. His religion
was his private affair. He would allow no human
being to interfere between him and his God. His
Irish friends, he hoped, would remember that,
though an American in every fibre of his being, he
loved, next to the principles of 1776, the principles
of Home Rule. While he lived he would oppose
any state tax on church property. To be honest
was the first commandment of his religion; and he
hoped, in Congress, to show that this religion influenced every act.

The card was effective; the Home Rule phrase
and that about church property helped him very
much, though he promised the Methodist minister
to lecture at an early date on "Roman Tyranny,"
—a promise which he did not intend to keep.

To be frank, Perseus believed that he was only
diplomatic, not dishonest; he often said to himself
that people did not know how good he was. His

wife's indifference about religion annoyed him. He held that a woman ought to be religious; but Clara laughed.

" The children shall choose their own religion," she said one evening, after one of the Cone City functions called a " coffee." Sixty leading Cone City ladies had eaten chicken salad and ices with her from three until six, and the probable conversion of one of their number to Catholicity had been discussed. " Cora Bramber is going to turn Catholic, and I must say I like her spirit."

" I thought you hated Catholics," Perseus said.

" I ? Good gracious, no! I think they are more consistent than other denominations. And I don't see why they should be held responsible for the awful things the Jesuits and popes did long ago. I'm sure the Puritans were bad enough."

" You wouldn't want the children to be Catholics, Clara."

" If they were rich and could do as they please, I think I would. But Providence, if there is a Providence, seems rather hard on people when he makes them Catholic and poor at the same time. The children must have some religion or other. I can keep straight without religion; I've a natural tendency towards respectability, and you're a good husband; but Perseus, I wouldn't trust anybody else. I'm thinking of sending Clara to a convent school."

Perseus set down his coffee cup in amazement—

he was in the act of making a collation from the remains of the afternoon feast.

" I won't have it," he said; " it would ruin the girl's prospects, Clara. Who'd marry a Catholic here, and if she goes to a convent, she might——"

" If there's anything that exasperates me," answered his wife, calmly washing the silver, " it's your foolish reverence for Cone City people. They're only people who came here to earn a living; they're the sort of people who go to Europe every year to complete an education that was never begun at home. If Clara has money, she might be a Mohammedan. Haven't you learned that yet ? She'll be *safe* in a convent school."

" Well, I'll lose the Methodist vote, that's all."

" No, you won't, nor the Baptist either. The anti-church-tax-property stand holds all denominations. Besides, haven't I given five hundred dollars for the Methodist chapel? You'll gain more Catholic votes than you ever had. Anyhow, I *will* have Clara well taken care of. I know our boarding-schools too well. The nuns may make her narrow-minded, but they'll keep her gentle. The others make their girls both narrow-minded and aggressive."

Perseus was silent. After all, it was like the sound of far-off bells, sweet to his ears, to think that his child might say the same old prayers and kneel before the tabernacle. Nevertheless he would not sacrifice anything for this. As Clara took the responsibility, he left it to her. He was resolved that the boys should not be handicapped by religion.

He took his wife to the opera-house that night to hear her brother lecture on " The Beautiful in Life." The theatre was crowded. The colonel was very florid in his speech. He said that beauty was religion, and if religion and the enjoyment of the beautiful were opposed, religion must go. " If God is a God of terror," he repeated, " God must go; when men's souls shall have attuned themselves to the grace of the Venus of Milo rather than to Churchly ideas of womanhood, when the use of money shall mean more beauty in life, then virtue and sensuous enjoyment shall be one and life be complete."

" I suppose you'd like Clara to hear that kind of stuff," Perseus' wife said as they drove home.

" It was very pretty," said Perseus; " I don't quite see what it means; it certainly makes religion very attractive. Like you, the colonel does not seem to need religion in order to be good."

His wife laughed. " I don't know about that; but I know what he means—he means free love. As for religion, we all need it. Do you know, if you had stuck to your religion I should have had more respect for you, and it is probable I might have become a Catholic myself. There are times, Perseus, when your silly admiration for Cone City makes you very tiresome. As for my brother, can't you see that he is not a good man ? He believes in God in his heart, of course he does!

The way he protests against it shows that he does. As for myself, I dislike any unreasonable and illogical belief founded on man's dictum and the Bible. But I don't know Catholicism. I might like it. We all need religion—my brother worse than anybody I know," she added with a short laugh. "There is nothing in our times, except religion, to keep a woman from dropping a husband she does not like and taking one she does; and no religion can do it effectively except yours—I beg pardon, I mean the religion you have ·progressed out of. There's Mrs. Churton—she's been divorced twice, and yet she's head and front among the Congregationalists."

"You don't mean to say that you'd——" Perseus almost gasped, as he turned to his wife.

"I don't mean to say anything but that Clara shall be fortified against the dangers that would beset me if I cared for any other man than you."

This was frank enough. Perseus shuddered as he heard it. He imagined his mother saying such a thing! No; toil-worn, uneducated, old-fashioned as she was, there was a bloom of innocence and womanliness about his mother which his wife lacked. Such frankness gradually built up a wall of distrust between them. Later, she differed with him almost habitually; and she was generally right. Finally, she came almost to despise him.

The question of the sale of the water-front came up. Perseus and Colonel Brodbeck opposed it. It meant robbery. It would open the door to monopoly. It was an outrage on the rights of the people. It was because of his course in this matter that he was sent to Congress a third time, and was enabled to second some of his brother-in-law's schemes very effectively. Frank Carney had been his constant supporter. Frank had now no legitimate business; he was devoted to politics, he lived by subsidies from the Hon. Perseus and Colonel Brodbeck. He was their slave, and the more self-respect he lost the more valuable he became. Somebody must do the dirty work in politics, and Frank's hand, once in the mire, did a great deal of it. His mother said this to him about Easter-time, when she was urging him to go to his " duty."

" I can't, mother," he said; " don't ask me. I'd have to get out of politics if I did. When I've made my pile," he added, with a rather timid attempt at a laugh, " I'll repent."

" They say that you and Colonel Brodbeck have robbed right and left. I can't bear to hear such things."

" Oh! it's newspaper lies. Don't you see the colonel is a big man for all that ? It doesn't make much difference in this country where you get money, so that you get it."

The old woman could only cry and wring her hands. She saw that her son had begun to drink, and it was said that he gambled. Prayer, constant and unwearying, was her only resource.

The railroad company wanted the water-front badly. Its counsel and directors knew that Colonel

Brodbeck and Perseus controlled the council of Cone City, of which the colonel was the attorney. Had the colonel and the Hon. Perseus a price? An answer to this question was easily obtained through Frank Carney. They had, and it was high. Perseus was at first inclined to be honest, but the colonel laughed at him.

"Nonsense," he said, "that sort of thing went out of fashion with religion. You felt yourself trammelled in the process of making your career by your Catholicism, and you gave it up. Why should you keep up the bondage after you've emancipated yourself? It ought to be a whole hog or none. There's no confession to be afraid of now."

Perseus laughed uneasily. He had the feeling "as if"—his mother would have said it—"somebody was walking over his grave."

His wife was shocked by the change of view on the waterside question. She spoke her opinion very plainly. "I might have known," she said in her most cutting tones, "that it was a risk to marry an apostate, but I never imagined this disgrace. Oh! my brother? My brother is an infidel, but you pretend to be a Christian still!"

After this Perseus knew that his wife despised him, though he had cleaved the ether and was a star. He winced under sarcasm; ridicule withered him; he distrusted her. What guarantee had he that she, not looking at their bond from the point of view of duty, might not desert him at any moment ? Clara, his daughter, was at a convent school; his boys were also away; his life was wretchedly unhappy—but it was growing richer in this world's goods every day.

The " deal " between the Cone City syndicate and the railroad company had been arranged very neatly through Frank Carney. There had been no tell-tale checks in the matter. Frank had delivered thirty thousand dollars to two of the most potent men. The council had been managed, but no one knew who did it, so that while popular indignation struck the council, it never even glanced on the colonel and his brother-in-law. It was cleverly arranged—there was no scandal; Perseus admired his diplomacy and his success, for thirty thousand dollars was a great sum in Cone City, and yet it was the beginning of disaster.

Frank Carney, good-natured, plastic, credulous, began to see that he was only a tool. He had been almost ignored in the division of the spoil. He feared Perseus and the colonel too much to find fault openly. But his discontent was growing. He was in this mood in the spring, when Easter came again. His mother met him one morning, just after old Mrs. Mahaffy's death; she stood and looked at him with yearning eyes. He had been drinking all night; but he was sober enough.

" What is it, mother ? " he said.

" What is it, dear ? I'm just thinking that I'd give the world to have my own boy back again."

In the early sunlight as she turned away, Frank saw a tear on her cheek.

"If God helps me, you shall, mother," he called after her; and then he said to himself: "She's worth it all; I'll surprise her; I'm tired of the mud."

IV.

It happened that the Hon. Perseus G. Mahaffy and Colonel Brodbeck were asked to speak before a spring meeting of the Farmers' Alliance one Saturday night. The colonel made an address which was not well received. It was not vaguely atheistical—it was not humorously atheistical; it was openly immoral—a plea for "affinities," an apology for a law granting easier divorces. It was hissed by the farmers who had tolerated his jokes on the Divinity and his amusing caricatures of modern Calvinism. Going home with Perseus and Frank Carney, his humor was ferocious. The "Beautiful"—not even Goethe's "Helena" or the march in "Lohengrin"—could have made him less savage. It was strange that the panaceas recommended by the colonel for other people rarely answered for himself.

The three were walking; it was a moonlight night. Perseus was well satisfied with himself; Frank Carney was moody. They were passing the arbor-vitæ hedge which separated his mother's little house from the road.

" Do you know, colonel, I have concluded to go back to my first love and get out of your infidel clique, and likewise out of politics ? You haven't treated me right; but that makes no difference now. I'm going into the insurance business at Oxhart next week, and I shall follow my conscience. I'm a Catholic at heart and I'll be one practically, with God's help, after this. A speech like the one you made to-night ought to make us all religious."

" Who hasn't treated you right ? " The colonel stood still and confronted Carney.

" You ought to know." They were standing near the new railroad embankment, and Carney paused near the edge to answer the colonel.

" I suppose you mean that as a threat," sneered the colonel. " I suppose you think we're afraid you'll go and confess certain little things to a priest. But you can't frighten us. If you want money, why don't you say so, instead of trying a monkey trick like this ? "

Frank Carney's face turned ashy.

" I don't want thieves' money."

He had no sooner spoken the words than the colonel raised his fist. Frank Carney tried to guard himself; the colonel struck him, and he fell down the embankment, a descent of twenty feet. He lay still among the stones; then he groaned. Perseus and the colonel went to the ladder at the side, and with some effort dragged him up to the hedge near his mother's house. There was a deep cut on his forehead, and another on the back of his head; his face was white.   The colonel felt his pulse.

" He can't live."

The wounded man opened his eyes, and his lips moved in a mute appeal.

" He wants a priest," whispered Perseus. " Stay with him, while I run to the town; it's not half a mile."

The colonel showed his white teeth.

" A priest, you fool!   Do you want him to ruin us with his silly nonsense ?   He knows too much. Let him confess to us; we'll keep his secrets."

" He must have a priest, colonel."

Again the dying man opened his lips and tried to raise his hands.

The colonel looked at Perseus in his ugliest way. " You're a nice person to be talking of priests—you that pretend to hate them.   I can't afford to have a priest come here; neither can you!"

Perseus stood irresolute.   He felt as if he were killing a soul.   But he had let the colonel's evil will dominate him so long that he could not resist it now.   At the same time his last hope of all better things seemed to die out as he steeled his heart against Frank Carney's whisper, " A priest."

Carney's voice grew stronger in his agony: " For God's sake, get me Father Lovel—he's not far— my mother.   It's all I ask.   I can't stand this much longer."

" *You* hear his confession, if you're so anxious about it," said the colonel, mockingly.

Perseus had become accustomed to wince at that tone. He turned away from the agonized face of his friend, and went down the road; and then it seemed to him that his own soul went to hell and a devil of despair took possession of his body. The colonel soon rejoined him, and spoke in his coolest voice.

" He's dead. The thing's awkward; but I just dropped my whiskey-flask into his pocket and rolled him down the embankment. Everybody knows he drank. That will account for it all when he's found. We'll say he left us at the Junction. The idiot!"

Nobody cared much, except Frank's old mother. She heard that he had died almost at her door. The whiskey-flask part of the story was mercifully kept from her. " It accounted for it all," as the colonel had predicted.

But the Hon. Perseus Mahaffy was never quite himself again. One night, in the autumn, he made a great speech at the closing dinner of the trustees of the County Fair. It was said to be the effort of his life. The colonel, who had noticed the change in him since the night of Frank Carney's death, watched his face intently. At first he sneered at the orator's grandiloquence; then his expression became more serious. When the Hon. Perseus began his peroration and was interrupted by cheers for the Star of Golung Creek, the colonel noticed a fixed look in his eyes, and when he again attempted to go on he stammered. Suddenly the words seemed to freeze on his lips; he looked at the large pyramid of fruit and flowers before him as if it were a human being of threatening aspect. The colonel jumped up and caught him as he was falling, crying out, " What's the matter ? "

" I thought I saw *his* ghost," he whispered. " It has killed me; for God's sake, send for a priest! "

" Nonsense! " returned the colonel. " What good will a priest do you ? Here, take this brandy."

Perseus thrust the little glass away from him.

" A priest! " he whispered again and again. But the group around him thought he was raving. Who among them had ever connected him with a priest ? The sneer came back to the colonel's face as he made room for the doctor. In less than an hour he was in convulsions. He never spoke again; the horror of it all was that his eyes remained open, and the look in their depth was as if he longed to speak. At last, a look of agony crossed his face as if he saw an awful thing. Then he died.

The doctor gave his disease a medical name; the colonel said to himself that it was superstition, acting on a weak mind. And his last words had been: " Success, gentlemen, is not measured by material prosperity. It consists in being true to ideals, in sacrificing all aims and objects which are not truth's. That is success in the sight of God. All other things named success are illusions."

His daughter did not forget the face of the old woman who had pulled her mother's frock at the funeral. She found out her name and made her acquaintance. Poor Mrs. Carney prayed for her son as only a mother in doubt about a son's soul can pray.

"If I only knew how he died!" Mrs. Carney wailed constantly; "if I only knew how he died! I've often thought your father might know whether he was prepared or not."

Clara understood her; she knew that the mother's thoughts were on her son's soul. She could say nothing; she did not dream that her father and the colonel knew only too well.

It happened that just before the summer vacation, Clara at the convent had finished a little picture of the Sacred Heart for Mrs. Carney. The chaplain, Father Morgan, was about to go to Cone City, and he had promised to take charge of it for her. Clara knew that the sight of his genial face would do Mrs. Carney good.

"Mrs. Carney," he said, reading the address. "Is that the mother of the poor young man who died under such strange circumstances last spring? Ah! indeed," he continued musingly, in answer to Clara's assent. "I saw him that very afternoon. I was hearing confessions in the German church, and he came to me just as I was leaving the box. He introduced himself and asked for some advice about the examination of his conscience. I answered him by taking him back to the box and hearing his confession. Poor young man!"

Clara's cheeks glowed, her eyes sparkled. She

had found out how Frank Carney died; now she knew that he had passed from earth with the cleansing dew of absolution upon him. She thanked Father Morgan and ran off to get permission from the mother-superior to go with him to Cone City; she gave her reason, and as a great and special favor it was granted.

" What would you like most to have? " she asked, when the old woman had greeted the priest and kissed her.

" To know that I should see my boy again in heaven, to know that he died well," she answered with a tremor in her voice. Then Clara and Father Morgan made her happy.

Colonel Brodbeck has begun to have more than a local reputation. His " *Life of the Honorable Perseus G. Mahaffy* " is much praised. The description of Perseus' " conversion " from Romanism to a serene state of religious indifference is particularly well done. His sister seldom sees him; she is in doubt. " If I were anything," she says, " I would be a Catholic, like Clara—that is, if all Catholics were like her. But Perseus' example and the example of so many like him make me pause. There's plenty of time." And she says to herself: " I'll send the boys to a Catholic school next year, in the hope that they will grow up unlike Perseus and the colonel."

When the Rev. Mr. Schuyler remonstrates with her, she tells him that she has tried Calvinism and agnosticism, and found them hollow; what is left to her but the Church ?   And then she wonders why Perseus turned away from it.   " He   must have been weak," she thinks, with a curl of her lip; she cannot say this to him; he has gone.

FRANCIS J. FINN, S.J.

THERE was a time, not so long ago, when there were no Catholic boys in fiction, that is, no boys of one's own species in the books which boys read as idealized pictures of their own lives. There were plenty of good little boys who were always undergoing persecution for the sake of their religion, and of smart boys who always had the best of an argument with the minister, but there were no pictures of the real American Catholic boy. In the great crowd of story-writers there was none to give a picture of the life of the American Catholic boy. Suddenly, while most of us were bewailing the fate of our children without books specially their own. Father Finn came. He has never told us whether he thought he had a mission to boys or not. Probably not, since "Tom Playfair" was written with no idea of publication. But the boys liked him and his books better than any books they had read, because he understood them and because when he wrote he became a boy again.

It is the kindness, the cheerfulness, the earnest sympathy, and the idealism of Father Finn that makes boys love him. By idealism we mean his power of illuminating the boy so that he sees himself as he would like to be; and his power, too, of showing the boys' teacher as he ought to be.

Father Finn takes the boy as he is; he has no illusions about him,—but he strives to make him better by showing that boys may be honorable and spiritual-minded without losing all the qualities which the growing man esteems and loves in his heroes. And what the boy loves in his heroes he strives to imitate.

Father Finn was born at St. Louis on October 4, 1859. He entered the Society of Jesus on March 4th, 1879, and was ordained priest in 1893. He was Professor in St. Louis University and in St. Mary's College, Kansas, and Professor of English Literature in Marquette College, Milwaukee.

Father Finn's published books are: "Percy Wynn," "Tom Playfair," "Harry Dee," "Claude Lightfoot," "Mostly Boys," "Faces Old and New," "Ada Merton," "Ethelred Preston." He is at present engaged on another story, which will no doubt be the equal of the others.

My Strange Friend.

BY FRANCIS J. FINN, S.J.

I.

A FEW days after Christmas, I was sitting in my room, nursing an incipient cold, and wondering when my health would permit me to return to the seminary. At this period of my life, I was heir to many ills, prominent among which was the dyspepsia. Headache in the morning from eight to ten, headache in the afternoon from two till about four, headache at night from seven indefinitely, then bed;—this constituted my daily order, dull enough surely in the reading, but painfully dismal in the realization.

The cessation of my morning headache was almost due, when my sister, singing gayly, tripped into my room with a letter, which she handed me with a mock bow.

"I am very much obliged to you, my dear, for bringing me this letter," I remarked; "but now really couldn't you dispense with your feminine war-whoop when you're in my room?"

" Oh, you great, big, dyspeptic bear," she laughed out, " you want me to take pattern after yourself, and go about like an unsuccessful undertaker ? "

I felt my gorge rising at her remark, and was tempted to say something ungracious and bitter, as she danced out through the door-way. That's the way with us dyspeptics; we have no sympathy for sweet human life, and are especially high with our near relatives.

Without stopping, however, to analyze my feelings, I tore open the letter and read:

FAIRMOUNT GROVE, *Jan.* 12, 1874.

MR. THOMAS MAXON:

Dear old Tom, I can never forgive myself the language I used previous to our parting. What a pity that supper ever came off at all. But I am now so heartily ashamed and penitent that I know you will forgive and forget. And now you can do me a great, a very great service, and I feel positive that you will not refuse me. I have heard that you are unwell. Come out here in the pure country air and spend a month with me. It will surely do you good, while beyond all doubt it will serve me untold gain. O my dear, dear friend (for I trust that you have already forgiven me, and are my friend again), come and see me. I have changed greatly, and am very miserable. The strange darkness that has come over my life, I may not, cannot tell. Some terrible power imposes silence upon me, though I would give worlds to confide it to you, dear Tom. But come, come; let yourself be the answer to this note. Ever your loving friend,

WILBER STONE.

I read this letter with mingled sentiments of pleasure and of pain; pleasure, that it reconciled me with the dearest friend of my boyhood; pain, that judging by the tenor of his communication, a terrible, saddening change had come upon him.

Wilber Stone and myself had been chums at college. Beginning together, we had gone on from class to class, dividing (let me say in all modesty) the honors between us. While studying Rhetoric, a prize was offered for the best essay on Longfellow. We were both admirers of the poet, and set to work at the task with ardor. The day before the essays were to be handed in, Wilber, on invitation, came to my house to see my paper. He read it carefully, praising what pleased him, and, like a true friend, frankly pointing out what he considered its defects.

" Well, Wilber," I said when he had finished, " suppose you let me see your own essay."

" Willingly," he answered, and took from his coat a bundle of manuscript.

I read it eagerly.

" It's no use my handing in," I remarked, when I had come to the end of it. " Your essay will certainly take first place: no boy in the class can come near it."

" You think it better than your own ? "

" Better! " I exclaimed warmly. " Why, Wilber, I couldn't write like that in a year's time. Yes, Wilber, my boy, I'm beaten squarely."

A strange look came over his face. But, instead

of continuing the conversation, he caught up his hat, bade me good evening, and abruptly left the house.

A month later the gold medal was awarded.

"The prize for the best essay on Longfellow is awarded to——" Here the vice-president of the college paused to clear his throat. I was sitting next to Wilber, and patted him on the back.

"Get ready to go up, old boy," I whispered.

Wilber's face was strangely pale; and so nervous had he grown that he was unable to return my smile.

"Is awarded," the vice-president continued, "to Thomas Maxon."

This was one of the greatest surprises of my school life. Amidst hearty applause, I found myself—how I got there I know not—on the stage, receiving from the hands of the president the gold medal. But I was far from being satisfied.

"Wilber," I said, when I had regained my seat, "this is a mistake."

"Next in merit," continued the vice-president, now that the applause had subsided, "George Murray and Francis Elaine."

"What!" I gasped. "Why you're not even mentioned. I'm going to ask our professor about this just as soon as this affair is over."

"No, no, Tom," whispered Wilber more nervous than before; "you mustn't do any such thing. You have honestly earned the medal."

I attributed his nervousness and his words to bitter disappointment.

" But I will," I answered hotly, for I was burning with indignation at what I could not but consider a cruel mistake.

My dear friend spent some time in persuading me not to make any inquiries in the matter; but he was unsuccessful.

" Mr. Warden," I said, touching my cap to my professor, as we met outside the exhibition hall, " how is it that Wilber got no mention for his essay on Longfellow? I read it, and felt sure that his was far superior to mine."

" The reason is simple," answered Mr. Warden. " Wilber neglected to hand in his essay."

Then the truth flashed upon me. I turned away with the tears standing in my eyes. The medal was now indeed valuable to me; it was the sacred memorial of a heroic act of friendship.

But poor Wilber, noble as he was, had grave faults. He exhibited two traits which made me tremble for his future. One was an ungovernable pride, the other, an outgrowth of the first, an unwillingness to take advice. He went through life " at his own sweet will."

The latter defect came into prominence during our year of philosophy. He grew captious about revealed truth, sneered at the classic answers to philosophical and theological difficulties, and occasionally gave voice to opinions which shocked me. Despite my protestations and the warning of some of the professors, who took a deep interest in him, he chose as a friend a fellow-student whose standing, both as to class and to character, was at the lowest. Insensibly there arose a coolness between us; not that we ceased to be friends, but that our plans and pursuits had become so widely divergent.

On the night of Commencement exercises, we philosophers, having finished our course, sat down to a parting banquet before separating in the great world.

The first hour passed pleasantly enough, though I noticed with uneasiness that Wilber was drinking freely. By and by the talk turned upon the valedictory which I had delivered.

"The allusion to Our Lord you brought in," said one, "was very beautiful, and, at the same time, came in so naturally."

Wilber gave a scornful laugh,—such a laugh that conversation came to a stop, and all eyes turned upon him.

Then, flushed with wine, he spoke such words of Our Saviour as I have not the heart to record.

Every one present was aghast at the blasphemous language; many looked at me. They knew that I was shortly to enter a seminary, and seemed by common consent to place me in the position of spokesman.

"Wilber," I said, rising, and the pain I felt at that moment I shall never forget, "I cannot stay in your company, if you choose to speak such language."

"Free country, young Levite," cried Wilber, his face hardening with pride. "We're not in the class-room now, Deacon, and I'll say just what I please."

Then he went on to utter further blasphemy. With a heavy heart, I left the room whilst he was still speaking, followed by all except Wilber and his evil genius, the classmate against whom he had been so vainly warned. On the following day Wilber departed for the East with his family; and though one year and a half had gone by from the time of that unhappy banquet, I had not seen him since.

On re-reading his letter, I decided to comply with his request at once, and accordingly I arrived at the depot near Fairmount Grove that afternoon at three o'clock.

What was my dismay when I saw awaiting me at the depot not the gay, handsome athletic Wilber of college days, but a sad, gaunt, hollow-eyed young man, so changed in appearance that I could hardly bring myself to believe it was the same person.

As he caught my eyes, his face lighted up with pleasure.

" O Tom, Tom! how glad, how very glad I am to see you."

I rushed forward to give him a hearty handshake, but he drew back with an air of timidity ill-befitting the bold Wilber of former days. Recovering himself by an evident effort, he took my hand in his. He held it for a moment in a cold, pressureless grasp, and then drew back as though he had done a guilty deed.

" Your hand is cold," he said nervously.

I looked at him closely, but the welcome on his face belied his actions. I was puzzled.

" You find something strange about me, Tom," he said in reply to my look, " but if you only knew all. Don't think that you are not most welcome. Here, jump in," he added, motioning to a sleigh that I knew to be his.

As we jingled along to Fairmount Grove, we fell into an earnest talk about old times in the course of which, however, through motives of delicacy, I avoided bringing in a single allusion to matters of religion, fearing that perhaps it might awaken unpleasant memories.

" So you are studying for the priesthood ? " he resumed after a short lull in our conversation.

" Yes, Wilber; and I hope to give my whole life to the service of God."

What was my astonishment when, at the mention of the sacred name, he released one hand from its hold upon the reins, and lifted his hat with an air of devotion that was a sermon in itself.

" Ah, Wilber," I cried in delight, " I knew it would end so; I knew that you would come back to the old way of looking at things."

He turned his face towards mine, and with a frightened, wistful expression in his eyes, asked:

" Tom, what does our divine Lord say about the scandalizing of little ones ? "

" It were better that a millstone were placed about the scandalizer's neck, and that he were cast into the depth of the sea."

" Just so," he responded with a sigh, and an expression that was pitiful, " and yet He is such a good, such a merciful God, too."

" Indeed, He is," I answered. " We can none of us begin to understand how tenderly God loves us."

" Say that again," he said softly, while a smile warmed his face into melancholy beauty.

I repeated my words, and continued to talk in the same strain, as I saw what evident pleasure the subject afforded him. When I had come to a pause, he added:

" And yet He is so terrible in His denunciations of those who scandalize His little ones."

" Yes," I made reply, " but there is forgiveness for them if they repent. But cheer up, Wilber; what makes you so sad ? "

" I have many reasons, Tom. Just one month ago mother died."

" Indeed!—your mother dead ? O Wilber! why didn't you let me know ? It must have been an awful blow to you."

" But that's not the worst, Tom. I knew for a month before that some one very dear to me was going to die."

I was again amazed.

" How in the world did you know that? "

" I can't tell, Tom, but listen "—his voice sank to a whisper—" what day of the month is this ? "

" The fourteenth of January."

" Very well, on the twentieth of January—"

here he paused while the lines upon his face indicated some terrible agony—" on the twentieth of January—O my God!—some one else dear to me will die."

The groan which accompanied his ejaculation sent a shiver through me; I began to fear that I was in the company of a madman. But he read my thoughts as though I had framed them in words.

" No, no: it is no hallucination; I am not out of my senses," he exclaimed; " nor can I now explain to you how I know such things; but what I say is true."

I made no reply, and my silence might have been awkward were it not for the fact that at this juncture we turned into the winding roadway which leads up to the spacious country house of Fairmount Grove. Standing at the gate was a bevy of boys and girls from the tot of three to the hoiden of fifteen, smiling and waving hats and handkerchiefs at my delighted self. I remembered them all—the " tigers " was my name for them—and, if signals of welcome go for anything, they remembered me.

" Hurrah!" cried Charlie, the oldest lad of the group, a cousin of Wilber's, " here's Uncle Tom come at last."

Though I was in nowise related to any of Wilber's cousins, they had insisted on calling me Uncle Tom from the first time that I showed myself to their delighted eyes in the full dress of young manhood.

No sooner had the horse come to a stop before

the gate than all the tigers, with the exception of the two older ones, sprang upon me with a series of joyful screams and friendly struggles, pulled me from my seat and out of the vehicle, and cast me down into a deep bank of snow, the more astute of them in the meanwhile emptying my overcoat pockets of various small packages, which, little rogues, they knew I would not fail to bring by way of a peace-offering.

We had a merry time of it on that winter afternoon, the tigers pulling me this way and that, forcing me to play the elephant, exhausting my entire stock of fairy tales, then clamoring for more, and, in fine, exacting of their Uncle Tom ample amends for his long absence. It was great fun for them, and, I may add without apology, for myself, too; for I love little children, and sincerely pity the man who does not.

Throughout this round of amusement, Wilber had contented himself with being merely an onlooker. He witnessed our rompings and tumblings with a strange, sad, timorous, yet pleased expression, and whenever he spoke to the children, it was in so sweet a voice, in so gentle a manner, that one would think he was addressing himself to superior beings. As we were going up the stairway at bedtime, I made a remark to that effect.

"You are right, Tom," he answered: "I do regard them as superior beings; for they are, God be thanked for it, pure and innocent, and whenever I am in their company, I cannot help bearing in mind that their guardian angels ever see the face of their Father who is in heaven."

Once more was I impressed with the thrilling, awe-inspiring reverence of his voice and expression. It was such a change in Wilber, who of all my school companions and friends had ever been the least reverent.

"Here," he continued, throwing open a door, "this is your room.   It is next to mine."

"Good," I said; "if I feel at all wakeful, which is not at all likely after the events of this day, I will give you a call."

With an air of secrecy, he closed the door, and said to me in a tone of voice which was little more than a whisper:

"Tom, my friend, if I should happen to come in here during the night at any time, you wouldn't mind it, would you?"

"Certainly not, Wilber: you shall be most welcome," I replied, though I must confess that I could not control a motion of astonishment.

"Thank you very much.   And, Tom, if you note anything strange or out of the way in my conduct in case I come in, you must try not to mind.   I should like to—to tell you all, if I dared; but I really cannot—at least, not yet.   Perhaps, the time will soon come."

"But at any rate, tell me this, Wilber: is not your health seriously affected? You look far from being a well man. You are very thin, and worn, and are excessively nervous."

" I can't tell—I can't speak out," he made answer in a voice that had become loud and hoarse. Then he caught at his throat as though he were choking, and resumed in a lower key: " *It* is wearing me away. Doctors have examined me, and have all been obliged to give it up; and no wonder. But good night, Tom. Suppose we shake hands: you are warm now."

He shook my hand with almost an excess of cordiality, and then quietly departed, leaving me to wonder and surmise far into the night.

I had not long been asleep, so far as I could judge, when an uneasy sensation to the effect that something or some one was in the room, began to trouble my slumbers. After a few struggles, I succeeded in awaking sufficiently to realize that a man was in the room. I sat up fully awake, and discovered by the pale light of the moon shining full through my window that Wilber, his face distorted by terror, was beside me.

" Come closer, Wilber," I said, endeavoring, despite an uncanny feeling, to put a note of cordial welcome into my voice.

" Oh, I am so glad that you are awake," he whispered. " Let me be near you. Let me take your hand. There, now, my dear friend, lie down again and try to go to sleep. Don't talk. You need your rest. All I ask is to be near you."

I ventured to make a few remarks, but he begged me to compose myself to sleep.

He sat beside me on the bed, meanwhile, holding

my hand, his large, lustrous eyes distended with fright. Occasionally, in a tone so low and indistinct that I rather apprehended than heard what he said, he muttered, " On the twentieth of January, one that is near and dear to me will die."

It is needless to say that I slept little. At the first break of day, he stole away quietly.

The following night witnessed a repetition of the same incident, whereupon I suggested to Wilber that he should make my room his own, a suggestion which he accepted with alacrity. His bed was removed to my room, and we were thus brought almost constantly together. From that time, and until January the nineteenth, all went well. Then came the twentieth of January.

" Tom," he said, on that memorable night as we entered our room, " may I ask a particular favor of you ? "

" Certainly, Wilber; I shall be only too glad to do you any favor in my power."

" Thank you, Tom. Please, then, stay up with me to-night; for I know that I shall not be able to sleep."

" With pleasure, Wilber; but how shall we pass the time ? "

" Tell me something about God's mercy, Tom; I love to hear you speak on that topic."

Fortunately, just previous to my visit, I had read and pondered over Father Florentine Bondreaux's excellent work entitled, " God, Our Father"; and so I could speak with some fluency on this beautiful subject. Wilber listened to me with an interest which was intense, although at times strange fits of trembling came upon him.

" But, Wilber," I said when one of these paroxysms had passed, " do you really entertain any doubts of God's mercy ? "

" No, no," he exclaimed earnestly, throwing out his hands with vehemence. " Not a man living, I dare say, has more reason to have faith in His goodness than I; and the very secret which is consuming me teaches me how very, very good He is."

" But if the secret is injuring you so much, why not tell it to——"

I stopped short; for an expression so unearthly and awe inspiring had come over his face, that it would be useless to attempt its description. To this day that expression haunts me. As it came upon him, he sprang from his chair, and, with bated breath, appeared to be listening. A moment passed; another and another, amidst a dead silence made horrible by the ticking of the great hall-clock; then, with a sob, he sank back upon his chair, and bending low his head, buried his face in his hands.

" Dead! dead!" he groaned.

" Who," I faltered, wiping my brow, for I too was possessed by fear. The clock sounded eleven, as he answered:

" Ah! I shall know soon enough."

The remaining hours of the night passed slowly; but from that moment Wilber became more composed. At the first gray dash of dawn upon the blackness of the eastern horizon, he fell into a heavy sleep, and, taking advantage of this, I threw myself upon my bed and was soon unconscious.

I had not slept beyond two hours, when I was awakened by some one pulling at my sleeve. It was Charlie, Wilber's cousin, to whom I have already referred. His eyes were wet with tears.

" Hello! " I exclaimed, " what's the matter, Charlie ? "

" Papa's dead," said Charlie, beginning to cry afresh. " He died at our house in town last night, and I shall never see him again."

II.

Charlie's father had been Wilber's best beloved uncle. Yet the bitterness of loss fell more easily upon my friend than the vague presentiment of it, and from that time he began to rest more quietly. I flattered myself, therefore, that the worst was over, and that Wilber's troubles had already touched their highest mark.

About eleven o'clock, on the night of February the fourth, however, I was aroused by some one clutching my arm. Looking up, I saw Wilber in such an agony, as God grant I may never again witness upon the face of any human being. His eyes, protruding from his head, gleamed with a strange light, his limbs were quivering and so unsteady that he swayed from side to side, while his face was moist and beaded with perspiration,

" Wilber, Wilber! what ails you ? " I cried.

" O my God! " he murmured.

There was no need for me to question further. I saw it all now. Another warning had come, and together we were to face the tortures of thirty nights of presentiment.

Like a drowning man he clung to my arm, and held it hour for hour, shivering and praying till the glad dawn broke.

The days that followed were indeed gloomy. Wilber appeared to be unequal to this fresh trial, and every hour seemed to set its seal of decay upon him. In two weeks' time he was hardly able to go about. His doctor, a man high in the profession, said that the case was baffling in every respect.

But strange to say, as Wilber's physical faculties grew weaker, his will and mind gathered strength. His gloomy fits became rarer, and he began to sleep quite soundly. In lieu of the weariness and unrest that formerly possessed his features, there came gradually a look of deep calm and abiding peace. Towards the end of February, he was obliged to keep to his bed.

On March the third, he called me to his side, and begged to be allowed to speak to me alone.

All left the room, and I seated myself upon his bed.

" Tom," he began, " you know what is going to happen soon. Some one near to me is going to die."

I bowed my head.

" Do you know who it is ? "

" No, Wilber."

" But I do," he answered with a certain triumph in his manner. " It's myself; and I am so happy, Tom, for I know who it is that will judge me."

He pointed to a picture of the Sacred Heart on the wall.

" That most loving Heart is the Heart of my judge."

Ah! how beautiful he looked, as his face softened with love and hope.

" I'm afraid, Wilber, that you are right. God is about to take you away. But I am glad, indeed I am, that you are in such peace."

" Before I do anything else, Tom, I want to tell you of that awful mystery—for I feel at last that I can talk of it. When you become a priest of God, it may be of service to you. Ah, Tom, sometimes I think that I might have become a priest, if I hadn't gone wrong. Then I'd have done some good, but now here I am a wreck. It's too late. ' Too late, too late, you cannot enter now.' "

His voice trembled as he quoted Tennyson's exquisite paraphrase.

" You remember," he went on, " my conduct on graduation night ? Well, I carried on in that way, blaspheming God and his saints, but always careful to keep such words and sentiments from my relations. When mother and I returned from our trip East, things went on smoothly till last Christmas a year ago. During the holidays, all my little cousins and nephews and nieces—your tigers, you know—came here for a visit, and for a few days we were a merry party. Shortly after New Year's day, I wanted to go to town to hear a certain lecturer who made fun of religion for one dollar a head. Somehow, my father came to hear of my purpose. He called me to his room, gave me a severe scolding, and ordered me not to leave home for a month. He was furious; but before he had said much—you know my pride, Tom—I was furious too, and there were high words between us. On returning to my room, I found a letter on my desk with news of the sudden death of one of my new friends. You know the kind of a friend that means, Tom, but I really had liked him very much.

" The dinner hour then found me in a most unhappy frame of mind. After some attempts to compose myself, I strode into the dining hall, where father, mother, and all those little children were already seated, and without looking at any one I threw myself into a chair.

" ' Wilber,' said my father, ' you forget your grace.'

" ' No, I don't. Bah! as if there were anything to be thankful for.'

" O Tom! you should have seen how pale and puzzled and frightened those little children became. And my dear mother! When I think of the sad look that came upon her sweet face, and see her put her trembling hand to her heart, I can hardly keep from weeping. And yet, brute that I was, I didn't soften in the least; no, not even when her trembling hand rested upon my cheek, and her dear eyes filled with tears.   My father could not speak.

" Poor mother was dazed; I could see it.   She could not credit her ears; with an effort she mastered herself and spoke.

" ' Come, my dear boy,' she said in her gentlest tones, ' you are not yourself.   God has been ever good to us, there is nothing we can ask for that He has not given us.'

" ' Indeed!' I exclaimed in the brutality of pride, ' there are a good many things He doesn't give us, seeing He's such a good God.'   Tom, I should have stopped there, at least.   For again my mother's hand went to her heart, her lips quivered and all the happiness of her life left her face; but, God forgive me, I went on and added: ' Why, for instance, can't I know beforehand when my friends are going to die ?'

" ' O Wilber!' and the words sounded as though they came from a broken heart, ' that I should live to see this day,' and my mother buried her head in her hands.

" I see it again, those little children, their innocent faces fixed in horror, my mother bent in grief, my father utterly at a loss what step to take.   There I sat gazing haughtily upon all, when suddenly I sprang to my feet and would have fled, but that I was rooted to the spot.   There was a cold, clammy grip upon my shoulder.   I turned, but there was no one behind me, and still that cold, chilling pressure, as of an icy hand moved slowly along my arm, till it caught my hand with a strength that I cannot describe, for it was not the strength of physical force, and words stop short of beginning to describe it. Then my hand, released of that awful grip, dropped powerless to my side, while in my ears I heard the sound as of a death-rattle. I gazed wildly about the room and saw that all were looking at me in utter consternation.

"I attempted to cry out, but it was impossible for me to utter a sound. At length the rattle ceased; the spell was broken, and I rushed from the hall, and sought refuge in my own room. For hours I paced up and down in the most terrible mental suffering; then, at random, I picked up a book, which chanced to be a collection of autographs, and opened it at these words:

"'I shall love thee, even after the cold hand of death hath touched thee.'

"I threw the book aside with my first sense of terror revived. An hour later I took up another book. This time it was the Bible. Perhaps you may guess what I read:

"'But he that shall scandalize one of these little ones that believe in Me, it were better for him that a millstone should be hanged about his neck, and that he should be drowned in the depth of the sea.'

"One month from that day, another of my former friends died. Then I knew what that strange occurrence meant. God had heard my wish, to punish and correct me. Three months later, the same dreadful feeling—and a month later my mother died. Tom, I had hastened her death; I had broken her heart.

"You know the rest, Tom; but you cannot see, as I do, how merciful God has been to me. Oh, He is indeed a good God, and what seems His severest chastisements are often His tenderest mercies."

Late the next evening, all the little ones gathered about the bed of the dying man. In faltering accents, he told them enough of his secret to repair, as far as could be, the dreadful scandal; and the sobs of his listeners were the only interruption.

"Wilber, my boy," said his father, "as you yourself say, God has been indeed most merciful to you."

"Yes, father, and I have often thought that, aside from my mother's prayers, He did it to reward me for the one heroic act of my life. It was heroic for me, when, through love for Tom here and to humble my pride, I gave up my chance for that Longfellow prize."

A few moments later, the hand of death had lost its power over him forever.

WALTER LECKY.

WALTER LECKY first made his mark not many years ago
in the columns of the Montreal *True Witness*. His
work, which was well considered, found favor with the public,
his advancement was consequently rapid, and to-day he is
known as one of the foremost of American Catholic writers.

He was born April 9th, 1863, and his early days were
passed in the town of Lawrence, Massachusetts. As
a child he attended a private school, and afterward went
for a time to Villanova College. At the age of eighteen
he turned his face Westward and reached Chicago,
where he became a "newspaper man," doing repor-

torial work on the *Times, Herald,* and *Mail.* A love of
adventure took him South, where he obtained work on the
Louisville Courier and the New Orleans *Picayune.* But his
restless spirit could not remain content in one place; he
travelled on foot to and through Mexico, and finally, having
come into some money, started for Europe. There he had
the pleasure of meeting many distinguished men, among
them Cardinal Newman and Pope Leo XIII. He witnessed the Passion Play at Oberamergau, and stood on the
summit of the acropolis of Athens. Finally, sated with
adventure and with his note-books filled to overflowing,
he returned to this country, and settled down in the mountain town which he has ever since made his home. It is
there, in the heart of the Adirondacks, that he met the
queer characters whom he has since described in his novel
"Mr. Billy Buttons."

A keen observer, an ardent lover of nature, Mr. Lecky
is seen at his best in his pathetic passages and his descrip-
tions of the woods and waters which are his haunts. Of
him it may be said as it was of Thoreau, he has " dedicated
his genius with entire love to the fields, hills, and waters."

Though vigorous in his denunciation of all shams, Mr.
Lecky is quiet and retiring in his manner and in deep sympathy with every form of human suffering. He is sincerely
loved by his neighbors, for whom he constantly labors. He
has built a hall and a library for them and has taught and
still teaches their children. In fact, he strongly resembles
the Père Monnier he has so charmingly drawn. His
published works are : " Green Graves in Ireland," " Down at
Caxtons," and " Mr. Billy Buttons."

Gilliman Ogley.

BY WALTER LECKY.

DRYBURGH was a small town. It had a few general stores, a grist-mill, a blacksmith's shop, and half a hundred private residences. Its people came from Vermont when Dryburgh was part of the forest, and by much toil and labor cut down the trees and made the soil productive. They were thrifty and saving—a combination which in the many years gave them a bank-account, and the airs which generally accompany a safe deposit. Their houses from log-huts were gradually transformed into pleasant cottages, of no known style of architecture; each owner, having years to study his tastes, built to satisfy his comforts. Dryburgh had one street, wide and tree-lined, giving, in the most sultry weather, coolness and shade. A bit of garden in front of each house, abloom with old-fashioned flowers—the seed, once a parting gift, when leaving their old homes to found the new, from some neighbor, who took this kindly way of being remembered —gave Dryburgh an air of culture. Somehow we do associate culture with cleanliness, flowers, and well-trimmed lawns. Yet of culture in its true sense, as referring to that knowledge which comes from books, the people of Dryburgh had little. The older and pioneer men and women had no leisure for books; and as that taste is rarely acquired in later life, they contented themselves with the editorials of a local paper, and the spicy columns of a farm journal that came weekly from the great city. This journal gave them a bundle of ideas to thrash nightly in one of the village stores. It kept them posted on legislation, and in well-rounded periods and fantastic metaphors ministered to their good humor with an exalted idea of the dignity and importance of the American farmer.

Dryburgh was a religious town with a periodical inclination to bigotry. Like most small towns, it had a sufficiency of churches. It mattered little that the baker's dozen of people were not forthcoming at a Sunday service; the ministers were conscientious, and, disdaining numbers and prizing the quality, hammered away for a good hour, forging the few to give testimony against sin. These few, though over-inclined to piety, were not generous; not even religion could command the beloved pocket-book. It was not surprising, then, that ministers could not afford to be leaders in dress. They made the best of their circumstance by marrying strong, thrifty, health-keeping girls, who could patch neatly, knit, fix over a bonnet, and for their outdoor exercise have a garden worth bending over the inconvenience of a picket-fence to see. It was a ministerial saying, coined by a clever Anabaptist exhorter, that " no minister in these parts could afford to have his wife run a drug bill." It was a truth vouched for by the other ministers—Baptist, Methodist, Dutch Reformed, Lutheran, Swedenborgian. Religion gave the people much of their social life, in the form of church parties of all kinds. As the revenue from a church supper is small, it was necessary to have them often—once a week at least. " The preparation for and consummation of such suppers," said the Methodist divine, " was a needed relaxation." This was the thought of the young, who found these suppers pleasant opportunities for wooing, and that without any fear of parental interference. Were they not under the watchful eye of the church—right under the noses of pastors whose watchfulness was proverbial; in full view of ancient spinsters, whose pleasantry was a shy at everybody's business? At these suppers, frequented by the sinner and saint alike, tongues were free, and, to use an old-time phrase, " rattled away at everything and on everybody." Here was a distributing agency for news. Every one brought a little, gave it willingly, and in return was privileged to carry away the budget. It was comfort after a hard day's work to sit down, especially for youth, by the side of a rosy girl, to a board which had none of your city lightness, but the solid, substantial character which appeals to the sons of toil. Pies and puddings, it is true, were there to round off the tail end—the merest fringe to pork and beans, potatoes, and other health-making foods. And the appetite—how it would wrinkle the wry faces of the nation's great army of dyspeptics! At a table where there is no appetite, where every one stares at his neighbor, where the music of fork, knife, and spoon is lacking, even the most brilliant conversation becomes dull. An air of weariness envelops the board, repressing all human spirits.

These Dryburgh suppers had all the qualities of a festive board. Youth, love, pride, and that delightful though heavy-footed old country lady, Dame Gossip. Some have been known to sneer at her presence as they saw her nestling among the divines. Yet these were base hypocrites, who in their innermost heart loved the old lady and but danced their mouth to the music of jealousy. It is a human way, though man has saddled the fox to carry his folly, that we despise the grapes that are beyond our reach. Jealousy is the acid that sours them.

It was at one of these suppers, held to reimburse for salary not forthcoming by ordinary means the Rev. John Powdery, the Swedenborgian—a man with a family not to be counted on one hand—that Brother Collins, the Anabaptist, whispered that a new gentleman had come to town. Whispering in Dryburgh was poorly developed. It had none of that artistic grace which one finds in the homes of the great. There whispers are dangerous if they shoot beyond your neighbor's ears. A Dryburgh whisper was in the ordinary tones of conversation; yet it was conceded to be a whisper, and as such unheard. It could never be a pivot around which conversation might revolve. After supper, however, whispers were considered public property and discussion of them was invited. Now the coming of a stranger to settle in Dryburgh, even for a few days, was an event to make bustle in every household. Questions were to be asked and assumptions made; to phrase it in Dryburgh's way, " bearings were to be taken," before anything definite could be said in public. Whisperings, no matter how fanciful, were legal; but woe betide the culprit that would in open speech state something that time would blow away. The women would brand him and hush their babies to sleep with the lying bugaboo's name. The ministers, whose two eyes rested prominently on the source of their bread and butter, followed the ladies; and in hints that were as thrown brick to the offender, held up to well-merited detestation " verily that abomination of abominations, the liar."

There is a Dryburgh tradition that becomes the property of even the passing stranger, of a young man who gave utterance to statements for the fun of making them. In a quiet way one Sabbath the Rev. Floyd Jenkins, then holding the Baptist living, read the story of Aman and Mardochai to his flock, which happened that day—possibly owing to a Saturday night hint—to crowd his church. With that story, by twists here and there, aided by his powerful imagination and the copious flow of words that, as a

brother said, " dripped from his mouth like water
from a soaked sponge," the Rev. Mr. Jenkins (here
I prefer to quote from a letter of the time written
by a lady well known for her gospel work) " made
his flock see the road liars were on—a road of per-
dition owned by Satan, and kept in good repair by
his wily majesty for their comfort.   On it he
showed Cain, Judas, and Jesuits—a nice crowd for
any young man to be in.   We were all in tears.
The Rev. Mr. Jenkins' speech was just grand, life-
full, soul-stirring.   Just think what effect was
in these words: ' To walk in truth is to be what
one seems; to scorn counterfeits, shun shams, or
the pathway hung about with shows and shadows
and pageants.'   I was doubled over in my pew
with expectancy.   I was braced up, I trust, for
many a day, by the next sentence—which was fairly
boiling: ' Truth lodged in the soul is like leaven
placed in the loaf: it works, it permeates, vitalizes,
revolutionizes.'   The young man for whose benefit
the masterpiece was done never repented.   He had
lived in the cities for a while, and laughed at his
neighbors for making such a fuss over a joke.   He
even went further—by wooing and marrying the minister's daughter, presenting, as he laughingly said,
the other cheek.   Then he went West, and many
who condemned him in the days of his youth, in
later years hearing of his success, speak of him now
with generous words.   The sermon had, however,
a lasting effect.   I might sum it up by saying
that it confirmed whispering on all topics, but

silenced open speech unless proofs were given in support."

The whisper of Brother Collins made the villagers alert and watchful of the new-comer. Had he money, or was he a poor man ? If the latter, said the nightly gossipers of the village store, what in thunder brings him here ? We have more poor than we need. There was a suggestion that he was a business man, which enraged the proprietor, who held a monopoly of the town's industry. His rage flew into such phrases as, "None but an idiot would come here to start in business;" " those who are in are there to their sorrow, and would like to sell out to-morrow at a loss. " Weeks went and the stranger added anxiety to every household by not divulging his plans, and by keeping within doors; giving no chance to be cross-examined by the few village fathers grown gray, who held as a sacred right their authority to ask any question under the guise of interest in those questioned.

One of the relics of Dryburgh's better days is a rambling brick ruin, used by the children as a place for their hide-and-go-seek games. Old men point to it and tell of the " circulating money," and " the work for all," when this ruin as a glass factory was in " full blast." Near the ruin is a red wooden structure, once the office of the glass company, but, following the fate of its brick neighbor, shaky and lonely-looking. Once a bright red, the storms in the years when it was in nobody's thought peeled off the paint and left a dusky rotten hue. Had it fallen at any time, it would not have caused the slightest talk. Its downfall was expected, and in heavy winds the prophets had always a subject for disaster. Judge, then, of Dryburgh's surprise when Simon Butler, the justice, announced that the ruin was about to be rented by the stranger, whose name—and he pulled out a large wallet from an inside pocket crowded with papers, selected one and adjusting his eye-glass proceeded—" was, as the paper that I hold in my hand shows, Gilliman Ogley."

The justice's information aroused inquisitiveness —a country gift.

" What does he intend to do with it ? " asked half a dozen. " It's of no earthly use, Mr. Butler," said Dr. Cronker, whose wisdom was appreciated. " Prop it as you will, it's bound to go; it cannot last a great while. Queer things never cease. I have two good houses to let and cannot get a tenant; yet here is an old affair that I wouldn't house hogs in—wouldn't take if it was made a present to me—rented! I am a man that don't say much—in fact, I'm the last to accuse any man—but, between us, that old barn of a thing was never rented for any good purpose."

There was a sense of wisdom in the listening faces —if, as some people think, a mingling of sourness and seriousness be the sign — and a shaking of heads, that told the doctor he threw their thoughts into words. The justice, little in size, corpulent and stately, dignified by nature and adding to it the

dignity of his office—an important one in Dryburgh
—gave his auditors a slight wink, cleared his throat
with a cough that was acknowledged by even his
enemies as original, and said he was now in a frame
of mind "to warn all whom it concerns that the
machinery of the law in this town is in most excellent form," and that "any man, or men, who
imagines this is a slow town, where you can do anything you want, without a tumbling thereto by the
aforesaid machinery of the law, put himself *ipsi facti*
in its coils, where, like a bird tangled in a thread, the
more he tried to get out the more he was caught."

The homely simile provoked a burst of laughter
from the listeners, and increased their pride in the
shrewdness and watchfulness of Justice Butler.

"Well, boys," said Dr. Cronker, "mind, I said
nothing about the stranger—he might be an acquisi-
tion to our town; but his renting such a building
seems so queer that I cannot get it out of my head;
it's either for something strange or it's a foolish
move."

"I have nothing to say," said the justice,
"absolutely nothing. Justice requires a tight mouth.
All I know is, that Mr. Ogley has leased the office
for the space of five years. On business matters I
found him very close. My experience I offered to
him—an experience of thirty years, meeting and
treating with all classes of people. He thanked me,
and said that he was a poor man and was about to
do business in a poor way, to knock a living out of
it; that's all. But I must tell you, boys, I was

honest.   I told him to save my soul I didn't know
a business that was not overdone in town.   It was
then that Mr. Ogley said, ' Would a marble-yard on
a small scale pay ? '   I nearly burst out in his face.
It took all my legal training to suppress myself.
' Why, dear Mr. Ogley,' said I, ' we die up here
so slow that one monument in a generation is about
as much as we put up, and then we have to see that
it wears well before we make up our minds to pay
for it.' "

" I wonder," said Dr. Cronker, " has he paid his
rent in advance.   This business of trusting strangers
who have seemingly nothing is not to my taste.
He may be honest, but I fail to see what is made
by putting honesty to a test."

" Speak of the devil and he'll put in an appearance," said one of the listeners.

" Right you are, my boy," said Justice Butler;
" here comes the gentleman himself."

" It's not every day you see a stone-cutter so
dressy," remarked Dr. Cronker; " he looks more
like one of the profession."

" Many a one afore you, doctor, that banked on
looks lost; and many a one coming behind you,
untaught by experience, will lose both capital and
interest," said a red-bearded farmer, stroking his
under-chin growth of hair, and watching with his
cold steel-gray eyes the effect of his philosophy
on the Solon of the law.   He was repaid when
Mr. Butler tapped him on the forehead, saying,
" Klinker will do: he's all right."

All eyes were turned in the direction of the stranger, who was accompanied by a merry-eyed, talkative girl of thirteen, who was continually changing from side to side, catching his hands and tugging at them with well-shown delight.

He was a man of middle age, wiry in build, with a military carriage. His features were pleasantly cut. When the hat was removed, the bristling black hair gave to the whole head a shapeliness which was agreeable, and an impression that the owner was, or should be, a lucky fellow. Faces throw impressions which are liable to toning down, or even radical change, as the years go by and contact and experience are ours.

The hands were white and small—an argument which might have been used with effect against Dr. Cronker's gratuitous assertion. The dress—and on that article Dryburgh holds an old opinion (you may hear it any night that you wish to bring up this subject in the village store)—dress makes a man, and the want of it a fellow; and between these words there is a distinction which, to borrow from Brother Powdery's great sermon on the ways of " Mr. Satan," is both special and profound. Gilliman Ogley had a good figure; the ladies admitted that, and to such authorities I respectfully bow. Nature has given their eye a quickening in this art that men, no matter how artful, can never possess. Dress would have set him out in a winning way, but it must be chronicled of him that he was indifferent to his shape's draping—careless of his clothes.

He will never know the peace of mind this little
failing procured him during his sojourn in Dryburgh.
The girl—(I am well aware that in the use of this
word I am departing from the well-established
phraseology of Dryburgh, which insists that from
the tenth to the fortieth year of female life the term
lady is only proper, and on sober thought I think
it is best to comply with my townspeople's rule, so—
the young lady)—was dressed in plain black, with
white cuffs and collar, simply, but so tastefully
that admiration dwelt in the mouths of the critical.
Comparisons were made; things dissimilar suggest
ideas; and be it said of Dryburgh that no idea went
naked.   If the critics would permit me an adjective,
I would write of corpulent ideas as being native to
the Dryburgh soil.   Gilliman Ogley's clothes were
neither torn nor patchy, but they were pitch-forked
on, and that in a hurry.   Miss Ogley's —for that
was the name of his daughter and companion—were
draped at leisure, the mirror advising; and all with
an eye to a graceful ultimate effect.

As Mr. Ogley approached the impatient-eyed
crowd, his dress brought forth a comment that
" he looked in his clothes like fury," a strong term
in these parts.

" He's not badly built," said Dr. Cronker, " but
work has thrown him to the one side too much."

This opinion was held in common, as was shown
by the audible grunt that welcomed it.

" He is about to join the crowd," said Mr. Butler,
becoming so grave that a small boy who makes his

mouth express his eye would call such gravity grinning.

" Perhaps there's some hitch in the lease; looks like it; it's the justice he's looking for. The only mill, justice, that everybody brings corn to is yours."

There was a loud laugh, for Dr. Cronker was called witty; and in the country, when a wit says something, you are supposed to see a joke and recognize the same by quick appreciative laughter.

" Just taking your afternoon stroll, Mr. Ogley ? The air is salubrious; full of this ozone; beats anything where it comes from; our country's full of it. And the young lady "—the justice removed his hat, dexterously showing his flat, close-cropped skull—" it will bring to her cheeks the color of a June rose; she will need no saspirillas or other concoctions to make blood. In a year she will be full of it. The doctor there can tell you a bit, if he wishes; if he didn't keep the drug store and make an odd ' spec ' on horses, he might starve. I have a joke on the doctor; I say, it is only for style that our folks buy drugs. I have been here a long while, but the only medicine I bought was a package of salts, and I believe my wife could hunt you up a dose yet."

Miss Ogley laughed that sweetest of all music, a young girl's blithe, hearty, untrammelled laugh. It swept away every prejudice and won the justice's heart, who took it as a compliment to his wit. What comfort there is in delusion! He is a sorry

fellow who considers it his duty to go up and down
the world disillusionizing his fellows.   It was an
inspired moment when the poet sang that if igno-
rance is bliss it is folly to be wise.   Yet the snarlers,
under the pretext of teaching wisdom, are ever
destroying our bliss.   To them a miry frog-pole is
dearer far than the loveliest visions.   Sticklers for
the real, let them shout in the crossways; the
majority of men will pass them by, travel, despite
their warning, in dream-land—suffer, if you will, but
paid a thousandfold for that suffering by the remembrance of those travel years.

Miss Ogley laughed and Justice Butler kept his
delusion.   That he died with it should be recorded,
for in after years it was his boast that Florence
Ogley's laugh was worth a dozen of his jokes; and
when it is known that the justice was in the habit
for years of giving but one, and that during the
festivities of the Fourth of July, the worth of the
compliment comes to view.

" How do you like Dryburgh," asked Dr. Cronker, waiving all introduction.   " I presume you
are Mr. Ogley.   We are a plain people, without
airs and frills, clap a stranger on the back at first
sight, and do our own introducing."

" Glad to meet you, gentlemen," replied Mr.
Ogley, " and especially you, doctor, who I understand have a house to let.   It happens to be just
the thing Florence and I need—very pretty and
comfortable.   I am willing to pay a fair price and
would like to move into it at once,"

Dr. Cronker was radiant in smiles, and full of apologies for his inability to let the cottage, "as so many people had spoken to him for it, who were old friends of many years."

"Well, doctor," said Mr. Ogley looking into his eyes, "what rent do you consider it worth ? or better, what do you get for such cottages ? Do not answer me if my question is in any way annoying. I am from the city, and have no just idea of village rentals."

"Well, a cottage like mine—use of the barn, garden, orchard—is cheap at fifteen dollars a month; saw the time when it was worth more, but times are hard and money tight."

"Doctor, I will give you sixteen dollars a month, and pay a year in advance, paying for any damage that you may declare during my occupancy."

The crowd winked to one another, some of them nipped their fellows. Dr. Cronker gave a delicate cough.

"Well, really, it is hard to go back on old friends; but, seeing you are a stranger and a business man at that, I will take on my shoulders all blame, and as soon as you deposit the money with the justice, you can have the key. Of course, the garden being set will be extra, and I claim the orchard this year."

"Very well, doctor; we will not dispute over these matters."

Gilliman Ogley went down the village street. As he turned into a lane which led to the lake, he remarked to Florence, who was full of wonder at the queer people of Dryburgh, " My dear Florence, money hath power, and selfishness and greed are everywhere—in town and country."

" Yes, papa, but I think a little more in the country."

" That, Florence, I do not know; in the city we hide it with putty and polish."

As Mr. Ogley and his daughter disappeared, the crowd took up the discussion, joined by Brother Collins, who always valued an audience.

" A queer man," remarked the sandy-bearded man, whose first hit made him prone, following the ways of human nature, to serve more from his dish.

" Not a bit of it," replied Dr. Cronker. " Not a bit of it! A business man with a city way of doing business! Catch anybody in the city going to rent a house and trusting to trust to pay the rent. We are away behind in this—away behind. See how quick we struck a bargain in a few minutes. It would take a week up here. Mr. Ogley saw that I was a business man and came to the point at once. In fact, my impression of him is that he has seen better days. I rather like to think of him as a contractor than as an ordinary mechanic. Adversity is to be pitied—but a man who meets it like Mr. Ogley deserves to be upheld. I am sure that is your thought, Brother Collins."

Brother Collins had that morning called on the Ogleys, to see, as was his wont, if they were of his flock. He was in a position to gossip.

" Well, doctor, it is very hard to know anything about that Ogley family. I questioned the young lady; then her father; but all I could get out of them was: ' You are very kind, Mr Collins, we assure you of our thankfulness; but we do not belong to your church.' Well, then I named him every church in town; he thanked me for my offices in his behalf, but accepted nothing. I fear he's one of those agnostics, and if so I pity the formative education of the young lady."

Brother Collins heaved a deep gurgling sigh.

" Humph," said Dr. Cronker, " it's nobody's business what he is, so long as he pays his debts and behaves. How many men are there in this town that bother with church? When they send their women, they think that's enough."

" Precisely," said Justice Butler. " You speak from a full hand. There are some of us, with all due reverence to this company, who think this visiting and offering religion is out of place."

" I am one of those," said Dr. Cronker, whose wife was leading-string in Brother Collins's church.

The divine twittered a little laugh, and with a bow went off, followed by the separating crowd, firm in their belief that no divine had a chance when confronted by Cronker and Butler.

In country towns men carry the news to their wives. This gives women the privilege, when visiting each other, of having something to feed on.

Said Mrs. Cronker to Mrs. Butler, over a mug of tea: " These Ogleys, I'm told, have no more

religion than the doctor's St. Bernard. Preserve
me from city folk. We think our husbands are
careless, but, my dear, there is no comparison—
none whatever. The justice and the doctor will
own up to some belief now and then, but these folk
to nothing. Just think of poor Brother Collins,
with all his kindness—and you know how lovely he
is—not being able to fathom these Ogleys! Such
people! I told Mr. Collins that they looked like
spiritualists. You know Mrs. Bixbee calls herself
a medium, and has her seances every Sunday night.
I am sure as my name is Mrs. Doctor Cronker, that
the Ogleys will be in that set.''

'' I don't care,'' responded Mrs. Butler, '' for
Ogley himself; he's just horrid; not to my taste.
And did ever you hear such a name in your life
as Gilliman? But the young lady just took the
justice's eye. She's just awful sweet. I wonder
who makes her clothes, they sit so well. Don't you
think they become her? I would like to have a
pattern of that waist for my Jenny. I think it is
awfully cute. The justice is going to invite her
down to the house to meet Jen.''

'' I would put down my foot,'' said Mrs. Cronker,
'' on any such invitation, until I knew what were
the religious principles of the child. I like this
child—rather I pity her—but we must remember
the Rev. Mr. Powdery's advice ' not to bind the
tare with the wheat.' Our children know nothing
of the world; little darlings of heaven, straying as
Brother Collins put it on Children's Day, ' far from

the battle-ground of care, in the land of bliss by the pathway of peace.'"

Mrs. Cronker wept; and Mrs. Butler, good old soul! joined her friend with a pitiful sob.

"Let us talk of something else," said Mrs. Cronker, rubbing her eyes with her fringed handkerchief; "time will show."

Here Mrs. Butler broke in with "Yes, time will show. Next Sunday all the eyes in the village will be on them. If they go anywhere it will be known."

Sunday came, slowly for the folks of Dryburgh. It was noted that sinners that day went to church. "It was curiosity, not the Word, they were after," was a woman's remark. I thought it cruel, but as I am a mere chronicler, in conscience I am bound to record it.

The Dryburgh school is pleasantly situated at the end of the town, in a shady maple grove, much used in summer-time for church picnics. It is very plainly built, and whether or not it was painted I am unable to state. Its present color is a dirty gray, making me, even at the risk of contradiction, hazard the guess that the only painting it ever had was with the winds as brush and the rain as paint. A few Irish farmers, heavily mortgaged with their wives and wagon-load of chattering, fun-making young Celts, came here for service once a month. They were unable to build a church, so the use of the school-house was allowed to this " handful of Romanists," as they were called, on condition that

they would give " annually a few loads of dry wood
for heating the school."   It was Justice Butler who,
against all opposition, procured them this privilege.
He had been in the same army corps with these
Celtic Catholic farmers, and was carried away by
their fighting qualities.   He knew they were honest
and brave men, struggling against many hardships,
working early and late to clear the mortgage, " and
if their religion was any consolation to them,
they were going to have it, even if he rigged up his
barn."   They on their part had always a vote for
their old comrade, and any law-business they had
was thrown in his way.   These farmers came early,
loitered around, the men smoking and chatting,
the women busied in making tidy the school-room,
the children romping around, now and then resting
to take a peep at their catechism.

There was a lull as a gentleman and a lady approached and asked " if this was the place were
Catholic service was held."

A large woman, holding a baby in her arms,
fluttered around for a few minutes, then called a
little urchin, who came suspiciously, and told him
" to find Myles McCaffrey for the gentleman and
missis."   Myles was, as she stumblingly said, " the
man who knows all about the church after the priest
himself."

Myles came trotting, pleasant-faced and smiling,
with information bubbling on the tip of his tongue.

" My name, sir, is Myles McCaffrey.   I come
here awhile always before the rest.   Just to do odd

turns around, before his reverence comes. I light fires when needed and fix the teacher's seat. Then the ladies, yer honor, make it into a snug altar."

"Well, Mr. McCaffrey," said Mr. Ogley, "if you show us seats we will be thankful; and my daughter Florence, you must know, Myles, will help the ladies to trim the altar."

"Bless her heart!" said the flattering Celt, "she's the best flower of them all."

The ringing of a little bell drew the worshippers within; and the priest, stately and grave, began the service.

A middle-aged lady thrummed indifferently Leonard's Mass. Note after note came, hurriedly, as if frightened; a few young uncertain voices kept the music company.

As soon as the service was over, the priest unrobed and came to where the strangers sat, hoping with fatherly care that they were properly attended to by Myles, as they happened to be seated before he noticed them. He invited them to come again.

"Certainly," said Mr. Ogley, "every time you hold service; and my daughter insists that you breakfast with us to-day—for that matter, that you stop with us while in the village. We are not rich, but I have no apology to make to a man of sacrifice."

"Yes, you must come," put in Miss Ogley; "we are the least of your flock, and that should be reason enough for your coming."

"But," said Father Denham, "I teach a village

lad Italian, and I generally breakfast with him; and as soon as the breakfast and lesson are over, I drive home; quite a drive—in the neighborhood of twenty miles."

"My! that is too much," said Mr. Ogley. "Bring the lad along. I have a few Italian books, and we will see, Father, if Florence is not your match in that tongue. If you come, I think you might get her to play the organ and train your choir. It is a little bit jerky—want of practice, I dare say. See now what attractions I hold out."

"I must submit, I suppose, and breakfast at your home," was the priest's response. "Just as soon as I settle a few matters with Myles, who is my merry man of all things, I will be with you."

On the way home Mr. Ogley said: "Florence, my dear, I have broken my resolution not to have any visitors save the priest, but it is a lad and it will be an easy matter to get rid of him."

"Oh! papa, if the priest brings him—and especially such a sedate priest—he must be bright and studious. The people here are so dull that a few lights should be a cause for thankfulness."

"Well, Florence, let us see him first. To find him studying Italian is a feather in his cap. See what you can do from our little store to make the priest's breakfast appetizing. There can be no doubt of his being educated in Rome. I knew that by his way of pronouncing Latin. Little housekeeper, make him think of your birthland.

Don't, I pray you, child, laugh if the lad murders the beautiful Italian. Everybody creeps."

The Ogleys were in front of their cottage. On Monday morning every passing villager had time to give a few moments to the old glass office. It bore on its front, in white-lead letters:

"Monuments Of Every Description Made to Order. GILLIMAN OGLEY."

Before the door stood a few marble blocks and a small monument crowned with a dove.

That Gilliman Ogley had gone to the " Romanist handful over at the school," sealed his fate.

The Dryburghers arose steady in purpose not to talk about anything save the strange religious belief of the Ogleys, a belief which meant social ostracism, at least from the women—and when they club against you, sociability is sparse; but seeing the sign and the monument and marble blocks, their astonishment took the form of a few day's dumbness; then tongues angrily wagged, assumptions were made, imagination let loose, charity and religion forgotten. This abated when a new minister took Mr. Powdery's place; then a change of subject was forthcoming—the new minister and his wife had to be passed upon.

Gilliman Ogley cared little about the village talk. Every morning he entered the old office, locked the door behind him, did something—what it was no one knew—and left every evening. No order for monuments came his way, and he sought none; so the curious spectacle—curious to village folk—of a man living on nothing was one of the things of Dryburgh.　Two callers came to his house; one the priest, when his duty brought him to the village; the other the lad he had introduced—a dreamy boy, full of talent and visions, laughed at by the village fathers, as most dreamers are, but somehow or other winning the friendship of the tongue-tied Gilliman and the confidence of Miss Florence.

He was an orphan boy, brought up by his grandmother, and this might have softened Gilliman Ogley's heart to him; or was it his name—Leigh Hunt Watkins—which appealed to one who loved the exquisite essays of the genial Cockney poet?

Be it whatever it was, young Watkins was a constant visitor at Mr. Ogley's cottage, and for this indiscretion had weekly homilies from his prophetic grandmother and unconcealed hostility from his neighbors.

Here it must be written that such persecution was taken in the spirit of Job.　Youth and, I was going to write, love—although I lean only on suspicion—build palaces with the stones tormentors throw.　To read Italian on the little cottage veranda under the careful guidance of Gilliman Ogley, to be mimicked by Florence, and to pay back sarcasm by culling her flowers; to listen to the Italian stories of Leigh Hunt or the mystic artist verse of Rosetti, was the height of boyish bliss, the dreamer's paradise.　The dreary town and its dull people were effaced; and in gayly decked barque

Leigh Hunt Watkins, like his namesake, sailed for the Hesperides.

What a blessed thing are the friends whose voices can waft us from dullard surroundings to the isles of the West!

With the death of the grandmother, Leigh Hunt Watkins bade Dryburgh a sorrowful farewell. A mercantile career in the great city was opened for him by rich relatives; and the dreamer from a country town with his head full of flowers, birds, and songs, and love romping through his blood making that glorious insanity which poetry has partly caught, went forth to join the ranks of the earners, to strive in the battle of life, to company with ugly realisms, and daily to walk on the ruins of his ideals.

Mr. Ogley had wished him well. Florence had allowed him to steal from her neck a little silver cross.

"A man that will be heard from some day," said Mr. Ogley the evening of his departure; " the most charming youth I have known; full of talent, but completely unsuited for a mercantile career. Poor fellow! you might as well try to cage a humming-bird. Like his namesake, he was born to live among books and flowers."

"Yes, papa, and how lonesome it will be here now! I only wished we lived in New York. Oh, dear me! what a dreadful place this is! Such horrid people!"

"But, Florence," and Mr. Ogley laughed, "you

must remember that you have lived here a few years seemingly content, and this sudden fit is rather difficult to explain; but if fortune favors us—and she has long kept away—we may live in New York some day. I also am a little weary of all this loneliness, and long for some one who would partake of my thoughts. No, Florence; I cannot blame you. Life only comes once, and to potter it out in Dryburgh would be sad waste. I trust he promised to write a letter now and then; it would be pleasant; you have time enough to answer."

"The Lord is merciful if we only wait long enough," said Mrs. Cronker; "young Watkins has gone to the city away from those Ogleys. The prayers of Brother Collins for that young man have not been offered in vain. Will he be saved, I wonder? These Ogleys have primed him well. It's my opinion they have made him a Jesuit. Just think of the grandson of Dan Watkins writing poems about the Madonna and telling Justice Butler that it be a Catholic priest that writ the hymn I'm so fond of —the one I sung at Moore's funeral. 'Yes,' says he, '"Lead, kindly Light" was so composed.' I trust he'll fall into good hands, but poison once in the vitals is hard to physic out. I wonder who's next on the list for contamination."

So runs the world, interesting from its diversity of opinions. We are saddled with motives, then accordingly judged. It is the old censure of the poet: man's inhumanity to man.

Dryburgh soon banished Leigh Hunt Watkins

from its ordinary conversation; he was only discussed when some memory recalled his name; and
thus the years wore on. The Ogleys made no new
friends. Dr. Cronker was delighted in having a
model tenant; the townspeople had given up guess-
ing how the Ogleys lived; the fountain that had
supplied gossip so long was dry.

Gilliman Ogley loved to sit on the little porch in
the warm evenings, and read his paper, or watch
his daughter busying herself among the flowers,
giving a cool drink to a drooping fellow, pruning the
ambitious, staying the weaklings. The paper lay
on an easy-chair ready to be read. One evening,
missing what had become a necessity, he called his
daughter, who approached him with a bundle of
manuscripts.

" I have something better than your old paper,
papa. Leigh has written a novel and had it accepted by a big publishing house. It is full of fun.
I have been reading and laughing all the afternoon.
I know the most of the characters. We can never
forget Dryburgh as long as we have Leigh's novel.
I see the Butlers, Cronkers, Collins, all that set,
strutting up and down the pages. If everybody
likes it as well as I do, it will make Leigh famous.
Just read Chapter III, where Justice Butler holds
court. How funny! Perhaps I had better read it,
as you look a trifle tired."

" Yes, Florence, read. I am weary, weary of
Dryburgh; but I see no chance of leaving it yet."

She read, throwing her whole soul into the reading, flashing out the fun with her laughing blue eyes.

As she read the weariness fled from her father's face, and a rippling laughter that she had not seen for years took its place. When the chapter was finished she looked towards him and listened.

" Florence, this is capital. By Jove, if I know anything this book will make Leigh famous! I knew he was clever, but I never looked to him to give us such a humorous book. I would like to take it to the shop and make a few drawings. I am on the spot, which means much. Leigh you could ask to show them to his publishers. All they can do in the matter would be to reject them, and that kind of thing will not hurt me. I am used to it," and a cynical shadow stole over Mr. Ogley's face.

" Oh! I wish you would, papa. Just think of a book by Leigh, and illustrated by you!"

" Foolish Florence! You rear a dream; the illustrations may not be needed."

It might have been a dream, but from that moment Florence Ogley saw it as a reality. She wrote to Leigh of her father's intention, and he procured time and a promise from the publishers to look over " Mr. Ogley's illustrations."

" Everything comes to the patient, Florence," said Mr. Ogley, opening the little wicket gate that led to his house. " The illustrations are done, and sent off in your name. Nothing venture, nothing win. If they are worthless——"

" Why talk that way ? You know that they will be as good as the text."

" Well, my daughter, it is right, I suppose, for you to hold an exalted opinion of your father—it enables him to bear the world's contrary verdict."

A few weeks came and went—weeks of longing on the part of Florence Ogley; weeks of hope and prayer for her father. At length the long-awaited letter came. It was noted in Dryburgh that on this day Miss Ogley actually ran from the post-office to her house, and throwing herself under the shade of a maple, opened the precious packet. How her heart beat! How the words went galloping! " The illustrations were accepted; the publishers declared they would sell any book." Mr. Ogley must come to New York, as the firm needed more of his work. And for all the Ogleys' kindness the book was to be dedicated to Florence, as a small token of Leigh's affection.

Leigh would return with Mr. Ogley and take a well-earned rest.

She rested her head against the trunk of the tree, happiness came to her dreams; beautiful dreams romped through her head. Dreams invited sleep, and that fairy princess came.

Mr. Ogley, returning home, found his daughter fast asleep with a crumpled letter held to her breast. Gently he took it and read. Tears ran down his cheeks. " If my wife were only alive," he muttered, " only alive! Perhaps people now may buy my pictures. All I wanted was to get a start—to get away from Dryburgh and exile, far from dulness and bigotry.   To live in the city once more is not a dream, but a reality, Gilliman Ogley."

Florence awoke: the father and daughter, eyes telling a tale, embraced.

"What is that you're killing yourself laughing at ?" said Justice Butler to Dr. Cronker.

"The funniest book that was ever penned—a book got up by young Watkins, and Ogley, who rented my place.   Ogley has become a great man. Guess what he was doing in the glass office while we were laughing outside—painting pictures.   They were sold the other day at auction; brought prices you and I couldn't touch.   I wanted to know more of that man, but I was led the other way by my wife. Men are foolish to be led by the noses, the women element holding the string.   My wife was always prophesying about these folk, and that Leigh was not going there for nothing, and something bad would happen some day.   Leigh was not going there for nothing; that bit of her talk is correct, I reckon, if the dedication to Mrs. Florence Ogley Watkins means anything, and I'm betting it does."

"Doctor," said the justice, removing his hat and scratching his head long and crosswise, "this is a slow town: the people know nothing.   Just think of the way they treated that great man.   I wouldn't wonder but that that Watkins boy, if he's clever enough to write books, might turn the laugh by

composing one on Dryburgh, and get Ogley to picture it."

"Serve them right.   Just what would wake them
up, and this book tells me that young Watkins can
do it thoroughly."

"Let me have a read at it as soon as you get
through, doctor," and Justice Butler went down
the street to his office.

Dr. Cronker put under his arm *Burghdry*, a
novel, by Leigh Hunt Watkins, illustrated by
Gilliman Ogley, and dedicated to Mrs. Florence
Ogley Watkins, and strolled off into the shade of a
maple to laugh at the music of a fellow-townsman.

CHRISTIAN REID.

Mrs. Frances C. Tiernan, whose books are published over the name of "Christian Reid," was born at Salisbury, North Carolina, where her people have lived from the first settlement of the country. Her father, Colonel Charles F. Fisher, was killed on July 21st, 1861, in the battle of Manassas, while in command of his regiment of North Carolina State Troops. His daughter was devoted to him, and his death greatly saddened her life. All attempts to lure her into society proved futile, for she neither asked any one to call on her nor accepted the invitations to visit which her neighbors sent. For years after, she lived a lonely life, with a maiden aunt as her only companion, in the Fisher homestead, an old fashioned brownish-gray house, with large columns in front, which stands in a grove of grand old oaks and cedars. During the summer she sometimes visited Ashville, but most of her time, when not writing, was passed in walking or driving about the beautiful mountain region. A zealous Catholic, Miss Fisher gave up part of the lot on which her old home stands and built a church upon it.

Miss Fisher began to write when she was very young, and the success of her first novel,'' Valerie Aylmer,'' which appeared in 1870, spared her the difficulties which beset most authors in their early efforts. Thereafter she wrote constantly for several years, publishing many books, of which '' Morton House,'' ''A Question of Honor,'' ''A Daughter of Bohemia,'' and '' Heart of Steel '' may be mentioned as the best.

In 1887 she was married to Mr. James M. Tiernan, and has since chiefly resided in Mexico, where her husband has large mining interests. Out of Mrs. Tiernan's stay in Mexico have come '' The Land of the Sun,'' '' Picture of Las Cruces,'' and '' Carmela.'' Her principal Catholic stories are '' Armine,'' '' A Child of Mary,'' '' Philip's Restitution,'' ''Carmela,'' ''A Little Maid of Arcady,'' and '' A Woman of Fortune.''

Besides the books already mentioned, Mrs. Tiernan has written: ''A Cast for Fortune,'' ''The Lady of Las Cruces,'' '' Mabel Lee,'' '' Ebb-Tide,'' '' Nina's Atonement,'' ''Carmen's Inheritance,'' ''A Gentle Belle,'' '' Hearts and Hands,'' '' The Land of the Sky,'' '' After Many Days,'' '' Bonny Kate,'' ''A Summer Idyl,'' ''Roslyn's Fortune,'' '' Miss Churchill.''

In the Quebrada.

BY CHRISTIAN REID.

AMONG the wildest heights of the Sierra Madre in western Mexico is the town or mining camp of Tópia, which occupies what would be in case of war an absolutely impregnable situation. It lies in a high, cup-shaped valley, with immense cliff-faced heights surrounding it like the walls of an amphitheatre, while its only gate of entrance, save some trails over the hills, is a deep pass, or *quebrada*, cut through the mountains by a river which in immeasurably distant ages forced a way for itself to the Pacific Ocean.

Up this *quebrada*, which is almost impassable in the rainy season because the waters of the river then completely cover its boulder-strewn bottom—the greater part of which is in the other season dry—all supplies for the town are conveyed on the backs of men or of mules. During the dry months there is a constant succession of long trains of the last-named patient animals, bearing immense packs, passing over the trail—for road it cannot be called—which winds upward among the rocks, crossing and recrossing hundreds of times the stream which flows down the pass. Of these trains the most important are the bullion trains, or *condúctas*, from the mines, which carry down the product of their reduction works in massive bars of silver to the mint in the city of Culiacan, to be conveyed back in a few days in the form of freshly-coined dollars stamped with the Mexican eagle. These bullion trains would have been in times past a mark for constant robbery, but since the government has suppressed brigandage with so strong a hand they are very seldom molested. As a measure of precaution, however, they are always accompanied by a guard of two or three armed men, and the leader or " conductor " is always a man of proved honesty and strong nerve.

Such a train set out one day from Culiacan, bearing many thousand dollars of freshly-coined silver for the Madrugada Mines in the mountains of Durango, and accompanied not only by the " conductor " in charge and his men, but by a young American, Philip Earle by name, who was going as consulting engineer up to the mines. Having had considerable experience both in Mexico and South America, this young man was not at all daunted by anything which he had heard of the difficulties of the way, nor by the remote and almost inaccessible situation of the place for which he was bound. All that concerned him was the large salary offered him at the mines, for he was particularly anxious to make money and to make it fast. So, bidding good-bye to his friends in the flowery city of Culiacan, he set forth with the bullion train for the mountains which lay, blue and remote, on the eastern horizon.

The journey of the first two days was common-place and monotonous enough to one who knew the country and was familiar with its customs. To one who was not, however, the nineteenth century, with its railroads and Pullman cars, would have seemed but a dream in this land where troops of mules and donkeys still transport all freight, where every man goes on horseback, and where at night the only places for lodging are the wayside *fondas* where the animals are turned into a *corral* while the traveller spreads on the ground the blanket which he carries and, with his saddle for pillow, sleeps—or does not sleep, as the case may be, to an accompaniment of the stamping of mules, grunting of pigs, and lowing of calves.

Earle had, however, travelled in remote parts of Mexico before, and these things were almost as much a matter of course to him as to his companions, the dark, sinewy, Arab-like men who formed the escort of the train. It was only when they entered the *quebrada* on the third day that he found himself impressed by any novelty in his surroundings. And indeed the person would have been singularly obtuse who was not impressed by the wonderful grandeur of this pass, which seemed a way opened by Nature into the heart of her remotest fastnesses.

Bold green hills and precipitous cliffs lined the sides of the narrow gorge, the bottom of which was covered with stones worn into round shape by the erosion of water through countless ages; and as the train of mules and men wound deeper and deeper into this wild cañon, with the great rock-faced heights towering above them, they were conscious of an increasing sense of altitude. They had left behind the oppressive heat and relaxing atmosphere of the *tierra caliente.* A cool, Alpine freshness was now about them, the gift of the giant hills, and a luxuriant wealth of verdure began to adorn the stern grandeur of the pass, mingled with fantastic masses of rock of every shape and hue, and the constant charm of rippling, flashing, pouring water. Strange to say, also, as they penetrated farther human habitations began to appear more frequently. So excellent was the grazing for cattle on the hill-sides, and so rich the soil wherever a foothold could be secured for cultivation, that every few miles some house of primitive construction appeared, nestling under broad, rustling shade on some little point of vantage between the mountains and the rock-strewn *quebrada.*

It was at the close of their first day in the pass, as twilight came on, with great masses of gorgeously tinted clouds flecking the narrow strip of sapphire sky over their heads, that Earle ranged his mule up beside that of the " conductor " and inquired where they would spend the night. It seemed a very pertinent inquiry at the moment, for they were then in a portion of the cañon so wild, so deep, so rugged that it seemed as if no human habitation could be near. But the Mexican replied without hesitation:

" At Las Huertas, señor."

"Las Huertas!" The young man looked around shrugging his shoulders. Nothing could have been less suggestive of gardens than this narrow pass in the heart of the frowning heights. "And how far are we from the place?" he asked.

"About a league," the other replied.

This meant an hour's longer riding, for progress in the *quebrada* was slow; so, resigning himself, Earle rode on. Half an hour later stars were shining out of the dusky violet sky, toward which the massive hills that lined their way towered in austere remoteness, and the murmur of the river was the only sound which met the ear except the plashing now and again of water as the train crossed some one of the many, fords. Earle, who had lighted a cigar to solace the way, was very far in mind from his surroundings as he mechanically followed the man who rode in advance of him around the shoulder of a jutting cliff, where great masses of rock—detached from above by the disintegrating processes of Nature —were scattered in piled confusion, amid which the mules slowly and in single file picked their way, when suddenly—*crack!*—the sharp report of a rifle rang out close at hand, and the startled rush of the animals, the cries and shouts of the men told Earle at once that the train was attacked. In the same instant that he realized this, two more reports sounded in rapid succession, and as he endeavored to control his wildly frightened mule he was suddenly aware of a dark head appearing above a rock close beside him, and the levelled, shining barrel of a gun. He spurred his already excited animal, and with a frantic bound it leaped forward just as a fourth report rang out. He was conscious of a stinging pain in his shoulder and of falling headlong from his saddle. After that he knew no more.

Even as his loss of consciousness had been by the road of pain, so was his return to it. Red-hot throbs and darts of physical anguish recalled his senses from the dark region where they had remained unaware of the body until thus recalled to it. He opened his eyes, and they rested on a face that seemed to him like the creation of a dream. Dark, delicate, gentle, tender, draped in the dusky blue folds of a mantle, it was so like in type to the well-known face of Our Lady of Guadalupe, which hangs on the wall of every house, palace, or hut in Mexico, that he could not believe it to be other than a vision until, meeting the gaze of his eyes, the vision spoke in a voice as soft as her glance:

" Did I hurt you so much, señor ? I was trying to do something for your wound."

" What can you do ?" asked Earle with a groan. " The ball must be in my shoulder, and only a doctor can take it out."

" We have sent to Culiacan for a doctor," she answered. " He may be here to-morrow, but meanwhile it is necessary that your wound should be bandaged."

" Bandage it, then," said Earle, setting his teeth with a groan.

He could not but acknowledge, however, that her touch was wonderfully deft and gentle, although she had not the skill of a surgeon or of a trained nurse. But the small dark hands, with the slender supple fingers of her race, had a soft skill of their own; and after she had bandaged the wound he looked at her gratefully.

" You did that very well," he said, " and it feels much better. But my head! I think it is injured worse than my shoulder. It struck a rock as I fell —that is the last thing I remember."

" It is badly cut, but not broken," she said. " I have examined and bandaged it. That blow was what stunned you. I don't think your shoulder is very badly hurt."

" But what occurred ?" he asked, suddenly remembering the scene last imprinted on his consciousness—the dark pass, the piled rocks, the sharp report of the rifles, the frightened mules, the shouting men, the gun levelled with deliberate aim at him, the bullet in his shoulder, the fall from his plunging mule. " Was any one killed ? " he asked. " Was the train robbed ? "

" No one was killed, señor—*gracias á Dios!* " she answered gravely. " But injured, yes. Don Ramon lies dangerously wounded, and so is Manuel Alvarez. The silver was carried off."

" By whom ? "

She shrugged her shoulders—apparently at the futility of the question.

" By robbers, without doubt, señor; but who they

were—*quien sabe?* It has been very long since any-thing of the kind happened in the *quebrada* before."

" Have they been taken?"

It seemed to him that she shrank, and that the soft tint of her face grew paler.

" No," she answered, catching her breath a little, " but the soldiers are out in search of them."

" Then it is not likely they will escape," said he with satisfaction. " Things of this kind are not played with in Mexico. They *catch* their robbers —and when they catch them, they shoot them."

" *Si*, señor," she assented faintly. There was no doubt now of her increasing pallor, and the hands still busied about his bandages trembled excessively. He noted these things, thinking to himself that her nerves were somewhat overwrought by such tragic happenings. Then it suddenly occurred to him to wonder where he was, and he asked the question.

" At Las Huertas, señor," she answered. She rose, adding gently: " I will bring you food—it is necessary that you should take something."

As she left him he lay looking at the scene which surrounded him and taking in its details, as far as his dulled and weakened faculties would permit him to do so. He perceived that he was lying on a cot under a straw-thatched shed, such as formed a front to all the adobe farm-houses of the country. The usual dark, unventilated rooms were behind, but in front was what might readily have been transformed into a paradise of beauty, for it was a part of the *huertas* at the mention of which he had smiled.

Through the glistening green foliage of a thick grove of orange-trees the sunshine flecked the ground in broken gleams; while under the arching boughs were to be caught glimpses of the rocky *quebrada*, with its towering heights, beyond, from whence came a constant murmur of the swiftly flowing river. This was for a little while the only sound which met the ear of Earle, then another reached him—a low, deep moan of pain. His eyes and attention thus drawn to his immediate neighborhood, he saw not far off, on a cot like his own, the recumbent form of Ramon, the "conductor" of the bullion train; while farther yet, stretched on a pallet on the floor, was another prone and bloody figure. "It is like a hospital after battle," he thought; "but where are surgeons, nurses, means of help for any of us? We shall probably all die from mortified wounds. My God! what a fool I was ever to have come here!"

He did not change this opinion even when, the next day, the doctor summoned from Culiacan arrived and speedily extracted the ball from his shoulder, declaring the wound not dangerous with proper care. The other men were also looked after and despatched to their homes near by. But when Earle pleaded to be taken to Culiacan, the surgeon promptly negatived the request.

"It would be exceedingly dangerous," he said, "to return to the hot country in your condition. No, you must stay here in the hills, and if you follow my directions carefully there is no reason why all should not go well with you. I will come back in two or three weeks, and you can then decide whether you will return with me or go up to the mines. For the present I will leave you in the hands of the pretty daughter of the house here, who is unusually capable, with natural qualities for nursing, if no training."

" There is something very soothing about her," said Earle, languidly.

It was this soothing quality, perhaps, which in the days that followed made him lean so upon this girl with the dark, tender face, so like the face of the Lady of Guadalupe. Once, when she was bending over him in some act of ministration, the resemblance seemed to him so striking that he said to her:

" Is your name Guadalupe? It should be."

She looked surprised. " No, señor," she answered. " My name is Innocencia."

" Ah! " He could not but smile, the name seemed so appropriate to the expression of her face—to her whole air and manner, which was that of a childlike innocence blended with the gravity and wisdom of mature womanhood. Lying on his couch of pain, with nothing to do but observe what went on around him, he had seen that not only himself but every one else in the house depended on this quiet, gentle, capable creature, who went about her daily tasks so silently and deftly. She appeared to be the only child of her parents, who leaned upon her in equal degree—her father a grave, taciturn, apparently careworn man, and her mother a fretful invalid who could render no assistance in

any household task. These tasks she performed
with wonderful neatness and despatch, yet never
permitted the stranger who so entirely looked to her
for all his comfort to feel himself in the least neglected. And through all her many and varied
duties she preserved ever the same gentle serenity,
the same sweet purity of glance and manner which
made Earle exclaim on hearing her name:

"That is charming! You could not possibly
have a name more appropriate to you—not even
Guadalupe."

He saw that she blushed and the lids with their
dark silken fringes fell over her eyes. "The
señor is very good," she said, "but he does not
know a great deal of me. It is possible that he
thinks better of me than I deserve."

"You deserve everything good that I could
possibly think of you," returned Earle with energy.
"You have been my good angel. I owe my life
to your kindness and care."

"And if that were so, señor, I should be very
glad," she answered with a sincerity which could
not be doubted. "Nothing could give me more
happiness than to believe that I had saved your
life."

"You may believe it," he said earnestly. "But
for your nursing, your constant care, I should surely
have died."

So far from dying, however, he was soon able to
walk about. And then it was that he fully realized
the exceeding picturesqueness and beauty of the

place where fate had thrown him. The hills, receding slightly from the *quebrada*, left a space a hundred or two yards in width, but in length perhaps half a mile, which was covered with the most luxuriant groves of orange and other fruit trees extending on each side of the house, which was set with its back immediately against the steeply rising mountains, covered with luxuriant forest growth. It was a delight to Earle when he grew stronger to wander out into these gardens, and in their leafy alleys—for the trees were planted in long rows—to try his strength in walking, or merely sit and absorb the marvellous beauty and tranquillity, the wild sylvan freshness, the sense of utter remoteness in the scene. And it grew daily more of a pleasure to him to watch for the appearance of Innocencia, as she would come to seek him at regular intervals with his food and medicine. He would establish himself at the end of the *huerta* farthest from the house, so as to prolong the pleasure of watching the advance of the slender figure, drawing nearer between the rows of trees, overarched by their foliage, amidst which gleamed the golden fruit. There was something so Arcadian in the whole environment that it made a perfect frame for that figure in its gentle grace, toward which his thoughts and feelings daily inclined with more of tenderness.

It is an old story, that of the heart of the convalescent turning toward the nurse who has become necessary to him. But there was something more than the ordinary reason to account for Earle's growing sense of attachment to this girl, who was so totally different from any woman he had ever known before, as different as this wild, remote, strangely beautiful chasm in the heart of the mountains was to the world left, it seemed to him, so far behind.

And the reason, too, was an old one. He had left, with a sore and angry heart, not only that world, but another girl whom he had loved for years, but who had refused to share the fortunes of his wandering life. " When you are able to return and live in civilization I will marry you," she had said, to which he had replied hotly that in such case she preferred the advantages of civilization to himself. " If you choose to think so," she had answered proudly. And so the matter had ended with a broken engagement and a disappointed man going to bury himself in the most remote portion of Mexico. His thoughts had been dwelling angrily, bitterly on Alice Wilmot at the very instant when the attack on the train was made; he had recalled her brilliant, scornful beauty as if it had been before his eyes, and then—after the dark interval of unconsciousness —it was on the tender face of Innocencia that those eyes opened. Was the one appointed to heal the hurt inflicted by the other, the mental as well as the physical wound from which he was suffering ? As the days went on he began more and more to think so, more and more to lapse into a dream of passive content.

But this content was suddenly and rudely shattered. It chanced that one morning he rose very early after a restless night, and wandered out into the leafy alleys of the *huerta* before the sun had appeared over the mountains and while a certain obscurity of dawn still lingered in the dewy, fragrant shades. As he sauntered along he was surprised suddenly to catch a glimpse of the familiar blue mantle of Innocencia in that part of the garden which bordered immediately upon the steep mountain-side. He turned at once and went toward her, with the pleasure which the sight of her always evoked quickening at his heart; and it was not until he had nearly reached her side that he perceived that she had a companion—a man, whose tall athletic figure was partially concealed by a clump of foliage as he stood, leaning on a rifle, before her.

Earle paused abruptly. Something in the attitudes of the two persons, and the sound of their low earnest voices, told him that this meeting in the early dawn was not an ordinary one. He would have retreated unseen, could he have done so; but as he paused the man glanced up, saw him, and, quick as thought, raised his rifle. Amazed, Earle stood still, offering an excellent target had the other fired; but at the same moment Innocencia also perceived him and with a low cry struck up the gun. She then uttered a few words rapidly and passionately. The man scowled, hesitated an instant, then, turning, quickly sprang up the mountain-side and was almost immediately lost to sight in the dense forest.

Innocencia stood looking after him for a moment before she walked slowly toward Earle, who still stood as if transfixed, the full significance of the scene having by this time dawned upon him. So she had a lover, this girl whom he had blindly thought so deserving of her exquisite name! And a lover whom she not only met in secret at unseemly hours, but who was so brutal a desperado that he lifted his gun without provocation to fire on an unarmed man. It was no wonder that he regarded her sternly as she approached, so pale that in the pallid, misty dawn she seemed the mere wraith of herself.

" Señor," she said, speaking faintly and with evident difficulty, " you are out—very early."

" Yes," Earle assented, " and I am sorry that chance should have brought me out to witness what I have seen. Yet," with sudden energy, " I am *not* sorry to learn the truth, however painful it may be. For I have thought so well of you that—"

" That it is now painful to you to think badly of me," she said, as he hesitated. She had regained the calmness which usually characterized her manner, although she was still very pale; and as she stood before him he could not but think that there was nothing of the culprit in her aspect. Instead there was a strange mingling of dignity and pathos. " It is true," she went on; " you cannot think otherwise than badly of me now, and you will perhaps think still worse when I ask you to do me the great favor not to mention to any one that you have seen—him who has gone away."

"I should not have thought of mentioning the fact to any one," Earle replied coldly. "It is no concern of mine that you choose to meet in such a manner and at such a time one who is so little of a man that he lifts his weapon against a stranger unarmed and unoffending."

"Pardon him, señor," she pleaded. "He is a hunted, desperate man, and he feared—"

"That I would recognize him?" A sudden swift intuition flashed upon Earle. "That was one of the robbers of the bullion train," he declared with positive conviction. "Perhaps the very man who shot me. You cannot deny it."

"Señor!" She clasped her hands and looked at him piteously, appealingly.

"My God!" said Earle, regarding her with eyes that burned with indignation. "I fancied myself in an honest, hospitable house, and instead I am in a haunt of robbers. I fancied *you* goodness incarnate, and instead you are—"

He paused, suffocated with passion; and as he paused she came nearer to him, holding out her clasped hands and lifting her eyes full of supplication.

"Of me, señor, think what you will," she cried, "but do not think for a moment that my parents know anything of this. My father's house *is* honest

—he would die sooner than harbor a robber within it. Oh, be just to him and believe this!"

" I am glad to believe it," replied Earle sternly; " but in that case how is it possible for you, the daughter of an honest man, to meet secretly one who is a highway robber, and a murderer as well at heart?"

She burst into an agony of weeping, burying her face in her slender hands, and it was several minutes before she could answer him. Then she said between her sobs:

" All that you say of him is true. I cannot deny it, and—*valgame Dios!*—I cannot tell you why I meet this man. Only, it would break my father's heart to know it, and I pray you, therefore, say not a word—"

" I have already told you that I will say nothing," Earle interposed abruptly. " But I shall make immediate preparations to leave this place, where I now feel that my life is unsafe."

Giving her no time to reply, he turned with the last words and walked away.

It was the afternoon of the same day that Earle, leaving the shady groves of Las Huertas, walked across the *quebrada* to its farther side, where the river flowed along the base of towering cliffs. Seating himself in the deep cool shadow cast by these, he gave himself up to very bitter reflections. On the exact nature of these reflections, especially as concerned the ineradicable depravity of feminine nature, it is unnecessary to dwell. They have been the reflections in all ages of those who leaped too rapidly from particular examples to general conclusions. Mingling in his thoughts the heartlessness of Alice Wilmot with the duplicity of Innocencia, he sat moodily gazing at the stream and wishing that it were possible to leave Las Huertas without an hour's further delay. But departure had proved more difficult than he had anticipated. Mules and a guide were to be obtained, all of which involved delay and required an exercise of patience to which he felt himself at present unequal. He had come out, therefore, to escape at once the annoyance of endeavoring to explain his sudden departure to his host, and the sight of Innocencia, which had become intensely painful to him.

But was he not to escape this sight after all? For, lifting his eyes suddenly, whom should he see hastening toward him across the rock-strewn space that lay between Las Huertas and the stream but Innocencia herself! She was running as fast as was possible over the stones, almost falling now and again, but recovering herself quickly and coming on with unabated speed. Earle regarded her approach with a wonder which grew into positive amazement when she at last reached him and paused, pale, panting, agitated as he had never seen her before. He sprang to his feet, thinking for an instant that she was about to faint.

"What is the matter?" he asked, assisting her to a seat on a stone. "What has happened?"

She looked up at him—a wild terror, as he now

perceived, in her eyes, and a passionate entreaty as well.

" Señor," she gasped, " he has been taken—the man whom you saw this morning—"

" Ah!" he said, with an instant hardening of feeling which was reflected in his face and voice. This, then, was what her agitation meant! Her villainous lover had been captured by the guards who had been searching the mountains for days; and she knew well what little chance of escape, what short shrift, there was for such criminals when once taken. Earle made no effort to speak other than coldly as he asked, " What then ?"

She cast an agonized look across the *quebrada;* and, following it, he saw a group issuing from the gate of Las Huertas and coming across the rocks toward him. It was a party of soldiers escorting a prisoner.

" Señor," she cried, catching his hand in both of her own, " they are bringing him to you, to see if you will identify him as—as one of those who attacked the *conducta*. When I heard that, I said that I would come in search of you; and I ran away before they could stop me, to beg you for the love of God to be merciful—to have pity—"

" Stop!" said Earle almost roughly, for the men were now half-way across the *quebrada*. " Let me understand you. Have they no proof against the man unless I can identify him ?"

" None, señor, none. They suspect him—ah, *valgame Dios!*—but they know nothing. It is all with you."

"Be quiet now," said Earle in the same sternly commanding tone. "They are almost here, and they must not suppose that you have appealed to me. Turn your face away or it will betray you."

As she obeyed him with one last piteous glance, he stepped forward so as further to shield her; and taking a few steps met the party, which had now reached him. They halted, salutations were exchanged between himself and the officer in command of the guards, and the latter then said:

"We believe, señor, that we have captured one of the robbers who attacked the *conducta* the night you were wounded. He bears a very bad name, but we lack direct evidence against him; and we have brought him to see if you can perhaps identify him, since we are informed that you alone saw one of the assailants on that occasion."

Earle looked at the prisoner, whose face he had hardly observed in the early morning. It was easy to observe it now, for he held his head haughtily erect, and his dark eyes were full of defiance under their level brows as they met without wavering those of the man whose word could send him to death. There was no fear in them and no appeal. Just so it was certain they would face the muskets which in a little while would be levelled to shoot him did Earle only say, "That is the man."

With the involuntary feeling of admiration which courage always evokes, Earle turned to the observant, expectant officer beside him.

"You will remember, señor," he said quietly,

" that the attack on the *conducta* took place at night. Therefore, although it is true that I saw one of the robbers just before I was shot by him, I could not be certain enough of his appearance to identify him, and I cannot possibly declare that this man is he."

" You positively cannot identify him as one of your assailants ?" asked the officer in a disappointed tone.

" I positively cannot do so."

" Then we need not trouble you further. *Adios*, señor."

" *Adios*, Señor Capitano."

Hats were lifted, the officer gave a word of command to his men and they turned back across the *quebrada* with their prisoner, the look of relief on whose face was visibly mingled with surprise.

Earle remained silently watching them until they were well out of earshot. Then he turned again toward Innocencia. But he was not prepared for her rising from the stone on which he had placed her, and, before he could divine her intention or prevent her, taking his hand and kissing it. Almost violently he drew it away.

" For God's sake, spare me!" he exclaimed passionately. " I need no further proof of how much you love this brigand—for that I am sure he is, though I have suppressed the truth in order to save him."

" It is because you have saved him, señor, that I thank you," she said in a tone of deepest feeling.

" I want no thanks," he replied angrily. " I have simply paid a debt. And I am glad to have been able to do so without perjuring myself. I did not recognize the man—how could I identify a face seen only for a moment in the obscurity of night ? But I have not the faintest doubt of his guilt, and I only refrained from expressing my conviction because, if *he* nearly took my life, I owe its preservation to *you*. And so, for your sake, I have spared him—though it might have been better, even for your sake," he added gloomily, " if I had identified him, and so insured his being shot."

" Do not say that, señor," she pleaded, growing if possible a shade paler, " for you would have broken not only my heart, but the hearts of my poor father and mother as well. He is my only brother."

" Innocencia ! "

It was a cry in which gladness, relief, reproach were mingled indescribably; but Innocencia went on without heeding, in her low pathetic tones:

" I did not intend to tell you, señor, for the sake of my poor father, who is so honest, so good, and to whom it is so sore a trial, so heavy a cross that his son is otherwise. To escape the disgrace he brought upon us, my father left his home beyond the mountains yonder "—she pointed eastward— " and came here, thinking that Cipriano would not find us and no one here need know with what a son God had afflicted him. But he discovered where we had gone and followed us. My father refused to allow him to enter his house. He went away, swearing that he should regret it. And soon after this, señor, occurred the attack on the *conducta.* I knew nothing of my brother's connection with it, but I feared, I trembled, and so did my father. And this morning, when I went out early to milk the cows, he—Cipriano—came down the mountain and spoke to me. He told me that he was closely pursued, that he would be shot if taken, and begged me to hide him. We were still talking, for I knew not what to do, when you came—and the rest you know."

"My poor Innocencia!" said Earle, taking her hands and regarding her with eyes in which compassion and pleasure were subtly mingled. "So this is the explanation. What a fool, as well as a brute, I have been!—a fool to think for a moment that you could have been guilty of what I imagined, and a brute to treat you in any case as I have done. Can you forgive me in consideration of the only excuse I have to offer—that I love you with all my heart, and that it maddened me to be forced to believe you unworthy of that love?"

"Señor!" She drew back as if frightened. "It is impossible"—she caught her breath—"it is not right that you should speak so to me—"

"And why not?" he asked impetuously. "Do you not know that you have healed my heart as well as my body, that I have daily learned to love you more, until now I cannot live without you—"

She drew her hands from his clasp, and retreating

slightly from him, stood looking at him, smiling a little sadly.

" Oh, yes, señor," she said in her musical accents, " you will easily learn to live without the poor Mexican girl who has had the happiness of repairing in some measure the evil her unhappy brother wrought, but who is not fitted to share your life. No, señor,"—as he attempted to speak—" say no more, I beg. You forget the great difference between your life and mine."

" It is true," Earle replied simply. " I forget everything, and desire to forget everything— except that I love you."

She shook her head. " But that is not right," she said. " There are many things which you should remember—your country, your friends—"

He made a gesture as if he abjured them. " I give them up," he said. " All that I ask is to stay here with you."

" Here—in the *quebrada* ! " She smiled again, almost pityingly. " Ah, señor, what a little time it would be before you would hate the *quebrada*, and perhaps poor Innocencia too, were she foolish enough to listen to you. But it is because you are still weak from your illness that you think these things. When you are strong and go back to the great world, of which you have talked to me, you will wonder that you ever thought of staying here or of loving a girl who is so poor, so igno- rant—"

" And so divinely good and tender," he cried,

taking her hand again. " Innocencia, what do I care for any of these things ? I care only for, I think only of *you*."

" Then think of me, señor," she said quietly, " as one whose duty is fixed. You have seen how it is—my parents are heart-broken over the loss of their only son. I am all they have and I will never leave them. That promise long since I made to God and to my own heart. But even if this were not so—if my parents had not such need of me, if my brother were not disgraced—I could not be so foolish as to listen to you, who would so soon regret your own folly—"

" Innocencia! "

She suddenly lifted her hand and pointed. "Yonder," she said, " comes the señor doctor from Culiacan, who will take you back with him. And it is better so."

" Hallo, Earle!" said the doctor when, having dismounted from his mule at the gate of Las Huertas, he came across the *quebrada* to his patient; " I am delighted to see you so much improved. And for your further improvement I have brought with me a most efficacious medicine."

" I have no need of any more medicine," said Earle, ungraciously. " I have taken enough of the stuff you left for me."

" Ah, this is medicine of another and better kind," returned the doctor. " It will give you all the strength you need to accompany me to Culiacan to-morrow."

" I have no intention of returning to Culiacan," said Earle. " I am going up to the mines."

" You are not strong enough yet for that trip," said the doctor, decidedly. " You must come back to Culiacan, and then take a companion with you when you start again for the mountains of Durango."

" A companion! " Earle glanced at the figure of Innocencia as, draped in her blue mantle, she was passing across the *quebrada* homeward. " I haven't the least desire for any companion who is likely to care to accompany me," he said gloomily.

" One never knows," returned the doctor, mysteriously, " what might turn up. It is the unexpected that happens, you know. Oh, confound it, Earle, I am a bad hand at either keeping a secret or breaking news! The long and the short of it is, that I have a letter for you from the most charming young lady in the world."

" For me! " Earle stared in amazement. " But I don't know a young lady in Culiacan."

" This young lady only arrived in Culiacan the other day, from San Francisco. She had heard some news which concerned her very much, and so she came. Here is her letter."

He produced from his pocket a letter which he handed to Earle, and then rising walked away.

With the feeling of one in a dream, Earle opened and read;

'PHILIP: We have both been foolish, and I apparently heartless. But I learned when I heard of your danger that I am not heartless, so I have thrown pride away and come to share all your dangers henceforth. Are you glad? If so, come quickly to

"ALICE."

When Earle looked up from the sheet which bore these lines of writing his eyes had a dazzled light in them, as if under amazement joy were dawning. But he turned his gaze to the spot where he had last seen Innocencia. She had disappeared.

MARY A. SADLIER.

Mrs. Mary A. Sadlier was born in Cootehill, County Cavan, Ireland, where her father, Francis Madden, Esq., was a highly respected merchant. Miss Madden began her literary career by poetical contributions to *La Belle Assemblée*, a London Magazine. Shortly after her emigration to America, Miss Madden was married to Mr. James Sadlier, the publisher. From this time forth, she embarked upon a literary career which lasted with but little interruption for almost half a century. She edited for some years the *New York Tablet*, being fortunate in such co-laborers

and contributors as Dr. Brownson, Hon. T. D. McGee,
Dr. Ives, Henry Giles, M. E. Blake, Dr. Huntington, Dr.
Anderson, and John McCarthy. In March, 1895, Mrs.
Sadlier received the Lætare Medal from the University of
Notre Dame, an honor conferred on few.

Amongst her best-known works are : " The Confederate
Chieftains " " Blakes and Flanagans," " Old and New,"
" The Hermit of the Rock," " Bessy Conway," " Maureen
Dhu," " New Lights, or Life in Galway," " Confessions of
an Apostate," " Elinor Preston," " MacCarthy More,"
" Daughter of Tyrconnell," " Old House by the Boyne,"
" Heiress of Kilorgan," " Red Hand of Ulster," " Aunt
Honor's Keepsake," " Con O'Regan," " Willy Burke,"
" Alice Riordan," " Fate of Father Sheehy," " Agnes of
Braunsberg," and jointly with her daughters a volume of short
tales, " Stories of the Promises." Mrs. Sadlier also com-
piled a catechism of " Sacred History," " A Young Ladies'
Reader," " Purgatory : Doctrinal, Historical, and Poetical."
Her translations include : " De Ligny's Life of Christ,"
" Orsini's Life of the Blessed Virgin," " Lambruschini's
Immaculate Conception," " Collot's Catechism," " The
Orphan of Moscow," " The Spanish Cavaliers," " Catholic
Anecdotes " in three volumes, " The Lost Son," " The
Castle of Rousillon," " The Year of Mary," " Legends of
St. Joseph," " Meditations on the Holy Eucharist," " Eas-
ter in Heaven," " The Pope's Niece," " The Bohemians,"
" Salim," " The Vendetta," " The Exile of Tadmor," " The
Poachers," " The Great Day," " Benjamin," " The Devil,"
" The Family," " The Priest's Sister and the Inheritance,"
" Ten Stories," " Tales and Stories."

Sban Dempsey's Story.

BY MARY A. SADLIER.

> Let not ambition mock their useful toil,
> Their homely joys and destiny obscure;
> Nor grandeur hear with a disdainful smile
> The short and simple annals of the poor.—GRAY.

THE old Catholic homesteads of Ireland have each and all their regular set of dependents or hangers-on, wholly apart from the domestics, yet belonging, as it were, to the family. What Catholic is there of the middle or upper classes, brought up in that country,

> "Where smiles hospitality, hearty and free,"

who has not a circle of these humble friends and followers associated with the memories of "auld lang syne"? A cherished place do they hold, these "well-remembered" beggars, in the heart's record of early life. They were the story-tellers of our youth, and had more to do than, perhaps, is generally believed with developing what nature gave of imagination. How eagerly the children of the family longed for the periodical visits of these successors of the *senachies* of old! Their presence was more joyfully welcomed than had they been royal personages.

Amongst the individuals of this class whom I best remember was an old man of the name of Shan Dempsey. He considered himself, and was by others treated, as above the ordinary run of beggars. He was as poor as poverty could make him. Yet somehow he always contrived to appear " a little decent," in an old, snuff-colored surtout much too long for his bent figure, gray corduroys, and indifferent woollen hose.

He had reached the last of Shakespeare's stages, so that the aforesaid hose were ever

" A world too wide
For his shrunk shanks,"

and his attenuated frame was bent almost double. Yet when he glanced up from beneath his shaggy eyebrows there was a sort of weird intelligence in his glance that both surprised and attracted one in some inexplicable way. It was the waning light of an intellect which had never borrowed either from art or culture, but which might have made some noise in the world had it been assisted and developed by instruction. As it was, poor Shan was confessedly illiterate, yet his natural shrewdness and quickness of perception gave him, like many other Irish peasants, a considerable knowledge of human nature.

He had been observant all his life long. The past seemed as vividly present in his memory as though the snows of fourscore winters had not silvered his head. Shan's reminiscences were mostly connected with the affairs of others. Seldom did they bear upon his own. It seemed to us children that some cloud hung over his own life, and the very indifference with which he affected to treat it made us the more anxious to know why he should be destitute when his only son was well-to-do, having a lucrative position as guard of a stage-coach and owning a small farm besides. For a long time Shan kept our curiosity at bay. When our questions pressed him rather hard, he would suddenly remember a romantic tale concerning some great family, and for the time made us forget Shan's secret, as we chose to call it.

" Well, then, it's no secret, after all," said the old man, one winter evening, when he sat in his accustomed place by the wide kitchen chimney, bellows in hand. He seemed to have a fancy for blowing that useful wind-instrument. " Sure, doesn't the whole country-side about the ould place know it. But, ye beat the world, childer, for pickin' out o' people. I b'lieve ye'll never be aisy till you know the ins and outs of it. Will you reach me a drink, Master John, dear, an' I'll tell you how it was, onst for all.''

The drink was given with unusual despatch, and Shan, after sitting a few moments with his old, twinkling eyes fixed on the turf fire, the bellows across his eye, his hand on the handle ready for use, he thus began his story:

"Well, I declare, childer," he said with visible effort, "it isn't much of a story, afther all. Still, as you want to hear it and it's something by common, thanks be to God! I may as well open my mind to you. But the sore's a deep one that I'm going to rip up. *Farear gar*, it is."

Another short pause and a few leisurely puffs at the fire, and Shan spoke again:

"It's thrue enough for them that tould you I might be well enough at home with Tommy, for he has ten acres of as good ground as you'd get from here to Ballyshannon. When I had them, better oats didn't come into the market than I brought; and as for the praties, why it 'id do you good just to look at them, laughin' in the basket after they were teemed. I'm tould nayther one no th' other's as good now with them, for the neighbors think there's a curse on the place of late years."

"A curse on the ground, Shan! How can that be ?"

"Listen, aroon, and you'll soon hear; that's what I'm goin' to tell you. I wasn't always as you see me now. Poor and lonesome as I am the day, I onst had as full an' plenty, an' as good a wife as ever broke the world's bread, and a houseful of fine, hearty childer, boys and girls, as God sent them. Tommy was the youngest, and, *mavrone*, sure we made a pet of him entirely, and for loathness to put him at hard work, it's what we let him grow up in idleness when all the others had to take their share of the work, rough and smooth, just as

it came. Many a time they grumbled hard to see
Tommy goin' about sportin' his figure at fair and
market, an' they workin' hard at home, though by
this time he was a'most as big an' strong as any of
them. Still they kep' it among themselves for fear
of frettin' the poor mother, that was weak and sickly
anyhow. At last she broke down altogether, an' it
was the first heavy crush my heart got when we
covered her up in the dry mould of Kilmarky. At
first there was nobody took on half so bad as
Tommy; but somehow or another he was the first
to get over it, and before many weeks went round
he was as brisk and merry as if the like never happened.

"Sure enough this went to my heart, and
I was so angry at the fellow for his want of gratitude that I couldn't keep my tongue off him.
When I did begin I tould him his own, never fear
but I did. It's what he only laughed at me, an'
said hard work wasn't to his likin', an' that he
believed he'd try his hand at something lighter.
I asked him what he meant to do, but he wouldn't
tell me at that time, all I could do. He cut his
stick that same evening, and the next we heard of
him he was stable-boy at the Head Inns, here in
town. Myself and the rest laughed when we found
out what the graceless fellow was at, for if our work
was hard, sure his wasn't aisy, an' we knew it 'id
soon cure him of his laziness.

" Every one in the house, barrin' myself, was glad
to be shot of him; but I missed him sorely, if it was

nothing else, on account of the poor mother that thought so much of him. Night and day I fretted and grieved, and at last I wanted so much to see his roguish face back at the hob, that off I set into town and done my best to bring him home with me. But if I was to lay the hair o' my head under his feet, sorra a step he'd come, only put me off with a laugh and made a joke of it. Well becomes the boys and girls at home if they didn't make game o' me when I got back, and said it was a pity Tommy wasn't tied on my back, so that I'd get enough of him. But at last when they seen I was keepin' so down-hearted, some of them began to get angry, and said that maybe I'd get more raison to fret before long. So I did, God help me! Take my advice, childer, and never grieve without good raison. It's not pleasin' to them above, as I know to my heavy sorrow."

Poor Shan stopped, gave a few blasts, pressed his lips very hard together, and winked several times to shake the gathering tears from his eyelids. No one spoke, for young as most of the listeners were, the sight of the old man's grief awed them into silence. When he spoke again his voice was thick and husky, but at a higher pitch than usual—probably because he feared it might fail him altogether.

" Not many days after I went to town," he continued, " the boys and girls were all out shearin' corn, barrin' my daughter Ally, that was washin' the vessels afther dinner-time. I was sittin' one side o' the fire makin' a potato-basket out o' some rods

I had, thinkin' o' poor Molshy and dronin' a kind
o' a song, when in walks a little ould-fashioned crab
of a lame beggar man, with a wallet on his back
a'most as big as himself.

"He had the quarest little red eyes ever you
seen in a man, and a hooked nose that was down
a'most over his mouth. Not a word he said—neither
'God save you' nor 'morrow be here,' but in he
stumped and popped himself down on a creepy
right forenenst me. He flung his bag down on the
floor, an' you'd think from the noise it made that
it was crammed with ould iron in place of potatoes
or anything that way.

" 'God save you, honest man!' says I at last
when I seen he didn't spake; 'did you travel far
the day ?'

" 'Farther than you'll travel in a year,' says he,
quite short; an' with that he turns round and claps
his ferret eyes on Ally. The *gersha* was smudgin'
an' laughin' in to herself, and no wonder she would,
for so quare an ould codger never came the way
before.

" 'What's the *gersha* laughin' at?' he says;
'maybe to show her purty teeth. They'll do, *a
colleen*, they'll do.'

" And the ould joker nodded and winked at her
as if he was a young chap ready for all sorts of fun.

" 'Ally,' says I, 'give the decent man his share
and let him be goin','—for myself didn't like the
looks of him or the way he was carryin' on.

"'I want no charity,' answers the beggarman,

'nothin' that's yours, barrin' what you'd hardly be willin' to give me.'

" ' An' what's that ? ' says I.

" ' That schemin' girl there,' says he.   ' If you give her to me I'll make it worth your while.'

" At this Ally laughed till you'd think she'd burst, but it was the other way with me.

" ' By this and by that,' says I, takin' up the tongs, ' if you don't get out o' my sight, you ould *leprachaun* of a creature, I'll smash every bone in your body.'

" ' Don't be makin' so free with the name of them that's your betters,' says the ould fellow, beginnin' to bristle up.   ' I ask you a civil question, Shan Dempsey: Will you or will you not give me your daughter Ally?'

" ' Get out o' my sight, I tell you, or I can't answer for what'll happen,' I cried, an' I made as though I would strike him.   He never answered a word, but looked up in my face in a way I'll never forget.

" ' Don't strike,' says he; ' don't, I warn you; if you do you'll only have once to rue it, an' that'll be your whole life.   I wish you well, though you mayn't think it, an' I came here for no harm.'

" ' Father, dear,' says Ally, coming behind me, ' let the man go quietly.   He's cracked,' added she in a whisper.

" ' I'm not cracked, Ally Dempsey,' says the quare ould customer, ' an' you'll know that, too, before long.   Still, I'm thankful to you for the soft

word, an' I'll give you a bed of down for it some
fine day, with a coach an' with soft cushions to take
your pleasure in. Fare you well till we meet
again!'

" I was so confounded that I couldn't get out a
word, if I'd die for it; an' as for strikin'—why the
tongs fell out of my hand as if I'd lost the power
of it, though I didn't, thank God! Without sayin'
another word, the beggarman ups with his bag,
threw it across his shoulder, and out he marched,
makin' a face at myself as he passed me by that
'id make you laugh if you were half dead. It did
set Ally agoin' again, an' she laughed till the tears
ran down her cheeks, throwin' herself down on the
very creepy where the ould fellow sat. I was vexed
to see her make so light of his impidence, an' somehow I didn't half like to see her pop down on the
stool the minute he rose from it. I hardly know
what I said to her, but I said plenty, for the tears
came into her eyes, and she looked at me with such
a pitiful face that I got sorry for spakin' so hard to
her, only I wouldn't own to it.

" ' Well, father,' says she, as she got up an'
began to put the vessels she had washed on the
dresser, ' it's a poor thing to be blamed for what a
crazy beggarman says and does, but I suppose we
must put up with it. God forgive you for all you've
said to me without rhyme or raison, an' I'm sure
it's more than you've said to Tommy the wildest
day ever he was.'

" This softened me down in a jiffy, and so I laid

my hand on the *colleen's* head, a silky, brown head it was, and bid her not take it so much to heart, for that I didn't mean half what I said. That was all Ally wanted, an' she started as merry as a cricket to give the others a hand at the shearin'. Towards evenin' she came back and put down some sowens to boil for the supper, an' then leavin' me to stir it, she took her pail and went off in search of the cows to milk.

" Whatever put it into my head, I went to the door an' stood lookin' afther her, an' sure enough I felt proud o' her as she tripped along over the green pasture, singin' like a thrush or a linnet. It was as fine an evenin' as ever came from the heavens, and the sun was just settin' behind Liscarron Forth.* I looked up at the Fairy hill, an' you'd think there wasn't a tree on it but was covered with goold. ' Ah,' says I, ' it's a pity the dark treachery's in you for all you look so smilin'.' Little did I think at the time the heavy woe it was goin' to send down on me."

Here Shan paused again, rubbed the back of his hand across his eyes, gave two or three heavy sighs, and when he did speak it was in a choking voice.

" That was the last sight I ever saw of my poor Ally—in life, anyhow. The ould *calliogh* that brought back the milk was no more like her than

---

* This is one of those primitive fortresses with which the earlier inhabitants of the country dotted the face of Ireland. They are called forths (i.e., forts) and raths indiscriminately, and are popularly regarded as the haunts of fairies.

I'm like Master Frank there—God between him
and all harm! She had Ally's clothes on, to be
sure, but that was all. They were all at their
supper when she comes in, an' down she sets the
pail with a grunt like a pig.

" ' 'Deed, then, an' it'll be a long time before
you'll get me to carry such a load agin,' says she.

" An' so it was, for she never did that nor anything else all the time she was on our floor. The
voice made us all look round, for we seen at onst
it wasn't Ally that was in it.

" ' Why,' says I, ' honest woman, where do you
come from ? Sure you're not our Ally ? '

" An' with that I thought of the ould beggarman, an' my blood ran cowld in my veins.

" ' If I'm not,' says she, puckerin' up her weazened face into a kind of a laugh, ' if I'm not, I'm
thinkin' I'm all you'll ever get of her. In regard
to where I came from, it's nothin' to you. Make
room at the table there till I get my supper. I
hope you didn't let the sowens burn, father, while
you stood with your mouth open lookin' afther me.
Bad scran to them cows, but I had hard work to
find them, an' when I did it was in the forth they
were, the thievin' villains.'

" She said this with such a wicked twinkle in her
ould eyes that we all knew she wanted to taunt us
about Ally, but we thought it best to say no more,
so the girls gave her a noggin of milk and made her
sit over to the table. Lord save us and bless us!
it 'id frighten you to see what the little ould thing

ate. Bedad, she left the rest of us stinted enough anyway, but we couldn't for shame's cause bid her stop, an' she ate on an' on till there wasn't a pratie left on the big wooden dish. If that was the beginnin', it wasn't the end of it. Every day of her life it was just the same, till at last we thought she'd ate us out of house an' home. The fun of it was, she wouldn't do a hand's turn in the house, but sat from mornin' till night in the chimney-corner, givin' ould chat to every one that came the way; an' a tongue like a razor she had, too, that 'id cut you to the very bone. We were all afeard to discommode her in the least, an' though we'd give the world to be shot of her, we'd as soon, any of us, put our head in the fire as say an ill word to her.

" Neither of the girls would sleep with her, so we made her a shakedown by herself in a corner of the room; an' Lord save us, she'd tumble into that at night and get out of it in the mornin' without ever bendin' a knee or even as much as blessin' herself. We knew well that luck or grace couldn't be in the house with such a haythen, but, then, what could we do? Some o' the neighbors advised us to bring the priest to her, and well becomes me, so I did. But what do you think of the ould sinner, when myself an' Father Terence—God be good to him!—got to the house, she wasn't in it, up or down! His reverence had a laugh at myself, for he wasn't willin' to come with me at the start on such an errand. He was hardly back at his own

house when we had her at the hob again, as large
as life, an' her laughin' till you'd think she'd split
her sides.   Two or three times she played us the
same trick, an' at last ne'er a one o' the priests 'id
come at all, for they said it was all nonsense and
shuperstition from first to last.   Well, as that
failed, all failed.   So there we were with that ould
damsel on us like a nightmare, atein' as much as
the three boys put together, an' doin' nothin' all
day long, only bitin' and snarlin' at every one of
us.   An' then to the back o' that was the loss o'
my poor *colleen*, one o' the best childer that ever
a poor man had.   It seemed to me as if all the
grief ever I had was nothin' to the loss o' her, for,
as I said to myself, if she only died a natural death,
an' was laid beside her mother under the green sod,
I wouldn't feel the tithe o' what I did.   But to
think of her bein' taken away where no one belong-
in' to her could ever get speech o' her, an' where
prayers or charity could do her no good!

" This was what troubled me most of all, an' I
could see by the boys an' girls that their hearts
were as heavy as my own, but somehow we couldn't
bring ourselves ever to speak of Ally to one another.
For in the fields we were too near the unlucky
forth, and in the house we daren't for fear of the
ould *calliogh* at the hob.   But she knew our thoughts
for all that.   One winter's evening, when I was
sittin' forenenst her, strivin' to smoke away the
sorrow that was like a load on my poor heart, she
looks over at me with her fiery red eyes, an' says

she, ' Shan Dempsey, sure it's nothin' but what
you brought on yourself. Maybe you wouldn't
grieve so much now for your graceless son Tommy
takin' a tramp—eh, father ? '

" ' Don't call me father, you ould—' I stopped,
for with all my anger I knew it wasn't safe to vex
her.

" ' Ha! ha! maybe I won't,' says she, with a
laugh as if it came out of a barrel; ' if you choose
to deny your own flesh an' blood, it's what I'll never
do, bad as you take me to be. Take it aisy, anyhow; an' above all, kape your tongue in bounds. I
think you ought to be the last man to say an un-
mannerly word to any one afther all that's come
an' gone.'

" With that she got up and stepped out into the
darkness, an' we didn't see her again till bed-time.
When we got her out we knelt down an' said the
Rosary, an' when we were done we looked at one
another, an' we all said into ourselves the prayer
that we daren't say aloud, not knowin' but the ould
hag was athin hearin' for all we couldn't see her.
It's like the Mother o' God heard the prayer of our
sorrowful hearts that night, for things took a turn
with us before many days went by.

" The month of October was comin' near an end,
an' myself and the childer were tryin' hard to have
the last of the praties in afore Holl' Eve night.
The weather was the finest that ever you seen for
the season, an' the nights were a'most as bright as
the days on account of the clear moonlight that was

in it. At last Holl' Eve came, an' we finished our job with the last o' the daylight, jist in time for the big supper. *Ochone!* but it was the sorrowful supper to me, for I was thinkin' all the time it lasted o' my poor darlin' Ally, an' whenever I looked across the table at the *calliogh* in the corner, every bit I ate was fit to choke me. But I couldn't ate, though I tried hard, on account of the night it was. I got up at last and took my caubeen off o' the peg, an' was makin' for the door.

"'Why, Lord bless us, father,' says my daughter Peggy, all of a fright, ' sure it's not goin' out you are on sich a night as this!'

"'Why wouldn't he?' says the thing in the corner, takin' the word out o' my mouth; ' what's amiss with the night, Peggy Dempsey ?'

"'Oh, nothin' at all,' says the poor girl, as white as a sheet; ' only we don't like to see father leavin' us to ourselves on a state night. Father, dear, don't—don't go out,' an' she most cryin'.

" Her sister and the boys were near as bad.

"'Nonsense, childer,' says I, mighty sharp, ' don't be makin' fools o' yourselves. I'll be back in a hurry. I'll only take a look at the night an' come in again.'

" Out I started, and when I seen the night was so fine I thought I'd take a stretch across the fields. I don't know how it happened that I made for the ould forth, for I'm sure I didn't intend it. But sure enough my head was full o' my poor Ally, an' I suppose my feet took me to 'ast where she was.

Anyhow, before I knew, I found myself at the head of the whin field close to the forth, an' when I looked up and seen where I was, my heart sank within me, for it was no place to be on Holl' Eve night, of all nights in the year. The best I could do was to bless myself, an' I done that in a great hurry. I was turnin' my back on the rascally ould place, when, what do you think but I heard a noise, like the rockin' of a cradle and a voice singin' soft and low.

" With that my heart rose to my mouth, for I knew the song and the voice too, for all it sounded as if it was down, down in the earth. I was most wild with joy, an' thought I wouldn't care if the whole fairy troop was athin hearin'. So I gave a kind o' little cry an' was for dartin' into the forth. But the voice from within spake out in a whisper—. begorra I thought it was at my elbow: ' Wise men never set foot in Liscarron Forth on Holl' Eve night. It 'id be no use to come in, anyhow. Go home and, the first chance you get, make the sign o' the cross over them, you know. Home, home! there's danger at hand.'

" Well, childer, you may be sure I wasn't long gettin' home—not on account of the danger, for somehow I never thought of it, I was so overjoyed. But I wanted to do what I was bid in regard to the thing at home, for I knew well enough it was her was meant. I thought it was the easiest thing in life to do it, an' the minute I got inside the door I was makin' over to her, sayin' that I wanted my pipe off the hob. My dear, she was on her feet in a jiffy, an' says she:

" ' Keep your distance, ould man, or I'll make you rue it the longest day you have to live. There's your pipe in the jamb hole.'

" Myself was so confounded, I didn't well know what to do. At any rate, I was too much afeard of the hag to slight her warnin'. So I pacified her as well as I could, an' took the cutty an' began to fill it with tobacco, makin' b'lieve I was laughin' all the time. The childer was busy duckin' for apples, so they didn't take any notice of what passed.

" I sat in one corner all the evenin' smokin' my cutty an' the ould hare forenenst me, as quiet as a lamb. But for all that, when she thought I wasn't lookin' she'd throw every eye at myself, that you'd think she wanted to pierce me through. Whiles I thought of makin' a dart over at her and doin' what I had to do. But the least move I made she was on the watch and I didn't half like the look of her fiery red eyes.

" At last the tricks were all over, and the childer began to prepare for bed. The *calliogh* never stirred till the fire was raked, then up she got an' waddled down the room. When she got to the door she half turned round and shook her finger at myself, with a look that made me shiver all over.

" ' Sure enough,' thinks I, ' she knows what's passin' in my mind. I b'lieve I'll not try it this night, anyhow.   I'll take my time an' come on her when she's not thinkin' of it.'

" For two or three days my ould hare and myself kept watchin' one another like two thieves. If I chanced to stir at all, even when I wasn't thinkin' of her, she set herself for me, with her two eyes shinin' like a cat in the dark, an' I declare to you I was afeard as much as to look at her.

" I was jist beginnin' to lose all heart, thinkin' I'd never get doin' what was laid on me, when one night—of all nights in the year it was the third after Holl' Eve—I was lyin' awake about the first cockcrow, thinkin' of Ally an' Tommy an' the poor woman I lost.   The clear frosty moon was shinin' in through the window at the head o' my bed, so that it was most as light as day.   I happened to set my eye on the room door, an' what does I see but it openin' of itself, very soft and aisy.   Well, sure enough I was a little afeard, but I couldn't keep from gettin' up on my elbow to see if there was anything in sight.   Not a thing could I see, but a voice whispered at my very ear: ' Now's your time!   Now or never!'

" I didn't ask who was in it, for the voice was my poor *colleen's*, nor I wasn't the bit daunted. All the fear was gone from me, an' I felt so strong and courageous in myself that I thought I wouldn't fear all the gentry * in the rath afore.

" I knew well enough what the *colleen* wanted,

* This is one of the many conciliatory terms applied to the fairies by the country people,

so up I gets an' down with me to the room t'other side of the kitchen, where the *calliogh* lay. I found that door open before me, too; but still when I got fairly into the room I stopped. Fear came upon me again, an' I felt the hair beginnin' to rise on my head. Still I thought of the warnin' I got, an' I made a step or two to'ast the shakedown on the floor. Not a sound did I hear from it—not as much as a breath; an' I couldn't see it, because it was in a dark corner at the foot of the girl's bed, where the moonlight didn't reach it.

"' Well,' says I to myself, ' it's on me to do it —it's for Ally's sake, an' with God's help I *will* do it. Now or never was the word the *colleen* said.'

" With that I put up my hand an' blessed myself, an' made a dart at the bed, an' made the sign o' the cross over it, though my hand shook like an aspen leaf. Childer, dear, the cry that came from the ould hag, I'll never forget to my dyin' day. It was as if I drove a knife into her heart.

"' O you black-hearted villain,' says she, ' you done it at last, but your luck ' ll be none the better for it. Take her now, an' much good may she do you! Ha! ha! ha!' The laugh was like the laugh of an evil spirit, an' it rung all through the house, an' I hard a noise like the whizzin' of ever so many wings passin' me by. I was most dead with fear, an' couldn't spake a word if it 'id save my life, but as God would have it the girls started up in a fright, and asked;

" ' In the name o' goodness, what noise is that? Father, is it you or your wrath that's in it?'

" ' It's me, childer, dear; don't be afeard, but get up an' light the candle.'

" They did, an' I tould them in the kitchen above what happened. Down we all went to the shake-down in the corner, an' we could hardly b'lieve our eyes when we seen the purty face of our darlin' Ally above the clothes, in place of the weazened ould *calliogh* that was in it at bed-time. At first we were goin' to wake Ally, but she was sleepin' so soundly that we thought it a pity. Well, we said to one another that we'd wait up till she'd waken, for you may be sure none of us could sleep, we were so overjoyed.

" So we got on our clothes, an' the girls lit the fire, an' we sat round it talkin' in whispers of the joyful mornin' we were goin' to have of it. How many things Ally would have to tell us an' we the same with her! We didn't disturb the boys, for we meant to give them a grand surprise in the mornin'. Every now and then some of us stole down on tip-toe to take a look at Ally an' see if she was stirrin'.

" But she wasn't, nor even breathin', though that didn't frighten us, for didn't we often hear of people brought back from the fairies that lay in a trance for hours an' hours. At last the daylight came peepin' into the little room. By degrees the dark corner where Ally lay was dark no longer, an' her face was plain in our sight. But it was a *dead face*, childer! a dead face! white an' cowld an' stiff as marble. The purty brown eyes never opened again, an' the voice that was music to my ears at the dead of night was silent forevermore.

" The ould wasp didn't go without leavin' her sting behind in our broken hearts. It was aisy to see that death was there. Still we wouldn't give up hopes that it might be a trance. So we kept Ally three days before we coffined her. There was no change on her, barrin' for the worse; so we put her in her last house, an' buried her in Kilmarky, longside of her mother. I thought my heart 'id break when I put the last shovelful of earth on her. But it didn't, you see, childer, it didn't. Well for me if it did."

There was dead silence for a few minutes after this. All were anxious to hear the sequel, but no one dared to break in on Shan's solemn musing, as he sat looking dreamily at the blazing turf on the hearth. At last he cleared his throat several times, and rousing himself as if by an effort, he looked round on the group of expectant young faces, with a faint attempt at a smile. " Death was newer to me then than it is now," said poor Shan. " I got well used to it athin the next three years, for by that time I hadn't a child in the world, barrin' Tommy, who was married an' doin' for himself. The boys and the girls dropped off one afther another—'deed they did, childer. They melted away before my eyes like snow off a ditch. The two girls died of decline, one of the boys of a pleurisy he took from a wettin' after a hard day's work, an' the other of a bad fever that was goin' at the time."

" Why, Shan, how did you live at all after them?" cried one of the youthful listeners, a bright, manly boy, his big round eyes dilated with wonder.

" Now, will you b'lieve what I'm goin' to tell you, childer," said Shan, with unusual solemnity, " I didn't feel half as bad about any of them as I did about Ally.   For all the others had the rites of the Church afore their death, glory be to God, an' I knew that their time was come, an' that their Maker was takin' them to Himself, where I'd soon be.   Still I was lonesome enough, you may be sure, especially when the last one went, my youngest boy, an' I found myself alone in the house.

" I might have been far worse. Only a day or two after poor Hugh's funeral Tommy came out to see me, an' brought me lots of tobacco an' tay an' sugar.   He tould me that if I wished, himself an' Jenny—that was his wife—'id come and live with me as soon as ever I liked.   He said it wouldn't answer him so well, on account of business; but still an' all, they'd do it if I wanted, for that Jenny's eyes had never dried since Hugh's death, thinkin' of how lonesome and desolate the ould man must be.

" ' An' you know, father,' he added, ' she's as good a servant as ever laid down two hands, for she lived three years with the mistress athin before we were married. So she'll give you a good bit and sup, an' kape you clean and comfortable. Faith she will, father; she's just the girl can do it,'

" Well, childer! myself can't tell you how overjoyed I was to find so much nature in Tommy and
his wife, an' to think that I'd have them for company an' to take some of the toil of the farm off
my hands.   'Deed I could hardly have been better
pleased if some of the childer were given back to
me from the grave.   An' it was good cause I had
to be joyful.   For afther Tommy and the wife came
home to me I had the life of a lord, a body might
say.

" Sich a son and sich a daughter-in-law as I had
couldn't be found anywhere.   Tommy had left off
his wild tricks altogether, barrin' the bit o' fun that
was in him.   That I didn't want him to get rid of,
for it kep' myself alive.   My dears, he was as sensible as a judge an' never said a word agin religion
as he used to do, an' that pleased me best of all.
He was away from us on the coach about half his
time, but when he was at home I tell you he worked
well.

" As for Jenny, if she was my own born child
she couldn't have done more for me than what she
did.   Not a hard turn of work she'd let me do—
not so much as to bring in a creel of turf; though I
used to do it when her back was turned, for I was
strong enough at the time, an' I'd rayther do it
than see her doin' it.

" Not but what she was abler than I was, for, you
see, she was a fine, strappin' woman, with every leg
an' arm on her so big an' so red that you'd wonder
to see them.   She was a likely girl to be sure, but

there was enough o' her to make two middlin' people.   I never had much *gra*, childer, for big
women, but Jenny was so kind an' good to me I
couldn't but like her.   She never went to fair or
market but she'd have the bit o' tobacco home to
myself, an' maybe some other kindness to the back
o' that.

" It was nothin' with her an' Tommy but 'father,
dear,' at every word, an' neither of them would do
the most triflin' thing without askin' my advice.
Them were happy days, childer, dear," said the
old man with a heavy sigh; " pity they didn't last.

" The only thing that I didn't like in my daughter-
in-law was a way she had of makin' little o' my
poor girls.   To hear her talk you'd think they were
both idle an' wasteful, an' had no care for their ould
father.   Well, this used to sting me to the very
quick, an' many a time I had a hot argument with
Jenny about it.   It was no use tellin' her she was
in the wrong, an' I soon see that she didn't want to
be set right.   At last I used to hould my tongue
an' let her talk on, though my very heart 'id be
tearin' asunder listenin' to what I knew well was
lies.   Still, Jenny was so good to myself that I
couldn't for shame's cause quarrel with her, an'
that's the way we lived together for as much as half
a year.

" I was never done tellin' the neighbors all round
what a treasure of a daughter-in-law I had, an' how
much Tommy was changed for the better.   Some
o' them seen with the same eyes I did myself, an'

they thought I was happy born. Far more o'
them used to shake their heads an' say: ' Wait a
bit, Shan! the big woman didn't take off her
brogues yet.'

" To be sure myself used to be a good bit put
out with them for throwin' a slur on Jenny. Sometimes, when they came out with worse than that,
or said I was too soft for a man of my age, an' that
my eyes 'id be opened some fine mornin', I'd take
it ever so hot, an' vow that I'd never darken their
doors again as long as I lived. The very best friend
I had in the world happened to have the very worst
opinion of my son an' daughter-in-law, an' that
grieved me more than all. I done all I could to
convince him, but. he was a dark, silent man, not
aisy to move from his own notions. All I could
say or do wouldn't bring him to say a soft word o'
them, espaycially Jenny.

" At last he called her a big ' stag ' up to my
very face, an' I couldn't stand that anyhow, so
Tarry an' I fairly quarrelled. For as good as three
months we never opened our lips to one another,
more than biddin' the time o' day, if we chanced to
meet. 'Deed it was ill our comin's, too, to fall
out, for Tarry an' me were no less than double
gossips.

" To make a long story short, childer, one winter's evenin' about a month or two after my quarrel
with Tarry Reilly, Jenny was down in the room
doin' somethin', an' Tommy an' me were settin'
above in the kitchen on either side of the hob.

" ' Father,' says Tommy, ' I'm goin' to say some-thin' to you on a little matter o' business, but mind if you don't like what I have to say, tell me so at onst, and the thing is ended.'

" ' Well, let me hear the word, anyhow, Tommy,' says I, lookin' over at him.

" ' I will,' says he, ' but you must come over near me, for I don't want the woman below to hear me. Do you know what came into my head last night, as I was sittin' on the back seat o' the coach an' it goin' like a bird flyin'?'

" ' Why, then, how would *I* know, Tommy? What was it, *avick?*'

" ' I was thinkin' that the care of the little spot o' ground must be too much for any man at your time of life, with sich a heavy load of trouble on you into the bargain. Says I to myself, wouldn't it be a good plan now if he'd make the house an' place over to me, an' let me give up this stravagin' way of life onst for all, an' stay at home an' mind it. My father then could have a little rest in his ould days.'

" With that up comes Jenny from the room an' say she:

" ' What's that you're sayin' to the ould man, Tommy? If it's in regard to him givin' up the bit o' ground it's what I'll never consent to. He'd find it quare now in the end of his days to be on your floor or mine. Not a word, now, Tommy, not a word. I know what you're going to say, *aroon;* an' to be sure it 'id still be his own floor he'd

be on when he'd be on ours. I know that as well
as you, Tommy, but the ould man doesn't know it.
He'd be afeard—and small blame to him for that
same—that he'd live to rue it. We're all well contented now, an' if you take that situation that was
offered you, Tommy,'—I chanced to look up at
Jenny, an' if my eyes didn't decaive me, she winked
at Tommy— ' if you do, you know, the ould man
can get plenty to come an' kape house for him. So
I tell you, again, don't think of sich a thing as him
givin' up the place to you.'

" Now myself was always aisy led—too aisy, as
poor Molshy—the heavens be her bed!—often tould
me. At first I thought I wouldn't do what Tommy
wanted, if he made a king o' me. But when I seen
Jenny, as I b'lieved, so much agin what was for
their own good, on my account, an' espaycially.
when she made mention of the situation that Tommy
could get, I began to ask myself what would I do
at all if they left me again. Sure there could be
no harm in it afther all, for wouldn't I have aisier
times and a good bit an' sup, as I had ever since
they came here, and besides, they'd be sure to stay
then. There was another notion in my head, too,
an' out it came first.

" ' I'll do it,' says I, dashin' the ashes out o' my
pipe on the hob, ' I'll do it, Tommy, if it was only
to spite Tarry Reilly.'

" ' How is that, father ? ' says Tommy, with his
eyes an' mouth wide open.

" ' Oh, never mind,' says I, ' that's none o' your

business.   I'm obleeged to Jenny for her good wishes in regard to me, but it's not her advice we'll take this time.   We'll go into town the morrow, if God spares us, an' get ould Douglas to make out the writin'.'

"And so we did, childer," said Shan, with rueful gravity.   "We went in on the edge o' our feet, Tommy an' me.   I made the house an' place over to him.   The scrivener wanted me to put in a clause that I'd have my livin' out o' it all my days, but I wouldn't hear o' sich a thing.   So all I had in the world was made over to my son Tommy.   Sure myself thought it a fine thing to get the care o' it off my shoulders.

"For about a week or so everything went on well, an' I seen no change worth spakin' of.   When .Jenny came home from the first market she was out, I got a little glimpse of what was in store for me.   She brought me no tobacco, an' at first I thought she had forgot it.   So I asked her for it, an' its what you'd think she'd bite the nose off me.

"'Where would I get tobacco for you?' says she; 'you gave me nothing to buy it.'

"'Why, Jenny, dear,' says I, 'didn't I give you a half-a-crown the other day to get some for me ?   You mind the day you went to Paddy Markey's shop, you only brought me an ounce, an' never gave me any change.'

"'How sharp we're gettin' all of a sudden!' says she, mighty cross.   'When you want tobacco, go an' buy it; you've less to do than I have.'

" Well, childer, there came a wakeness over me
so that I was ready to drop. I asked Jenny to give
me a drink of water, an' she made as if she didn't
hear me, an' walked away with herself into the
room. So I had to do without the water, an' I got
waker and waker every minute till I thought I was
goin' to die. I didn't. God had greater trials in
store for me, blessed be His name! It 'id be too
long to tell you the treatment I got afther that from
both Tommy and the wife. The good cup o' tay,
the smoke o' tobacco, an' all the good eatin' an'
drinkin' went from me by degrees. The hardest
turns about the house were laid on me, till my very
life was a burthen to me with sorrow an' the height
of hardship.

" The worst of it was that the neighbors had no
pity on me. They all said it was my own fault,
an' that as I made my bed now I must lie. What
do you think, but it was Tarry Reilly had the most
compassion on me, afther all. When at last Jenny
tould me one day to go an' look for my share, as
many a better man had done, an' that they had
enough to do to support themselves an' the child
they had, it was to Tarry's corner I went. Though
I wouldn't be a burthen on him an' his, an' took to
the road as Jenny bid me, I was welcome to the
best bit an' sup they had, an' a bed in the warmest
corner, as often as I chose to go.

" But Tarry died some four or five years agone,
an', *mavrone*, but I lost the good friend when I lost
him. The childer all make me welcome, to be

sure; still, they can never be to me what their father was. For we were gossoons together, an' grown men, ay! an' ould men together too. We had a heart likin' for one another, an' when poverty an' ould age, an' worse than all, the unnatural treatment of my own flesh an' blood, sent me on the *shaugh-ran*, I could never say I wanted a friend as long as Tarry lived.

" His death was another sore crush to me an' a heavy loss, but I got over that, too, like all the rest, thanks be to God that never shuts one door on His poor creatures but He leaves another open. As for Tommy an' his wife, I b'lieve they're not much better off than I am. Though Tommy said he'd give up the coach when he got the farm, he never did for all that. The idle, lazy habits he got about that inn an' them horses he never got over, an' never will. They have a scrawl of young childer about them, so that Jenny can't get much out. So between one thing an' another, nothin' seems to go right with them. The farm is so little use to them that they might as well not have it.

" So, you see, childer, they didn't make much of it afther turnin' out the poor ould man that owned it. Sure, sure, that same's no wonder, for when was a bad undutiful child known to prosper! If they do, it's only for a while. For the curse of the evil-doer is upon the man or woman that shuts their heart agin the father or mother that God put over them."

Reader, this was Shan Dempsey's story, and I

wish I could say that it ended here. The conclud-
ing words of the broken-hearted father were fearfully impressed on the minds of all who heard him
by the sad fate of his unnatural son, who fell from
the top of a coach a year or two after and broke his
neck. He left his wife and children to beg their
bread, as he had driven his father to do before.
The old man did not long survive this most dreadful of all his misfortunes, and in him we lost the
last of our old story-tellers. May his doom be a
warning to all foolishly indulgent parents, and his
story be of interest to the readers. It belongs to
the days

> "When fairies were in fashion
> And the world was in its prime."

ANNA T. SADLIER.

Anna Teresa Sadlier, daughter of Mrs James Sadlier, was born in Montreal, Canada, and was educated chiefly at Villa Maria, the principal Convent of the Congregation de Notre Dame, in that city. Like her mother, she has spent about equal portions of her life in New York and Montreal. She has been a frequent contributor in prose and verse to most of the American Catholic periodicals as well as to some English and Canadian ones. She has written a great many short stories. One of her earliest literary ventures was ''Seven Years and Mair,'' a novelette published by the Harpers in their Half Hour Series. Her principal original published works are '' Names that Live'' and ''Women of Catholicity,'' two volumes of biography. On these Miss

Sadlier spent much labor, but not unavailingly, for they possess no little value from a historical point of view. In two of the sketches which are distinctively American she drew largely from the Jesuit '' Relations '' and the Memoirs of Père Olier, and she had the advantage of access to the annals of the Ursulines of Quebec and of the Congregation of Notre Dame of Montreal. Of her work it may be said as she says of the writings of Marie de l'Incarnation, it possesses '' rare excellence in a literary point of view, and as a historical record is unsurpassed for clearness and accuracy. The style is delicate and *spirituelle*, while forcible and consistent; the work is marked by a keenness of perception, a subtle grasp of points at issue, an attention to detail which is never wearisome, and a breadth of thought embracing the whole extent of what lies before it.'' Her other books are ''Ethel Hamilton'' and ''The King's Page.'' Her translations from the French and Italian include : '' Ubaldo and Irene,'' ''Mathilda of Canossa,'' ''Idols,'' ''The Monk's Pardon,'' '' The Outlaw of Camargue,'' '' The Wonders of Lourdes,'' ''The Old Chest,'' ''Consolations for the Afflicted,'' ''A Thought of the Sacred Heart for Every Day of the Year,'' ''Words of St. Alphonsus,'' '' Lucille, or the Young Flower-Maker,'' ''The Two Brothers,'' '' Augustine, or the Mysterious Beggar,'' ''Ivan, or The Leper's Son,'' '' The Dumb Boy of Fribourg'' and ''The Recluse of Rambouillet.''

Mistress Rosamond Trevor.

*LEAVES FROM THE JOURNAL OF THE ABOVE
LADY, BEING A NARRATIVE OF CERTAIN
EVENTS IN THE COLONIES OF MARYLAND.*

BY ANNA T. SADLIER.

*The Fifteenth Day of June, in the Year of Our
Lord* 1644.—I marvel much if my father did, indeed, regret that day of St. Cecilia, in the year
of 1633, upon which he set sail for these shores.
My mother declared that he wept bitter tears on
passing the castle of Yarmouth, overhung by
November mists.   Excessive the grief which could
draw tears from eyes habitually cold and stern.
Perchance time hath wrought a change.   A youthful portrait showeth him, light of heart, buoyant
of spirit, as Philip himself.

Philip!   It is a pretty name.   How deeply did
he carve it upon the oak!   Above it mine—Rosamond! " Rose of the World," he said.   How wondrous are those oaks, " standing since the world
was young!" as sayeth our dear, dear Father White.
Yet I am wroth with him because of the confusion
into which he threw me at table yester e'en.

" If God and my superiors so will," he said, " I shall stay yet awhile at St. Mary's. I, who christened Mistress Rosamond, and have otherwise ministered unto her, must needs officiate upon a certain happy occasion. What say you, Philip ? "

" In truth, your Reverence," began Philip.

But the dessert being ended, I fled, first curtsying to his Reverence and to my father.

My father, methought, looked graver than his wont. This jesting recalleth, perchance, that it was Father White who married him in England, and christened me some eight years before the departure for these countries. Hence in my eighteenth year I take this journal for my confidante, recording the petty events of my daily life. How solemn the thought of my beauteous mother, dead long-since! Often do I stand before her picture painted in wedding finery. Her eyes would seem to question that adventurous, hazardous future into which she was going unawares. Dare I look forward? Shall the years, too, transform my Philip? But, no—the thought is monstrous.

His countenance becomes illumined as he discourses with Father White upon the conversion of these pagan Indians. I am, in sooth, more in terror of these hideous, painted beings, notably the Susquehannas, than I am solicitous for their souls. This is paltry. Even Philip hath so declared it. What noble plans he has against the time he shall have made his fortune. I must be worthy of these noble souls, amongst whom my lot is cast. I must

aid in this holy work of conversion. Yet I tremble at sight of these grim chiefs, streaked with red
and yellow, feathers upon their head, and a fish of
copper or other metal upon their brow. It is sad
to reflect that these beings, created by the most
high God, should worship corn and fire, and invoke
an evil spirit whom they call Ochre. At least I
can pray for them.

The Twenty-seventh Day of the Month of June.
—At eighteen should not one be grave and circum-
spect ? Yet have I confession of folly to make.
Last night a ball was given by his Excellency,
Governor Leonard Calvert. It was surpassing
beautiful. Gay uniforms, rich costumes. Those
splendid gentlemen were most kind to me, no doubt
for my father's sake, who is in high repute amongst
them. His Excellency spoke first of my father's
high services and next of my auburn ringlets and
the pearl necklace, out of which he made a most
graceful comparison. My heart, I confess with
shame, was more pleasurably moved by these
praises than betimes it is when Philip speaks of
higher things. And if the blossom of vanity be
sweet, the fruit thereof is exceeding bitter. Hence
arose my first quarrel with Philip. Repeating to
him certain fine phrases of one Captain Evelyn concerning my foot in its high-heeled slipper, Philip,
flushing, laid his hand upon his sword. Unsuspect-
ing I added, thinking to please him, the pretty
compliments of our Governor. I further remarked
that it was passing strange that a man of such fine

parts as his Excellency should have grown old unmarried.

"Perchance he showeth therein his customary wisdom," said Philip, in a tone which I had never before heard. "Moreover my lord Leonard Calvert is not old, but still much in request as a cavalier."

"He is most fair of speech," I said; whereat Philip's anger broke forth, and he accused me of being overfond of the commendations of strangers.

"It is but a vain coquette who seeketh praise from all men," he cried.

Whereat my spirit being aroused, I retorted that I was no coquette, and that perchance he was too sparing of such commendations. At this moment Captain Evelyn offered me his hand for the dance. After which I spoke no more with Philip, but went home in much sadness and vexation of mind.

This morning after Mass I received a brief note from Philip, worded thus:

"My Rose of the World, forgive me. Greatly have I misdemeaned myself in rudeness of speech to you. Write, I do beseech you, to assure me that your gentle spirit bears no malice."

I penned a tiny epistle and despatched it to

The Most Honorable Philip Fairfax,
Gentleman, at the Island of St. George.

He is gone thither for a short period with some officers. He is a St. George himself, so brave, so excellent, and so zealous for the conversion of the savages.   Last night I prayed to be worthy of him, and I laid the string of pearls at Our Lady's feet.

How thoughts jostle each other with scant ceremony in one's mind.   Great was the divine goodness in saving the vessels which brought thither my father and the other colonists, all men of fortune, high lineage, and professing our holy Catholic faith. It being the anniversary of St. Clement, the name of that Saint was given to the island where a landing was first effected.   Possession was taken " in the name of Our Saviour and for our Sovereign Lord the King of England."

After solemn Mass our own Father White with his companions, and aided by his Excellency Governor Calvert, took upon their shoulders a huge cross, which they carried to some distance and set up.   The devout assemblage, kneeling, recited the Litanies of the Cross.   Truly were they mindful of the saying of the Lord Cecil Baltimore, " that his first and most important design, which should also be the aim of all who go to these shores, is not to think so much of planting fruits and trees in a land so fruitful, as of sowing the seeds of religion and piety."

Like a page from the annals of the first Christians was that celebration of the most blessed festival of the Annunciation, 1634.

The Twenty-first Day of the Month of July, Present Year.—To-day I shall be busy.   Gooseberries, plums, and mulberries have been gathered from the woods, to be made into compotes and confections of

many sorts.   Adelaide has likewise a store of gums
and balsams for the preparation of plasters, unguents, and perfumes.   She declares that I must be
initiated into those arts which it behooves a woman
to know before departing from my father's house
to govern a household elsewhere.   When I argue
that time presses not, she but rebukes me for my
levity.

" When he whom the Lord hath appointed hath
his dwelling in readiness, thither must you go," she
says, " to do your appointed work."

She positively affrighteth me.   She should have
been a heretic of the colonies of New England—
which indeed she hath been until converted by
Father White.   I opine that, being a Dissenter,
she fled thither to escape persecution, but of this
she speaks no word.   Duty is her idol.   Imagination she scarce knows by name.   How wroth was
she that I should strive to catch the sunlight falling
through the linden on the casement!   I affected to
believe it gold.   Little knows she what romances I
steal into unguent pots or seal up in pickle jars.

Wondrous skilful is she in all household matters.
But now she has brought to completion a wine
thick as oil, concocted of berries from the neighboring wood.   What homilies she reads me as I stand
by her side in the store-room!   Philip may have
cause to bless her if I profit by her teaching.   Pre-
paring these mulberries, I bethink me that Philip
proposes to cultivate mulberry-trees for the feeding
of silkworms near the manor he is building on

land bestowed by the king. He fancies it may become a lucrative industry. My father shakes his head, but who knows ?

The Nineteenth Day of the Month of August.— After the middle day repast yesterday I stole into the woods adjoining. It was a veritable stealing, for Philip declares that wild beasts are in its depths, and Adelaide with sour looks cries out that it beseems not a maiden to go thus far unattended. Excellent soul! I would not for a kingdom's wealth that she accompanied me with homilies and texts for each tree and clump of moss. She can flatter, this grim Adelaide, betimes. Last evening she declared to Philip that the Lord till His good time was reserving for the honored Master Fairfax the treasure of a good housewife.

" My claim," cried I, " rests upon little better foundation than some skill in peach conserving."

" Sweetness," returned Philip, " is a safe basis for a life's happiness."

" It may cloy," I said gravely, " as confections do ferment."

" Nay, and the peaches be sound and sugar without alloy ? " said Philip. Whereat I cried:

" To drop metaphor, what nature is without alloy? Not mine, good sooth. I know not if bitterness would not best preserve me."

" Sunshine purifies! " laughed Philip.

" Can its rays dispel the mists of vanity ? " I said, " for strong within me is the desire to seem fair.

Looking upon my mother's portrait, I would fain
be as comely.''

'' All brides are fair,'' said Philip; '' so perchance—''

But I fled around the dairy wall, for Philip's eyes
were full of laughter. How sweetly the blackbird
sang above our heads, my love and I. Peradven-
ture it was the same bird I heard in the fir-trees.
I love those sombre firs, with strange whisperings
as of some we see not. In the silence and mystery
of the woods one's better self is uppermost. Perchance the soul responds to the touch of solitude.
Beautiful are the oaks, larches, and cypresses
touched by the sun. Philip tells me that ships will
be built some day from this same timber, and will
help him to grow rich. He is rich enough, and how
full of schemes for the hereafter! The very word
makes me to sigh unreasonably. But Father White
will endure no sighs. '' Joy, cheerfulness, hope are
the Christian's heritage,'' he says. '' The shadow
of the cross should banish other shadows.''

The Fourteenth Day of the Month of September.—
Philip hath been away for a fortnight on some
military expedition with the Governor. Trouble is
ever impending at Kent Island, from the wiles of
one Master Claiborne, the evil genius of this colony.
Kent Island is sixty miles hence—but a step to the
voyages he has taken, declares my father. To me
it seems so far. There is comfort in the reflection
that thought can bridge unmeasured distance. On
laying by my trinkets in the jewel case I bethought

me of the hopes entertained by Philip and others, that gold and gems should be found in these countries.

This belief is occasioned by the native men and women decking themselves with articles of un- wrought gold and strings of pearls—indubitable proof that such are found here. How proud shall I be of an ornament made from Philip's mines! Such is the glory of a new country. One never knows. There is room for hope and endeavor.

Twentieth Day of the Month of September.—Oh, joy! Philip hath returned. This evening Adelaide permitted me an hour's walk with him in the elm avenue. My heart sang like a thrush, though our discourse was mostly of sober tone. I knew full well it was with no vulgar boastfulness that Philip, in speaking of the origin of these colonies, said, with the air of pride that so well becomes him:

" They were all gentlemen, Rosamond, in fortune and lineage; but they were more—they were con- fessors of the faith."

" They came thither," he added, " to worship God in freedom and bring truth to these aborigines My lord Cæcilius Baltimore might well exclaim that the English nation, renowned for so many ancient victories, never undertook anything more noble than this. For it is the work of Christ, the King of Glory."

" A noble character that of my Lord Baltimore, our *Pater Patriæ*," I said.

" No less noble is our Governor," said Philip,

with a smile, " though he should write sonnets to auburn ringlets."

Philip, noting my confusion, turned to sober themes again.

" Here they have made asylum, not alone for those of our faith, but for the oppressed of every creed and race. These shores have been made the refuge from intolerance, always through the good counsels of their Reverences."

" Our good and gentle Jesuits," I said, eagerly.

" Say rather our high-hearted and whole-souled Jesuits," said Philip, who had been a student with the Society for years. " You will join me in the sentiment, sweetheart, God bless the Jesuits; for what should these poor colonies of Maryland have been without them ? "

" From my heart, Philip, God's blessing on the Jesuits!"

We fell to discussing the incidents which befell " The Ark " and " The Dove " on their voyage thither, accompanied for many miles upon the high seas by the good ship " Dragon." How the portentous sunfish gave token of the storm, during which " the Dragon " parted company with them and walked no more upon the deep.

" A brave sight must it have been," I said, " when those brave men knelt to receive holy absolution from the Fathers. After which, Father White, turning aside in prayer, besought the Divine Master to remember that for the honor of His name this expedition had set forth. Scarce was his prayer concluded when the storm ceased. How beautiful must have been the sunlight which followed!

" Our exiled hearts recked little of beauty," said my father's voice coldly and so suddenly that I started. " We gave God thanks, in truth, but with the resolution of servants doing a Master's will, thankful for sunlight, prepared to buffet storms. Child, you speak of what you know not. Better beseems you the knowledge of pasties and needle-work. Philip, lad, you may mar a promising house-wife. Let not a woman's mind run riot on serious themes, or your pasties will be of lead and your hose unmended."

Cold and scornful as were tone and words, I knew they came not from the heart, which conceals its high purposes under such an exterior. My father hath had many a stern experience. When my father had left us Philip took my hand.

" Sweetheart," he said, " we men, though of rude exterior, sympathize more than might appear."

" Alas for all womankind were it not so," I said; " sympathy is our life. Failing it, God's grace alone keeps us from growing hard."

" Let sympathy and trust be our mutual aim," said Philip, and solemnly we made the pledge.

" Good night, Rosamond."

" Good night, Philip."

Our voices died with the twitter from the nest in the laurel-tree which alone broke the stillness of coming night. Philip, watching till I had gained the stone steps, waved farewell. Adelaide, who had called me divers times from the casement, rebuked me, saying:

" The Lord loveth a prompt and cheerful spirit, quick to obey."

" A cheerful spirit am I, Adelaide," I said, full of happiness.

" The Lord keep you so," said Adelaide.

To which I responded heartily, " Amen."

In the corridor I encountered my father. To my amazement he detained me.

" I grieve," he said, " if I have broken in but harshly on thy pretty foolishness. Keep the spring while it is yours, lest winter come in dreariness excessive."

Never had I beheld him so moved, but at supper his countenance was once more impassive.

" At eighteen one is of necessity an egotist," he said to Master Gerard, who sat beside him; " for women this feeling perchance hinders them from meddling in concerns beyond them."

Perchance I am an egotist in my love and happiness. Our Lady guard me from the fault.

Twenty-sixth Day of the Month of September.— Sympathy is founded on a true understanding. Therefore do I make such study of the history of these countries as enables me to enter into Philip's feelings. From a manuscript loaned me by Father White, I learned that the most noble George, Baron Baltimore, sought in the colony of Virginia asylum for those of his faith. So sorry was his reception, that he was fain to turn northwards to the Bay of Chesapeake. An oath was tendered him denying the spiritual supremacy of the Pope, which that brave gentleman rejected with scorn. He procured grants from the king, and set about the work of colonizing. But it was his son, the Lord Cæcilius, who completed such arrangements, and sent thither the Most Honorable Leonard Calvert, with his brother George, with Masters Hawley and Cornwallis, and many more brave spirits, guided by three Fathers of the Company of Jesus.

No human creature was wronged by the advent of these worthy pioneers. The savages were most fairly compensated for their lands, from which they had previously resolved to depart, in terror of the formidable Susquehannas. When the great chief Archihu heard from Fathers White and Altham of their mission of peace, he said:

"It is well. We will eat at the same table. My people shall hunt for you, and we shall have all things in common."

In our settlement of St. Mary's, one mile's distance from the river of the Potomac, each man was accounted free to worship God as he desired. Error was tolerated side by side with truth, as chaff amongst the wheat, God winnowing in His own good time.

So this Maryland had its origin in peace and good will to all men.

The Twenty-eighth Day of September.—We sat at dinner to-day to the number of forty, a somewhat motley assemblage. His Excellency gave me his hand to the dinner-table, uttering many pleasant speeches during the repast. Masters Cornwallis and Hawley and other friends were mingled with two Swedes from the Province of Pilaware or Delaware, a Quaker from the Hampshire colonies, three Anabaptists, and other Dissenters from the English of Virginia. All were of a certain distinction, having fled to our colonies through persecution. They are worthy of respect and sympathy, for though we hold them in error, they have suffered much for conscience. Alas! could our Catholic charity and toleration for our neighbor but spread through these countries!

Near my father sat a huge man, discoursing in a big voice across the table to Father White, who regarded him with kindly interest.

"He is mayhap somewhat over-forward in relating all that hath befallen him for conscience' sake," I whispered to Master Cornwallis, who sat upon my left.

"I discover in him a resemblance to the son of Saul," said he, as he broke some filberts to lay upon my plate.

"Wherefore?" asked I, surprised; for scriptural quotation, save with such as Adelaide, is not in vogue amongst our people.

"Because he hath never trimmed his beard nor washed his garments."

I was forced to laugh, though I misliked the jest as savoring of discourtesy to a guest at our table.

For the laws of hospitality, observed with so much punctilio in our Maryland, are doubly binding where these exiles are concerned. Our Maryland gentlemen do vie with each other in good offices to them.

The Second Day of the Month of October.—A day of mingled bitter and pleasant flavor. Father White departs to dwell amongst the Indian tribes one hundred and twenty miles distant. Father Fisher will be superior, aided by others from England. For, in addition to the conversion of the Indians, many heretics have renounced their errors and embraced the faith. Divers others attend our Catholic sermons.

Adelaide and I proceeded early to the dwelling of the Fathers. She brought with her some excellent butter and a batch or two of bread, all of her making, with other delicacies. These shall be stored, with cheese, corn, beans, and flour, in a small chest. Another shall contain essentials for the Mass, and holy water for Baptism. The missionaries go provided, too, with trifling objects, such as bells, needles, combs, to please the natives. I laughed heartily, picturing those great, solemn chiefs, whom I so dreaded, receiving with pleasure these infantile gifts. Adelaide would have been scandalized at my levity had not Father White joined heartily in my mirth. He likewise showed me a tent to serve as sleeping-place, and a table to be an altar. I shuddered as I thought of the perils to which this beloved friend would be exposed. Adelaide having not yet completed her preparations, and my father being absent from home, we remained to supper, Adelaide attending me as I drank my tea from a coarse earthen cup. To her chagrin I performed a like office for her.

Philip came later to make his farewells to Father White. How delightful the half-hour we spent in the study, though my heart was heavy at thought of our dear Father's departure! But sorrow cannot last in his presence: he smiles it away. He said beautiful things to Philip and me of our future lives and of the good we might accomplish in these colonies. The windows were open, for the air was warm, and the light of the moon poured in, forming a halo around that fine head as he spoke.

" I shall be bodily amongst you often," he said, " as ever in spirit. My ministry will necessitate visits to St. Mary's. If duty permits, in due season I shall be here to give Rosamond to you, Philip. At your side she will play the part of one of those bright spirits whose feast we keep to-day. And with happy confidence I shall know, Philip, that you are worthy of the trust."

After a time Philip inquired as to the reports concerning the chief Tayac, for it was to his country that Father White was bound. The latter replied that, as far as human judgment can be trusted in such matters, the tale was worthy of credence.

" Tayac was vouchsafed a dream, which has conduced to his conversion," he said. " In it he beheld Father Gravener and my unworthy self, no doubt as superior of our house. Both were in company with a stranger of rare beauty, clad in snow-white garments."

We fell to talking of a similar vision vouchsafed to one Unwanno, who beheld the selfsame Fathers, and heard a voice declaring that they loved the tribes and would bring them blessings.

"Who can inquire into the mysteries of the Most High?" said Father White, looking towards the moonlit sky as for solution of the problem. "Who dare say whether such things be His manifestation or a trick of the senses?"

Our minds were diverted by the appearance of the other Fathers, all of whom joined with Father White and ourselves in jest and laughter—a rebuke to all the Puritanism of the world.

As Philip and I went homeward, saddened and yet calmed by the influence of that happy presence we had left, the moon shone exceeding bright upon the distant Potomac—Altomeck the savages style it; the Fathers have rechristened it St. Mary's. The islands which they met they named for Our Lady, St. Clement, St. Catherine, St. Cecilia, St. George. The promontory jutting into the Potomac was christened St. Michael. As the descending sun of evening falls thereon, one might fancy that mighty spirit standing there, clad in shining armor.

The Tenth Day of the Month of October.—Our interest—that is, Philip's and mine—had been awakened of late in one employed as my father's secretary. Philip declares that, my father consenting, this Master Gerard shall be overseer of the new domain. A sad story, but great grace hath compensated him for much evil. He is of gentle birth and breeding. In England he squandered a fortune. Adelaide compares him to the prodigal son.

" He hath spent his substance in riotous living," she says, " wherefore the Lord afflicted him. For the riches of the unjust shall be dried as a river."

However it be, he was constrained to sell himself into bondage amongst the English of Virginia. He was ransomed by the Fathers and afterwards became a Catholic. So great is his fervor that it edifies all who observe him, especially during Mass. His countenance is sad, but uncommon peaceful. Perchance is he happier than in prosperous days, though it is sad to be severed from home and kindred. He has much skill in music, and is an adept at arms. Amongst our serving people are two likewise delivered from bondage and professing the Catholic faith. Adelaide treats them with much respect as " the Lord's freedmen."

Fifth Day of November.—Ill tidings have come. Father Gravener, having had a relapse of fever, has perished amongst the Indians. I pray earnestly for his soul. God grant him sweet rest after his toils for the kingdom of God. Father White is likewise stricken with that pestilent disease, but is in a way to recovery. How deplorable, when the Indian harvest fields lie so white!

" Perchance it is not yet God's time. Blessed be His name," observed Father Fisher tranquilly.

First Day of December.—Little have I said in these pages of troubles with the neighboring colonies of Virginia, and with one Master Claiborne, before mentioned, who lays claim to the territory of Kent Island, despite the pleasure of our sovereign lord the king. My Lord Baltimore has had to chastise his insolence and quell disturbances arising through his arts. Religious rancor has of late arisen, and upon this blessed soil, which we of the Catholic faith would have made free to all, must ourselves suffer the bitterness of persecution. Rumors of trouble are rife. Peace has been the calm before a storm. My father looks disturbed. Father White is visiting St. Mary's—welcome as the dove to the ark.

Second Day of the Month of December.—At a late hour Fathers White and Fisher arrived, proceeding to my father's study. I marvelled at so late a visit. Their Reverences departed speedily, engaged in anxious converse with my father, even to the very door. He has ridden forth, though it be close upon midnight. I am full of forebodings.

Fifth Day of the Month of December.—Early on the third day of the present month Philip brought tidings that, after an attack upon St. Mary's by the colonists of Virginia, our Governor and others had surrendered themselves upon conditions which were already violated. Three brave gentlemen have already suffered death. My father is at large, though he was in attendance upon the Governor. Philip rode away with Master Gerard. We have passed a day of terror and suspense. As the hour of ten struck from the timepiece in the hall, the sound of galloping hoofs reached us. Each nerve within me vibrated. My senses were on the alert to a painful degree, my eyes starting from their sockets.

" Though armies assail me I shall not fear," muttered Adelaide, " for the Lord is my strength, my helper and deliverer."

She stood in the great hall, a lantern raised above her head. I, fearing the very shadows upon the armor or warlike implements, crept close to her side. The knocker was sounded with vehement haste.

" Deliver us, O Lord, from the hand of the wicked," cried Adelaide, " and from our fear."

As the knocking continued, she opened a small panel in the door, saying:

" If the Lord hath sent you, make yourself known to His servants."

" Open, open, without delay," cried my father's voice.

The command was joyfully obeyed. He entered with Philip, Master Gerard, some servants, and two gentlemen closely muffled, whom I presently recognized as Fathers White and Fisher. Their countenances of wondrous serenity were in strong contrast to the flushed and wrathful ones of my father and the others.

" Adelaide," said my father, " prepare instantly such food as may be taken upon a journey. Master

Gerard, see that horses be in readiness. Your Reverences be seated and partake of some refreshment. In an hour's time we ride for our lives to the frontier.''

'' We must indeed go into hiding for the moment,'' said Father White, '' but personal considerations cannot permit us to be long absent from our work.'' He added smilingly, '' Nor must we needlessly terrify our little Rosamond. With our dear Lord's aid all will be well, and for His greater glory.''

Their Reverences riding forth supperless, Father White still feeble from fever, were accompanied by my father. He peremptorily ordered Philip and Master Gerard to remain.

'' Need may arise,'' he said; '' the town is in sore confusion. The dwellings of all Catholics are menaced.''

I wrung my hands in anguish of spirit, whilst Philip secured and barricaded the house—that peaceful dwelling which my father had erected on coming to the colony.

'' Alas! '' thought I, '' when we heard of like doings in neighboring colonies, how little did we guess it would so soon be our own case!''

Philip having completed arrangements, counselled me to seek shelter in a retired part of the house.

'' In the hour of peril you shall not banish me,'' I said.

'' I am but a poor commander if so youthful a soldier proves contumacious,'' said Philip, smiling.

" Command what you will, so that it be not to leave you," I said; " my place is at your side now and forever."

I had never spoken so boldly. I read in Philip's face his pleasure at my words, though Adelaide reproved me for overforwardness of speech.

Philip beguiled the time by relating the events of the evening. Sad havoc had been wrought with the Fathers' dwelling. Their furniture and books had been destroyed.

When the moment had come for flight, an attack was made by some Catholic gentlemen at the farthest side of the house, to divert the attention of the assailants. Meanwhile my father and Philip stood ready with horses for the Fathers to mount. The feint being unsuccessful, a certain number of the enemy remaining before the dwelling, Master Gerard stationed himself in the doorway, crying that he desired to encounter the caitiff crew single-handed. Having thus drawn attention upon himself, the Fathers were enabled to depart, though with much reluctance. Philip declared that they feared lest life or limb should be lost for their preservation. My father at length threatened to convey them thence by force.

The mob meanwhile clamored against " impostors," " false teachers," yet how deeply are these very heretics beholden to these ecclesiastics; and as to their meddling with state concerns, often have I heard my father relate that Fathers White and Altham refused a seat in the first colonial assembly of Maryland, praying to be excused from taking part in secular affairs.

" How base, how cruel the ingratitude!" cried I.

" It is infamous," said Philip; " I shall shake the dust of our Maryland from my feet if she do not teach them a lesson."

" The Lord hath permitted that His anointed be tried in the crucible, as gold in the fire," said Adelaide. Her cheeks were wet with the first tears I had ever seen there. I could not refrain from embracing her, to her confusion, in presence of the honored Master Fairfax.

" I pray you, hold my young lady excused," she said; " her heart is ever greater than her judgment."

" A small fault in a prospective bride," said Philip.

But I was too heavy-hearted to note his speech or the smile accompanying it.

Sounds of strife began to reach us with terrifying distinctness. Our discourse ceased, save for whispered conferences between Philip and Master Gerard, who, heavily armed, grimly awaited events. How careworn his countenance beside the open, joyous one of Philip! Sad and stern his expression. This came to me afterwards. I could but sit with clasped hands, praying silently. Adelaide in a loud voice repeated psalms and versicles from Holy Writ. During that harrowing night musket-shots were fired about our dwelling, with shouts and maledictions:

" Down with the traitor, the friend of lying

priests! Burn his dwelling. Perchance the pestilent Mass-mongers are within."

Thundering knocks sounded upon the door, with cries of " Open, or we burst it! "

" That oak was not grown in Virginia, caitiffs! " cried Master Gerard through a loophole, wherein he had placed his musket. A storm of blows fell upon the door. Glass was shivered by musket-shots. I sat with covered face, praying, oh, how earnestly!

Master Gerard and Philip used their rifles with good effect, as did the servants above; but as the cries of " Burn the nest of traitors! " became more frequent, Philip resolved to make terms with those outside. To this was Master Gerard resolutely opposed, his blood being up.

" You shall enter and search," said Philip,— " no priests are here,—provided you commit no violence."

" No dictation of terms," said a voice.

" Then stay without," cried Master Gerard furiously, " and let incendiaries look to it. Herein are soldiers who will open so deadly a fire that Virginia shall be filled with widows."

Terms were, however, agreed upon, Philip recalling my father's great credit with our lord the king, which was the reason the house had not been sooner fired. During the search, which Philip conducted in person, four stragglers, evidently intoxicated, reached the distant room whither Adelaide and I had retired. I should have swooned away in fright,

for, despite the expostulations of Adelaide, they
were determined to venture upon obtrusive pleas-
antries with me. Suddenly a powerful blow struck
down the foremost ruffian. Master Gerard, of
deadly pallor, his eyes aglow with anger, cried:

" You hounds, had I a whip at hand, I should
teach you how a gentleman keeps his kennels." In
an instant he was at bay against four brutal assailants. Adelaide drew me forcibly away. Later I
saw her tying up an ugly wound in my defender's
arm. He only smiled when I wept at sight of the
thrust, saying with a courtier's grace:

" In some causes wounds are sweet."

By morning his manners had resumed their
wonted quietude. None could guess how brave,
how impetuous he is.

The Nineteenth Day of the Month of December.—
Our beloved Fathers have contrived to get over the
frontier, where they have taken shelter in a species
of cistern. Philip and Master Gerard convey pro-
visions to them by night, and are loud in commendation of their courage and patience. Now it is a
jest at their sorry shelter or foodless state, which
often continues for hours. Even when they return
to their missionary labors, the small sum sent for
their maintenance being intercepted, they will have
no guides through the trackless forests. Most grievous do they esteem it to have no wine for the Holy
Sacrifice.

My father declares that henceforth there will be
no certainty of peace for persons of our faith. I

account it glorious to suffer in that cause, if God willeth. He can give strength to our weakness. Yet is my nature enamored of sweetness and light. Should a bird twitter in yon elm, or a rose burst into bloom in the garden, I should be filled with a thousand dreamy fancies. While winter lasts it is impossible. Therefore let me dwell upon reality.

The Thirtieth Day of April in the Year of Our Lord 1645.—I have had no courage to write down my feelings or fancies since that grievous time when our dear and saintly Fathers while on an apostolic mission to the tribes were seized, loaded with irons, and sent over seas. This was done under an iniquitous law concerning "Missionary Popish Priests." My tears flow as I write; a word serves to awaken the grief and indignation of Philip and my father. I feel that we shall see our Father White in Maryland no more, even if he bears up under hardships and indignities. Alas that this should befall him upon that free soil, where his own wise counsels of forbearance and toleration did so happily prevail while Catholics were in the ascendant! God grant us grace to pray for our enemies.

"There is but one weapon to be employed— prayer," was Father White's last counsel to his friends. My Lord Baltimore is righteously indignant and, it is said, will seek redress at the throne. But it will not make good our loss.

The Third Day of the Month of August.—Save for a disturbance upon St. Ignatius' Day, peace has been unbroken. Our Catholic citizens did desire to celebrate the patronal feast of the college by fire-works and discharge of artillery. A party of evil-disposed Englishmen from a neighboring fortalice attacked the dwellings of our Catholic gentry, much damage being done. Our own was once more defended by Philip, Master Gerard, and my father. My father received a wound in the sword arm, which being hastily dressed by Adelaide, he seized his weapon in his left hand and returned to the attack. Philip had like to have perished but for the timely intervention of Master Gerard, whom I shall always love. Surely never was home defended by more gallant gentlemen.

The Eighth Day of September. Feast of Our Lady's Nativity.—Peace hath returned. All upon Kent Island have taken the oath of fealty to my Lord Baltimore, who has appointed Sir Robert Vaughn military governor there. Peace! how sweet after long disquiet! The sun lies upon the lawn, as a loving hand stretched in benediction over the spot, for sake of those who walked thereon, but shall walk this earth no more. These troubles in-clined my naturally light heart towards melancholy. Father White's superiors have refused him permis-sion to return, despite his desire. How I should rejoice to see him stand once more, a venerable figure, in cassock and beads, under the oaks he loved so well!

The Ninth Day of September.—In the dusk I could perceive the red roof of Philip's house, soon to be mine. It is a solemn thought. I, Rosamond

Trevor, shall leave this home which has been mine since early childhood, and that before the festival of Christmas. To me all change is unutterably sad, though I must not let Philip divine my thoughts. I shall even look upon the brighter side. How wondrous it will be to come and go without hindrance from Adelaide, and to give my orders and have in safe keeping a bunch of keys. There is a strange fascination in that bit of roof outlined against the sky and shadowed by an elm.

I shall miss old Adelaide, though she were severe betimes. And my father would seem to grow less stern. Yestere'en he laid a caressing hand upon my hair, saying that I grew like my mother. Father White declared that he " was one of the noblest-hearted gentlemen in St. Mary's." Soon must I bid farewell to many a familiar spot: my bed of heart's-ease, planted when I first saw Philip; the carnations that we tended together, the robin's nest which he saved from destruction; and the elm avenue, where Philip first spoke of love. Then there is the confection-room, where Adelaide taught me housewifery. It overlooks the stone court whence Philip used to peep at me bedabbled with flour, or anointed with the unguents I was engaged upon.

Lastly, I shall say good-bye to my mother's portrait. I shall stand before it in my wedding-dress, with pearls about my throat. I shall look into her silent eyes, seeking to read her thoughts, and from the shadow of her presence go forth over the threshold into the new life.

Philip is approaching. How handsome and noble he is! My sad thoughts fly at his approach. I must put my whole heart into his hopes and aspirations to make them mine. How comical Adelaide looks with her cap askew upon her head as she gravely cites to Master Gerard, in yonder casement, a text against the pursuance of warfare as a profession! As if *he* could be other than a soldier!

From that day ends the journal of Mistress Rosamond Trevor, but mention occurs of her at a banquet given to " His Most Honorable Excellency," Leonard Calvert, Governor of Maryland. At the head of the table presided the beautiful and gracious Mistress Fairfax, who had been of late given in marriage to the most honored gentleman Master Philip Fairfax. This was in the manorhouse erected upon the lands granted in perpetuity to Master Fairfax by the king's highness.

JOHN TALBOT SMITH.

Rev. John Talbot Smith is an original, forceful writer who has selected as the scene of his many stories the mountain towns bordering on Canada, with their rough, uncultivated men and women as his characters. No more picturesque people is to be found in New England and New York than the French Canadian with his happy disposition, his wife, a model of thrift inherited with her French blood, his large family, his church, and national feasts. Diametrically opposite to him in character and mode of life is his Irish-American neighbor, his enemy at first, but subsequently his friend and later his relative by marriage. From a long acquaintance with these people Father Smith has learned to know them intimately, not only from daily association, but through his priestly relations. He has studied them and describes them, their life and their surroundings, with wonderful fidelity.

Father Smith was born at Saratoga, New York, in 1855. He went to the Christian Brothers' school in Albany, and made his classical and seminary course at St. Michael's College, with the Basilians at Toronto. He was ordained in 1881, and appointed curate in a little mission on Lake Champlain, where he laid in the backgrounds of romantic scenery and the characters to be found in his stories. In 1883 he was made pastor in Rouse's Point, and subsequently held an official office in the diocese of Ogdensburg. On the death of P. V. Hickey, the editor and founder of *The Catholic Review*, Father Smith became editor of that paper, a position he filled for nearly three years; as a journalist he was masterful and brilliant, but perhaps too independent in his ideas and his expression of them. Since his retirement from journalism he has lived in New York as chaplain to the Sisters of Mercy on Madison Avenue, and has devoted himself entirely to literature and journalism. He contributes to the daily papers and to the magazines, and at regular intervals produces a volume of fiction or more serious matter. His published works are: "A Woman of Culture," "Solitary Island," "His Honor the Mayor," "Saranac," "The Prairie Boy," "History of the Diocese of Ogdensburg," and "Our Seminaries," an essay on the training of young men for the priesthood.

The Baron of Cherubusco.

BY JOHN TALBOT SMITH.

IN some doubtful, untraced way history has left
upon me the impression that a baron of the early
ages when barons began to be was a hard, tyrannical,
ignorant man, who drank great quantities of spirits,
beat his wife and his daughters, was envious of his
growing sons, had a few streaks of generosity in
him, and, above all things, hated and oppressed the
poor. Whether the ancient average of barons justi-
fied this impression I have not yet had time to
discover. So much that was history twenty years
ago has since become fable, that he would be an im-
prudent man who would venture to defend the historical impressions of his youth before examining
the latest authorities; but I always acted on the
impression when speaking or thinking of Mr. Turnham of Cherubusco, the principal citizen of our
village, and the gracious friend who had appointed
me, a struggling lawyer and a pugnacious Catholic,
to the position of town-clerk. It was not a very
high distinction, to be sure, to be principal citizen
of Cherubusco—a hybrid, nondescript village on
Lake Champlain; but to the people who dwelt there

it was a deeply interesting position, and had a considerable deal to do with their personal comfort, occasionally also with their material prosperity; and it was one reason why I looked upon my patron as a modern type of ancient baron that he made the common people of the town as miserable as possible when the fit seized him, and sold them comfort at the price of a degrading vassalage. It would not be charitable to detail all the enormities, private and public, personal and distributive, which he practised in a year. He was not such a monster as I considered an old-time baron. He drank spirits in quantity, and enjoyed an occasional " toot," as my neighbors name a period of intoxication, but it was not a matter of scandal for any one; he swore in his office, among his cronies, and promiscuously in the absence of children and clergymen; he had no religious belief of any definite character—in his own expressive language being a " free nigger "—and his morality was of a pattern with his religion, clouded, uncertain, wavering, leaving him no better than he should be; but he *was* the kindest, most indulgent householder that ever lived, was deservedly loved by the members of his family, and had an amiable wife and rather handsome children, in spite of a discouraging personal appearance. For Turnham, briefly, had a stiff leg and a face all hair and spectacles. So much of his skin as was visible above the tide of glass and hair was either muddily pale or fiery with an erysipelous affection, always shaded by the wide brim of a homely felt hat. A more malignant appearing face I had never seen; a fiercer expression no piratical pirate ever wore. As he walked the street, dragging his stiff leg after him like an evil genius or a familiar spirit, and bowed to the passing villagers, I interpreted the looks he gave them to mean, '' Be careful, now; you know me: at any minute I might cut the earth from under you;'' and the same look seemed to say to strangers, ''*You* don't know me; but I'm a terror, and I might cut the solid earth from under you if you said a cross word.'' He had cut happiness out of so many persons' lives that my interpretation was reasonable, and the title of baron, so far as it represented my idea, was clearly applicable to him.

Still, barons are men in spite of their odd characteristics and noble title, and are as apt to cry when pinched as better men. Mr. Turnham had his good points. One of his best was the fancy he took for me; for this fancy, while not doing me much good, brought him much annoyance from his brother barons. It was urged against my appointment that I was a Catholic, that I was too young, that I could not be trusted to keep business secrets from the priest, that better men wanted the position of town-clerk; to which objections he replied, with his malignant grin, that he loved Catholics more than hypocritical Protestants, that he hated old men, that no secrets were intrusted by him to any one, and that he didn't care a button if Bishop Potter was after the office of town-clerk—no one should get it that year but me. By this declaration

he unflinchingly stood.   Furthermore, he made me
his confidant in most matters of business and politics—a position which I, being a very young fool
and having fifteen years before me in which to make
up for present blunders, accepted with confidence
and courage.   Behold me, then, on a fine morning
in the month of June, seated in confidential discourse with my patron, our heels elevated in a
fashion plainly intended to keep our brains from
scattering, and he fairly glaring upon me for the
opposition which I offered to his plans concerning
the coming village election.

"So you don't believe in buying votes," said he.
"On principle ?   Or are you one of these Young
Men's Christian Associations, that shout for C. S.
Reform, in chorus, and in side streets, dark-night
solos buy up all the votes they can git ?"

I omit the baron's profanity.

"On principle," I answered benignantly.   "It's
wrong.   It's against the constitution and the law.
It's un-American.   It's an injury to the poor fellows
who are tempted.   George Washington wouldn't
approve of it.   Neither will I."

After sending the venerable Washington to a part
of the other world in which the baron seemed to
have a vested interest, judging from the authorita-
tive way in which he assigned lots there, and glaring
at me several moments, he said:

"Do you mean to hold that principle all your
life ?"

"I hope I shall," I replied, with the proper

humility of manner and an interior conviction that hope was utterly crushed by certainty. I was only twenty-one.

"Then let me tell you," said he viciously, "you'll never git a bigger office than town-clerk. You might as well git out now as wait till yer kicked out to make way for men that have purer principles."

"That's good!" said I. "I'll wait till I'm kicked out, and it won't be the men with purer principles that'll do all the kicking."

"And what *do* you propose to do at the election?" irritably. "Sit 'round, an' talk, an' stare, an' have old Whiting an' Stacy an' the rest of 'em askin' what you're doin', and all the rest of it?"

"Don't mind me," I said. "Let me have my own way, and I'll do as much work as the best man among 'em, in my own fashion. If they find any fault after election, I'll resign."

"Well, it's a satisfaction that all Catholics are not so strict in their way of thinkin'."

"If they aren't they ought to be. They're not Catholics. It must be a satisfaction to you to see most Protestants acting as you do. I suppose you will have the usual whiskey-barrel on tap in this room for the poor Frenchmen and the thirsty gentry of the town. I can read the future of America in election whiskey."

He glared for a few minutes and closed the conversation with a laugh, muttering some indistinct thunders concerning papists, and flinging his books and papers through the room savagely. I lost myself presently in a sad meditation on vote-buying as a means of political promotion. There was little doubt of my inability to hold even so inferior a position as town-clerk long while my principles remained at variance with the universal practice of Cherubusco politicians. If Catholic morality were not quite so stern on that and some other points of political and business life, how rapid would be the rise of ambitious Catholic lawyers with a good stock of principle and little cash on hand!

"I think," said Turnham after a time, "you had better hint to Joe Miron—he's a papist, you know—that I don't like his talk around town. He's restive. It looks as if he wanted to bolt the straight ticket."

"He has a right to bolt."

"And if he does," continued the baron, "let him understand that he'll get no more work in this town, if I can help it."

"He has a big family," I said, "a good wife and five children. They are not the kind to be left to starve on account of a vote."

"Just let him know how it will be," he replied indifferently. "They won't starve, you kin bet, but they'll suffer some trouble. That's good for papists. It's the only thing keeps the critters down."

Two persons entered the office in succession, transacted some business, and departed. One was a feeble, sickly woman in rags pathetically clean, the other a nervous, well-dressed business man.

" Well, Henriette! Good-morning, Sol Dotler! Come to pay the rent, Henriette ? "—he knew very well the day would never come when the poor woman would be able to pay it. " Six months due to date—eighteen dollars. I'll let you off for ten, seein' it's a hard time for the poor."

Henriette looked at the spectacles and whiskers, fumbled nervously with her rags, and began to tremble.

" The same old story," he said, after she had made a few vain efforts to speak. " No money, not able to work! Well, let it go for this time, Henriette! I'll make it up out o' Sol Dotler."

The woman went out shedding grateful tears. The nervous business man cursed the baron in a friendly fashion, and was cursed in turn, as he asked for the note which he intended to take up that morning. It was a small sum, one hundred dollars, for the use of which for one month the baron received the sum of thirty-five dollars.

" Not a bad job," he said to me a moment later. " A little business o' that sort would help you along, my boy, if you have a few hundreds to loan."

" Thus runs the world away," and a heavy heart carries the young Catholic who tries to run after it in our time, and I suppose in any time. He must strip himself of every principle of his faith, if he wishes to keep up with it, of love of his neighbor, love of his country, and love of religion, carrying only in his gripsack the shirt of convenience and expediency, and the trunks and hose of pharisaical morality. So the baron had often told me; nor could I doubt his word after a thorough examination of his and the wardrobes of all the other barons of the country! The items mentioned were not always to be found in their entirety among these nobles, but I observed that when their destruction left them morally naked public opinion drove them either into retirement or into business in the city on a large scale. The baron, being a family man, still held his scanty wardrobe together by dint of much patching and darning, and with the help also of a class of clients whose leader and mouthpiece was just entering the office on the heels of the reflections which had passed through my mind after the last remark of Mr. Turnham.

He was a small man in working-clothes, wrinkled, rudely jointed, and old. His thick gray hair was cut straight across his neck by the domestic scissors. His whole appearance had the home-like finish peculiar to old brooms and well-used furniture; so that the natural dignity of his manner was more remarkable by contrast, and left an agreeable impression. His wrinkled face was weighted with an expression of sorrow. He bowed to us both in a grave way, and, turning to the baron, opened his mouth to speak, but the under-lip trembled so much that he sat down suddenly and covered his eyes with his hand to hide the tears that fairly spouted through his fingers.   The baron's face grew a shade paler at this sight.

" Dupuy," said he, " your boy's dead."

" An' little gell, too," moaned Dupuy.   " Bot' die las' night."

The baron started up with a groan, and hopped up and down a few times in real distress.   He, too, was the father of boys and girls.

" It's too bad, too bad! " he said.   " This diphtheria is the worst thing in creation.   How did it happen, Cyriac ?   I thought they were gittin' well yesterday.   I could swear the girl was all right."

He came to the Frenchman's side and sat down to listen to a father's details of his children's death-struggle.

" M' ole 'oman," said Cyriac, with a visible effort, " watch Leah; I tek care o' Joe, me.   I clean de t'roat one, two, tree, much taime.   She git bettair, poor Joe; *mais* lit'le gell he no git bettair.   Very weak all de taime—choke.   O seigneur, c'est terrible! " as the memory of her suffering came back to him.   " I mek him dhrink de wine et de bif-tea, you see.   All de sem ma little gell no git vary sthrong—weaker, weaker, 'n' I t'ink, me, his bre't' stop, raight up.   Two o'clock d' ole 'oman cry 'loud, ' O mon Dieu! Leah die.'   I run to him.   It is so.   Leah die, easy, easy, easy, laike go to sleep—no pain, no scream, no not'ing'," finishing the description with a gesture of falling easily to sleep.   " Poor Joe hear her moder say he die, 'n' git frightened, you see, 'n' call me raight off.

' Wot's de madder wid you, Joe ? You 'fraid ? '
' No, p'pa, no 'fraid me. Mek de pr'ers fo' de
soul. I go after Leah.' ' You go after Leah, *petit
fou?* . Leah no die. Moder 'fraid laike you, 'n'
scream. You stay wid Leah, Joe.' *Mais* no fool,
Joe. She say all de taime, ' Mek de pr'ers, p'pa,
mek de pr'ers.' Purt' soon she go after Leah—
easy, easy, too, comme de raison. Ah! seigneur,
tout est perdu."

He spoke in broken tones, and with the last
words burst into a fit of sobbing. The baron
pressed his hand and turned his face away to hide
the tears that moistened his fierce eyes. When his
eyes were dry again he turned to me.

" Mighty hard, isn't it ? " said he. " An' they
were alone, too; no one with children 'ud go near
'em. It's the black diphtheria. Did you git any
one to lay the children out, Cyriac ? "

" I fix 'em tout seul," said Cyriac briefly, with
an expressive shrug of the shoulders.

" Well, I suppose it can't be helped, Cyriac.
I'm sorry for you—very sorry. It's hard to lose
your children after bringin' 'em to that age; but
it's the way things are done in this world, an' we
can't help ourselves."

" Mes enfants se reposent dans les bras du bon
Dieu," said Cyriac, clasping his hands tightly with
a sincere but painful effort at resignation. I translated the sentence for the baron, and was rewarded
with the usual glare. He could not presume to
dispute the existence of heaven at that moment,

and raged to have me find him temporarily muzzled. Old Dupuy informed us that the children would be buried that evening at sundown, and was made happy by Mr. Turnham's promise to attend, as, owing to the malignity of the disease, the ceremony would be private and no services held in the church until the next morning. The baron here saw fit to mention a little matter of business. It would have been in better taste to leave poor Cyriac to his heavy misfortunes, only that Mr. Turnham was not to be held back from any measure by the mere dictum of good taste. And, to tell the truth, the matter was not calculated to interfere with Cyriac's sorrow. It was as if one had said to him, Your hat is awry, or, Button your coat and it will sit better, while he was wiping away his tears.

"To-morrow, Cyriac, if you don't mind," said the baron casually, "we'll talk over that bolt of the Duquette boys. It looks as if they mean to hold off till the other party buys 'em."

A deeper shade settled on Dupuy's face, and I saw that he looked at his horny fingers, as if a new and startling difficulty had sprung suddenly from the deformed brown joints.

"I t'ink, me, it is de pries'," he said slowly, with a long-drawn sigh. The baron stared at him with his mouth open, and Cyriac met the stare with a cringing smile.

"Purt' bad boy dem Duquettes, M'sieu' Tu'n'am," he said gravely, seeing that the baron did not or would not understand the smile, whose

meaning was perfectly clear to me. "Bad Cat'-
lique, no go t' churc', all taime drunk, no spik
French—French no nice f'r dem. Las' mont' big
change. Dey mek de confession, tek pew in de
churc', no drink no more—big change. I t'ink,
me, it is de pries'."

Now the baron understood, and his face showed
some such expression as must have rested on the
face of the first Roman emperor who discovered the
presence and the power of the Pope in Rome.

"That's the new priest," he said briefly. Cyriac
nodded. "Has he said anything to you?"

Cyriac shrugged his shoulders doubtfully.

"Tell me," shouted the baron, bringing down
his fist with a crash on the desk, "did he speak to
you?"

"Turnham," I suggested gently, "let me remind
you—"

"You—" But it will not do to record his answer.
Had I said simply, remember his dead children,
and left myself out of the suggestion, its effect
would have cooled him instantly. Cyriac was frightened, but calm and polite.

"She say some word," he replied, "an' I t'ink,
me, she no say a word. 'Cyriac Dupuy'"—imi-
tating the tone and manner of the priest—"''f you
see the mans to buy 'n' sell de vote, tell me, *tell*
me all taime.'"

"That's all?" said the baron, holding his wrath
in check until he was bursting like a boy in smoth-
ered laughter.

" All," replied Cyriac briefly, standing up to make his low, old-fashioned bow, with his hat describing a circle in his hand.

" It's just as well, Cyriac," drawing a paper from his open safe and shaking it at him with a most baronial air. " When the priest comes foolin' around you and talkin' o' the wickedness o' buyin' votes, just think o' that an' you're safe." An extra shade of humility lodged in Cyriac's wrinkles. " I won't stand no curé's nonsense. He may keep you from voting as I want you to, but he can't stave off a mortgage. I'll squeeze you, my boy—I'll squeeze you."

" Turnham," I said, disgusted, " remember his children." The baron blushed. No one acquainted with him would have noticed the purple current stealing behind his hat, whiskers, and spectacles. He hopped over to Cyriac, going out of the door, and slipped a bill into his hand while gently patting his back.

" It's all right," he said gently; " we'll settle this another time, and I'll surely be at the funeral."

My youth alone excused the antics in which I indulged after the door closed on the Canadian. I gravely jumped over several chairs, walked around them, stood on my head, and turned a boyish cartwheel to the musical accompaniment of the baron's profanity. On this occasion he swore more like an emperor than a baron, if we suppose that felicity and fluency follow a person's rank. If verbal electricity could be stored in a material atmosphere, the office would have exploded on the spot.

"That accounts," said he, "for the Duquettes" —the only words which were not pure exclamation in a five minutes' discourse.

"I'm glad of it," said I; "I rejoice in it. I don't know much about Father O'Shaughnes- sy—"

"What!" cried he, "is that his name?"

"What's in a name?" said I. "Wait till you see the man. He's so small that it seems ridiculous he should have so powerful a name. I'll tell you what he did in Buckeye county two years ago." The baron, who had been stupefied at the name, looked interested. "A Democratic judge, who lived across the way from him, had a sewer which emptied into the priest's garden, and because it was cut off brought the matter into court, meanly pre- ferring that his neighbor should die of typhoid than to dig a way for his sewerage. The judge was the county head of his party. An election was near; the priest went into it, and the county, for the first time in sixteen years, went Republican. I'm glad he's here. You won't buy any more Frenchmen. You won't shake mortgages at them when they talk of voting as they please. You won't see them running like chickens at the cluck of a hen whenever you crook your finger. Best of all, you will now need me and my methods to hold these people on your side. Influence now is more than money. I can coax where you can't bribe or threaten. Do

you see ?   Do you understand your position ?
Father O'Shaughnessy will skewer you like a fly on
a pin, and I say again I'm glad of it."

" Oh! you *air*," snapped he, with his most intense nasal drawl. " You *air* glad of it, you son
of a wild Irishman, you ignorant papist, — —!
Well, I'll show you just what that priest amounts
to!   I'll buy more Frenchmen than I ever did.
I'll buy your Irishmen; I'll buy the hull town, if I
need it.   And the barrel of whiskey 'll stand jest
where *you're* standin'; and I'll set every p'isonous
Kanuck 's drunk as Noah, and I'll march 'em up to
the polls jest as usual, an' have 'em vote under my
eye; an' if they don't, the niggers!—if they cut and
run, the sinners!—I'll cut the earth from under
'em; I'll fling 'em out of the town into Canada as
poor as they came into it; an' as for you an' your
notions, if you want to stand by Father O'Shaughnessy—"

" That's my name, sir," said a thin, precise voice
at the door.   The baron had been hopping about
the office, and, being close to the door when it
opened, fairly bawled the name into the visitor's
face.   The little man was not as much surprised as
the baron, and his keen gray eyes studied the stupid
expression on Turnham's face as calmly as though
it were a brass door-knocker.

" Come in," said Turnham feebly, as he hopped
to his desk and mechanically struck a business atti-
tude.   " Won't you sit down ?"

" Thank you," said the precise voice.   " I want

a ton of coal sent up to the house this afternoon, if possible."

" I'll send it up," said the baron briskly. At this point I ventured to introduce the two magnates.

" You have good work to do here," said Turnham roughly, as a salve to his recent confusion, " in sendin' the children to school. They don't go, the half of 'em."

" Pay their fathers decent wages," said the priest, " and the children will attend. Can a dollar a day eight months of the year support five persons decently ? If the school is all they say it is, I don't blame them for remaining away."

" How is that ?" said the baron angrily, for the school was his pet device and chief diversion.

" Another time I'll explain, sir. Briefly, do you believe in teaching Latin and physiology in a town whose people are born to labor hard all their lives ? I wonder you never asked yourself the question before. Excuse me now, as I am in a hurry. I'll give you a chance to answer in a day or two."

He bade us good morning and went out hurriedly, leaving the baron to chew his pen-holder and to confide to me his impression that the priest was a vain busybody and needed a good fright in order to settle him in his proper position.

" Does he think," said he, " that priests only should study Latin ?"

" Between you and his reverence," I replied, " Cyriac Dupuy will be torn to shreds at election time."

Poor Cyriac! As he stood looking into the double grave which held the two bodies dearest to him in this world, the fabled America of his childhood seemed as desolate and bleak as Anticosti, and he sighed in his quiet and polite way over the peace enjoyed in his native Canadian village, where death was never so violent and unkind, where great disasters by land and sea were heard of but once in a lifetime, where mortgages were practically unknown, and where votes, voting, bribery, and barons were institutions that concerned only the rich and had little concern with the sorrows and joys of the poor.

The peace that Cyriac dreamed of, although he thought it a Canadian possession, was really the natural peace of careless childhood; but because he had left Canada a child, to begin his apprenticeship to labor and sorrow in the States, it seemed to him happiness was a growth of his native soil—as it seems to all of us, whether success or sorrow meets us in the last days. And Cyriac, had he been compelled to return to Canada, would have looked for it as naturally as for the roses which grew in the front yard and the delicious peas that covered the paternal acre. Candidly, America, in the person of the baron, had been kind, and yet unjust, to him. He had reached Cherubusco in his fifteenth year, when the baron was a baby almost; but the baron's father had given him work and encouragement and favor, and had urged him to learn English well and to become a citizen of the country. He did not succeed with the English, and, because party spirit was not very warm in earlier days, was not hurried to the other. As a matter of business, Turnham, junior, on succeeding his father, pointed out to him that were he naturalized he might make a few dollars on his vote at each election; whereupon Cyriac went through the usual formalities, and, on receiving a certain sum for depositing a bit of paper in a box one election day, began to think that the American Constitution was a great thing. He spread the news among his fellows, and immediately after it became the French fashion to haggle on election day with politicians, and to return home in the cool midnight a few dollars ahead of the world or full to the brim with bad whiskey. You can fancy the astonishment with which I first heard an honest and virtuous Canadian openly grumble on receiving for his vote a dollar less than his neighbor, and the deeper astonishment with which I listened to a committee of barons bemoaning the treacherous designs of Catholics on the bulwarks of American freedom. Yet this moral turpitude really existed, and the defenders of the aforementioned bulwarks were deepening it daily, adding to it, in fact, and were bound to hold the ignorant, innocent Canadians to their attacks on the bulwarks, if they had to send half their forces to the enemy's rear and bayonet them into battle.

How it happened that Cyriac became the scape-goat of his countrymen amid his bitter misfortunes is accounted for by two circumstances: that he marshalled the hosts of bought voters for the baron,

and that he one day brought out the goose pimples
of patriotic horror on Father O'Shaughnessy by
artlessly mentioning how much he sold his vote for
each year. From that unguarded admission dated
Cyriac's woes. He had the duties of citizenship
sharply explained to him, and was made acquainted
with the criminality of his acts. The priest and the
baron both threatened him, the one with terrors of
the law, the other with the mortgage; and as he
looked at the steady alternatives he thought, with
the poet, "In truth, how am I straitened!"
However, the mortgage was such a fixed, dread
certainty, and Father O'Shaughnessy's temper being
a still unknown quantity, Cyriac determined to
appeal to the priest for a milder interpretation of
the law. He spoke to him after the funeral service
was over.

"M'sieu' le Curé," said he with grave politeness,
"I laike to spik de few word wid you, m'sieu',
'bout de vote."

Monsieur le Curé bowed with a very cold face—
so cold, in fact, that Cyriac hastened to
say:

"I know, me, you spik thrue, m'sieu'. I mek
mysel' vary sorry dat I sell de vote, *mais* I know
nottin' f'r de counthry, 'n' M'sieu' Tu'n'am say,
'All raight, all raight, Cyriac; you mek some
monay, I git some vote—all raight, *all* raight,
ALL raight.' I no t'ink, me, all wrong. M'sieu'
Tu'n'am big man f'r de counthry, m'sieu', vary
big man. Mek de work f'r poor pipple, mek de

house, len' de monay, git de job—vary good neighbor, oh! *vary* good neighbor."

After this prologue Cyriac twisted his hat and
waited for a reply which might give him a chance
to declare the object of his visit.   Monsieur le Curé
O'Shaughnessy, however, was as dumb as if he were
born so. Cyriac came to the point then desperately.

" Purt' soon, m'sieu', dey mek de vote f'r 'lection.
Some buy, some sell.   No mattair f'r de raight or
de wrong; buy, sell all same. I t'ink, me, no
harm "—he hesitated for the right words to express
a delicate and embarrassing thought, and then said
in tumultuous patois: " If all others can buy and
sell, why not I, for this one time—only for this one
time ? "   It was his last hope, and Monsieur le
Curé knew it and laughed rather heartlessly in his
face.   Not for that—oh! no—but at his reasoning.
He caught the emphasis on the last words and their
piteous eagerness.

" Why for this one time, Cyriac Dupuy ? " he
asked, and saw at once by the expression on the
man's face that it was the proper question to put.
" Why for this one time, Mr. Dupuy ? "

More hat-twisting and hesitation.   It was so
dead a certainty, that mortgage, why need the
priest be made acquainted with its existence ?
Cyriac looked out sadly on the green lawn where to
his mournful fancy the document which the baron
had menaced him with stalked like a sheriff outside
Congress awaiting his noble prey; and as his gaze

wandered up to the new-made graves, and he compared the grief of that day with the new griefs that priest and baron were making for him, a few resistless tears streamed over his face. He was a man, and therefore ashamed of them; and because Father O'Shaughnessy took his emotion coolly, being used to tears, he sat down and in mingled English and patois explained his straitened position.

"It is too bad," said the priest when he had finished, "and I consider Turnham a cruel man. But if worse were to happen you, Cyriac, if you were to be thrown out naked, you could not engage in this detestable traffic in votes. You must let your fellows alone. You can vote as you please. But to sell your vote, to buy others, to do this dirty work—no! no! no! Let your house be sold, let everything go; but be honest, Cyriac, and true to the teachings of your Church."

Cyriac knew somewhat of those teachings, but saw no connection between religion and voting, and was minded to tell the priest that the catechism said nothing about it. Yet why dispute? The priest had pointed out the law and the right, and he was bound to follow both at any cost. If there were no mortgage the cost would be trifling; *now* it included his little possessions, the savings of a lifetime. He rose to depart in silence, with his despair and his resolution written on his seamed face.

"You will do as I have advised?" said the priest kindly.

"Purt' hard, m'sieu'; *mais*," shrugging the shoulders, "I must."

"And if you suffer for it," added the priest, "never fear but that I will do all I can for you."

Which was small consolation to Cyriac, whose business eye saw the immense disproportion between his poverty and the baron's wealth.

"I lose de house," he said briefly, and his Reverence felt the implied reproach without anger.

"Better to lose that than your honest name, Mr. Dupuy. Better to be poor and to lose your dear earnings than to be a shame to Canada and a danger to this country. Better to have no house than to own one at the price you are to pay for yours."

His tone impressed the poor man, if his words did not. Cyriac could not see the relation of vote-buying to shame and danger and dishonesty, and felt no emotion on hearing these stately sentences; but he knew "f'r sure" that the priest and the Church regarded it as a great crime; he was therefore tied to the necessity of avoiding it forever. What a dull pain beat against his heart all that day! He thought with mournful satisfaction that, while himself and his old wife would lose their home, the children were never again to be in danger of losing theirs. Who held a mortgage on a graveyard, or who would throw the dead from their shelter? Cyriac had never read the annals of the Gironde.

The baron had been present at the funeral, and had noted sourly the interview with the priest. Was it that circumstance which tightened his nervous, vicious grasp on Cyriac's arm at their next meeting ? He dared not look in the baron's face, and would have given much to be able to forget the many favors father and son had heaped on him. They weighted him heavier than the mortgage. Turnham was breathing hard, and the beads of sweat started out on his forehead, as he came face to face with his henchman and with a terrible thought which Cyriac's sad face suggested.

" Cyriac "—his voice shook like a leaf—" my two boys have the diphtheria. What if they should die ? "

" Mon Dieu ! " cried Cyriac as the remembrance of his own suffering rushed upon him, " c'est effray- ante. Git de bes' doctor. Clean de t'roat vary much, 'n' pray on de bon Dieu."

Pray to the good God ! It was the very last remedy which would occur to the baronial mind ; but in his excited state, recalling the number of faith- cures which had taken place in certain parts of the country, and knowing the depth and strength of Cyriac's faith, he said, and to this day denies that he said :

" Dupuy, *you* pray for 'em. If faith an' pra'er kin save, you're the man for that business."

And his voice broke into a wail pathetic enough to veil the ridiculousness of the remark from the humorous ear.

Cyriac volunteered his services in nursing the boys, and was brought to the house by the grateful baron. In a village which had suffered much from the ravages of diphtheria it was difficult to secure the services of a neighbor. The baron, indeed, would not have asked so great a favor. He was rather anxious than otherwise that friends with children in their family should remain away, and never opened his door to a knock until the visitor was made acquainted with the fatal presence within. His haggard face would then be thrust through the barely opened door and business transacted briefly. In four days he did not once come to the office. Day and night he and Cyriac haunted the sick-rooms of the children, sleeping fitfully, talking mournfully of life's chances, working with might and main to fight off the disease. In the critical moments when man and medicine could do no more, and nature had hard work to assert itself, he stood in silent agony, squeezing the old man's rough hand and muttering :

" I know *now* what you suffered," with his hard eyes fixed on the young faces. Meanwhile Cyriac was praying " on de bon Dieu," and the baron was solicitous to know if he prayed still.

Occasionally pressing business of an unusual nature made it necessary for me to intrude on his grief. I was struck with the intensity of anguish and anxiety expressed in his face, never having credited him with a human feeling so deep and sincere. He heard my account listlessly, and in like fashion gave me my directions.

" How are the boys? " I asked when about to go.

" Would you like to see them ? " he said, with a

gesture of hopelessness. It was the fourth day—
the day of the crisis. " But I forgot. You have
brothers and sisters. It is not the place for you."

And although I protested, he would not permit
me to enter the sick-room.

" I don't want any human being to suffer this
way," said he, unconsciously laying his hand on his
heart, while his eyes wandered drearily towards the
inner chambers. He was suffering in all truth, and
I thought it best to defer some information concerning the election until another time. Such tenderness! such affection! I could not believe it. And
yet in how many instances of his life had I seen the
baron as charitable and human-hearted as he was
often hard and cruel! Ten minutes after I left his
house four day-laborers presented themselves before
him to protest against a wage of ninety cents a day.

" How much do you pay for your board ? " said
he.

" Three dollars a week," said the laborers.

" That leaves you a hundred dollars a year, boys,
to dress on and spend. If you had any more you'd
drink it. You're all single, an' it's quite enough
for you. If you had women an' children to look
after I might raise you twenty cents."

Vainly they pleaded, argued, threatened. After
cursing him heartily for a stingy devil, and being
cursed uproariously in turn, they departed. It was
my good fortune to encounter him later in the day.
The information I held could not be longer kept
from him, humiliating as it was to my pride. The

electioneering processes were all disordered. Father O'Shaughnessy, in a quiet way, had sat on vote-buying among the Canadians, and there was a general break along the line. Nor could I, with all my persuasiveness, after all my boasting, induce even a handful to promise their votes for the baron. I humbly explained the situation to him. Cyriac happened to be in the room looking for a medicine-bottle.

"Do you hear that?" said the baron. The old man shrugged his shoulders and smilingly shook his head. He was out of politics this year.

"You've got to straighten things out," said the baron boldly. "I'll let you off duty. Go an' see the boys. Promise 'em anything they ask. Git 'em all into line, an' after they vote we'll settle with 'em."

Cyriac listened to these directions, given with old-time freedom and directness, as the condemned listens to the Sheriff's legal reasons for taking away his life; then he shook his head and continued his search for the bottle.

"Cyriac, sit down here," shoving a chair towards him. Cyriac sat down seriously. "What nonsense has the priest been stuffin' ye with now? You ain't goin' back on us at the last minnit without warnin', be you? If you were goin' to do that, why didn't you let us know days back when we could have filled yer place? Oh! no; you've got to come to time this onct, an' next year, if you say so, we'll count you out."

"Counting-in is the fashion this year," said I, referring to a recent political event.

"Just so." And a smile glimmered for a moment on the waste of beard. "You've got to count me into office this year, Cyriac," patting his knee kindly, "and after that stay at home. Your priest is foolin' you. Everybody buys and sells votes. It's the custom of the country. It may be wrong where the priest comes from; it is *not* wrong here. I won't ask you to buy a vote. Go an' talk to the boys. Square 'em up; straighten 'em out. Git 'em to promise their votes; see that they vote right, an' I'll do the rest. Ain't that fair?"

It looked fair, but, as we all knew, the looks did not here indicate the disposition.

"No use," said Cyriac nervously. "I no more buy de vote, me."

"Well, well," said the baron, with a patient sigh and a curious inspection of the wrinkled face whose owner so stubbornly defied him. "You don't see what I mean. You needn't buy. Talk to the boys. Why won't you do that?"

"To talk is to buy," answered Cyriac, with shrewdness and dignity.

"It's the last time I'll ask you to do it, Cyriac. We can't do without your influence now, an' if you go back on me I'm fixed for this year. You won't be able to stand this town if I lose an' the boys know I lost through you. The place 'll git too hot for you."

Cyriac felt the force of this statement, which the

baron proceeded to amplify, and his distress and anguish were evident. He brushed his hair and fidgeted woefully, and once or twice I thought he was about to surrender, for this year at least. So did the baron, who, when he had worked up the old man's feelings to a proper pitch, pushed him gently towards the door, saying, as if the matter were settled:

"Do your best with the boys, Cyriac, an' the hull thing 'll be forgotten to-morrow."

Houseless, childless, friendless, driven from the town which had given him a home for forty years! A more violent temptation was never thrust upon any man, and Cyriac was not to be blamed for the momentary yielding before these terrible consequences. He walked to the door in a dream, seeing on one side his poverty and exile, his defiance of Monsieur le Curé on the other. The thought of crime did not occur to him, for he could see no crime in vote-buying. Nor did he know how wildly consequences had been exaggerated by the baron, and how determined a friend he had in Monsieur O'Shaughnessy. His temptation was real, if its circumstances were not, and so he turned submissively away, put on his hat, turned the knob, and hesitated. It was a flash of baronial genius which prompted Turnham to supplement that hesitation as he did. He drew from his pocket the mortgage on Cyriac's house, showed it to him silently, and tore it into bits so small that no art could ever again make it a legal instrument. The old man shook as if with an ague, stretched out his hand to protest, while the unwilling tears streamed over his pallid face.

" M'sieu' Tu'n'am," said he, brokenly, " your fader vary good, you bettair. Me go back on Kennedy [Canada]. You 'ave de house raight off, but no more buy de vote."

With these words he left the room, and the baron stood gazing now at the door, now at the litter of torn paper on the carpet, while the clock ticking on the shelf seemed hammering the dead stillness into the very furniture.

" Beaten by a damned Frenchman!" hissed my patron as he threw himself and his leg out of the room.

Beaten! Yes, the baron was beaten, routed, horse, foot, and artillery, by the same power which had beaten imperial Cæsar; and he felt very sore over it. Being a shrewd politician, however, he was determined to make the most of altered circumstances, and my mock regrets at being compelled to rank him with the judge of Buckeye County were received with equanimity. His children were getting well, and when the election came off matters went so very smoothly and prosperously that he could afford to be chaffed about sacerdotal influence. Cyriac came to the polls, deposited a vote for his sometime master, and returned home to finish the packing of his household goods. Quite enough votes for any purpose were still to be purchased in Cherubusco, and the baron was elected by a reduced but still handsome majority. Father O'Shaughnessy voted for him on my recommendation—a fact which made his first visit of ceremony to the baron's office an agreeable occasion. He talked cordially on the questions of the day, read the baron a lecture on bribery with a general application, and asked him to prevent gentlemen who held mortgages on the property of the poor from using said mortgages improperly; which my patron promised to do, and consequently Cyriac did not go to Canada. He resumed in time the old affectionate relations with Turnham, but no word was ever spoken to him of vote-buying. The baron was content with legitimate service from him, and to this day falls into a deep melancholy when reminded of the occasion of his henchman's victory over him.

CHARLES WARREN STODDARD.

CHARLES WARREN STODDARD was born at Rochester, N. Y., on August 7th, 1843, and as a child of twelve removed to California with his parents. There he remained for two years, when he returned to New York and attended school till 1859; then he once more joined his family in California. In 1864 he made the first of five journeys to Hawaii, a country to which, till then, comparatively few foreigners had gone. On his second voyage there, in 1868, five years before the advent of Father Damien, he visited the Leper settlement at Molokai. Fifteen years later, at the time of his last journey to the Sandwich Islands, he was the guest of the great Apostle of the Lepers. In 1873 he was sent on an extended excursion to Europe as special correspondent of the *San Francisco Chronicle*, and in that character drifted about for four years, from place to place, going as far as Asia and Africa. Thoroughly appreciating the genius and ability of its correspondent, the *Chronicle* restricted him neither to time nor place, and it was while acting for that journal he produced his " South Sea Idyls," than which there is nothing more beautiful of its kind in English. Weary of his wanderings, Mr. Stoddard at last determined to "settle down," and in 1885 he accepted the position of Professor of English Literature at Notre Dame University. This he held for two years, when he was obliged to resign through illness and seek renewed health in the Blue Grass region of Kentucky.

In 1889, when the Catholic University of America was opened in Washington, Mr. Stoddard was tendered the chair of English Literature, which he has since filled to entire satisfaction.

Mr. W. D. Howells, the distinguished author and critic, speaks of the "South Sea Idyls" as "the lightest, sweetest, wildest, freshest things that ever were written about the life of that summer ocean ;   *   *   *   there are few such delicious bits of literature in the language ;   *   *   *   they always seemed to me of the very make of the tropic spray which ' knows not if it be sea or sun.' "

Mr. Stoddard's published works are : " Poems," " South Sea Idyls," " Summer Cruising in the South Seas," " Marshallah, A Flight into Egypt," " A Trip to Hawaii," " The Lepers of Molokai," " A Troubled Heart, and How it was Comforted at Last," and " Hawaiian Life, being Lazy Letters from Low Latitudes."

Joe of Lahaina.

BY CHARLES WARREN STODDARD.

I.

I WAS stormed in at Lahaina. Now, Lahaina is a little slice of civilization beached on the shore of barbarism. One can easily stand that little of it, for brown and brawny heathendom becomes more wonderful and captivating by contrast. So I was glad of dear, drowsy little Lahaina, and was glad also that she had but one broad street, which possibly led to destruction, and yet looked lovely in the distance. It didn't matter to me that the one broad street had but one side to it, for the sea lapped over the sloping sands on its lower edge, and the sun used to set right in the face of every solitary citizen of Lahaina just as he went to supper.

I was waiting to catch a passage in a passing schooner, and that's why I came there; but the schooner flashed by us in a great gale from the south, and so I was stormed in indefinitely.

It was Holy Week, and I concluded to go to housekeeping, because it would be so nice to have my frugal meals in private, to go to Mass and Vespers daily, and then to come back and feel quite at home. My villa was suburban—built of dried grasses on the model of a haystack, dug out in the middle, with doors and windows let into the four sides thereof. It was planted in the midst of a vineyard, with avenues stretching in all directions under a network of stems and tendrils.

> " Her breath is sweeter than the sweet winds
> That breathe over the grape-blossoms of Lahaina."

So the song said; and I began to think upon the surpassing sweetness of that breath as I inhaled the sweet winds of Lahaina, while the wilderness of its vineyards blossomed like the rose. I used to sit in my veranda and turn to Joe (Joe was my private and confidential servant), and I would say to Joe, while we scented the odor of grape, and saw the great banana leaves waving their cambric sails, and heard the sea moaning in the melancholy distance,— I would say to him, " Joe, housekeeping is good fun, isn't it? " Whereupon Joe would utter a sort of unanimous Yes, with his whole body and soul; so that question was carried triumphantly, and we would relapse into a comfortable silence, while the voices of the wily singers down on the city front would whisper to us and cause us to wonder what they could possibly be doing at that moment in the broad way that led to destruction. Then we would take a drink of cocoa milk and finish our bananas and go to bed, because we had nothing else to do.

This is the way that we began our co-operative housekeeping: One night, when there was a riotous sort of a festival off in a retired valley, I saw in the excited throng of natives who were going mad over their national dance a young face that seemed to embody a whole tropical romance. On another night, when a lot of us were bathing in the moonlight, I saw a figure so fresh and joyous that I began to realize how the old Greeks could worship mere physical beauty and forget its higher forms. Then I discovered that face on this body,— a rare enough combination,—and the whole constituted Joe, a young scapegrace who was schooling at Lahaina, under the eye—not a very sharp one—of his uncle. When I got stormed in and resolved on housekeeping for a season, I took Joe, bribing his uncle to keep the peace, which he promised to do, provided I gave bonds for Joe's irreproachable conduct while with me. I willingly gave bonds—verbal ones—for this was just what I wanted of Joe: namely, to instil into his youthful mind those counsels which, if rigorously followed, must result in his becoming a true and unterrified American. This compact settled, Joe took up his bed,—a roll of mats,—and down we marched to my villa, and began housekeeping in good earnest.

We soon got settled, and began to enjoy life, though we were not without occasional domestic infelicities. For instance, Joe would wake up in the middle of the night, declaring to me that it was morning, and thereupon insist upon sweeping out at once, and in the most vigorous manner. Having filled the air with dust, he would rush off to the baker's for our hot rolls and a pat of breakfast butter, leaving me, meantime, to recover as I might. Having settled myself for a comfortable hour's reading, bolstered up in a luxurious fashion, Joe would enter with breakfast, and orders to the effect that it be eaten at once and without delay. It was useless for me to remonstrate with him : he was tyrannical.

He got me into all sorts of trouble. It was Holy Week, and I had resolved upon going to Mass and Vespers daily. I went. The soft night winds floated in through the latticed windows of the chapel, and made the candles flicker upon the altar. The little throng of natives bowed in the impressive silence, and were deeply moved. It was rest for the soul to be there; yet, in the midst of it, while the Father with his pale, sad face gave his instructions, to which we listened as attentively as possible,—for there was something in his manner and his voice that made us better creatures,—while we listened, in the midst of it I heard a shrill little whistle, a sort of chirp, that I knew perfectly well. It was Joe sitting on a cocoa-stump in the garden adjoining, and beseeching me to come out, right off. When service was over, I remonstrated with him for his irreverence. "Joe," I said, "if you have no respect for religion yourself, respect those who are more fortunate than you." But Joe was dressed in his best, and quite wild at the entrancing loveliness of the night. "Let's walk a little," said Joe, covered with fragrant wreaths, and redolent of cocoanut-oil. What could I do? If I had tried to do anything to the contrary, he might have taken me and thrown me away somewhere into a well or a jungle, and then I could no longer hope to touch the chord of remorse,—which chord I sought vainly, and which I have since concluded was not in Joe's physical corporation at all. So we walked a little. In vain I strove to break Joe of the shocking habit of whistling me out of Vespers. He would persist in doing it. Moreover, during the day he would collect crusts of bread and banana skins, station himself in ambush behind the curtain of the window next the lane, and, as some solitary creature strode solemnly past, Joe would discharge a volley of ammunition over him, and then laugh immoderately at his indignation and surprise. Joe was my pet elephant, and I was obliged to play with him very cautiously.

One morning he disappeared. I was without the consolation of a breakfast even. I made my toilet, went to my portmanteau for my purse—for I had decided upon a visit to the baker,—when, lo! part of my slender means had mysteriously disappeared. Joe was gone and the money also. All day I thought about it. In the morning, after a very long and miserable night, I woke up, and when I opened my eyes, there, in the doorway, stood Joe, in a brand-new suit of clothes, including boots and hat. He was gorgeous beyond description, and seemed overjoyed to see me, and as merry as though nothing unusual had happened. I was quite startled at this apparition. "Joseph!" I said in my severest tone, and then turned over and looked away from him.   Joe evaded the subject in the most delicate manner, and was never so interesting as at that moment.   He sang his specialties, and played clumsily upon his bamboo flute,—to soothe me, I suppose,—and wanted me to eat a whole flat pie which he had brought home as a peace-offering, but-toned tightly under his jacket.   I saw I must strike at once, if I struck at all; so I said, "Joe, what on earth did you do with that money?"   Joe said he had replenished his wardrobe, and bought the flat pie especially for me.   "Joseph," I said, with great dignity, "do you know that you have been steal-ing, and that it is highly sinful to steal, and may result in something unpleasant in the world to come?"   Joe said "Yes" pleasantly, though I hardly think he meant it; and then he added, mildly, "that he couldn't lie,"—which was a glar-ing falsehood,—"but wanted me to be sure that he took the money, and so had come back to tell me."

"Joseph," I said, "you remind me of our noble Washington;" and, to my amazement, Joe was mor-tified.   He didn't, of course, know who Washing-ton was, but he suspected that I was ridiculing him.   He came to the bed and haughtily insisted upon my taking the little change he had received from his customers, but I implored him to keep it, as I had no use at all for it, and, as I assured him, I much preferred hearing it jingle in his pocket.

The next day I sailed out of Lahaina, and Joe came to the beach with his new trousers tucked into

his new boots, while he waved his new hat violently
in a final adieu, much to the envy and admiration
of a score of hatless urchins, who looked upon Joe
as the glass of fashion, and but little lower than the
angels. When I entered the boat to set sail, a tear
stood in Joe's bright eye, and I think he was really
sorry to part with me; and I don't wonder at it, because our housekeeping experiences were new to
him,—and I may add, not unprofitable.

II.

Some months of mellow and beautiful weather
found me wandering here and there among the
islands, when the gales came on again, and I was
driven about homeless, and sometimes friendless,
until, by and by, I heard of an opportunity to visit
Molokai,—an island seldom visited by the tourist,—
where, perhaps, I could get a close view of a singularly sad and interesting colony of lepers.

The whole island is green, but lonely. As you
ride over its excellent turnpike you see the ruins of
a nation that is passing like a shadow out of sight:
deserted garden-patches, crumbling walls, and roofs
tumbled into the one state-chamber of the house,
while knots of long grass wave at half-mast in the
chinks and crannies; a land of great traditions,
of magic and witchcraft and spirits; a fertile and
fragrant solitude. How I enjoyed it; and yet how
it was all telling upon me, in its own way! One
cannot help feeling sad there, for he seems to be

living and moving in a long reverie, out of which he dreads to awaken to a less pathetic life. I rode a day or two among the solemn and reproachful ruins with inexpressible complacence, and, having finally climbed a series of verdant and downy hills, and ridden for twenty minutes in a brisk shower, came suddenly upon the brink of a great precipice, three thousand feet in the air. My horse instinctively braced himself, and I nervously jerked the bridle square up to my breastbone, as I found we were poised between heaven and earth, upon a trembling pinnacle of rock. A broad peninsula was stretched below me, covered with grassy hills; here and there clusters of brown huts were visible, and to the right the white dots of houses to which I was hastening, for that was the leper village. To that spot were the wandering and afflicted tribes brought home to die. Once descending the narrow stairs in the cliff under me, never again could they hope to strike their tents and resume their pilgrimage; for the curse was on them, and necessity had narrowed down their sphere of action to this compass,—a solitary slope between sea and land, with the invisible sentinels of Fear and Fate forever watching its borders.

I seemed to be looking into a fiery furnace, wherein walked the living bodies of those whom Death had already set his seal upon. What a mockery it seemed to be, climbing down that crag,—through wreaths of vine, and under leafy cataracts breaking into a foam of blossoms a thousand feet below me;

swinging aside the hanging parasites that obstructed the narrow way,—entering the valley of death, and the very mouth of hell, by these floral avenues!

A brisk ride of a couple of miles across the breadth of the peninsula brought me to the gate of the keeper of the settlement, and there I dismounted, and hastened into the house to be rid of the curious crowd that had gathered to receive me. The little cottage was very comfortable, my host and hostess friends of precious memory; and with them I felt at once at home, and began the new life that every one begins when the earth seems to have been suddenly transformed into some better or worse world, and he alone survives the transformation.

Have you never had such an experience? Then go into the midst of a community of lepers; have ever before your eyes their Gorgon-like faces; see the horrors, hardly to be recognized as human, that grope about you; listen in vain for the voices that have been hushed forever by decay; breathe the tainted atmosphere; and bear ever in mind that, while they hover about you,—forbidden to touch you, yet longing to clasp once more a hand that is perfect and pure,—the insidious seeds of the malady may be generating in your vitals, and your heart, even then, be drunk with death!

I might as well confess that I slept indifferently the first night; that I was not entirely free from nervousness the next day, as I passed through the various wards assigned to patients in every stage of decomposition. But I recovered myself in time to observe the admirable system adopted by the Hawaiian Government for the protection of its unfortunate people. I used to sit by the window and see the processions of the less afflicted come for little measures of milk morning and evening. Then there was a continuous raid upon the ointment-pot, with the contents of which they delighted to anoint themselves. Trifling disturbances sometimes brought the plaintiff and defendant to the front gate for final judgment at the hands of their beloved keeper. And it was a constant entertainment to watch the progress of events in that singular little world of doomed spirits. They were not unhappy. I used to hear them singing every evening: their souls were singing while their bodies were falling rapidly to dust. They continued to play their games, as well as they could play them with the loss of a finger-joint or a toe, from week to week: it was thus gradually and thus slowly that they died, feeling their voices growing fainter and their strength less, as the idle days passed over them and swept them to the tomb.

Sitting at the window on the second evening, as the patients came up for milk, I observed one of them watching me intently, and apparently trying to make me understand something or other, but what that something was I could not guess. He rushed to the keeper and talked excitedly with him for a moment, and then withdrew to one side of the gate, and waited till the others were served with their milk, still watching me all the while. Then the keeper entered and told me how I had a friend out there who wished to speak to me—some one who had seen me somewhere, he supposed, but whom I would hardly remember. It was their way never to forget a face they had once become familiar with. Out I went. There was a face I could not have recognized as anything friendly or human. Knots of flesh stood out upon it; scar upon scar disfigured it. The expression was like that of a mummy, stony and withered. The outlines of a youthful face were preserved, but the hands and feet were pitiful to look at. What was this ogre that knew me and loved me still?

He soon told me who he had once been, but was no longer—our little unfortunate "Joe," my Lahaina charge. In his case the disease had spread with fearful rapidity: the keeper thought he could hardly survive the year. Many linger year after year, and cannot die; but Joe was more fortunate. His life had been brief and passionate, and death was now hastening him to his dissolution.

Joe was forbidden to come near me, so he crouched down by the fence, and pressing his hands between the pickets sifted the dust at my feet, while he wailed in a low voice, and called me over and over, " dear friend," "good friend," and "master." I wish I had never seen him so humbled. To think of my disreputable little protégé, who was wont to lord it over me as though he had been a born chief,—to think of Joe as being there in his extremity, grovelling in the dust at my feet; forbidden to climb the great wall of flowers that towered between him and his beautiful world, while the rough sea lashed the coast about him, and his only companions were such hideous forms as would frighten one out of a dream!

How I wanted to get close to him! but I dared not; so we sat there with the slats of the fence between us, while we talked very long in the twilight; and I was glad when it grew so dark that I could no longer see his face,—his terrible face, that came to kill the memory of his former beauty.

And Joe wondered whether I still remembered how we used to walk in the night, and go home at last to our little house when Lahaina was as still as death, and you could almost hear the great stars throbbing in the clear sky! How well I remembered it, and the day when we went a long way down the beach, and, looking back, saw a wide curve of the land cutting the sea like a sickle, and turning up a white and shining swath! Then, in another place, a grove of cocoa palms and a melancholy, monastic-looking building, with splendid palm-branches in its broad windows; for it was just after Palm Sunday, and the building belonged to a sisterhood. And I remembered how the clouds fell and the rain drove us into a sudden shelter, and we ate tamarind jam, spread thick on thin slices of bread, and were supremely happy. In this connection I could not forget how Joe became very unruly about that time, and I got mortified, and found great difficulty in getting him home at all; and yet the memory of it would have been perfect but for this fate. O Joe, my poor, dear, terrible cobra! to think that I should ever be afraid to look into your face in my life!

Joe wanted to call to my mind one other reminiscence—a night when we two walked to the old wharf, and went out to the end of it, and sat there looking inland, watching the inky waves slide up and down the beach, while the full moon rose over the superb mountains where the clouds were heaped like wool, and the very air seemed full of utterances that you could almost hear and understand but for something that made them all a mystery. I tried then, if ever I tried in my life, to make Joe a little less bad than he was naturally, and he seemed nearly inclined to be better, and would, I think, have been so but for the thousand temptations that gravitated to him when we got on solid earth again. He forgot my precepts then, and I'm afraid I forgot them myself. Joe remembered that night vividly. I was touched to hear him confess it, and I pray earnestly that that one moment may plead for him in the last day—if indeed he needs any special plea other than that Nature has published for her own.

"Sing for me, Joe," said I; and Joe, still crouching on the other side of the lattice, sang some of his old songs. One of them—a popular melody—was echoed through the little settlement, where faint voices caught up the chorus, and the night was wildly and weirdly musical. We walked by the sea the next day and the day following that, Joe taking pains to stay on the leeward side of me —he was so careful to keep the knowledge of his fate uppermost in his mind: how could I dismiss it from my own, when it was branded in his countenance? The desolate beauty of his face plead for measureless pity, and I gave it out of my prodigality, yet I felt that I could not begin to give sufficient.

Link by link he was casting off his hold on life; he was no longer a complete being; his soul was prostrated in the miry clay, and waited, in agony, its long deliverance.

In leaving the leper village I had concluded to say nothing to Joe other than the usual "*aloha*" at night, when I could ride off in the darkness, and, sleeping at the foot of the cliff, ascend it in the first light of morning, and get well on my journey before the heat of the day. We took a last walk by the rocks on the shore, heard the sea breathing its long breath under the hollow cones of lava, with a noise like a giant leper in his asthmatic agony. Joe heard it, and laughed a little, and then grew silent, and finally said he wanted to leave the place—he hated it; he loved Lahaina dearly: how was everybody in Lahaina?—a question he had asked me hourly since my arrival.

When night came I asked Joe to sing, as usual; so he gathered his mates about him, and they sang the songs I liked best. The voices rang, sweeter than ever, up from the group of singers congregated a few rods off, in the darkness; and while they sang, my horse was saddled, and I quietly bade adieu to my dear friends the keepers, and, mounting, walked the horse slowly up the grass-grown road. I shall never see little Joe again, with his pitiful face, growing gradually as dreadful as a cobra's, and almost as fascinating in its hideousness. I waited, a little way off, in the darkness— waited and listened till the last song was ended, and I knew he would be looking for me, to say *Good night*. But he didn't find me; and he will never again find me in this life, for I left him sitting in the dark door of his sepulchre,—sitting and singing in the mouth of his grave,—clothed all in death.

PRINTED BY BENZIGER BROTHERS, NEW YORK.

STANDARD CATHOLIC BOOKS

PUBLISHED BY

BENZIGER BROTHERS,

CINCINNATI:
848 Main St.

NEW YORK:
36 & 38 BARCLAY ST.

CHICAGO:
178 Monroe St.

ABANDONMENT ; or, Absolute Surrender of Self to Divine Providence. By Rev. J. P. Caussade, S.J. 32mo, *net*, 0 40

ANALYSIS OF THE GOSPELS of the Sundays of the Year. By Rev. L. A. Lambert, LL.D. 12mo, *net*, 1 25

ART OF PROFITING BY OUR FAULTS, according to St. Francis de Sales. By Rev. J. Tissot. 32mo, *net*, 0 40

BIBLE, THE HOLY. With Annotations, References, and an Historical and Chronological Index. 12mo, cloth, 1 25
Also in finer bindings.

BIRTHDAY SOUVENIR, OR DIARY. With a Subject of Meditation for Every Day. By Mrs. A. E. Buchanan. 32mo, 0 50

BLESSED ONES OF 1888. By Eliza A. Donnelly. 16mo, illustrated, 0 50

BLIND FRIEND OF THE POOR: Reminiscences of the Life and Works of Mgr. de Segur. 16mo, 0 50

BROWNSON, ORESTES A., Literary, Scientific, and Political Views of. Selected from his works, by H. F. Brownson. 12mo, *net*, 1 25

BUGG, LELIA HARDIN. The Correct Thing for Catholics. 16mo, 0 75

—— A Lady. Manners and Social Usages. 16mo, 1 00

CANONICAL PROCEDURE in Disciplinary and Criminal Cases of Clerics. By the Rev. Francis Droste. Edited by the Right Rev. Sebastian G. Messmer, D.D. 12mo, *net*, 1 50

CATECHISM OF FAMILIAR THINGS. Their History and the Events which led to their Discovery. 12mo, illustrated, 1 00

CATHOLIC BELIEF ; or, A Short and Simple Exposition of Catholic Doctrine. By the Very Rev. Joseph Faà di Bruno, D.D. Author's American edition edited by Rev. Louis A. Lambert. 200th Thousand. 16mo.
Paper, 0.25 ; 25 copies, 4.25 ; 50 copies, 7.50 ; 100 copies, 12 50
Cloth, 0.50; 25 copies, 8.50; 50 copies, 15.00; 100 copies, 25 00

"When a book supplies, as does this one, a demand that necessitates the printing of one hundred thousand [now two hundred thousand] copies, its merits need no eulogizing."—*Ave Maria.*

"The amount of good accomplished by it can never be told."—*Catholic Union and Times.*

CATHOLIC FAMILY LIBRARY. Composed of "The Christian Father," "The Christian Mother," "Sure Way to a Happy Marriage," "Instructions on the Commandments and Sacraments," and "Stories for First Communicants." 5 volumes in box,   2 00

CATHOLIC HOME ANNUAL. A Charming Annual for Catholics.   o 25

CATHOLIC HOME LIBRARY. 10 volumes. 12mo, each, o 50
  Per set,   3 00

CATHOLIC MEMOIRS OF VERMONT AND NEW HAMPSHIRE. 12mo, cloth, 1.00 ; paper,   o 50

CATHOLIC WORSHIP. The Sacraments, Ceremonies, and Festivals of the Church explained. BRENNAN. Paper, o.15 ; per 100, 9.00. Cloth, o.25 ; per 100,   15 00

CATHOLIC YOUNC MAN OF THE PRESENT DAY. By Right Rev. AUGUSTINE EGGER, D.D. 32mo, paper, o.15 ; per 100, 9.00. Cloth, o.25 ; per 100,   15 00

CHARITY THE ORIGIN OF EVERY BLESSING. 16mo, o 75

CHRIST IN TYPE AND PROPHECY. By Rev. A. J. MAAS, S.J. 2 vols., 12mo,   *net*, 4 00
  "By far the most serviceable manual that has hitherto appeared in the English language on a most important subject."—*London Tablet*.

CHRISTIAN ANTHROPOLOGY. By Rev. J. THEIN. 8vo, *net*, 2 50

CHRISTIAN FATHER, THE : what he should be, and what he should do. Paper, o.25 ; per 100, 12.50. Cloth, o.35 ; per 100,   21 00

CHRISTIAN MOTHER, THE : the Education of her Children and her Prayer. Paper, o.25 ; per 100, 12.50. Cloth, o.35 ; per 100,   21 00

CIRCUS-RIDER'S DAUGHTER, THE. A novel. By F. v. BRACKEL. 12mo,   1 25

CLARKE, REV. RICHARD F., S.J. The Devout Year. Short Meditations. 24mo,   *net*, o 60

COCHEM'S EXPLANATION OF THE MASS. With Preface by Rt. Rev. C. P. MAES, D.D. 12mo, cloth,   1 25

COMEDY OF ENGLISH PROTESTANTISM, THE. Edited by A. F. MARSHALL, B.A. Oxon. 12mo,   *net*, o 50

COMPENDIUM SACRAE LITURGIAE Juxta Ritum Romanum una cum Appendice De Jure Ecclesiastico Particulari in America Foederata Sept. vigente scripsit P. WAPELHORST, O.S.F. 8vo,   *net*, 2 50

CONNOR D'ARCY'S STRUGGLES. A novel. By Mrs. W. M. BERTHOLDS. 12mo, 1 25

COUNSELS OF A CATHOLIC MOTHER to Her Daughter, 16mo, 0 50

CROWN OF THORNS, THE ; or, The Little Breviary of the Holy Face. 32mo, 0 50

DATA OF MODERN ETHICS EXAMINED, THE. By Rev. JOHN J. MING, S.J. 12mo, *net*, 2 00

DE GOESBRIAND, RIGHT REV. L. Christ on the Altar. Instructions for the Sundays and Festivals of the Year. Quarto cloth, richly illustrated, gilt edges, 6 00

—————— Jesus the Good Shepherd. 16mo, *net*, 0 75

—————— The Labors of the Apostles: Their Teaching of the Nations. 12mo, *net*, 1 00

—————— History of Confession; or, The Dogma of Confession Vindicated. 16mo, *net*, 0 75

EGAN, MAURICE F. The Vocation of Edward Conway. A novel. 12mo, 1 25

—————— The Flower of the Flock, and the Badgers of Belmont. 12mo, 1 00

—————— How They Worked Their Way, and Other Stories, 1 00

—————— A Gentleman. 16mo, 0 75

ENGLISH READER. Edited by Rev. EDWARD CONNOLLY, S.J. 12mo, 1 25

EUCHARISTIC GEMS. A Thought about the Most Blessed Sacrament for Every Day, By Rev. L. C. COELENBIER. 16mo, 0 75

EXAMINATION OF CONSCIENCE for the use of Priests who are making a Retreat. By GADUEL. 32mo, *net*, 0 30

EXPLANATION OF THE BALTIMORE CATECHISM of Christian Doctrine. By Rev. THOMAS L. KINKEAD. 12mo, *net*, 1 00

EXPLANATION OF THE GOSPELS of the Sundays and Holydays. From the Italian, by Rev. L. A. LAMBERT, LL.D. With An Explanation of Catholic Worship. From the German, by Rev. RICHARD BRENNAN, LL.D. 24mo, illustrated.
Paper, 0.25; 25 copies, 4.25; 50 copies, 7.50; 100 copies, 12 50
Cloth, 0.50; 25 copies, 8.50; 50 copies, 15.00; 100 copies, 25 00

"It is with pleasure I recommend the 'Explanation of the Gospels and of Catholic Worship' to the clergy and the laity. It should have a very extensive sale; lucid explanation, clear style, solid matter, beautiful illustrations. Everybody will learn from this little book."—ARCHBISHOP JANSSENS.

FABIOLA ; or, The Church of the Catacombs. By CARDINAL WISEMAN. Illustrated Edition. 12mo, 1 25
Edition de luxe, 6 00

FINN, REV. FRANCIS J., S.J. Percy Wynn ; or, Making a Boy of Him. 12mo,   o 85
———— Tom Playfair; or, Making a Start. 12mo,   o 85
———— Harry Dee; or, Working it Out. 12mo,   o 85
———— Claude Lightfoot ; or, How the Problem was Solved. 12mo,   o 85
———— Ethelred Preston; or, The Adventures of a Newcomer. 12mo,   o 85
———— Mostly Boys. 16mo,   o 85

Father Finn's books are, in the opinion of the best critics, standard works in modern English literature ; they are full of fascinating interest, replete with stirring and amusing incidents of college life, and admirably adapted to the wants of our boys.

FIVE O'CLOCK STORIES ; or, The Old Tales Told Again. 16mo,   o 75

FLOWERS OF THE PASSION. Thoughts of St. Paul of the Cross. By Rev. Louis Th. de Jésus-Agonisant. 32mo,   o 50

FOLLOWING OF CHRIST, THE. By Thomas à Kempis.
With reflections. Small 32mo, cloth,   o 50
Without reflections. Small 32mo, cloth,   o 45
Edition de luxe. Illustrated,   from 1 50 up.

FRANCIS DE SALES, ST. Guide for Confession and Communion. Translated by Mrs. Bennett-Gladstone. 32mo, o 60
———— Maxims and Counsels for Every Day. 32mo,   o 50
———— New Year Greetings. 32mo, flexible cloth, 15 cents ; per 100,   10 00

GENERAL PRINCIPLES OF THE RELIGIOUS LIFE. By Very Rev. Boniface F. Verheyen, O.S.B. 32mo,   *net*, o 30

GLORIES OF DIVINE GRACE. From the German of Dr. M. Jos. Scheeben, by a Benedictine Monk. 12mo,   *net*, 1 50

GOD KNOWABLE AND KNOWN. Ronayne. 12mo, *net*, 1 25

GOFFINE'S DEVOUT INSTRUCTIONS on the Epistles and Gospels. With Preface by His Eminence Cardinal Gibbons. Illustrated edition. 8vo, cloth, 1.00; 10 copies, 7.50 ; 25 copies, 17.50; 50 copies,   33 50
This is the best, the cheapest, and the most popular illustrated edition of Goffine's Instructions.

"GOLDEN SANDS," Books by the Author of :
Golden Sands. Third, Fourth, Fifth Series. 32mo, each, o 60
Book of the Professed. 32mo.
Vol. I.   *net*, o 75
Vol. II.   Each with a steel-plate Frontispiece.   *net*, o 60
Vol. III.   *net*, o 60
Prayer. 32mo,   *net*, o 40
The Little Book of Superiors. 32mo,   *net*, o 60
Spiritual Direction. 32mo,   *net*, o 60
Little Month of May. 32mo, flexible cloth,   o 25
Little Month of the Poor Souls. 32mo, flexible cloth,   o 25

GREETINGS TO THE CHRIST-CHILD. A Collection of Christmas Poems for the Young. 16mo, illustrated, o 50

GROU, REV. J., S.J. The Characteristics of True Devotion. Translated from the French by the Rev. ALEXANDER CLINTON, S.J. A new edition, by Rev. SAMUEL H. FRISBEE, S.J. 16mo, *net*, o 75

——— The Interior of Jesus and Mary. Edited by Rev. SAMUEL H. FRISBEE, S.J. 16mo, 2 vols., *net*, 2 00

HAMON'S MEDITATIONS. See under MEDITATIONS. 5 vols. 16mo, *net*, 5 00

HANDBOOK FOR ALTAR SOCIETIES, and Guide for Sacristans and others having charge of the Altar and Sanctuary. 16mo, *net*, o 75

HANDBOOK OF THE CHRISTIAN RELIGION. For the use of Advanced Students and the Educated Laity. By Rev. W. WILMERS, S.J. From the German. Edited by Rev. JAMES CONWAY, S.J. 12mo, *net*, 1 50

HAPPY YEAR, A; or, The Year Sanctified by Meditating on the Maxims and Sayings of the Saints. By ABBÉ LASAUSSE. 12mo, *net*, 1 00

HEART, THE, OF ST. JANE FRANCES DE CHANTAL. Thoughts and Prayers. 32mo, *net*, o 40

HIDDEN TREASURE; or, The Value and Excellence of the Holy Mass. By ST. LEONARD OF PORT-MAURICE. 32mo, o 50

HISTORY OF THE CATHOLIC CHURCH. By Dr. H. BRUECK. With Additions from the Writings of His Eminence Cardinal Hergenröther. Translated by Rev. E. PRUENTE. 2 vols., 8vo, *net*, 3 00

HISTORY OF THE CATHOLIC CHURCH. Adapted by Rev. RICHARD BRENNAN, LL.D. With a History of the Church in America, by JOHN GILMARY SHEA, LL.D. With 90 Illustrations. 8vo, 2 00

HISTORY OF THE MASS and its Ceremonies in the Eastern and Western Church. By Rev. JOHN O'BRIEN, A.M. 12mo, *net*, 1 25

HOLY FACE OF JESUS, THE. A Series of Meditations on the Litany of the Holy Face. 32mo, o 50

HOURS BEFORE THE ALTAR; or, Meditations on the Holy Eucharist. By Mgr. DE LA BOUILLERIE. 32mo, o 50

HOW TO GET ON. By Rev. BERNARD FEENEY. 12mo, paper, o 50; cloth, 1 00

HUNOLT'S SERMONS. Sermons by the Rev. FRANCIS HUNOLT. Priest of the Society of Jesus and Preacher in the Cathedral of

Treves.   Translated from the original German edition of
Cologne, 1740, by the Rev. J. ALLEN, D.D.   12 vols., 8vo, 30 00
Per set of 2 vols.,   *net*, 5 00
Vols. 1, 2.   The Christian State of Life.
Vols. 3, 4.   The Bad Christian.
Vols. 5, 6.   The Penitent Christian.
Vols. 7, 8.   The Good Christian.
Vols. 9, 10.   The Christian's Last End.
Vols. 11, 12.   The Christian's Model.

His Eminence Cardinal Satolli, Pro-Delegate Apostolic: "... I believe
that in it is found realized the desire of the Holy Father, who not long ago in an
encyclical urged so strongly the return to the simple, unaffected, but earnest and
eloquent preaching of the word of God. ..."
His Eminence Cardinal Gibbons, Archbishop of Baltimore: ... "Contain a
fund of solid doctrine, presented in a clear and forcible style.   These sermons
should find a place in the library of every priest. ..."
His Eminence Cardinal Vaughan, Archbishop of Westminster: "... I cannot praise it too highly, and I think it might find a place in every priest's
library."
His Eminence Cardinal Logue, Archbishop of Armagh, Primate of all Ireland: "... What is of real service is some work in which the preacher can find
sound, solid matter.   I believe Father Hunolt's Sermons furnishes an inex-
haustible treasure of such matter. ..."

IDOLS; or, The Secret of the Rue Chaussée d'Antin. A novel. By
    RAOUL DE NAVERY.   12mo,   1 25

INSTRUCTIONS ON THE COMMANDMENTS and the Sacra-
    ments. By ST. LIGUORI.   32mo.   Paper, 0.25 ; per 100, 12 50
    Cloth, 0.35; per 100,   21 00

KONINGS, THEOLOGIA MORALIS. Novissimi Ecclesiæ Doc-
    toris S. Alphonsi.   In Compendium Redacta, et Usui Venerabilis
    Cleri Americani Accommodata, Auctore A. KONINGS, C.SS. R.
    Editio septima, auctior, et novis curis expolitior, curante HENRICO
    KUPER, C.SS.R.   The two vols. in one, half morocco, *net*, 4 00

LEGENDS AND STORIES OF THE HOLY CHILD JESUS
    from Many Lands. Collected by A. FOWLER LUTZ. 16mo, 0 75

LEPER QUEEN, THE. A Story of the Thirteenth Century.
    16mo,   0 50

LIBRARY OF THE RELIGIOUS LIFE. Composed of "Book of
    the Professed," by the author of "Golden Sands," 3 vols. ; "Spirit-
    ual Direction," by the author of "Golden Sands" ; and "Sou-
    venir of the Novitiate." 5 vols., 32mo, in case,   3 25

LIFE AND ACTS OF LEO XIII. By Rev. JOSEPH E. KELLER, S.J.
    Fully and beautifully illustrated. 8vo,   2 00

LIFE OF ST. ALOYSIUS GONZAGA. From the Italian of Rev.
    Father CEPARI, S.J. Edited by Rev. F. GOLDIE, S.J. Edition
    de luxe, richly illustrated. 8vo,   *net*, 2 50

LIFE OF THE EVER-BLESSED VIRGIN. From Her Concep-
    tion to Her Assumption. 12mo, imitation cloth,   0 30

LIFE OF FATHER CHARLES SIRE. By his brother, Rev.
    VITAL SIRE. 12mo,   *net*, 1 00

LIFE OF ST. CLARE OF MONTEFALCO. By Rev. JOSEPH A.
    LOCKE, O.S.A. 12mo,   *net*, 0 75

LIFE OF THE VEN. MARY CRESCENTIA HÖSS. 12mo, *net*, 1 25

LIFE OF REV. MOTHER ST. JOHN FONTBONNE. By Abbé Rivaux. 12mo, *net*, 1 25

LIFE OF ST. FRANCIS SOLANUS, APOSTLE OF PERU. 16mo, *net*, 0 50

LIFE OF ST. GERMAINE COUSIN. 16mo, 0 50

LIFE OF ST. IGNATIUS OF LOYOLA. By Father Genelli. 12mo, *net*, 1 25

LIFE OF ST. CHANTAL. See under St. Chantal. *net*, 4 00

(LIFE OF) MOST REV. JOHN HUGHES, First Archbishop of New York. By Rev. H. A. Brann, D.D. 12mo, *net*, 0 75

LIFE OF FATHER JOGUES. By Father Felix Martin, S.J. From the French by John Gilmary Shea. 12mo, *net*, 0 75

LIFE OF MLLE. LE GRAS. 12mo, *net*, 1 25

LIFE OF MARY FOR CHILDREN. By Anne R. Bennett, née Gladstone. 24mo, illustrated, *net*, 0 50

LIFE OF RIGHT REV. JOHN N. NEUMANN, D.D. By Rev. E. Grimm, C.SS.R. 12mo, *net*, 1 25

LIFE OF OUR LORD AND SAVIOUR JESUS CHRIST and of His blessed Mother. Adapted by Rev. Richard Brennan, LL.D. With nearly 600 illustrations. No. 1. Roan back, gold title, plain cloth sides, sprinkled edges, *net*, 5 00

No. 3. Morocco back and corners, cloth sides with gold stamp, gilt edges, *net*, 7 00

No. 4. Full morocco, richly gilt back, with large figure of Our Lord in gold on side, gilt edges, *net*, 9 00

No. 5. Full morocco, block-paneled sides, superbly gilt, gilt edges, *net*, 10 00

LIFE OF OUR BLESSED LORD. His Life, Death, Resurrection. 12mo, imitation cloth, 0 30

LIFE, POPULAR, OF ST. TERESA OF JESUS. By L'Abbé Marie-Joseph. 12mo, *net*, 0 75

LIGUORI, ST. ALPHONSUS DE. Complete Ascetical Works of. Centenary Edition. Edited by Rev. Eugene Grimm, C.SS.R. Price, per volume, *net*, 1 25

Each book is complete in itself, and any volume will be sold separately. Volumes 1 to 22 are now ready.

Preparation for Death.	True Spouse of Christ, 2 vols.
Way of Salvation and of Perfection.	Dignity and Duties of the Priest.
Great Means of Salvation and Perfection.	The Holy Mass.
	The Divine Office.
Incarnation, Birth, and Infancy of Christ.	Preaching.
The Passion and Death of Christ.	Abridged Sermons for all the Sundays.
The Holy Eucharist.	Miscellany.
The Glories of Mary, 2 vols.	Letters, 4 vols.
Victories of the Martyrs.	Letters and General Index.
	Life of St. Alphonsus, 2 vols.

LINKED LIVES. A novel. By Lady GERTRUDE DOUGLAS.
8vo,   1 50

LITTLE COMPLIMENTS OF THE SEASON. Simple Verses for
Namedays, Birthdays, Christmas, New Year, and other festive
and social occasions. By ELEANOR C. DONNELLY. 12mo, *net*, 0 50

LITTLE MANUAL OF ST. ANTHONY. Illustrated. 32mo,
cloth,   0 60

LITTLE MANUAL OF THE SODALITY OF THE CHILD
JESUS. 32mo,   0 20

LITTLE PICTORIAL LIVES OF THE SAINTS. With Reflections for Every Day in the Year. Edited by JOHN GILMARY
SHEA, LL.D. With nearly 400 illustrations. 12mo, cloth, ink
and gold side,   1 00
10 copies, 6.25; 25 copies, 15.00; 50 copies, 27.50; 100 copies, 50 00

The book has received the approbation of the following prelates: Arch-
bishop Kenrick, Archbishop Grace, Archbishop Hennessy, Archbishop
Salpointe, Archbishop Ryan, Archbishop Gross, Archbishop Duhamel, Arch-
bishop Kain, Archbishop O'Brien, Archbishop Katzer, Bishop McCloskey,
Bishop Grandin, Bishop O'Hara, Bishop Mullen, Bishop Marty, Bishop Ryan, of
Buffalo; Bishop Fink, Bishop Seidenbush, Bishop Moreau, Bishop Racine,
Bishop Spalding, Bishop Vertin, Bishop Junger, Bishop Naughten, Bishop
Richter, Bishop Rademacher, Bishop Cosgrove, Bishop Curtis, and Bishop
Glorieux.

LITTLE PRAYER BOOK OF THE SACRED HEART. Prayers
and Practices of Blessed Margaret Mary. Sm. 32mo, cloth, 0 40
Also in finer bindings.

LITTLE SAINT OF NINE YEARS. From the French of Mgr.
DE SEGUR, by MARY McMAHON. 16mo,   0 50

LIVES, SHORT, OF THE SAINTS; or, Our Birthday Bouquet.
By ELEANOR C. DONNELLY. 16mo.   1 00

LOURDES. Its Inhabitants, Its Pilgrims, Its Miracles. By R. F.
CLARKE, S.J. 16mo, illustrated,   0 75

LUTHER'S OWN STATEMENTS Concerning his Teachings and
its Results. By HENRY O'CONNOR, S.J. 12mo, paper,   0 15

MANIFESTATION OF CONSCIENCE. Confessions and Communions in Religious Communities. By Rev. PIE DE LANGOGNE,
O.M.Cap. 32mo,   *net*, 0 50

MANUAL OF THE HOLY FAMILY. Prayers and Instructions
for Catholic Parents. 32mo, cloth,   0 60
Also in finer bindings.

MANUAL OF INDULGENCED PRAYERS. A Complete Prayer
Book. Arranged and disposed for daily use by Rev. BONAVEN-
TURE HAMMER, O.S.F. Small 32mo, cloth,   0 40
Also in finer bindings.

MARCELLA GRACE. A novel. By ROSA MULHOLLAND. With
illustrations after original drawings. 12mo,   1 25

MARRIAGE. By Very Rev. PÈRE MONSABRÉ, O.P. From the
French, by M. HOPPER. 12mo,   *net*, 1 00

MARRIAGE, Popular Instructions On. By Very Rev. F. GIRARDEY, C.SS.R. 32mo, paper, 0.25; per 100, 12.50; cloth, 0.35; per 100, **21 00**

The instructions treat of the great dignity of matrimony, its indissolubility, the obstacles to it, the evils of mixed marriage, the manner of getting married, and the duties it imposes on the married between each other and in reference to their offspring.

MEANS OF GRACE, THE. A Complete Exposition of the Seven Sacraments, of the Sacramentals, and of Prayer, with a Comprehensive Explanation of the "Lord's Prayer" and the "Hail Mary." By Rev. RICHARD BRENNAN, LL.D. With 180 full-page and other illustrations. 8vo, cloth, 2.50; gilt edges, 3.00; Library edition, half levant, **3 50**

"The best book for family use out."—BISHOP MULLEN.
"A work worthy of unstinted praise and heartiest commendation."—BISHOP RYAN, of Buffalo.
"The wealth of matter, the admirable arrangement, and the simplicity of language of this work will make it a valuable addition to the household library."—BISHOP BRADLEY.

MEDITATIONS (BAXTER) for Every Day in the Year. By Rev. ROGER BAXTER, S.J. Republished by Rev. P. NEALE, S.J. Small 12mo, *net*, 1 25

MEDITATIONS (HAMON'S) FOR ALL THE DAYS OF THE YEAR. For the use of Priests, Religious, and the Laity. By Rev. M. HAMON, SS., Pastor of St. Sulpice, Paris. From the French, by Mrs. ANNE R. BENNETT-GLADSTONE. With Alphabetic Index. 5 vols., 16mo, cloth, gilt top, each with a Steel Engraving, *net*, 5 00

"The five handsome volumes will form a very useful addition to the devotional library of every ecclesiastic."—HIS EMINENCE CARDINAL LOGUE.
"Hamon's doctrine is the unadulterated word of God, presented with unction, exquisite taste, and freed from that exaggerated and sickly sentimentalism which disgusts when it does not mislead."—MOST REV. P. L. CHAPELLE, D.D.
"We are using them daily, and are delighted with them."—MOTHER M. BLANCHE, Mother House Sisters of Charity, Mt. St. Joseph, O.
"Having examined the 'Meditations' by M. Hamon, SS., we are pleased to recommend them not only as useful and practicable for religious, but also for those who in the world desire by means of mental prayer to advance in the spiritual life."—SISTERS OF ST. JOSEPH, Flushing, L. I.

MEDITATIONS (PERINALDO) on the Sufferings of Jesus Christ. From the Italian of Rev. FRANCIS DA PERINALDO, O.S.F. 12mo, *net*, 0 75

MEDITATIONS (VERCRUYSSE), for Every Day in the Year, on the Life of Our Lord Jesus Christ. By the Rev. Father BRUNO VERCRUYSSE, S.J. 2 vols., **4 00**

MEDITATIONS ON THE PASSION OF OUR LORD. By a PASSIONIST FATHER. 32mo, **0 40**

MISTRESS OF NOVICES, The, Instructed in her Duties. From the French of the ABBÉ LEGUAY, by Rev. IGNATIUS SISK. 12mo, cloth, *net*, 0 75

MOMENTS BEFORE THE TABERNACLE. By Rev. MATTHEW RUSSELL, S.J. 24mo, *net*, 0 40

MONK'S PARDON. A Historical Romance of the Time of Philip IV. of Spain. By RAOUL DE NAVERY. 12mo, 1 25

MONTH OF THE DEAD. 32mo, 0 75

MONTH OF MAY. From the French of Father DEBUSSI, S.J., by ELLA McMAHON. 32mo, 0 50

MONTH, NEW, OF MARY, St. Francis de Sales. 32mo, 0 40

MONTH, NEW, OF THE SACRED HEART, St. Francis de Sales. 32mo, 0 40

MONTH, NEW, OF ST. JOSEPH, St. Francis de Sales. 32mo, 0 40

MONTH, NEW, OF THE HOLY ANGELS, St. Francis de Sales. 32mo, 0 40

MR. BILLY BUTTONS. A novel. By Walter Lecky. 12mo, 1 25

MÜLLER, REV. MICHAEL, C.SS.R. God the Teacher of Mankind. A plain, comprehensive Explanation of Christian Doctrine. 9 vols., crown 8vo. Per set, *net*, 9 50
The Church and Her Enemies. *net*, 1 10
The Apostles' Creed. *net*, 1 10
The First and Greatest Commandment. *net*, 1 40
Explanation of the Commandments, continued. Precepts of the Church. *net*, 1 10
Dignity, Authority, and Duties of Parents, Ecclesiastical and Civil Powers. Their Enemies. *net*, 1 40
Grace and the Sacraments. *net*, 1 25
Holy Mass. *net*, 1 25
Eucharist and Penance. *net*, 1 10
Sacramentals—Prayer, etc. *net*, 1 00

———— Familiar Explanation of Catholic Doctrine. 12mo, 1 00

———— The Prodigal Son ; or, The Sinner's Return to God. 8vo, *net*, 1 00

———— The Devotion of the Holy Rosary and the Five Scapulars. 8vo, *net*, 0 75

———— The Catholic Priesthood. 2 vols., 8vo, *net*, 3 00

MY FIRST COMMUNION : The Happiest Day of My Life. BRENNAN. 16mo, illustrated, 0 75

NAMES THAT LIVE IN CATHOLIC HEARTS. Cardinal Ximenes—Michael Angelo—Samuel de Champlain—Archbishop Plunkett—Charles Carroll—Henry Larochejacquelein—Simon de Montfort. By ANNA T. SADLIER. 12mo, 1 00

NATALIE NARISCHKIN, Sister of Charity of St. Vincent of Paul. By Lady G. FULLERTON. 12mo, *net*, 0 75

NEW TESTAMENT, THE. 32mo. Limp cloth, *net*, 0.20 ; levant, *net*, 1.00 ; French calf, red edges, *net*, 1 60

OFFICE, COMPLETE, OF HOLY WEEK, according to the Roman Missal and Breviary, in Latin and English. New edition, revised and enlarged. 24mo, cloth, 0.50 ; cloth, limp, gilt edges, 1 00
Also in finer bindings.

O'GRADY, ELEANOR. Aids to Correct and Effective Elocution. 12mo, 1 25
——— Select Recitations for Schools and Academies. 12mo, 1 00
——— Readings and Recitations for Juniors. 16mo, *net*, 0 50
——— Elocution Class. A Simplification of the Laws and Principles of Expression. 16mo, *net*, 0 50

ON CHRISTIAN ART. By EDITH HEALY. 16mo, 0 50

ON THE ROAD TO ROME, and How Two Brothers Got There. By WILLIAM RICHARDS. 16mo, *net*, 0 75

ONE AND THIRTY DAYS WITH BLESSED MARGARET MARY. 32mo, flexible cloth, 0 25

ONE ANGEL MORE IN HEAVEN. With Letters of Condolence by St. Francis de Sales and others. White mar., 0 50

OUR BIRTHDAY BOUQUET. Culled from the Shrines of Saints and the Gardens of Poets. By E. C. DONNELLY. 16mo, 1 00

OUR LADY OF GOOD COUNSEL IN GENAZZANO. By ANNE R. BENNETT, née GLADSTONE. 32mo, 0 75

OUR OWN WILL, and How to Detect it in Our Actions. By the Rev. JOHN ALLEN, D.D. 16mo, *net*, 0 75

OUR YOUNG FOLKS' LIBRARY. 10 volumes. 12mo. Each, 0 50 ; per set, 3 00

OUTLAW OF CAMARGUE, THE. A novel. By A. DE LAMOTHE. 12mo, 1 25

OUTLINES OF DOGMATIC THEOLOGY. By Rev. SYLVESTER J. HUNTER, S.J. 3 vols., 12mo, *net*, 4 50

PARADISE ON EARTH OPENED TO ALL ; or, A Religious Vocation the Surest Way in Life. 32mo, *net*, 0 40

PEARLS FROM FABER. Selected and arranged by MARION J. BRUNOWE. 32mo, 0 50

PETRONILLA, and other Stories. By E. C. DONNELLY. 12mo, 1 00

PHILOSOPHY, ENGLISH MANUALS OF CATHOLIC.
Logic. By RICHARD F. CLARKE, S.J. 12mo, *net*, 1 25
First Principles of Knowledge. By JOHN RICKABY, S.J. 12mo, *net*, 1 25
Moral Philosophy (Ethics and Natural Law). By JOSEPH RICKABY, S.J. 12mo, *net*, 1 25
Natural Theology. By BERNARD BOEDDER, S.J. 12mo, *net*, 1 50
Psychology. By MICHAEL MAHER, S.J. 12mo, *net*, 1 50
General Metaphysics. By JOHN RICKABY, S.J. 12mo, *net*, 1 25
A Manual of Political Economy. By C. S. DEVAS, Esq., M.A. 12mo, *net*, 1 50

PICTORIAL LIVES OF THE SAINTS. With Reflections for Every Day in the Year. Edited by John Gilmary Shea, LL.D. 50th Thousand. 8vo,   2 00
     5 copies, 6.65 ; 10 copies, 12.50 ; 25 copies, 27.50 ; 50 copies, 50 00

PRAYER-BOOK FOR LENT. Meditations and Prayers for Lent. 32mo, cloth,   o 50
     Also in finer bindings.

PRAXIS SYNODALIS. Manuale Synodi Diocesanæ ac Provincialis Celebrandæ. 12mo,   *net*, o 60

PRIEST IN THE PULPIT, THE. A Manual of Homiletics and Catechetics. Adapted from the German of Rev. I. Schuech, O.S.B., by Rev. B. Luebbermann. 8vo,   *net*, 1 50

PRIMER FOR CONVERTS, A. By Rev. J. T. Durward. 32mo, flexible cloth,   o 25

PRINCIPLES OF ANTHROPOLOGY AND BIOLOGY. By Rev. Thomas Hughes, S.J. 16mo,   *net*, o 75

REASONABLENESS OF CATHOLIC CEREMONIES AND PRACTICES. By Rev. J. J. Burke. 12mo, flexible cloth, o 35

RELIGIOUS STATE, THE. With a Short Treatise on Vocation to the Priesthood. By St. Alphonsus de Liguori. 32mo, o 50

REMINISCENCES OF RT. REV. EDGAR P. WADHAMS, D.D., First Bishop of Ogdensburg. By Rev. C. A. Walworth. 12mo, illustrated,   *net*, 1 00

RIGHTS OF OUR LITTLE ONES ; or, First Principles on Education in Catechetical Form. By Rev. James Conway, S.J. 32mo, paper, o.15 ; per 100, 9.00 ; cloth, o.25 ; per 100,   15 00

ROSARY, THE MOST HOLY, in Thirty-one Meditations, Prayers, and Examples. By Rev. Eugene Grimm, C.SS.R. 32mo, o 50

RUSSO, N., S.J.—De Philosophia Morali Prælectiones in Collegio Georgiopolitano Soc. Jes. Anno 1889–90 Habitae, a Patre Nicolao Russo. Editio altera. 8vo, half leather,   *net*, 2 00

ST. CHANTAL AND THE FOUNDATION OF THE VISITATION. By Monseigneur Bougaud. 2 vols., 8vo,   *net*, 4 00

ST. JOSEPH, THE ADVOCATE OF HOPELESS CASES. From the French of Rev. Father Huguet. 24mo,   1 00

SACRAMENTALS OF THE HOLY CATHOLIC CHURCH, THE. By Rev. A. A. Lambing, LL.D. Large Edition, 12mo,   *net*, 1 25
     Popular Edition, illustrated, 24mo.
     Paper, o.25; 25 copies, 4.25; 50 copies, 7.50; 100 copies,   12 50
     Cloth, o.50; 25 copies, 8.50; 50 copies, 15.00; 100 copies,   25 00
     "Am glad you have issued so practical a work, in a shape in which it ought to reach every Catholic family."—Cardinal Satolli, Delegate Apostolic.

SACRED HEART, BOOKS ON THE.

Devotions to the Sacred Heart for the First Friday of Every
Month. By P. HUGUET. 32mo, 0 40
213. Imitation Levant, limp, gilt centre, round corners, edges
red under gold, 1 35
Imitation of the Sacred Heart of Jesus. By Rev. F. ARNOUDT,
S.J. From the Latin by Rev. J. M. FASTRE, S.J. 16mo,
cloth, 1 25
Month of the Sacred Heart of Jesus. From the French of
Rev. Father HUGUET. 32mo, 0 75
New Month of the Sacred Heart, St. Francis de Sales. 32mo, 0 40
One and Thirty Days with Blessed Margaret Mary. From
the French by a Visitandine of Baltimore. 32mo, flexible
cloth, 0 25
Pearls from the Casket of the Sacred Heart of Jesus. A Col-
lection of the Letters, Maxims, and Practices of the Blessed
Margaret Mary Alacoque. Edited by ELEANOR C. DONNELLY.
32mo, 0 50
Month of the Sacred Heart for the Young Christian. By
BROTHER PHILIPPE. From the French by E. A. MULLIGAN.
32mo, 0 50
Sacred Heart Studied in the Sacred Scriptures. By Rev. H.
SAINTRAIN, C.SS.R. 8vo, *net*, 2 00
Revelations of the Sacred Heart to Blessed Margaret Mary;
and the History of her Life. By Monseigneur BOUGAUD.
8vo, *net*, 1 50
Six Sermons on Devotion to the Sacred Heart of Jesus. From
the German of Rev. Dr. E. BIERBAUM, by ELLA McMAHON.
16mo, *net*, 0 60
Year of the Sacred Heart. Drawn from the works of PÈRE DE
LA COLOMBIÈRE, of Blessed Margaret Mary, and of others.
32mo, 0 50

SAINTS, THE NEW, OF 1888. By Rev. FRANCIS GOLDIE, S.J.,
and Rev. Father SCOLA, S.J. 16mo, illustrated, 0 50

SECRET OF SANCTITY, THE. According to ST. FRANCIS DE
SALES and Father CRASSET, S.J. 12mo, *net*, 1 00

SERAPHIC GUIDE. A Manual for the Members of the Third
Order of St. Francis. 0 60
Roan, red edges, 0 75
The same in German at the same prices.

SERMONS, HUNOLT. See under HUNOLT.

SERMONS ON THE BLESSED VIRGIN. By Very Rev. D. I.
McDERMOTT. 16mo, *net*, 0 75

SERMONS for the Sundays and Chief Festivals of the Ecclesiastical
Year. With Two Courses of Lenten Sermons and a Triduum
for the Forty Hours. By Rev. JULIUS POTTGEISSER, S.J. From
the German by Rev. JAMES CONWAY, S.J. 2 vols., 8vo, *net*, 2 50

SERMONS, SHORT, FOR LOW MASSES. A complete, brief course of instruction on Christian Doctrine. By Rev. F. X. Schouppe, S.J. 12mo, *net*, 1 25

SERMONS, SIX, on Devotion to the Sacred Heart of Jesus. From the German of Rev. Dr. E. Bierbaum, by Ella McMahon, 16mo, *net*, 0 60

SHORT CONFERENCES ON THE LITTLE OFFICE OF THE IMMACULATE CONCEPTION. By Very Rev. Joseph Rainer. With Prayers. 32mo, 0 50

SHORT STORIES ON CHRISTIAN DOCTRINE: A Collection of Examples illustrating the Catechism. From the French by Mary McMahon. 12mo, illustrated, *net*, 0 75

SMITH, Rev. S. B., D.D. Elements of Ecclesiastical Law.
Vol. I. Ecclesiastical Persons. 8vo, *net*, 2 50
Vol. II. Ecclesiastical Trials. 8vo, *net*, 2 50
Vol. III. Ecclesiastical Punishments. 8vo, *net*, 2 50
—— Compendium Juris Canonici, ad usum Cleri et Seminariorum hujus regionis accommodatum. 8vo, *net*, 2 00
—— The Marriage Process in the United States. 8vo, *net*, 2 50

SODALISTS' VADE MECUM. A Manual, Prayer Book, and Hymnal. 32mo, cloth, 0 50
Also in finer bindings.

SOUVENIR OF THE NOVITIATE. From the French by Rev. Edward I. Taylor. 32mo, *net*, 0 60

SPIRITUAL CRUMBS FOR HUNGRY LITTLE SOULS. To which are added Stories from the Bible. By Mary E. Richardson. 16mo, 0 50

STORIES FOR FIRST COMMUNICANTS, for the Time before and after First Communion. By Rev. J. A. Keller, D.D. 32mo, 0 50

STORY OF JESUS SIMPLY TOLD FOR THE YOUNG. By Rosa Mulholland. 24mo, illustrated, 0 50

SURE WAY TO A HAPPY MARRIAGE. A Book of Instructions for those Betrothed and for Married People. From the German by Rev. Edward I. Taylor. Paper, 0.25; per 100, 12.50; cloth, 0.35; per 100, 21 00

TALES AND LEGENDS OF THE MIDDLE AGES. From the Spanish of F. De P. Capella. By Henry Wilson. 16mo, 0 75

THINK WELL ON'T; or, Reflections on the Great Truths of the Christian Religion. By the Right Rev. R. Challoner, D.D. 32mo, flexible cloth, 0 20

THOUGHT FROM ST. ALPHONSUS, for Every Day of the Year. 32mo, 0 50

THOUGHT FROM BENEDICTINE SAINTS. 32mo, 0 50

THOUGHT FROM DOMINICAN SAINTS. 32mo,   o 50

THOUGHT FROM ST. FRANCIS ASSISI and his Saints. 32mo,   o 50

THOUGHT FROM ST. IGNATIUS. 32mo,   o 50

THOUGHT FROM ST. TERESA. 32mo,   o 50

THOUGHT FROM ST. VINCENT DE PAUL. 32mo,   o 50

TRUE SPOUSE OF CHRIST. By St. Alphonsus Liguori. 2 vols., 12mo, *net*, 2.50 ; 1 vol., 12mo,   1 50

TRUTHS OF SALVATION. By Rev. J. Pergmayr, S.J. From the German by a Father of the same Society. 16mo, *net*, o 75

TWELVE VIRTUES, THE, of a Good Teacher. For Mothers, Instructors, etc. By Rev. H. Pottier, S.J. 32mo, *net*, o 30

VISIT TO EUROPE AND THE HOLY LAND. By Rev. H. F. Fairbanks. 12mo, illustrated,   1 50

VISITS TO THE MOST HOLY SACRAMENT and to the Blessed Virgin Mary. For Every Day of the Month. By St. Alphonsus de Liguori. Edited by Rev. Eugene Grimm. 32mo,   o 50

WARD, REV. THOMAS F. Fifty-two Instructions on the Principal Truths of Our Holy Religion. 12mo, *net*, o 75

—————— Thirty-two Instructions for the Month of May and for the Feasts of the Blessed Virgin. 12mo, *net*, o 75

—————— Month of May at Mary's Altar. 12mo, *net*, o 75

WAY OF INTERIOR PEACE. By Rev. Father De Lehen, S.J. From the German Version of Rev. J. Brucker, S.J. 12mo, *net*, 1 25

WENINGER'S SERMONS.

Original Short and Practical Sermons for Every Sunday of the Year. Three Sermons for every Sunday. 8vo, *net*, 2 00

Sermons for Every Feast of the Ecclesiastical Year. Three Sermons for Every Feast. 8vo, *net*, 2 00

Conferences specially addressed to Married and Unmarried Men. 8vo, *net*, 2 00

WHAT CATHOLICS HAVE DONE FOR SCIENCE, with Sketches of the Great Catholic Scientists. By Rev. Martin S. Brennan. 12mo,   1 00

WOMEN OF CATHOLICITY: Margaret O'Carroll—Isabella of Castile—Margaret Roper—Marie de l'Incarnation—Margaret Bourgeoys—Ethan Allen's Daughter. By Anna T. Sadlier. 12mo,   1 00

WORDS OF JESUS CHRIST DURING HIS PASSION, explained in their Literal and Moral Sense. By Rev. F. X. Schouppe, S.J. Flexible cloth,   o 25

WORDS OF WISDOM. A Concordance of the Sapiential Books. 12mo, *net*, 1 25

ZEAL IN THE WORK OF THE MINISTRY; or, The Means by which every Priest may render his Ministry Honorable and Fruitful. From the French of L'Abbé Dubois. 8vo, *net*, 1 50

CATHOLIC NOVELS BY AMERICAN AUTHORS.

MR. BILLY BUTTONS.

By WALTER LECKY. 12mo, cloth, special design on cover, $1.25.

Walter Lecky has in a few years reached an enviable place among the Catholic writers of this country. This book, of which the scene is laid in a little town of the Adirondack Mountains, abounds in vivid bits of description, suggestive of Thoreau in their appreciation of nature, in dramatic and touching situations, and the quaint characters of Billy Buttons, Cagy, Weeks, etc., are sketched to the life. Nothing quite like this has been given to the public before, and we feel sure Mr. Billy Buttons will be heartily welcomed.

THE VOCATION OF EDWARD CONWAY.

By MAURICE F. EGAN. 12mo, cloth, special design on cover, $1.25.

This is a novel of modern American life. The scene is laid in a pleasant colony of cultivated people, on the banks of the Hudson, not far from West Point, and the military element enters into the story. The tone is Catholic, but not controversial, and the hits at the fads of the day are softened by a sense of humor, evidently the result of keen observation, modified by wide experience. A competent critic pronounces this the best novel Mr. Egan has yet written.

A WOMAN OF FORTUNE.

By CHRISTIAN REID. 12mo, cloth, special design on cover, $1.25.

Christian Reid is the most prolific of all the Catholic novelists. Over a score of novels have come from her pen, and in all of them "the author has wrought with care, and with a good ethical and artistic purpose, and these are essential needs in the building up of an American literature." The heroine of the present story is a Southern girl of rare beauty and wealth, and of a very independent and perhaps wilful disposition. The scene is laid in this country and various cities of Europe.

PASSING SHADOWS.

By ANTHONY YORKE. 12mo, cloth, special design on cover, $1.25.

Novels the scenes of which are laid in New York have an interest for people in all parts of the country. "Passing Shadows" is a New York story, the scene of which is laid, for the most part, in the lower east side of the city. It is a simple tale of love in a neighborhood that has not been much exploited by Catholic writers. It is a reflection of Catholic life, and for this reason will be acceptable to many.

BENZIGER BROTHERS, NEW YORK, CINCINNATI, CHICAGO.

www.ingramcontent.com/pod-product-compliance
Lightning Source LLC
Chambersburg PA
CBHW021722110726

47902CB00005B/1309